Wrong Turn

Peri Jean Mace Ghost Thrillers #10

Copyright © 2018 Catie Rhodes.

Published by: Long Roads and Dark Ends Press

Cover artwork by Book Cover Corner

Content Editing by Word Webber Press

Copy Editing by Julie Glover

Proofreading by Deborah Digrispino

ISBN Ebook: 978-1-947462-19-9

ISBN Print: 978-1-947462-18-2

First Printing, 2018

Rhodes, Catie.

Wrong Turn/ Catie Rhodes. — 1st ed.

Visit the author website: www.catierhodes.com

SERIES LIST

Forever Road (Book #1)

Black Opal (Book #2)

Rocks & Gravel (Book #3)

Rest Stop (Book #4)

Forbidden Highway (Book #5)

Rear View: Prequel (Book #6)

Crossroads (Book #7)

Dead End (Book #8)

Dark Traveler (Book #9)

Wrong Turn (Book #10)

Last Exit (Book #11)

WRONG TURN

PERI JEAN MACE GHOST THRILLERS #10

CATIE RHODES

Another for my sweetie. Thanks for understanding when I'm so wrapped up in a story that I can barely remember my name.

1

———

THE HOUSE, a white brick ranch with pretty turquoise shutters, didn't look like a witch's house. But the hemlock and henbane growing in the flower beds hinted we'd found the right place. I parked my truck a little way down the block and left the engine running. Too hot to do otherwise.

Tanner, sweat beading his forehead, fiddled with the truck's air conditioner until he had it running full blast. He gave me a smile.

I smiled back, but fatigue wavered behind my eyes. I took a sip of Vietnamese-style coffee. It was sweeter than I liked, but I hoped the combination of sugar and caffeine would keep me rolling just a little longer. The two days spent driving from Archer City, Texas, to Natchitoches, Louisiana, had me whipped.

It wasn't just the drive that had kicked my ass. My hot boyfriend had kept me awake most of the night. I reached across the truck and tucked his hair behind his ear. He grabbed my hand and planted a sweaty kiss on it. I took another sip of the sweet coffee mixture. Come to think of it, it was a nice change from my usual strong, bitter coffee.

Summervale Carnival had a yearly engagement here. They had invited Sanctuary to join in as long as we kept it on the down low. Nobody else wanted to come to humid north Louisiana at the end of August, but Cecil voted us all down. Sitting in front of this witch's house, I suspected his ulterior motive for this visit to sportsman's paradise.

Across the truck, Tanner held his condensation-beaded plastic cup of Vietnamese coffee to his forehead. "Why are we here?"

"Cecil didn't say any more than I told you—this Queenie woman might have a solution for getting rid of the scar tissue spell." The scar tissue spell had been placed on me in infancy. It kept me from accessing the full measure of my witching abilities. Eventually, it was going to get me killed.

"What are we waiting for?" Tanner adjusted the air-conditioned vent until it blew directly in his face. The livid red streaks decorating his broad cheekbones worried me. The humidity in this part of the Southeastern US didn't agree with my California-born boyfriend. He'd already puked once.

"Cecil said he'd be here at one." I lit a cigarette and picked at the lighter's safety label with my fingernail.

Tanner put his hand over mine to still my restless fingers. "Look at me."

I blew out a long breath but did what he said. More than just my lover, Tanner had grown into my closest confidant. We talked naked in the dark of night. We spent the miles driving from place to place talking on phones. Hours-long conversations about everything and nothing. Now Tanner fixed me with his gaze. Jewel green, sexy, and wild.

"Whatever Queenie the Witch says won't be all bad. If it is, you and I will find another way."

I wanted to believe him, but nothing ever came easy for me. There was no reason to believe this would be any different.

Someone tapped on my window. I turned to see my great-uncle Cecil wiping sweat from his face with a plain white handkerchief. He motioned me to follow him and walked toward the witch's house.

"You can stay in the air conditioning." I opened my truck door.

Tanner grabbed my arm. "How could you think I'd want to stay?"

As close as we'd gotten, I didn't feel comfortable having Tanner hear me get bad news. One day he'd get tired of the bad news and head out for greener pastures. I wanted to put that off as long as possible. There was no way to tell Tanner that without making him mad, so I shrugged and said, "Come if you want."

He reached for the door handle, and the relief I felt shamed me. How had I let myself turn into such a wimp? Cecil raised his eyebrows when he saw Tanner trailing behind.

"I didn't tell Queenie there'd be three of us," he said in a low voice when we reached the porch.

"Do you think she'll be upset?" I had never even heard of Queenie until Cecil told me I'd be meeting with her.

"Hell if I know," Cecil stage whispered. "Last time I spoke with her, she and her husband were running house repair scams in the Deep South. That's been thirty, thirty-five years ago."

This visit with Queenie the Witch was beginning to worry me. "Why do you think she can even help?"

"Because Queenie always knew where to find the Wanderer." Cecil spoke out loud now, voice sharp with impatience.

Cecil hadn't yet explained who, or what, the Wanderer was or how he might help. When pressed, he'd only say, "The Wanderer just knows. If anybody can help, it's him." But what if I didn't want his kind of help?

Hinges whined as the front door swung open. "Cecil Paul, are you and these young folks just gonna stand out here and argue, or are you going to ring my doorbell?"

Cecil's lips cracked into a grin, spreading wrinkles across his face. He turned and held out his arms. "Queenie! Sugar, you look just the same."

The two embraced, laughing. I studied Queenie. Black hair shot with liberal white threads. Face as wrinkled as Cecil's. Crepey skin hanging off skinny arms. Either it hadn't been three decades, Cecil's eyesight was failing, or Queenie didn't look the same at all.

I pushed away the less-than-nice thoughts. Queenie had agreed to help, even though she didn't know me from a frog on the porch. Tanner took my hand, twining his fingers through mine. I glanced at him for reassurance. He winked and squeezed tighter.

Cecil and Queenie broke their embrace. Cecil, still squeezing her arms, said, "Thank you so much for making time for us."

Queenie mock frowned. "For you? Anytime."

Cecil gestured at me, pride shining in his eyes. "This is my great-niece, Peri Jean Mace."

"Leticia's granddaughter?" Queenie cocked her head and studied me like a cut of beef she might be considering in a butcher shop.

I nodded.

"I suppose you'll do." Queenie's dark eyes sparkled with humor, and she grabbed me in a hug and squeezed with a strength I hadn't suspected. She let go of me and took in Tanner.

"Tanner Letts, ma'am." He held out one deeply tanned hand.

Queenie stared at it for several beats, making no move to take it.

Cecil said, "Tanner is Peri Jean's...ah...friend. He's a trusted member of Sanctuary. He decided to join us at the last minute."

Queenie nodded and took Tanner's hand. Instead of shaking it, she turned the palm up and traced one of the lines. She raised her eyes to Tanner's. "Passion. Loyalty. You're a catch."

His sun-browned cheeks flushed, and he cast his eyes down. Queenie let go of Tanner and held open the door for us. We filed inside and stood in the entry hall. An old wall mirror threw my reflection back at me. I winced. The humidity had turned my black hair into ropy clumps that looked like something out of a painting of Medusa.

Queenie closed the door and led us through a spacious living room where a huge TV showed a peaceful ocean scene. The plain beige carpet and tasteful furniture could have been in anyone's home. Not what I expected at all.

Queenie motioned us into the dining room. "This is where I work."

She went straight to the oblong dining room table and straightened the black tablecloth covering it. A tuxedo cat jumped onto the table and meowed. Queenie gave the cat a pat and went to a shelf of different colored candles.

I took one step into the room. Queenie's considerable power rushed out in warning. It swirled around me, testing, probing. My black opal necklace, which magnified my gifts and warned me of magic nearby, shot painful electric jolts into my chest. I stopped right inside the door. Cecil, oblivious, sat at the table. The cat hissed at him.

Tanner stopped next to me. "What is it?"

I shook my head, keeping an eye on both Queenie and the cat. She turned, holding a virgin purple candle, and gasped. She spoke in a harsh, unfamiliar language to the cat. It jumped off the table and came to rub against my legs. The black opal's pings softened to a bearable level. The magical force lost its menace and welcomed me inside.

"Faustus thinks every person of power is a threat. He likes us to have all the power." Queenie sat the purple candle on the table and two vials of oil next to it. "Since we're working for you, dear, you'll need to dress the candle."

I moved to the table, taking slow steps to keep from tripping over Faustus, who trilled at me. I'd spent enough time with my raven familiar, Orev, to understand Faustus was laughing at me. Little rat-turd muncher. I held my left hand over each of the two vials of oil, testing to see which one had the magic that fit mine, and picked up the one on the right.

"We're contacting the Wanderer?" I needed to know so I could set my intent before I rubbed on the oil.

Queenie nodded. "I'll contact him on your behalf."

I picked up the candle and the oil and walked to a table that had several animal skulls on it. Placing my hands on the table, I drew on the energy of the bones, the wood, and the magic of the beeswax Queenie had made the candle from. The lights flickered. Intent set, I cleared my mind of everything else and rubbed the oil from top to bottom to draw things to me instead of push them away.

"Someone taught her well," Queenie said to Cecil.

"It wasn't me." But the pride on his face said he took credit for me anyway.

"Oh, I know that. You were always too busy chasing women to learn the old ways." Queenie took the candle back to the table and motioned me to follow.

For the first time, I noticed only three chairs around the table. Suddenly I understood Queenie's reaction to Tanner. She'd set up the table for three participants. Three as a number held great power. Now she'd have to add a fourth person. It might throw off the balance of what she had planned.

"Queenie, Tanner won't be upset if he can't participate in the ritual," I said quickly. "He knows he's gate-crashing."

Queenie gave me a wink. "No, sweetie. If I understood Cecil Paul correctly, this is serious stuff we're discussing. Your lover needs to hear whatever is said."

My cheeks flamed because Queenie had hit on why I almost didn't want Tanner here. Letting him in on too much personal business solidified his spot in my life. And I wanted to keep it loose and easy. Every little merge tangled things further, made it harder and more painful for one of us to change our mind and leave. But Queenie was already dragging a chair away from the wall. Tanner hurried to help her, placing it exactly where she told him.

She took an object covered with black lace out of a cabinet behind her chair and placed it on the table. Next to it, she set the purple candle and motioned for me to light it. Queenie and I sat at the same time.

She pulled the black lace away to reveal a black crystal ball. "My power is much like what I feel coming off you, Peri Jean. By that, I mean I won't be conducting a traditional ritual. Instead I'll use both your power and mine to tell me what you want to know."

I nodded to let her know I understood and agreed.

Satisfied, Queenie turned to Cecil. "I'm afraid I'll need you to explain why you need the Wanderer. He doesn't like being disturbed for frivolous reasons, and if I facilitate such a thing, the responsibility will fall on me."

Again I speculated on who this person—or creature—was. And I questioned the wisdom of hunting him down.

Before I could tell Cecil we needed to get out of this place and leave this nice lady to her TV programs, he launched into the story of how I came to have a spell covering my magical core. Queenie listened with her faded brown eyes fixed on Cecil's face, nodding every few sentences. When he stopped talking, she sat in silence, her wrinkles arranged into a frown. She started to speak a couple of times but shook her head.

"So Leticia is the one who chose this for Peri Jean?" Queenie looked me over again, as though seeing me for the first time.

I nodded. "From what I understand, yes."

Queenie nodded again. "I'm sure she had her reasons. Why don't you tell me your reasons for wanting the spell removed."

"Two different times I've dealt with a spirit called the Coachman. In life, he was a man named Oscar Rivera. " I paused to take a calming breath. Just thinking about Oscar made my chest tighten.

Queenie drew back from me, face set in distaste.

"You know him?" I asked.

"Heard of him." The distaste stayed on her face.

"Both times, he almost killed me because I couldn't access my full power." I stopped because I wasn't sure what else to say.

Cecil spoke up. "This is her destiny, Queenie. The challenges intended for her will come whether or not she's ready." He leaned forward. "In addition, she may not be able to pass our family's power on to the next generation without full control of it."

"And that's the really important thing." Queenie raised what eyebrows she had left and gave Cecil a not-very-nice smile.

He leaned back in his chair. "This power has been in our family for millennia. It's important that it continue. Is it not important to you that your family's power continue?"

Queenie appeared to think that over, but she wasn't really considering. She was gathering her energy. It moved in the air, cooler and sharper than my power. Reality rippled around Queenie. Tendrils of it moved near her sagging ears. She put her hands on the black crystal ball and took a deep breath.

"Put your hands on the ball, Peri Jean." Her voice had gone guttural.

I leaned forward and did as she asked. Soon as my fingers touched the black sphere, Queenie's power sang in my fingertips, testing me, pressing against what little bit of Priscilla Herrera's mantle I had access to.

"Now Cecil Paul." Her voice rang deeper with more power.

Cecil wiped his hands on his dress pants and put his fingertips on the ball. He closed his eyes and breathed deeply. The power stabilized to a low hum.

"Now Tanner Jackson Letts," Queenie commanded.

Tanner jerked next to me. Queenie knew his middle name. He took a deep breath and put his fingers on the ball, throwing me a nervous glance. Power vibrated around the woman's little old lady shell, greater and more terrible than anything I had in my arsenal. Just went to show things aren't always what they seem.

Queenie's strong voice cut into my thoughts. "Cecil Paul, join me in thinking of the Wanderer, in remembering all we know of him."

Both elders leaned their heads forward in concentration. A low hum came from Queenie.

Threads of bright light shot through the black sphere like rainbow lightning. Different colored threads touched each person's fingers. When it got to my fingertips, a light shock carried through my body. It tried Cecil again, but came back to me. The shock grew more intense.

"Don't pull away," Queenie said. "Just let it test you."

The light shot power into my fingertips over and over again until an ache spread up my arms. My black opal grew warm on my chest, then hot enough to burn. It would leave a red mark. My raven familiar, Orev, cawed outside Queenie's house. Faustus hissed in response. I opened my eyes to find Queenie staring at me.

"You are the one," she said and took her fingers off the black sphere. The rest of us followed suit. Queenie picked up the swath of lace and draped it back over the black ball. She stood from her seat and blew out the candle.

Finally I could stand it no more. Patience had never been my strong suit. "Did you find out anything about the Wanderer?"

Cecil blew out a breath and shook his head. "She means no disrespect, Queenie. She's young and impatient."

Queenie barely acknowledged either of us. "You're not ready for contact with the Wanderer. He'll only help you on the last leg of your journey. You have at least several more trials to complete. More to discover about yourself. Keep your mind open."

I leaned back in my chair and tried to keep the disappointment off my face. Pissing off Queenie might create an ass whipping I didn't want to experience. But I was disappointed. We'd come all the way to Natchitoches, Louisiana, for nothing.

"If you want to move forward, stop living in your own life like a ghost." Queenie pointed one arthritis-warped finger at me.

What did that mean? I couldn't keep from frowning as I puzzled over it. Meanwhile, Queenie stood and walked us to the front door. Remembering the customs of our kind, I dug in my pocket for the fold of cash I kept there.

"Do you take donations?" I asked Queenie.

She held out one hand and said her line. "Whatever you feel appropriate."

I put the entire wad of cash in her hand. Fear can motivate generosity as well as anything else.

Queenie made the money disappear. "Don't be so disappointed. Today was a success."

"How so?" I couldn't hide my incredulity. The money I'd given Queenie would have bought groceries for the month.

Queenie smiled as though she knew my thoughts as well as her own. "The Wanderer will meet with you when the time is right. He is now aware of your need."

She closed the door on any answer we might have made. The deadbolt clicked home. It was a clear message that we needed to go. Tanner and I followed Cecil to the economy car he and Shelly pulled behind their motorhome. He unlocked the door and stood back for the heat to boil out.

"Follow me downtown. We got in too late last night to get meat pies, and I'm ready for one or two." Without waiting for an answer, Cecil got in the car and started it.

"Are meat pies barbecue?" Tanner asked on the short walk to my truck.

I answered with a glare. Tanner's obsession with Texas barbecue—the culture and the food—left the permanent taste of smoked meat in my mouth. The only smoke I wanted to taste all the time was cigarette smoke.

The restaurant Cecil chose consisted of a long, narrow room full of tables for four. Despite the lunch hour being over, people jammed the place. The smell of frying food made my mouth water.

Cecil ordered a plate of corn fritters as an appetizer. Tanner had never even heard of the deep-fried balls of batter embedded with corn kernels. He wolfed one down and refused another.

"Too heavy," he said, face pale and beading with sweat.

I finished my corn fritter and reached for another. The food wasn't too heavy for me. I loved deep-fried anything. But worry churned in my stomach.

Cecil voiced my feelings. "Queenie scared me. What might be in store for you?"

"Nothing good." I had several pissing matches running in the background.

The threat of Oscar Rivera hung over me like a storm

cloud and would until I vanquished him from this plane. I'd destroyed the Six Gun Revolutionaries Motorcycle Club. And I owed favors to several chthonic beings who could choose to call in their markers any time.

CECIL PINCHED the bridge of his nose between his thumb and forefinger. "Other battles you've been through have lessened the scar tissue, yes?"

Yeah. And they almost killed me too. Cecil didn't like whiners, so I kept the thought to myself and just nodded.

"Then there's nothing to do but be careful." Cecil dug into his meat pie, which had come while we talked, and chewed with his eyes closed. His wife, Shelly, would have had a shit fit at him for eating so much fried food.

I finished my meal in silence, wondering how much more I could stand before I fell over from exhaustion.

Cecil went back the RV park to rest before the carnival started that evening. Tanner and I set off to see the sights of Natchitoches. Established in 1714, the city was the oldest permanent settlement in the 1803 Louisiana Purchase.

Guzzling cold drinks and pouring sweat, we explored the carefully preserved downtown buildings. Along the banks of the Cane River Lake, right off the downtown, Tanner pointed to a sign advertising the Christmas Festival of Lights.

"We should come back in a few months." He kissed me.

"I'd like that." It felt good pretending to be just another couple in the honeymoon phase of a relationship.

The day ended as most days did with Tanner, our

clothes in a pile on the floor and our bodies tangled together. Had I known how much things would change in just a few hours, I'd have cherished it more.

———

I LAY in the dark trying to figure out what had changed. Maybe it had been a nightmare, the kind waking up erases so completely you're left with nothing but an unsettled feeling. But I didn't think so. Something was different.

The shadows of my camper seemed the same. The basket of laundry sat on the table where I'd left it, silently scolding me for being too lazy—or horny—to fold it before I went to bed.

Tanner slumbered next to me, a heavy arm and leg thrown across me, pinning me to the bed. He slept the sleep of the dead, slow even breaths puffing against my hair. He hadn't woken me with a sudden movement. What then?

The air conditioner rumbled overhead, shaking my little camper with its noise. It may have woken me when it kicked on. The unit blasted cold air into the small space, but the late August heat and humidity still burned like fever under my skin. But it wasn't the only thing that kept me from falling right back to sleep.

Queenie had said I had more trials to face before the Wanderer would help me with the scar tissue. Trials, most of which turned out to be life-threatening, scared the pudding out of me. This trial would likely come at exactly the wrong time. But what could I do? My thoughts began to fragment as the languor of sleep slipped over them. My eyes drooped.

A shadow moved near the bathroom at the back of the camper. I sucked in a deep breath. My heart lunged into action, pumping blood and adrenaline through me. Someone was in here with us.

My body tensed. Had I left the door unlocked? No. I'd locked the door as Tanner tugged off my clothes a few hours earlier. The shadow slowly taking shape in the darkness belonged to someone who'd broken into my little home. I nudged Tanner. He responded with a sluggish grunt and tightened his grip on me.

Great. It would take force to wake him up, and right now I wanted to believe the shadow didn't know it had woken me. I reached for the mantle. Even though I didn't have full control of the power it contained, the few hours' rest had me fully charged. I gathered energy, pulling on everything in the room, even the electricity.

Once the shadow neared, I'd give him or her a blast of something they might not live through.

The bathroom light flicked on. I jerked with shock, eyes burning, and threw up one arm to shield my eyes, squinting at the blurry figure. There was something wrong with his head. It brushed the camper's ceiling and seemed to bend with it.

Next to me, Tanner's slow breaths stopped. He was awake. Good. At least he'd help me fight.

The shadow spoke. "Peri Jean Macccccc." He dragged out my last name, making it hiss. All of a sudden, I knew who it was. Mohawk. I couldn't mistake that voice.

His skinny body came into focus. Now I could identify his bleached blond Mohawk as the part of him brushing the ceiling. In spite of the heat, he still wore a leather jacket, ripped black pants, and heavy jack boots. Made sense. Aren't snakes cold-blooded?

Faster than my vision could track, Mohawk rushed at the bed. I let out a sissified scream, clawed at Tanner like a damn girl, and hollered, "Don't let him take me."

Tanner, with no regard for his own safety, rose to meet Mohawk. The covers fell off his naked body and puddled at his knees. Tanner drew back his fist. His back muscles bunched, and he let one punch fly at Mohawk. The creature from the dark outposts dodged Tanner's fist the same way he'd have avoided walking through a spider's web.

My hope sank. Of course Mohawk could counter any physical attack and beat it. He wasn't even human. My friend and mentor, Mysti Whitebyrd, called beings like Mohawk chthonic beings. The only way we had any chance of beating him was to use magic.

Shoving the covers off my naked body, I crouched next to Tanner, drawing on our combined magic, and let loose a bolt of electric fire. It slapped into Mohawk's chest and died there in a puff of smoke. The smell of singed leather competed with the being's swampy, snake stench. He opened his mouth, let his snake fangs show, and hissed. The sides of his neck flared out like a cobra's.

One skinny, long-fingered hand flashed out, grabbed my arm, and yanked me off the bed. Tanner let out a warrior's yell and leapt on Mohawk. The snake man held my arm so tight the bone began to ache. In a second, my lower arm began to tingle from having the blood flow cut off. With his free hand, Mohawk plucked Tanner off him like an errant kid and slung him back on the bed.

Tanner rolled to his feet and tensed to launch himself at Mohawk again. The monster held out one hand. A flash of light, not unlike the one I'd tried to blast Mohawk with, blazed into Tanner. He fell on his side, holding his chest and gasping.

I quit fighting to get away from Mohawk and launched myself at him, jabbing at his eyes with my fingers. He let go of my arm to fight me off, curled his other hand into a fist, and slammed it into my sternum. Pain bloomed in my midsection. My legs folded, and I sank to the floor of my camper, where I lay naked and curled into the fetal position, struggling to breathe.

Tanner, a red welt forming on his chest, got to his feet. He was ready to fight again. Mohawk pointed one finger at him. "Stop now, Tanner Jackson Letts, or I'll kill you."

No. I wouldn't let Mohawk kill Tanner. He didn't even deserve to be in the middle of this. I tried to draw breath to speak. My injured sternum spasmed, refusing to let me draw more than the shallowest wisp of oxygen. I held up one hand to Tanner and shook my head.

Tanner frowned and gave Mohawk a death glare. His battle-scarred fists clenched.

Mohawk flicked his forked tongue at Tanner. "One more attack, and I'll consider Peri Jean Mace in violation of our agreement."

"She'd never make a deal with a piece of shit like you."

Tanner's chest rose and fell with each breath. A vein throbbed in his forehead. He was ready to go to war.

Mohawk's woody brown eyes flicked over my naked body. His pupils expanded, and his nostrils flared. He chuckled. "If that's what you believe, you don't know this woman very well."

A chill started at the base of my spine and spread over my body. I shook my head again at Tanner, silently pleading.

Recognition flooded his face. The fury went out of his green eyes as though a switch had been flipped. Shoulders slumped, he dragged on his clothes, retrieved mine, and helped me into them. I had a hard time uncurling my body. Each pull on my abdominal muscles sent stabbing pain through my bowels.

Mohawk sat at my camper's table watching our progress. He drummed long, sharp fingernails on the table and checked the time on his phone every few seconds.

When I could speak, I said, "Why did you break into my home?"

"We have a bargain. I can tell you haven't forgotten. Did you think you could fight your way out of it?"

I shook my head. Tanner set a glass of cold water in front of me, face set in hard planes of anger. We exchanged a glance. I'd told him as little as possible about Mohawk and the deal I'd made. Some part of me had hoped it would just go away. I should have known better. Never taking my eyes off Mohawk, I sipped the water.

"I'm not a cheater. I do what I say I'll do. But you promised to contact me through the marble. I thought you'd changed your mind and come to just take me." If I failed to fulfill my end of the bargain with Mohawk, I'd forfeit my freedom. Become his slave. Bear his offspring. I shuddered at the thought.

"Then you *do* want to attempt to find the book?" Mohawk checked his phone again. Like he had anything more interesting to do than harass me.

"Anything to get you out of my life." I took my first deep breath, and then another just to make sure I could do it again.

"At the risk of sounding like a broken record, I want to remind you that coming with me voluntarily would satisfy all debts." Mohawk set down his phone and leaned forward. "I am willing to grant your freedom in five years' time. You only have to..."

"She's not going anywhere with you," Tanner shouted.

Nausea roiling in my sore stomach, I ignored Tanner and spoke to Mohawk. "No. I'll get the book. Whatever it takes, I'll get it."

Mohawk sat back in his seat and watched both of us for several long seconds. Finally, he heaved a deep sigh, reached into an inside pocket of his jacket, and withdrew an old, wrinkled photo. He set it on the table.

A young woman with wispy blond hair blowing in a long-dead wind stared out at a vista of tree-covered hills. A minidress with a geometric pattern showed off her shapely legs. The garment's cut suggested the picture might have been taken in the late sixties.

The young woman clutched a huge book to her chest. On the visible end of the book was metal twisted into a circles and dots pattern that raised the hair on the back of my neck. Even the years separating me from this book were not enough to hide the wrongness of it. It probably didn't help that Mohawk had already hinted at what it did to people who read it.

"This is the book? The one you want me to find?" I reached out to touch the picture with my index finger but drew it back. I didn't even want to touch an image of the nasty thing. Tanner crowded in for a closer look.

Mohawk nodded. "This human is the last one to possess the book." He slid out of the bench seat and took the few steps to the camper's door.

"Wait." I shot out of the bench seat, shoved around Tanner, and went after Mohawk. "I need more information. I don't even know her name."

Mohawk spun to face me. I halted in my tracks. He tilted his head, dead eyes boring into me. His tall, stiff hair scratched against the cabinet over my sink.

"Why would I help you? I've told you how I'd like this to end." He ran one skinny, cold finger over my face.

Cold horror radiated outward from where he touched. I backpedaled away from Mohawk and sat down in the seat he'd just vacated hard enough to jar the breath from me.

"You have..." Mohawk looked at his phone again. "Oh, let's make this fun. You have seventy-two hours from right now. Failure means you belong to me."

My lungs constricted, and my mouth dried up. A lifetime as Mohawk's consort would drive me mad. Blood roared in my ears. Mohawk smiled.

"This is your last chance to come with me voluntarily. As promised, I'd release you in five years. But if you play this out and fail?" He clucked his tongue. "You'll be mine for the rest of your natural life."

"Now wait a minute…" Tanner, who'd gotten control of his anger, took a step toward Mohawk.

The creature hissed and pointed one finger at him. "Interfere, and you'll die crying for your mother."

I grabbed Tanner's arm, sweat stinging my forehead and scalp, and pulled him close. Tanner put one arm around me. The three of us glared at each other, barely breathing. One drop of sweat rolled down the back of my head, down my neck, and left a cold trail down my back. Mohawk's pupils grew larger until they spread over most of his eye. A smile twitched at the corner of his mouth.

"Last chance." He sang the words.

I shook my head. "I'll find the book."

He laughed and stepped out into the night, leaving the camper's door hanging open.

Tanner walked to the door, closed it, and locked it. He turned to me, green eyes burning bright and intense. "All right. Time to come clean about that asshole and whatever he's holding over you."

I took a deep breath. "You remember me telling you about the hag that almost killed Hannah?"

"It attached itself to you, and to get rid of it, you had to buy it out of slavery." His face slackened. "That was the hag's owner? Sweetie, why did you…" He put both hands over his face and took deep breaths. Finally he dropped them. In a deceptively calm voice, the one he used before he started screaming, he asked, "What happens if you don't find the book?"

My voice trembled when I spoke. "He admires the line of witches I'm descended from. He wants to have a child with me."

Tanner's face fell in shock. "But I thought you were... couldn't have kids."

I shook my head. "It can be fixed by a healer. I've just never..."

Never what? Wanted to risk having a child? Wanted to see how badly whoever fathered it could screw up both our lives?

"But any child you had with him wouldn't even be human." Tanner's face paled, and he swallowed hard.

I imagined the result of a union between Mohawk and me. A sour wave of nausea shot up my throat. I ran into the bathroom, fell to my knees in front of the toilet, and barfed.

2

———

TANNER HELD my hair while I called dinosaurs. When I was finished, he wiped my face with a cold cloth. I sat on the floor, eyes closed, leaning against the tiny door to the camper's only full-length closet space, too weak to move just yet.

Tanner ran more cool water on the cloth and wiped my forehead with it. I felt a rush of love for him. I opened my eyes to stare at his not-quite-handsome face and his brilliant eyes.

Sweet Tanner, so sincere and helpful. We exchanged a smile. With one arm, I pushed myself off the floor. Tanner pulled me to a standing position. I got out my toothbrush and brushed the awfulness out of my mouth.

He watched me. "Tell me about this book. What does it do?"

I spat out toothpaste and turned on the faucet to wash it down. "Best I can understand, it instigates murder and mayhem."

Tanner frowned in the mirror.

"Mohawk was once worshipped as a god. He compelled his followers to draw symbols on the walls of caves. These symbols drove his worshipers into a violent religious frenzy."

Tanner, who'd dealt in magical items all his life, thought this over. "The symbols probably created a mild hypnotism. So you're saying the symbols from the caves ended up in these books?"

I nodded. "There's three of these books. Mohawk wants this one back into play."

Tanner made a disgusted face. The gravity of my task hit me. I was going to release evil into the world to save myself from an awful fate.

I examined myself in the mirror. Could I really be so selfish? Tanner stood behind me in the mirror and put his arms round my waist.

"I know what you're thinking." His whisper sent a shiver through me. "You can't look at it that way. You have to value yourself enough to fight for your own survival. Whatever it takes."

He released me, helped me back to the table, and sat me in front of that creepy picture while he rummaged in the refrigerator. He was about to make me ingest some of the awful sports drink he loved. And I felt so bad I'd probably do it.

I studied the picture while he filled a glass with ice. The woman holding the book had a sweet face ruined by evil, dead eyes. Her fingers curled around the edge of the book possessively. Was she dead or alive? I concentrated on the picture. Sometimes I could tell if a person in a picture was alive or dead. But this time, I only got a whiff of dry, dusty air. I turned the picture over. Scrawled on the back were the words "Devil's Rest, 1973."

Tanner set my neon-colored drink in front of me. "Any ideas?"

"No." I hid the lie by putting the condensation-covered glass to my forehead. Tanner couldn't know about Devil's Rest or 1973. He'd only want to help, and it might get him killed. No. I had to do this alone.

A plan pieced itself together. I'd get in my truck and leave everything, including Tanner, here. My friends and family would be pissed, but they'd be safe.

Tanner watched me, brows drawn together. "You're lying." One hand flashed out and snatched the picture from me. He held it close to his face, studying it.

Don't turn it over. Please. I sat still as possible, as though that would make my hasty prayer come to pass.

Tanner squinted at me across the table. "What are you hiding?"

Not waiting for an answer, he put the picture close to his face again, memorizing details. I held my breath and begged the universe to make him give it back. *Don't let him see the name Devil's Rest.* Tanner moved the picture a few inches away from his face, eyes moving back and forth. He turned over the picture. I wanted to scream at him to drop it, but Tanner had a stubborn streak.

Now he raised his eyes to mine. "What's Devil's Rest?"

I shook my head.

He pushed the picture across the table. "I see plans forming behind those dark eyes. Tell me."

"I'm leaving as fast as I can. Before anyone wakes up." I put my fingers on top of the picture.

"What? Why?" Tanner, always eager to involve others, never understood the wisdom of going the course alone.

"They'll want to help." I said the words as though my family's help came with cooties.

"The more of us there are, the faster we can get it done." Tanner drank down his own over-sweet sports drink.

"No way. Mohawk doesn't want me to find his book. He wants me to fail so he can make me his slave. If they get in the way, they're toast." I finished off my sports drink in three big gulps with a grimace and a shudder.

Tanner thought this over in his usual solemn way, head lowered, hair fallen across his face. After a few seconds, he nodded. "You're right. Let me go get a shower and pack. We'll leave a note for them."

This was the hard part. "You can't go either, sweetie."

He stood, came around the table, and shoved his way into the booth seat next to me, crowding me in. "I go where you go." Before I could answer, he kissed me.

A few seconds later, I pulled away, heart hammering, body flushed. "I'm serious. You can't go."

Those eyes, molten green and hot as asphalt at the end of August, hardened. "Why not?"

"There are a thousand ways this could go bad." I cupped his face in both hands, hoping to soften the blow. "I need to know you're safe."

Tanner snarled and pushed my hands down. "You don't trust me."

I shook my head. That wasn't it. I trusted Tanner with everything I had. My body, my life, my belongings. The person I didn't trust was myself. Things tended to go wrong around me, and people got hurt. Like Wade Hill. There was one who'd never speak to me again.

An expedition like this could change everything. Tanner and I had gotten together in the midst of extreme danger. Another bout of extreme danger might be too much. I cut the thoughts off cleanly. What needed doing? Pack for Devil's Rest. Go talk to Hannah.

I climbed over Tanner to get out of the booth style dining table and went to my bed. There I lifted my mattress to access the storage underneath and pulled out both my witch pack and the traveling hatbox I used for a suitcase. The latter had been a gift from Hannah. She'd bought it in Austin from an artist who'd painted runes and ravens all over it. I hefted the hatbox onto the table, opened it, and began tossing in the freshly laundered clothes.

Tanner followed. "That Queenie woman was right about you."

"Huh?" Busy calculating what I'd need for three days—because nothing mattered after that—I barely heard Tanner.

"Look at me." He grabbed my wrist, hard enough to make me gasp at first, then loosened his grip. "Stop packing." He spun me to face him. His eyes burned into mine. "That woman said you live like a ghost in your own life.

That's what you're doing right now by not wanting me to go with you."

"Hey, you're right. Let's all go. Go tell Dillon and Finn to get the kids ready to travel." I threw another handful of underwear into my hatbox. "No, wait. Let's go get Hannah first. She really needs some more fucking trauma in her life."

Face reddening, Tanner narrowed his eyes into angry slits. "Don't blow me off." His voice rose to a shout on the last couple of words. Someone's dog started barking. He took a deep breath and spoke nearly in a whisper. "Do not blow me off. You know exactly what I'm talking about."

I yanked my wrist away from him. "No. I most certainly do not. All I know is my whole life is a circus of tragedy and danger, and I don't want you dragged into it."

Maybe a quick session of mattress rodeo would soothe his hurt feelings. I sidled close to him and brushed my lips against his.

He wasn't finished saying his piece and talked against my lips. "Then let me go with you. Finding stuff like this book is what I do. I can help you."

I drew back to stare at him. What he said was true. But what else came with it? Danger for him. Maybe death. I shook my head.

"Let me go take care of this. I'll make up for it when I get back." I trailed my fingers down his bare chest.

He moaned and planted soft kisses along my jawline. "I know exactly what you're trying to do right now."

"Me too." I popped open the button on his pants and dipped my fingers inside, still thinking about the time and getting out of here before people started stirring, and tugged him toward the bed.

Tanner didn't let me pull him. He planted his bare feet and stood like a statue. "You're avoiding the subject. I said you live in your life like a ghost. In order to keep from thinking about it, you're trying to get me naked."

I glanced down at the front of his pants. "You want to be naked with me."

He put his arms around my waist and pulled me against him. "But I also want to talk to you about this."

"About what?" I let my chest rub against his.

His eyes slid closed, and he pulled me against him hard enough to make us both grunt. He shook his head and pushed me away.

"Listen, please." He held up one hand. "That lady, Queenie, said you walk in your own life like a ghost. I know what she's talking about. You tiptoe around like you don't belong here rather than just living. Not wanting me to go is part of it."

My face heated. "That's not true."

He rolled his eyes and huffed out an ugly laugh. "Of course not."

I closed the distance he'd put between us, pressed my lips against his hot skin, and slipped my arms around his waist. "I can't risk you going with me and getting hurt, maybe even dead. What if I lose and he takes me as his... concubine?" The idea made my mouth dry, and I swallowed hard. "He'll kill you if you fight him. Or he might kill you for fun. Or he might take you as well. This is no game."

"And what we faced together a few months ago was a

game?" He cupped my chin and tilted my head to look at him.

I shook my head. "No. It wasn't a game either."

"I helped you then, and I want to help now." He slid one hand under my shirt and ran his fingers over my bare skin. I shivered.

"Not this time." I tugged him toward the bed, to make that the last thing we did together, rather than argue.

But Tanner pushed my hand away and stepped around me to open the door. The sound of frogs singing drifted into the camper. "I'm going to shower and pack my bag. If you're not here when I get back, we're done."

Knowing I was beat, I waited until the door slammed before I got up and finished my packing. I grabbed my bags and a wad of cash I kept for rainy days and slipped out of the camper.

———

NEXT DOOR, in Tanner's seventies era camper, the lights shone and the sound of water hitting the walls of the shower drifted through the night air. Sadness rose up, swelling in my chest. I took out my phone and dialed Brad Whitebyrd's number. He picked up on the fourth ring, his voice thick with sleep.

I didn't bother with pleasantries. "Get up, get out here, and stop Tanner from leaving in about ten minutes."

"Who is it?" Jadine's voice asked.

"Peri Jean, what is this about?" Brad groaned.

"Mohawk's ready for me to find his book." Brad knew

all about my bargain with Mohawk from his sister, Mysti. "Tanner wants to help, and he can't. Stop him." I hung up and walked to Hannah's camper, teeth clamped on my lower lip to keep from getting all weepy. *Control yourself.* I heard Priscilla Herrera in the command and was still puzzling over how I felt about that when the door to Hannah's motorhome swung open.

She peeked out. "Hurry if you're going to leave him behind."

She motioned me inside her luxury liner. A divorce settlement from her husband, a major league baseball player, let her do everything first class.

"Did our argument wake you?" I hoped not. I didn't want to hear what Hannah thought about the things Tanner and I had said to each other.

She shook her head. "I was already awake. Leon likes to leave early."

I raised one eyebrow. I knew they'd been dating but hadn't realized they'd progressed to the point of sleep-overs, even sneaky ones. Sounded like a good arrangement right then. At least everybody in the world didn't know their business. I might try it with Tanner's replacement. My heart gave a little ache at that.

"I didn't hear much, really." Hannah rubbed my back. "I only know what I do because Tanner said that last bit to you after the door was open. So Mohawk's back?"

Hannah amazed me. She could take a few random facts and figure out a world of information.

"I've got seventy-two hours to find that stupid book or I

become his bride." I screwed up my courage to ask her the question I'd come to ask.

Hannah made a face. "Do you want me to come with you? I can be packed and ready in ten minutes."

I shook my head. "I meant what I told Tanner. I don't want anybody else involved in this. Too dangerous. That's why I'm here. I need your gun."

I stood still, my heart thundering. I'd never asked anybody for a gun in my whole life. This was the first time I honestly thought one might help me.

Most people would have asked me a zillion questions. Hannah just nodded and walked to the back of her fancy motorhome. A cabinet opened and closed. She came back holding a little zippered pouch in zebra print.

"This one's not registered to anybody. I got it after the business with King and the Six Guns. I keep thinking Corman's going to come back to finish things." She held the cute little pouch out to me. I took it, surprised at its weight, and tucked it into my hat case.

Hannah cleared her throat. "The only thing is...well, I hate to say this. But I don't think it'll kill Mohawk."

I raised my head so we could look at each other while I had my say. "It's not for him. It's for me. I won't let him take me alive."

Hannah and I stared at each other for several long seconds. She held out her arms. I went to her, and we hugged tight.

I spoke first. "If we don't see each other again, I want you to know I've been grateful to have you in my life."

She pulled back from me and put her hands on either side of my face. "Same. I love you."

We hugged again, this time harder. I pulled back and said, "I need to go before Tanner gets out of the shower."

She nodded and wiped at her cheek. "If you do make it back, you need to think about what Tanner said. About tiptoeing through your life."

"Thought you didn't hear much." My skin heated as I tried to remember everything Tanner and I had said.

"I heard that. And he's right." She opened the door for me, indicating she'd said her peace.

I walked out but turned back to her. "He won't be here when I get back. And he's wrong anyway."

She smiled. "Tanner might surprise you. Most guys would have taken the piece of ass and let you go."

My face heated. *Didn't hear anything, my ass.*

Brad Whitebyrd sat on the hood of Tanner's truck when I came out of Hannah's motorhome. I walked over, climbed up, and gave him a hug. He put both arms around me and rested his cheek on my shoulder.

"You should call Mysti. She'd help you." He ended the hug and stared hard at me.

"So would everybody in this camp, including your wife. It might get them killed." My voice trembled on the last word.

Brad hung his head. He wouldn't offer up his pretty bride as a sacrifice to my drama, and I'd never ask him to.

"Goodbye," I whispered.

Orev perched on the rearview mirror of my truck. "Caw caw caw."

I opened the truck's door and laid a towel on the passenger seat while he worked his way inside. Then I climbed into the driver's seat and drove out of there like the devil was riding my bumper.

A few miles down the road, I stopped at a convenience store and looked up Devil's Rest on my phone. It was south and west of San Antonio. At least seven hours from my current location. I got on Louisiana State Route 6 and drove into the darkness of the new morning.

That final bit of nighttime and the lonely highway woke up the ghosts of my regrets. Tanner. Leaving the way I had was a bitch move, one he didn't deserve. I'd become attached to him and then let myself get scared about it. I should have done things differently. I should have said goodbye to my family.

"I'm sorry. I'm sorry," I whispered, tears dripping from my jawline.

The yellow stripes disappeared under my headlights with no answer. Maybe there wasn't one.

I crossed the Texas-Louisiana border just as the sun peeked over the tall pine trees. It rose blazing into a sky already white with humidity and chased away the velvet of the morning like a mean dog protecting his yard. I kept driving and stopped in Lufkin at a McDonald's for breakfast but couldn't make myself order more than coffee, which I drank while sitting on the hood of my truck, smoking. I offered Orev cat food, but he flew off and came back later with a snake which he ate right in front of me.

I turned away and text messaged Cecil about what had happened and what I'd be doing. He tried to convince me to wait for the family to join me, but I wouldn't even tell him the name of the town where I was going. Cecil finally gave up, told me he loved me and to call if I decided to quit being a jackass and accept his help. I wanted to ask if Tanner had left Sanctuary but couldn't bring myself to do it.

I got in my truck and checked the map function on my phone to see how much farther to Devil's Rest. Five and a half hours from Lufkin.

Just to torture myself, I went into my contacts and pulled up Tanner's. A picture of him smiling, the sun peeking out from behind his head. I had treated him shabbily, like he didn't matter. He'd responded the only way someone with any self-respect could. By removing himself from my life.

My finger hovered over the call button. The urge to call him itched, nearly impossible to resist. It wouldn't cost me anything but pride to apologize. He certainly deserved it. But I couldn't make myself call. After a couple of wasted minutes, I put the phone away, started my truck, and got back on the road.

I pushed the speed limit as hard as I could, ever aware of the minutes passing. As I moved west, the trees got shorter, and the sky stretched open, endless and blue, the sun a frying egg in the middle. The landscape grew sparse, the road ribboning out with waves of heat rippling above it. My phone said it was eighty-two more miles to Devil's Rest.

Those final miles beat with urgency. Any minute saved might be the one that allowed me to find the book. A green sign that said Devil's Rest and pointed left onto a rutted and forgotten-looking asphalt road marked the final turn. I fishtailed as I made it.

THE TOWN of Devil's Rest would have reminded me of Gaslight City had it not been for the huge expanse of sky hovering over it. In East Texas, the pines would have hidden the sky, wrapped it in their web of secrets. Devil's Rest's stark openness made it seem harsher, more mean. I drove through town on a street called Veterans Drive, not sure how to proceed.

I had the picture of the woman holding the book, but I didn't know her name. I didn't even know where she'd lived or what the book had compelled her to do.

Tanner's knowledge of magical items would have been useful here. The voice sounded like some creepy mixture of Priscilla Herrera and me. I ignored it and the flash of remorse it brought. I pulled into the slant parking in front of a row of buildings and already had the truck in park before I realized I was facing a bridal shop, with an out-of-date wedding dress in its dusty window. *It would have to be a bridal shop.*

I took out my phone again and scrolled through the pictures I'd taken of Tanner over the course of our short relationship. I got stuck on the one we'd gotten a fellow tourist to take on the ferry from Galveston Island to the Bolivar Peninsula. Tanner had one arm hooked over my shoulders, and we were staring into each other's eyes, laughing.

I'd made a mistake. Story of my life. And now I had to sit here in front of a bridal shop mourning it. Screw that. I started the truck, backed into traffic, and cruised to the other end of the small downtown.

An older one-story building caught my eye. The awning was shaped into long diamonds. Inside each diamond was a neon letter. They spelled Phil's. Another sign on the window read "Home of Phil's World Famous Monkey Burger!"

Gross as it sounded, my stomach rumbled. I whipped into the parking lot. Soon as I opened the truck's door, Orev scrambled over me and took flight. I let him go and walked across the parking lot to the diner. A cowbell clanged when I opened the aluminum framed door. People turned to stare. I pretended not to see and walked inside.

The sign over the counter said "Order Here," so I stood in line behind a blond woman with her two kids. The kids wanted dessert more than hamburgers. A minor skirmish ensued. By the time it was my turn, I'd had plenty of time to study the menu. My stomach had stopped rumbling and started roaring.

"What's a monkey burger?" I asked the cashier, who wore a nylon uniform that looked like it probably forced your skin to sweat.

She snorted. "You know how many times I gotta answer that every day?"

I shrugged and shook my head. "'Least one more, I guess."

She sighed. "A monkey burger is two hamburger meat patties, grilled onions, a slice of ham, and ranch dressing. Meal comes with one side and a drink."

"Why's it called a monkey burger if…" I began.

She held up one hand to stop me. "The burger is named for Phil's daughter. When she was little, Phil called her his little monkey. This is her favorite kind of hamburger. So it's a Monkey Burger."

I might have asked if Phil's Monkey Burger was really world famous, but the look on the cashier's face suggested she'd had just about enough questions from me. I kept my questions to myself and ordered the monkey burger meal with onion crisps just because they sounded good and an unsweet tea with half lemonade.

The clerk took my money and gave me a big plastic number. "Set this on your table. We'll bring it out to you."

I chose a booth at the back of the diner and took out the picture of the woman holding the book to look at while I waited. Someone in this little nowhere town probably knew who she was. All I had to do was figure out how to find them.

I'd seen a sheriff's office on the way into town. They might be able to help, especially if the woman with the book did something awful, but they also might take offense to me poking around in the county. I'd dated the sheriff of a little nowhere county for a while. He could be a real prick when he thought a stranger might be nosing around.

One narrow building in the downtown had claimed to be a library. They'd have back issues of newspapers. But unless the librarian knew the woman in the picture, it would be a needle in a haystack search. For the first time since I'd told Brad to leave his sister out of it, I wanted to call Mysti Whitebyrd. She'd help with no questions asked. But she also might come to Devil's Rest. If I lost this game with Mohawk, she'd die before she let him take me.

I sat in my booth, watching people come and go, and wanting to scream in frustration. My time was running out, second by second, and I was no closer to finding the book than when I'd started hours ago. The woman I'd been standing behind in line used her phone to take a picture of her young son with ketchup smeared on his face. That gave me an idea.

Image searches. Someone might have uploaded this very image online with an explanation of who the woman in the picture was and what she did. To find it, all I had to do was run an image search. I should have thought of that to begin with.

Before I could get out the picture Mohawk had given me, a woman wearing the same type of uniform as the girl who'd taken my order appeared at my side. She set down a plate holding the biggest burger I'd ever seen, a separate basket of crispy fried onion pieces, my drink, and a squeeze bottle of ketchup.

My mouth began to water. *Eat now. Mess with the picture later.* I thanked her and dug in.

As I ate, I realized it had been over twenty-four hours since my meal of Natchitoches meat pies. Tanner and I had chosen to enjoy each other the night before instead of having supper. Hungrier than I thought possible, I polished off the hamburger, most of the onion pieces, and got a refill on the tea and lemonade.

Remembering my plan to do an image search on the picture Mohawk gave me, I cleared back my plates and wiped the smears of grease off the table. I set out the picture and stood to get the right angle hovering over it. The waitress came back to bus the table.

"You were hungry." She picked up the plates. "Sure you don't want some dessert? We got..." Her gaze fell to the picture, and the smile faded from her face. "Damn it. Can't you people leave well enough alone?"

I glanced down at the picture. Its mere presence was obviously some kind of social faux pas in Devil's Rest. Normally I'd have been embarrassed enough to sweat bullets. Not this time. Relief nearly turned my muscles to jelly.

"You know who this is?" I tapped the edge of the picture.

She rolled her eyes at me and shouted over her shoulder. "Phil? Phiiiiiil? We got another one."

A fiftyish man with swarthy skin, a big, fleshy nose, and a stained paper apron covering his clothes came out of the kitchen. "What is it?"

"This one's got a picture of Loretta Nell." The waitress reached for the picture, but I snatched it up. No telling what she and Phil would do to it, and it was the only clue I had.

Phil watched me slide the picture into my bag with narrowed eyes. He punched one stubby finger at me. "You people are a disgrace to the human race. What happened here happened a long time ago."

Every instinct begged me to cower and apologize. These people had seemed nice enough before the waitress saw the picture, and the hamburger had been delicious. But the last couple of years had taught me something. Once you shit in a bed, it will always be a bed that's been shit in.

There was no way I'd win Phil over, get him to buy me a cup of coffee, and tell me a story. Right now, I could do one of two things. Get all the information I could or run.

"What happened a long time ago?" I asked.

A lady with a hairspray halo twisted in her seat and snarled worn teeth at me. "You know good and well what you came here for."

I shook my head truthfully. A little tendril of fear worked its way through me. I had fucked up, and this little scene could go a lot of different ways, none of them any good.

Phil grabbed me by the arm and tried to pull me away from the table. I pulled out of his grasp and snatched up my bag. This pissed Phil off. He grabbed me under one arm, held me off balance, and marched me toward the door. The other customers forgot their meals and yelled encouragement at Phil, a few of them clapping.

My fear grew legs and ran rampant, showing me images of what a crowd like this could to do me. If they hurt me bad enough, I wouldn't be able to look for the book. I staggered along, trying not to fall, and prayed I could make it to the parking lot and relative safety.

Then someone stuck out their foot. I went sprawling. Phil's painful grip was the only thing that kept me from face-planting on the floor. I tried to regain my footing, but with Phil yanking me along, the best I could do was take big clown steps the rest of the way to the door.

The waitress held it open so Phil could sling me onto the rough asphalt. I'd been thrown down enough to know to roll with it and not try to catch myself. One elbow got a good scrape, but I ended up on my feet.

Phil charged toward me, teeth bared in fury. I held up both hands, already reaching for the power of the mantle. It crackled against my skin and warmed the black opal.

"Stop right there, Phil." I spoke as calmly as I could, given my elbow had already started to drip blood onto the parking lot.

Phil took one more step, but then he seemed to sense something. Fear widened his eyes for a flash, but then they narrowed again in rage. "My momma was one of the ones killed by those pieces of garbage. You axe me, ever' one of them motherfuckers got exactly what he or she deserved."

The waitress spoke from the door. "Your kind coming here, stirring shit up, disrespects the people of this town."

Both Phil's and the waitress's eyes blazed crazed fury in my direction. Several faces crowded the plate glass windows.

I backed toward my truck, hands up, mouth shut, and magic at the ready. I recognized the look in their eyes. This kind of zeal couldn't be talked down. Couldn't be reasoned with. But it could escalate into something deadly.

The people who'd burned down my grandmother's

house and tried to beat me and my friends to death had looked just like this. Possessed. Wild. Ready to drink blood and howl at the moon.

Heart trying to lodge in my throat, I opened the door to my truck, barely holding my magic at bay. It was so close to the surface, I'd have to release it in some way or it might make me sick. Before I could get the door closed, Orev swooped inside. He cawed at me. *Hurry.*

"I agree," I said and started the truck.

My phone buzzed with a text message. I reached to take it out of my bag, and my concentration slipped. The plate glass window of Phil's exploded outward.

I put the truck in gear and backed out in a big hurry. Phil, esteemed inventor of the World Famous Monkey Burger, ran after me for a few hundred yards, screaming obscenities and shaking his fist.

It wasn't until I was passing the Devil's Rest city limits sign that I realized I'd gotten not one but two really good clues to the identity of the lady in the picture. Her name had been Loretta Nell, and she'd been involved in murder.

I did a U-turn and drove back through Devil's Rest, toward the only lodging I'd seen.

3

———

THE DEVIL'S Rest Guest Houses consisted of two facing rows of pastel painted cabins separated by a narrow concrete lane. Each cabin had its own carport, and the sign outside advertised free internet. Even if it was slow as molasses in January, I'd still be able to research Loretta Nell. Just knowing who she was and what happened could go a long way toward figuring out what happened to the book.

I parked in front of a church next door and took out my phone. Sure enough, Devil's Rest Guest Houses Wi-Fi signal showed up. Bingo. I tapped on it.

A box popped up. It read "Enter Your Password." I groaned. Of course they wanted a password. Otherwise everybody and their dog would be using their signal to surf.

I took a closer look at the pastel cabins. Might be a nice place to rest and set up home base. Get a hot shower that lasted more than the five minutes the RV hot water heater allowed.

I moved the truck into the Guest Houses' parking lot. The first cabin was marked "Office." I went inside. The smell of disinfectant and flower-scented air freshener hit me, and the idea of a warm shower and a bed with clean sheets began to sound as necessary as the internet.

A woman with a curly cap of iron-colored hair raised her head, took one look at me, and shook her head. "You ain't staying here. Get out of our town."

The flat way she said it rocked me. Gossip traveled faster than the bullet train here in Devil's Rest. In the couple of minutes it took me to drive to Devil's Rest Guest Houses, someone had called this old bitch and warned her I might be coming. No use arguing.

Skin burning with humiliation and indignation, I backed toward the door and pushed it open one-handed. I turned and came face to face with a beanpole of a man. Thin lips set in a snarl, he held a short handled hatchet in one hand.

He leaned around me to speak to the woman at the desk. "She giving you problems, Mama?"

"Better not be." The woman fixed me with a steady glare, magnified by her thick-lensed glasses.

I shoved past the guy and hurried to my truck, glancing often over my shoulder, and burned rubber out of the Devil's Rest Guest Houses. Once it was out of sight, I slammed the flat of one hand into the steering wheel.

Whatever killing Loretta Nell had done in this town had marked it. But it also must have been pretty famous if people came here on pilgrimages. It must be all over the internet. To hell with it. I didn't need a motel room to research. I whipped onto the shoulder and dragged my phone out of my bag.

A message from Tanner hovered at the top of the screen. "Let me know you're okay."

I squirmed again over the way I'd acted and unlocked the phone's screen. No bars and no service. It figured. I put the phone down and pulled back onto the sun-bleached highway.

I drove away from Devil's Rest, remembering the map had shown another town not far south. I'd drive a few miles and see if I came to it. Right past the few businesses on the outskirts of town, I spotted a sign that made me slow down.

Old-fashioned as sock hops and ducktails, the red sign's white letters, each overlaid with a strip of neon, read Devil's Slumber Inn. Underneath the name the word "Vacancy" flashed, almost invisible in the bright sun. The sign's orange arrow pointed toward a one-story L-shaped row of rooms with orange doors. I crept into the empty parking lot, shoulders tensed.

This could turn out just like things had at the Devil's Rest Guest Houses. There could be some Brylcreemed golden oldie waiting to chase me out. Town like this, the locals probably didn't have much excitement. Today must've been a kind of Mardi Gras for them.

The Devil's Slumber Inn didn't look like much. It was the kind of place where Mysti Whitebyrd would take in the clean, rolled-up bedspread she kept in the trunk of her

Toyota sedan and exchange it for the motel's. The guest houses would probably have been immeasurably nicer, but I was running low on options. The town I remembered seeing on the map might be ten minutes or an hour away. With no phone service, there was no way to find out.

The red neon sign on the motel office's glass door flashed "Open." Underneath hung a hand-lettered sign that said "Clean Rooms. WIFI for guests only, so don't ask." Only one way to find out if they'd rent me a room. I sighed and climbed out of the truck. Orev hopped out and took off flying.

"Don't go far. They might not let me stay," I called after him. The bird kept going. I went inside the motel's office.

An electronic bell dinged, and someone yelled, "Just a minute."

The voice had come from an open door at the back of the office that led down a dimly lit hallway. Probably a small apartment for the owner or caretaker.

I picked up a faded brochure advertising a nearby spring-fed lake. All the people pictured wore outdated clothing and hairstyles. Stuff from before I was born. The hair on the back of my neck rustled, warning me again something was very amiss in this little hidden hamlet of hell.

A young guy hurried into the office holding a thick sheaf of printed pages. He set them down on the counter and squinted at me. "You don't look like a roadhouse chippie."

I drew back from the assessment.

Laughing, he held up one extremely pale hand

speckled with fine, dark hair. "Sorry. Miz Hester, the owner of the guest houses, already called to warn me you'd be coming by. She told me you had trashy, long black hair and wore eyeliner like a roadhouse chippie."

I did a slow burn. Prejudice based on what I was—a psychic medium—had dogged me my entire life, getting worse when my witch powers began to manifest. I'd almost been killed for being something I couldn't help.

Nasty people like Miz Hester needed a lesson in compassion. Part of me wanted to march back over there and give it to her. But Mohawk's book and the ticking clock attached to it took precedence. The guy settled his stormy blue eyes on me and quirked his lips in a smile that probably got him laid often.

"Good thing for you I don't share Miz Hester's desire to rid this town of nosy-rosies. Making enough money to keep this place open is more important to me." He leaned forward, eyes still fixed on mine, and said, "Plus, I think you're hot."

I took a step back, a little repulsed by this odd guy and his overt come-on. "You'll rent me a room?"

The smile again, this time accompanied by a wink. "Sure, why not?"

I dragged out my brand-new credit card.

He shook his dark head. "Cash if you've got it."

I hadn't thought to stop by a bank, which limited my cash reserves, but I nodded.

The guy quoted me a price that was neither cheap nor expensive, and I paid for two nights. Once he had my cash, he held out one hand for me to shake. "Name's

Dwight Carr, owner and operator of the Devil's Slumber Inn."

We shook. Dwight's hand was cool and dry against mine and stronger than I'd expected. Something wasn't right about this guy, and it wasn't just the come-on. I pulled my hand away, resisting the urge to wipe it on my pants.

"You let me know if I can be of service. And I mean any service." He slipped me a raunchy wink.

I bit back a smile. The young women who came here to find out about Loretta Nell probably kept Dwight in free ass. Well, he wouldn't be getting a piece of mine. But I did have a question for him.

"Actually, you can help me. What do you know about this Loretta Nell person?" I watched Dwight's face carefully for the flash of anger I'd seen on the other residents of Devil's Rest.

Dwight's smile only broadened. "Only if we can play some show-and-tell. I want to see the picture you flashed at Phil's Monkey Burger, the one that caused such a ruckus."

I hesitated, overcome with an irrational fear that Dwight might take the picture from me and rip it up. But my time was running out. Showing him seemed the only way to move forward. I slid the picture out of my purse and set it on the counter, thumb and forefinger holding it to the worn Formica. Dwight tried to take the picture. I shook my head but offered no explanation.

"Can you turn it around to face me?" The amused glint never left his eyes. I did as he asked. Dwight leaned forward. The smirk fell off his face. "Where'd you get this? I heard rumors about Loretta's book, but there's not one picture of it floating around."

Instead of answering, I put the picture back in my bag. "We're playing show-and-tell, Dwight, and it's now your turn. Who's Loretta Nell, and what did she do that has this town on a gag order?"

Dwight's eyes chilled. Fear pricked at the base of my spine. Awareness of how alone I was out here filled my heart and made it thud harder. Dwight reached under the counter and dug around. I stiffened, muscles screaming at me to run, but I held still. He straightened and set a brass key down on the sheaf of papers.

"You're in room five."

I reached for the key, but he put his hand over it.

"How about we go to room five, and I'll give you the whole story on Loretta Nell and the Messengers? I've got some primo giggle smoke." He pulled the key just out of my reach.

I'd had enough of Dwight. For all the time he'd wasted, he could have told me Loretta Nell's life story. If he decided not to let me stay here, it might be a blessing in disguise.

"I appreciate the offer, but I don't smoke dope." I packed as much disdain as I could into my refusal, even though I really had nothing against pot. I just didn't smoke it. "Tell me about Loretta Nell."

The smile finally fell from his face, and he gave his pretty eyes a practiced roll. "I can't believe you're here with that picture and don't know anything. But all right. Loretta Nell Grimes came here in the early nineteen-seventies with a bunch of other hippies. They called themselves the Messengers."

What a weird name to call their group. Had they chosen it because they delivered a message from Mohawk's book? I didn't ask. The less Dwight knew about why I was here, the better. Something flickered behind his eyes, as though he knew my thoughts, but he continued talking without missing a beat.

"The Messengers rented a farmhouse outside town and told everybody they were going to live off the land." Here, he snorted as though it was the corniest, most typical thing he'd ever heard. "They stayed to themselves, so people got to thinking they weren't so bad. Besides, there'd been a couple of pretty brutal murders, whole families, and a couple of kidnappings. People had bigger things to worry about."

Had one of these been the murder of Phil's mother? My monkey burger rolled around on my stomach. Dwight watched me, eyes gleaming in a way I didn't like at all.

"But this one sheriff's deputy, Freddy Stephens, figured out those hippies were the ones doing the killing." He drummed his opened palms on the countertop and hummed some tune. "Freddy Stephens and some other lawmen raided the farm. It turned into a standoff, and all those murdering hippies ended up full of bullet holes. Except for Loretta Nell. They never found her body." The smile slid back onto his face. "Now...you tell me where you got that picture."

"A collector." The word popped out before I had much time to think about it. I'd helped Tanner move a few magical artifacts. He always called the people who wanted them collectors.

"Of pictures?" One of Dwight's eyebrows cocked, stark black against his pale skin.

I suddenly wanted to tell him to give my money back. My truck would be an okay place to sleep for the next two nights. Maybe I could use the public library's internet. Even if I had to pay for it.

"Come on. Maybe I can help you." This time he wasn't flirting. He was curious what I had going on.

"The collector I'm working for wants Loretta Nell's book." I kept it short and simple.

Dwight nodded slowly. "The book. Yeah. Your picture's the first I've seen to prove its existence. I'd only heard rumors. Supposed to be some kind of book of the dead. Sacrifice to the god, and you're all powerful." He waggled his fingers and made a woo-woo sound. He had to take his hand off the key to put on his little finger puppet show, and I snatched it. My fatigue made me clumsy, and I dragged the sheaf of papers off the desk.

"Shit," I yelled as papers fluttered to the floor.

Dwight hurried through a swinging half-door separating the counter from the reception area and knelt to help me pick up the papers. I dropped to my knees to help him.

"I got it," he snapped.

I ignored the little turd and began picking up papers. They were covered with row after row of email addresses. Dwight saw me looking. His shoulders slumped, and the confidence fell off him.

"This place doesn't get the most business. I've been trying a little email marketing." Red spots blazed high on his cheeks.

Devil's Rest didn't seem like a place to get rich. And I didn't think emailing all these people would get him more business. Different strokes. "So about the book. Any ideas where I could start looking for it?"

"I've been out to that farmhouse dozens of times. If that book was there, I think I'd have found it." Dwight went back to stacking his email addresses, popping them against the counter.

Something about this place, and Dwight, made me itch. I lifted the sleeve of Tanner's too-big Foo Fighters shirt and scratched my arm. Dwight's eyes widened at the sight of my raven tattoo. I dropped the sleeve.

He straightened. "You know, you might have better luck searching for Loretta Nell's book at the farmhouse your-self. Why I don't I give you directions?"

"I'd appreciate that." I had already started formulating a plan. If this had been a made-for-TV movie, sweeping victory music would have been playing in the background.

Dwight reached under the counter again and pushed a home-printed brochure at me. "Map's ten dollars. Cash."

Inwardly growling, I dug out the ten-spot and snatched the map.

"What's the internet password?" I wanted to knock the smile off Dwight's face.

"Loretta." Dwight's laughter followed me into the hot parking lot.

———

I GLANCED at room five and turned over the brass key in my hand. Should I go to my glamorous room and try out Dwight's internet access to learn more about Loretta Nell and the Messengers? After all, I'd gotten a room so I could access the web.

The lengthening shadows gave me my answer. No. Better to use the last of the daylight to visit the farmhouse.

I got into my truck, turned on the air conditioning, and studied the map. A big red *x* marked the farmhouse. Unless Loretta Nell escaped the police raid, which I doubted, she'd died in the farmhouse or on the grounds. The best and easiest way for me to find out about the book would be to contact her spirit.

Loretta Nell herself could tell me the location of the book. I'd banish her for her trouble, get the book, and see if I could salvage my relationship with Tanner. The more I thought about it, the less I wanted to see him walk away. He mattered to me unlike any man—even Chase Fischer —had.

Come to think of it, maybe I did have an immediate use for Dwight's internet. I still hadn't answered Tanner's text message. Even though there was still no phone service, there was internet as long as I had Dwight's silly password. I logged in and tapped out a quick email.

———

Tanner,

No cell service out here in the wilds. Hope you are

checking your email.

Things are okay. I'm here in Devil's Rest and think I have a line on this book. Maybe I'll be finished faster than I thought.

Please forgive me for the way I acted.

xoxox PJM

I tapped send and had to wait several seconds for the confirmation ding. Dwight's internet sucked. But hadn't everything about this trip?

I spent a few minutes hunting through my witch pack and the covered bed of my truck to make sure I had everything I needed. Then I started the truck and put it in gear.

Dwight's map instructed me to reset my vehicle's trip meter before I left the Devil's Slumber Inn. Then I was to drive exactly ten point two miles south of Devil's Rest and turn onto an unmarked dirt road. The helpful note on the map said the road's official name was Stephens Ranch Road, but dark tourists kept stealing the sign. The county eventually quit bothering to replace it.

Stephens Ranch Road turned out to be hard to miss. A tall, rusted metal archway with a big *S* on either side marked a dirt road winding into the hills. I turned onto it, bumped over the cattle guard, and drove along feeling pretty good about things. If it all went well, I could be headed back to my friends and family tonight.

But then the road came to a fork, both branches stretching off into nowhere. I took out the ten-dollar map and studied it more carefully. It didn't show a fork in the road. Had I turned off on the wrong unmarked road? I didn't think so. All the landmarks had matched up with Dwight's cheesy map.

I took the road to the right because I didn't want to waste the time to backtrack. According to the map, the farmhouse was three miles from the state highway. I'd gone a mile and a half, so I'd either be there soon or not.

The road took me up a steep incline that switched back and forth up the side of a hill. I chugged along at little more than a crawl because each second made me more sure I'd chosen the wrong branch. Now I'd have to find somewhere to turn around or back down the way I came. Turning around would be a bitch because this little road was barely wide enough to accommodate my truck.

At two and three-quarters of a mile, the hill flattened out into a grassy clearing overlooking miles of rolling green hills below a deep blue sky broken only by a few puffy clouds. The place seemed vaguely familiar, but the Texas Hill Country was full of views like this one.

Something moved at the edge of my vision. I turned to see three men getting out of a truck parked on the far edge of the clearing. They sauntered toward my truck. The chubby one in the middle with sunburned cheeks waved. One of his two companions, a pig-faced guy wearing a muscle shirt to show off his nice body, smiled at me. The third one, nondescript with his mousy hair flopping in his face, marched along with his head down like he was going to war.

My body tightened. I had two choices. I could slam the truck in reverse, do a quick donut, and haul ass back down the road I came in on. Or I could see if these men might give me directions.

A stinging combination of apprehension and doubt simmered in my guts, the bane of womanhood. I'd been on my own most of my life and considered myself a capable woman. But the hardest part was knowing when to take a chance on people being normal and helpful and when to run. It could go either way. Once it did, things would happen fast, and it would be too late. I made sure the gearshift was in drive and kept my foot on the accelerator.

The chubby guy with sunburned cheeks smiled wider and hollered, "You lost, lady?"

The other one, with the ugly face and the nice body, yelled, "Looking for the old Stephens farmhouse?"

I started to nod, but then it hit me that the third guy with the floppy brown hair had disappeared. Where had he gone? I took my eyes off the first two guys and searched for him. As I stared out the windshield, Floppy Hair leapt onto the hood and jeered at me. My fear snapped. I screamed.

The other two men laughed and closed the distance faster than I'd given them credit for being able to move. The chubby one yanked at my door and frowned when it wouldn't open. He yanked again.

"Open this door, you bitch." He beat on the window with a meaty fist. Now that I could see his eyes, I knew I never should have stayed. They glinted pure, wild crazy.

The pig-faced one, eyes just as wild as Chubby's, pulled a hammer out of his back pocket and hefted it in one hand as though testing the weight.

Go, go, go. I snapped into action, jamming my foot down on the gas pedal. The truck shot forward.

Pig-Face bleated a high-pitched squeal but couldn't jump out of the way in time. The truck moved him. I tensed for the huge bump of running him over, but it never came. Chubby chased my truck, beating his fist on the side, his face so contorted with rage he barely looked human. I swerved toward him. He tried to jump away and fell into a cactus. His pain-filled scream made something inside me wake up and blink sleepily at the world.

Anger always simmered close to the surface for me. Now it came at me full steam. I wanted to hurt Pig-Face and Chubby again. The urge was so strong, vivid, bloody images accompanied it. But I'd had a lifetime's practice controlling my anger—or at least knowing when to run before I got my ass whipped.

I put more pressure on the gas pedal and made a U-turn, cruelly steering my truck over the rough terrain. An ATV buzzed to life and burst out of the bushes near the mouth of the road, racing to block me from leaving. Floppy Hair sat on the back. His hair streamed out behind him like a banner.

I gunned the engine even harder. Floppy Hair and I reached the road at the same time. He gave me demonic grin that would never pass for normal, accompanied by a satisfied raise of his eyebrows. As though to say "got you now."

Maybe some women would have stopped to keep from damaging their vehicle. Others might have stopped because they didn't want to run over Floppy Hair. I wasn't either of those women. I swung the steering wheel toward the ATV and never let off the gas. Floppy Hair could do nothing but let me hit him or get out of the way. He chose the latter, missed the road, and jounced down the steep hill. I hoped the ATV rolled over and killed his sorry ass.

I hightailed it back to the *Y* in the road and sat hunched over the wheel, taking deep breaths and shaking. Part of me expected my would-be attackers to come chasing after me. But I'd fucked them up pretty bad. It would take them a while to regroup and work up their nerve again. If they came back, I'd show them my magic. Make all of us sorry.

I stared down the other fork in the road. Would traveling it bring me just as bad of luck as the first fork? My instincts yelled at me to get back to the motel and find someone to come back out here with me. But who?

I'd run off a perfectly good boyfriend, perhaps the nicest I'd ever had, five hundred miles ago. My conscience didn't want him here anyway. The same went for my friends and family. Even so, I wished for them with all my heart.

A familiar black form came to rest on a scrubby little tree's gnarled branches. Orev. My raven familiar would come with me. He cawed as if saying, yes, he would. His thoughts met mine, and I saw what he'd seen as he flew here.

Go back toward the main road a bit. There was a place where I could turn around if I was careful. If I drove slowly, the men wouldn't be able to tell if I'd left the property or if I'd gone down the other fork looking for the farmhouse.

Orev was right. I did as he suggested, coming upon a grassy crossroads I'd barely noticed before. The turn-around done, I drove back to the fork and took the road I didn't choose before, driving slowly so as not to create a dust cloud. This was going to work out. I'd find the farmhouse, summon Loretta Nell, and get the book. Easy as chocolate pie.

The narrow little road went on for so long I figured I'd somehow gotten lost again. But then I rounded a curve and saw a faded red barn. Beyond it stood a white shape that could be nothing but a house. I stopped the truck, twisted in my seat, and stared behind me for the telltale puff of dust from another vehicle following. The shadows had lengthened with the ending day, but other than that, nothing had changed.

I continued my snail's pace, still determined not to throw up dust for anybody to see. In the distance, the barn had looked small and quaint. As I got closer, I realized it was a towering building that covered as much ground as three houses. Beyond were mazes of pens and corrals. All empty with boards buckled and warped by the intense Texas heat.

In back of the barn lay a pile of junk that would have been the envy of any hoarder. A bicycle sat balanced on its handlebars. The wheel's rim had been torn away, and the spokes pointed at the sky like meat skewers. Imagine falling on that. My skin tightened, and I glanced away.

I drove toward the farmhouse but didn't see the graffiti until I got almost to the yard. The white chipped paint had been covered over with phrases like "Josie did it. She killed them all. Josie is just like Loretta Nell," and my personal favorite, "Josie is the devil."

I stared at the words. Dwight hadn't mentioned anybody named Josie, but he had mentioned a group called the Messengers. Maybe she'd been one of them.

I parked near a sagging picket fence that used to be white but was now mostly gray. I slung my witch pack over my shoulder and grabbed the padded case holding my stang in one hand and a pot of grave dirt in the other.

The faded fence's gate was warped shut. I had to put down the grave dirt and the stang to power it open. The hinges let out a groan. It echoed over the empty property. The air around the old farmhouse went still.

The sense of someone, or something, watching pricked at my skin, so intense that I did a slow circle, scanning the horizon for those assholes back at the hill. Nothing moved. I was alone, but only in the sense of being the only living person for a few miles.

Had I come here without talking to Dwight first, I'd have still known a bunch of people died here. It hung over the house like a swarm of flies. This old farmhouse was the kind of place where ghost hunters said they saw something.

If I believed Dwight, and I had no reason not to, the people who died here were murderers. Bad folks. Sometimes dark, ugly shadows came to claim evil souls. But sometimes hell didn't even want them. They were left to walk the earth, lonely and angry, terrorizing whoever they could.

I stared into the farmhouse's second-floor windows.

The glass had been busted out and littered the ground near my feet. Rust-colored splotches decorated the crabgrass and broken glass.

Blood? That didn't make sense. Dwight had said the cops took out the Messengers in the early nineteen-seventies.

A board above creaked, and a shadowy figure passed across one of the windows. The whispers of the dead filled the back of my mind. Yes, a spirit here would talk to me. Even if I had to force them.

I steeled myself, climbed the leaning steps, and picked my way across the porch, mindful of dry-rotted boards. The front door swung open on its own, letting out a stale cloud of pent-up heat. Chest tight, heart hammering, I walked inside.

Dust motes floated over the narrow, empty living room. I opened my second sight and looked around. Nothing here. But the black opal heated on my chest, pulsing, and Orev cawed outside. A board creaked overhead.

"*Up here, witchy-witch.*" The sing-songy voice came from both inside and outside my head.

Loretta Nell Grimes? Only one way to find out.

I picked my way across carpet so dust covered I couldn't even tell what color it had been. The narrow staircase climbed one side of the room, going straight up the wall. Climbing these stairs could end with me lying in a pile of broken boards with a rusty nail sticking out of my eye, but the spirit was upstairs. I needed to make contact if I wanted to find the book. The black opal pulsed again, as though in agreement.

4

———

I SLUNG the stang in its padded case over my shoulder to free up one hand. Gripping the shaky banister with all my strength, I took the first step. The wood groaned but held me. Body tensed, ready to fall, I took the next step. And the next.

By the time I reached the landing, sweat covered my body, and I trembled all over, breath coming in gasps. Climbing with fear of falling hurt more than pushing a lawn mower all day. I longed for a cigarette but didn't dare light up in this old tinderbox.

"Come," the voice whispered all around me.

The black opal gave one long pulse. With the hair on the back of my neck burred out like a dog's hackles, I tiptoed down the hallway. The door at the end slowly swung open, the hinges squealing like the pig-faced guy when I hit him with my truck. I swallowed hard and forced myself to keep going.

The room at the end of the hall was where I'd seen the

shadow pass across the windows. I crept inside. The air stunk like death and chilled my skin despite the end-of-day heat.

The room held a bed pushed against the far wall with a dusty comforter bunched up. The nightstand hung open where it had been rifled either by thieves or thrill-seeking jerks. The room's air shimmered with dark energy. The mantle uncoiled inside me like a snake seeking sun, ready to fight, and Orev cawed outside. The supernatural was with me, in me, all around me, but I still couldn't see the ghost.

"Got you," whispered a female voice, right next to my ear.

The temperature dropped from a little chilly to cold enough for my breath to puff out in front of me. She was here. I readied my energy to fight a spirit, but the seconds ticked past with no more activity. My shoulders relaxed, and I took a more careful look around the room.

The way the comforter lay on the bed made it look like someone was underneath it. Creepy. I couldn't quit looking at it. The fabric rustled. A puff of dust dotted the dying daylight. The comforter rose, the fabric draping over a human shape. My breath caught in my throat. Terror began to uncoil in my stomach. Then I caught myself.

Spirits did stuff like this to scare the living. It was a great trick, and it probably scared the poopy-poo out of ghost hunters. But I wasn't one of those. I was Peri Jean Mace, psychic medium and witch. A woman of power. This spirit was the one who'd better watch out. I drew myself to my full height of five-feet-nothing.

"Loretta Nell?" My voice trembled. *What the hell?* I cleared my throat. "I just want to talk."

The comforter flew off the bed, trailing dust, and came right for my face.

I didn't have time to yell, to move, to do anything before it wrapped around me in a musty cocoon. A surprised scream escaped me. I sucked in a lungful of musty fabric odor and began to cough. The supplies I'd so carefully collected to summon Loretta Nell dropped to the floor in a heavy crash.

I staggered sightless around the room, knocking into furniture and walls, trying to pull the comforter away. My thoughts fractured into terrified blocks of information. *Can't see. Can't breathe.* Fear fluttered in my midsection like a trapped bird. Something moved against my legs.

I stopped in my tracks. *What was that?*

The comforter shifted against my torso. I held my breath, heart thundering in my chest. A woman's high-pitched laugher tinkled in my ear. My throat closed, its dry sides grinding against each other. Something was inside the comforter with me.

Wild terror eclipsed any rational thought, and I screamed.

Icy fingers scrabbled over my face, fingernails scratching and tearing. Stinking breath, straight from the grave, filled my nostrils. Panic ripped through me. I grabbed fistfuls of comforter and pulled as hard as I could. It wouldn't budge.

My horror, fully unspooled, spread thorny vines through my bloodstream. *Stay calm. Stay calm.* Mysti always chanted those words when things got out of control. I whispered them to make them seem more real. "Stay calm. Stay calm. There is a way out of this."

The specter writhed harder against me, its frantic whispers filling my head. *"Mine now. Mine now. All mine."*

Images of gnashing teeth and spurting blood flashed behind my eyes followed by a shaking image of people kneeling before a crude effigy of a snake that looked to be made of human intestines.

My sanity broke like a glass shattering on the floor, bits spraying in every direction. I drew in a dusty breath and screamed. Fight or flight kicked in. I took a few running steps, tripped, and pitched forward. My shoulder clipped something, probably a wall, and then there was nothing.

No. The window. I'm falling out the window. I tried to scream, but my voice wouldn't come.

Orev's caws came, along with the sound of his wings flapping. He hit me, flying against the force of my fall. Then there were more birds. The harsh caw of crows joined Orev's throaty croak. They pushed me back into the room.

Orev stayed with me, cawing, pulling at the ghost until it detached from me. The nasty comforter crumpled to the floor.

The ghost flew away from Orev and flashed around the corners of the room, running so fast my eyes couldn't track it. I opened my second sight.

That gave me a clearer image of the spirit. A young woman with a puff of cottony blond hair flitted around the room, disappearing, then appearing again. Loretta Nell would have been pretty had it not been for the expression on her freckled face. It was wild, pure vicious animal.

Normally, I'd try to calm a ghost before attempting to communicate. Instinct told me there was no point this time. I had enough power to force Loretta Nell to talk to me. It felt disrespectful as hell to do that, but she'd tried to kill me. To hell with being nice.

I got a bundle of sage out of my witch pack and used my cigarette lighter to get it started. Waving it around my body, the same way I'd do with soap in a shower, I cleansed her negative taint off my person. My fear and panic floated away with each inhale of the heady smoke.

Under my breath, I chanted, "*All negative feelings, all negative impulses, get thee out of me,*" over and over until I felt them go. Then I shook my hands to rid myself of the last of it.

Good thing I'd brought the supplies to make a strong circle. It would have been too risky to communicate with Loretta Nell otherwise. Her violent death and evil, hate-filled life had left behind a murderous force. She'd tried to drive me out the window to my death. I remembered the blotches on the ground outside and shivered. Had she done the same to others?

Sacrifices. That's how she keeps the power.

Thinking I understood what was going on calmed me. I took a few cleansing breaths and centered myself. The time had come for Loretta Nell to go on to her reward. I reached for the mantle. We'd talk, and then I'd send her packing. Let the entities in the dark outposts have her.

I zipped open the padded case and pulled out my

shroud-wrapped stang. The power of the wood vibrated through my arm and pinged when it touched the black opal. The mantle zipped toward this new power, thrumming through my hand and into my fingertips.

The two magics touched. A flare of light flashed and rippled through the air around me. It whooshed against my skin like the percussion at a heavy metal concert.

Loretta materialized in one corner. She fixed her blazing, insane eyes on me and hissed, teeth bared. They were stained red with blood. My stomach crawled at the sight of her, threatening to expel my monkey burger. I forced my mind back on task. *Set up the contact.*

My pot of grave dirt had turned over and spilled on the nasty carpet, but there was still enough left to do what I needed. I righted the pot and pulled it near my feet.

Holding the stang in one hand, I leaned my head back and imagined a dome of light surrounding me. I made it the brightest possible light, so bright the idea of it hurt my eyes and burned against my face like summer sun.

The musty smell went away, replaced with the smell of warm grass and healthy fertile soil. Somewhere nearby, birds chirped.

I took a deep breath, filling my lungs with the clean air, and called the corners.

"I call to the power of North
I call to the power of East,
I call to the power of South,
I call to the power of West
Join me."

Around me, the points of the compass fell into place

with a flash of power. The golden bubble surrounding me grew with them and strengthened.

"I call to the power above

And to the power below."

The dome lengthened into a sphere and clicked closed. Now it was time to call the elements. I centered my concentration and let the mantle flow throughout, its power dizzying.

"I call to the element of water." Humidity settled over my skin, and the sound of a brook babbling reached my ears.

"I call to the element of air." A soft, warm wind filled my circle, chasing away the last of the cold and leaving behind the smell of sunshine and flowers.

"I call to the element of earth." The wood in the house's walls, in its floors, sang to life. A low hum filled my head as it spoke to me.

"And I call the element of fire." A blast of flint filled my nostrils, but fire was also my power. The mantle opened like a ripe flower, filling me to bursting and dancing with anticipation.

I drove the stang into the grave dirt. The circle clanged like a bell being rung. The air around it rippled. A blast of heavy air hit me, moving through my hair and my eyelashes.

Now I was as safe as I could be while dealing with something as repugnant as Loretta Nell.

I dug in my witch pack and found my offering bowls. Into one, I poured olive oil. Into the other, I dumped a little cherry-scented pipe tobacco. I knew so little about Loretta Nell that I could only guess what appealed to her.

I took out the picture of Loretta Nell, studied the crafty smile curving her lips, memorized the way her arm rested over the huge book she held pressed to her chest.

Then I put my hand on the stang and called her. I'd pull Loretta Nell's spirit through the stang so that I had power over her. This would prevent her from hurting me, which she'd already proven she wanted to do.

"Loretta Nell Grimes." My voice came out guttural and deep, as it often did when I communed with the spirit world. "I call your spirit. Accept these offerings, and answer my questions."

The floor beneath my feet rumbled. My body tensed, but I pushed away the distraction. I couldn't freak myself out. If I did, I'd lose control of this situation.

"Loretta Nell Grimes." The name came out in a growl. "Come. Let us visit. Accept your offerings."

The stang heated underneath my hand and then cooled. Magic rumbled through it and flowed into my body. She was with me.

The tobacco began to smoke. Tiny red embers glowed within it. Then a puff of smoke whooshed out as though someone had inhaled and exhaled. It went from brown and moist to gray ash in a second. The oil simmered, rippling and moving, and then boiled down to nothing.

"Loretta Nell, I understand you've been through an ordeal. Show me where the book in this picture is, and I'll help you feel better." I held out the picture to make sure she saw it.

The photo fluttered between my fingers. Good. She

knew what I meant. Sometimes older spirits no longer understood living ideas.

"Take me to the book in the picture, Loretta Nell." I couldn't ask her. I had to sound in control, confident and sure what I wanted her to do.

Loretta Nell manifested, clearer than ever. She wore the same geometric patterned dress from the photo. Dirt blackened her bare feet. The musk of her body odor filled my nose. She cocked her head at me, the way a dog does when a human speaks to it. Finally she nodded. She understood. I let a little relief seep into my muscles.

"I'll show you." With one thin, graceful hand, she motioned me to follow.

The beauty of making a circle with the stang in the pot of grave dirt was that I could take it with me wherever I went. I picked up the pot and followed Loretta Nell.

———

LORETTA NELL'S form floated in front of me, a small gap between her feet and the floor. She led me down the staircase and out the front door. It swung closed behind us with a click that hit me as ominous and final.

We crossed the yard and went through the warped gate I'd left standing open. Dry, dead grass crunched beneath my feet. Because I was using my magic, the smell of its nutrients filled my nose. The flow of its energy joined mine.

Loretta Nell led me to the barn. Its huge sliding door yawned open, a maw of blackness waiting inside to swallow us up. Had the door been open when I first saw the barn? I couldn't remember. But I knew one thing. I wasn't going into that darkness with no light. I stopped walking and dug in my pocket. My keychain had a tiny light that wasn't much good for anything except desperation.

Just a little bit more. I'll have the book. I can be done with this whole thing. I can go find Tanner, see if I can salvage our relationship. The inner pep talk bolstered my cringing nerves. I thumbed the keychain light and walked into the darkness, mind full of rattlesnakes, spiders, and other stinging dirt monsters.

Shock molded me to a spot right inside the doorway. I'd expected dark emptiness with a tiny cone of light around me. But inside the barn, a warm, moving light, like that of fire, danced. The walls wavered dimly in the flickering light. Sprays of blood covered them. Bodies hung from the walls.

A dark shadow slanted over the bodies. The shadow gathered light, which first defined a head and shoulders. A flickering image of Loretta Nell came together in front of the wall. She stood erect, chin high, like an artist before her work. Maybe that's what it was to her.

"Why are you here?" She fixed me with emotionless eyes the blue of storm clouds.

We'd been over this, but I answered anyway.

"The book in this picture." I took it out again and held it up.

"You can't have it. The Serpent God charged me with the duty of spreading his word." Loretta Nell waved one hand at the bodies behind her. As though she'd pulled a switch, their stomachs opened, and ropes of intestines fell to swing between their legs.

Bile stung the back of my throat. I took deep breaths until I was sure I wouldn't spew monkey burger lava all over my magic circle. My stomach settled.

"The Serpent God has sent me to retrieve the book. He demands you release it." I let the mantle give my words a little magical push. Some spirits needed a little convincing.

Loretta Nell's blue eyes darkened with fury. Her cute face contorted. "No! The Serpent God wants me to have the book. I am his favorite daughter."

I took a more careful look at Loretta Nell. Was she the child of Mohawk? I opened my third eye and looked for the taint of otherworldliness on her but only saw an angry, dead human.

"Loretta Nell, you can move on from this. Whatever happened in your earthly life is done. There's more." I raised one arm and pointed at the wall. A bright light opened and grew. "I can send you there. You can heal and find peace."

"Noooooo! My job is to arrange cleansings." She waved her hand again.

I flinched, expecting further mutilation of the corpses behind her. Instead, the world around me faded.

Loretta Nell stands in front of a room full of young adults. On the walls are pictures of Jesus Christ on the cross, of Daniel in the lion's den. It hits me that she's in a church.

"What is that slut up to now?" The words come with a tickle of hot breath against my ear.

I turn and find myself face to face with a teenage girl. She wears cat-eye glasses with black frames etched with white flowers. Dancing hazel eyes meet mine, and she claps one hand to her mouth and giggles through her nose.

Mind reeling, I force a smile to my face. Do I know this chick?

Nerdy brown pigtails and a pretty, oval-shaped face. No. I don't know her. Then why is she talking to me? She must think I'm someone else.

I glance down to see a powder blue double-knit skirt covering my lap. The outdated fabric stops well above my knees to show off suntan-colored pantyhose. Matching vinyl shoes with a hideous brass buckle adorn my feet. Ick.

I look around the room. More double-knit polyester. More butt-ugly colors. Button-up collars and shaggy hair for the boys.

They all look ready to go home and watch Janis Joplin, who isn't dead yet, on the Dick Cavett Show. And I'm one of them. Cold fingers walk up my back.

Am I me, Peri Jean Mace? Surely not. This girl beside me wouldn't be giggling with a thirty-something woman. I grab the tooled leather purse sitting next to me and rummage through, fingers stumbling over a plastic makeup compact. I open it and stare at an unfamiliar heart-shaped face. The girl has pretty brown eyes, fair skin, and brown hair with a widow's peak. Definitely not me.

Loretta Nell clears her throat at the front of the room. "I know all y'all probably wonder why I—the bad girl of Fairview Baptist Church..."

"She's not a bad girl. Just a slut." The girl next to me giggles, but so do a lot of other kids.

I want to tell them all to shut up. Loretta Nell brought me back to the time of I Dream of Jeanie and bell-bottoms to show me something. The sooner I see it, the sooner I can get out of this unfamiliar body.

Loretta Nell reddens. "Fine. I just want to read something to y'all."

She opens the book, Mohawk's book.

My heart begins to thud. I don't want to hear this after all, and I don't want to see what it did. I concentrate, trying to push myself out of the vision.

Loretta Nell begins to read. The words sound like gibberish at first, but then my brain relaxes and I hear them for what they are.

"You are a wave sweeping over the earth, reaping the red harvest. You feel this wave, rising inside you. You are of a single power. You are of a single purpose. You were made to reap the harvest. You were made to cleanse this earth of the undeserving." Loretta Nell reads on, but the words all mean the same thing.

A boy in front of us turns and winks at me. A memory belonging to the girl whose body I'm in flashes. In it, this winking boy mashes his lips against hers, hand squeezing one breast so hard it hurts. She tries to push him away, and he shoves his knee between hers. She slaps his face. He slaps her back and walks away.

Anger burns in the body I'm borrowing. Loretta Nell's recitation from Mohawk's book seeps into the anger, stirring it. My skin heats with is fever.

That boy—his name is Kevin—needs to be taught a lesson. He needs to be cleansed from the earth. Boys like him, boys who think they can get away with treating girls like toys, shouldn't be allowed to get away with it.

Around me, other kids shift in their seats, a few murmuring. Our fury joins together. It gains strength.

My anger trips into fury as I stare at the back of Kevin's head. I could hit it and hit it until the skull cracked open and I saw his brains.

From the back of the room comes, "You nasty bitch. I'll teach you to spread rumors about me." A pained scream follows.

The fury inside my head pounds, begging me to show Kevin I won't take his shit. I grip my purse strap in both hands, slip it over Kevin's head, and yank down with all my weight.

The pigtailed girl beside me watches with parted lips. Every once in a while, she licks them. Her hazel eyes flash, and she's on me, yanking at my hair.

"You bitch, you think you're better than everybody else." Her fingers search for my eyes.

I let go of my purse to stop her, and Kevin leaps over the back of his seat, arms outstretched. He tackles me to the floor, planting his knees on my chest. He slams his fists into my face over and over. The sound of my skull shattering is like the crack of a wet branch.

In the background, Loretta Nell is shouting, "In his name. In his name. All in his name, you snotty assholes."

A familiar voice woke me from the vision of hell on earth.

"Peri Jean! Look at me. Do not take another step. Peri Jean!" A clattering sound followed the words.

Something popped against my ankle. It stung. The vision faded. I came to, surrounded by a huge, blueberry sky studded by a million pinpricks of starry light. Nothingness stretched out before me. Orev perched at my feet, head reared back to give me another peck.

"Peri Jean, please listen to me. Please." This time I recognized Tanner's voice. He wasn't supposed to be here. I'd let him go because he might get hurt or killed. But now it was too late. He was here, and he wouldn't leave until we did what we came to do. That snapped me back into the real world.

I stood on the barn's roof, a long, damn way to the ground. Panic beat at my chest. Had I climbed up here? I didn't remember. What had happened in that barn? I'd lost control.

A wave of fear swam in my head. My foot slipped. A scream tore from my throat. Heart slamming, I fought for balance.

"You'll never have the Serpent God's book," Loretta Nell's voice, perfumed with the grave, blew into my face. "It was entrusted to me."

I fought for control, sucking oxygen deep into my lungs and letting it out slowly. My thundering heart slowed. Things began to make sense again. Loretta Nell thought me a thief. I'd just explain. Once she understood this was what Mohawk wanted, we'd be okay.

"The Serpent God sent me to retrieve the book." My voice only shook a little.

"Liar." Loretta Nell's anger rose, chilling the night air.

"No. The Serpent God wanted to have a child with me. I didn't want to do that, so I agreed to retrieve the book..." I quit talking as freezing hands pressed against the small of my back and gave me a hard shove.

I locked my knees and pushed back. One foot slid on the barn's tin roof, slick with dew.

"Noo," I squealed and let myself go down on one knee.

Maybe that would keep me from overbalancing and toppling over the edge. I had seen the barn in daylight and knew how far it would be to the ground. The memory of that pile of junk, those bicycle spokes pointing at the sky, flashed behind my eyes. A whine escaped my lips.

"The Serpent God would never bestow his offspring on you. I was his chosen daughter, the keeper of his word, and you're a worthless little shit stain." She shoved me again.

I slid on the slanted roof, feet kicking for purchase. My heel caught a rough spot. I lay gasping, trying to slow my heart. If I allowed myself the luxury of panic, I'd die. I had to think.

Tanner's voice came from below. "Listen to me. There's all kinds of broken shit down here. It'll kill you if you fall. Hear me?"

The image of those bicycle spokes loomed large in my memory. A falling sensation swept through me. I squeezed my eyes shut.

"Yeah." I barely got the word out.

"Hang tight, baby. I'm coming up there to get you. Just be still." His footsteps crunched on the dead end-of-summer grass.

I wanted to tell him not to, but I couldn't. Uncontrollable shivers ripped through me. My teeth chattered. Tears leaked from my eyes.

Loretta Nell. Where was she? I twisted to see if she was still behind me. The wraith glowed against the dark night sky, malice radiating off her.

The world flashed, and that rage I'd felt in the vision came back. It pulsed at my temples and throat. Told me to get up and fight her.

I pinched the inside of my arm as hard as I could. The thoughts stopped. I turned over and lay flat on my stomach, the tin cold through my dew-dampened clothes, to watch Loretta Nell. My heart beat so hard I should have been able to hear it banging on the tin.

Loretta Nell inched toward me. Mad light danced in her eyes, but she controlled way more energy than most spirits. She had taken me into a vision, pulled me into a deep enough trance that I almost walked off the roof of this barn to my death. Then she'd forced the return of the emotions I'd felt in the vision. So far, she was winning.

I reached for the mantle. It gave me no more than a weak buzz. Perfect. In order to use my magic well, I had to be calm and in control. Right now, I was all out of sorts. Sweating, shivering, scared. So I used a method I'd developed where I called my power a little at a time.

First I concentrated on the air. I focused until I felt the slight wind drying the sweat on my back. I sniffed until I smelled the promise of dawn. Then water. I went through the same process of feeling the humidity on the air, the sheen of dew still standing on the barn's roof. Then earth, the best one of all. I heard the rattle of the trees as the wind moved them, smelled the sweet scent of their leaves. Then I called fire. Thunder rumbled in the distance, and a little bolt of lightning popped. I pulled the fire of that lightning into me, let it fuel my power.

Loretta Nell moved even closer, kneeling to watch me like a cat waiting for a mouse to move. All she needed was the writhing tail.

"It's too late," she hissed and launched herself at me.

I gathered the mantle and aimed it at her. Spirit mediumship was my talent. A form of necromancy, spirit mediumship allowed me some control over spirits. The best forms of control required spell casting. But right then, I just threw power at Loretta Nell.

"Get the hell away from me," I screamed and blasted her with all the magic I had. The rage from the vision came back, and I poured it into my one shot at sending her away.

She glowed even brighter for a second. In that second, my imagination put on a dog and pony show. It convinced me I'd just empowered Loretta Nell to give me the most gruesome death I'd ever imagined.

But that didn't happen. Not quite. Loretta Nell brightened until the light coming off her almost blinded me. Then she began to fade. She opened her mouth, elongating her face into a horror mask, and let out a howl so loud it vibrated through my body.

My ears popped. My back teeth ached. I slapped my hands to my ears, but it didn't help because the howl was coming from inside my head. Then she winked out of existence, and I was alone on the roof.

I lay on my back, gasping, and stared at the endless blanket of stars.

"Peri Jean?" Tanner's voice came from nearby. He put his forearms on the roof and hooked his leg over the side. "You all right?"

"Got a headache." I put my hands over my ringing ears.

"I bet. That was some scream. I bet your throat'll be sore tomorrow too." He crept over to me, the old tin bowing beneath his weight.

"I screamed? All I heard was Loretta Nell." I got my legs under me and tried to stand. Tanner had to grab my arm to keep me from overbalancing.

"You screamed too. Loretta Nell—that a ghost? You get her to tell you where the book is?" Tanner took my arm.

Warmth spread through me, making the awful day seem a teeny bit less bad. I grabbed his hand and brought it to my cheek.

"I'm sorry I treated you the way I did." The words kicked my Texas-sized pride right in the gonads, but they needed to be said. "Had you talked to me that way, I'm not sure I'd have come looking for you."

Tanner pulled his hand away and held his ground. He wanted more. I didn't blame him.

"I want you here. I'm grateful for your help." I wracked my brain for more right words, but Tanner closed the distance and put both arms around me. He'd live with what little I had given him.

"It's gonna be hell getting down from here," he said against my head.

Even though I wanted to cry from the frustration of nearly a whole day wasted, I laughed because Tanner was here. I didn't have to do this alone.

5

TEN HARROWING MINUTES LATER, Tanner and I climbed
down the rickety ladder connecting the barn's ground floor
to the loft. My stang lay a few feet from the pot of grave
dirt, which had been overturned. I retrieved both items,
muttering to myself.

"What?" Tanner said from behind me.

I faced him. "Loretta Nell must have gotten me to break
my protective circle while she had me in that vision."

I explained what I'd seen in my trip into Loretta Nell's
past but couldn't quite put words to that pure, white-hot
rage. Tanner recoiled as I detailed the experience. I didn't
blame him. What I'd seen, and my reaction, turned my
stomach.

"I might have a theory on how she got control of you
and why she wanted to bring you out here, if you want to
hear it." Without waiting for my answer, Tanner shone his
flashlight on the walls.

Gone were the dead bodies. Reddish brown stains

marked where they'd hung. Age darkened the stains, blurring their edges. But that didn't stop me from making out the purposefully rounded corners of a sigil. Fear crawled up my back.

Tanner pointed the flashlight at several more sigils. "It's like somebody's temple of worship."

"Did she control me with these?" I muttered the question to myself.

Tanner answered. "From what you're telling me, this Loretta Nell can do a lot more than the average ghost. And I might even know how it ties to the book."

"Let's talk about it outside." I tightened my grip on my stang, tucked the pot that had formerly contained grave dirt under my arm, and led the way outside.

Tanner took my arm and led me around the side of the barn. "Loretta Nell was able to invade your consciousness because of the power in those symbols on the wall. I'm thinking those symbols were probably taken right out of Mohawk's book. You agree?"

"I'll agree for now." I'd take every chance I could to smart off.

Tanner twisted enough to give me the slow smile that had won my heart over the past months and put his arm around me. He whispered in my ear, "You're going to pay for that later."

"Promise?" I planted a kiss on his lips. "Now finish telling me your theory about Loretta Nell."

"The Serpent God was worshipped by some religion or cult. Religions and cults have leaders, priests and priestesses. Think about it." We came to a stop in front of a pile of junk.

"You're saying Loretta Nell was a priestess and, therefore, has special powers. That works. She told me she was Mohawk's favorite daughter." I thought it might be possible, even though I didn't quite understand how it worked.

"That's exactly what I'm saying." Tanner gestured at the junk around the side of the barn. "This is what you'd have fallen on."

I couldn't make out details in the darkness, but metal glinted in the moonlight. Tanner pulled out his flashlight again and flicked it on. Now I could make out part of the bicycle frame, twisted spokes aiming at the sky. I shivered. Tanner tugged me away from the wreckage and toward our trucks parked in front of the house.

I trudged along behind him. Loretta Nell's ghost had tricked me from the first minute I got out that silly bundle of sage and tried to cleanse myself. As a priestess of Mohawk's followers, or favorite daughter, she had power I wasn't prepared to combat.

"I don't know what to do now." I said to Tanner's back.

"I brought my scrying mirror. Why don't we see if I can pick up a trace of the book?" He twisted and tried to smile, but it didn't reach his eyes.

We walked back to where he'd parked his beat-up old truck next to mine in front of the farmhouse. The vintage two-tone paint job glowed against the darker rust spots.

"Why don't we leave?" I wanted away from this haunted place before Loretta Nell returned. She surely would since I hadn't completed the banishing ritual I'd planned to do.

Tanner shrugged. "We can go, but if the book is some-where on this property, this is our best chance of picking up its psychic signal."

I considered just getting out of here. But my time was running out. If Tanner's scrying mirror worked, we could be on the road away from Devil's Rest as soon as we had Mohawk's book in hand. I nodded my okay.

Tanner began preparing to scry.

He placed a worn square of a striped, woven blanket in the bed of his truck and set his black scrying mirror on the fabric. Next to that he placed his incense bowl. From his pocket he drew a plastic packet with a little incense in it. He sprinkled this in the bowl and lit it, blowing gently to get the smoke going.

A new problem hit me. I gripped his arm to get him to stop. "This isn't going to work. We don't have a piece of the book like we did with Miss Ugly's skull lamp, and I don't have a connection with the book like I did with the wheel of life."

I let go of Tanner and dug around in my truck until I found an unopened pack of cigarettes. As I lit up, I realized I did have a connection. Mohawk had bitten me with his snake fangs. "Wait, I do."

I explained about the snakebite. Tanner made a disgusted face, but his preparations to scry for the book became more urgent.

Tanner jogged back to the truck's cab and came back with two cheap prayer candles in glass containers. He lit them and placed them next to the incense. The candles flickered in the light wind, their glow playing over Tanner's face.

Something in my chest twinged, deep enough to make me squirm. I liked him too much. It would never end well. Worries and thoughts jammed together. I smoked faster, consumed by it all, until I caught Tanner watching me.

He tucked a hank of hair behind his ear and lowered his head. He held out one hand to me. I took it and forced the worry out of my mind. A hum of magic passed between us. My black opal heated.

I didn't have much power left, but our bond as lovers connected us. Together we had enough. The smoke from the incense drifted toward us, tracers following behind. It enveloped both of us. The black opal pulsed with each heartbeat. The hum of magic increased.

Tanner ran the index finger of his free hand over the mirror and let his eyes slide closed. I did the same. The spot where Mohawk had bitten me flamed to life, whatever venom he'd left throbbing all the way up my arm. Tanner's breathing deepened. The candles began to gutter as though being blown by a hard wind. He gave my hand a soft squeeze, and we opened our eyes at the same time.

The scrying mirror at first just reflected the light of the sputtering candles, but then it opened to a blue, cloudless sky that overlooked the kind of green, hilly vista one could see from every high point in this part of central Texas. Then it went dark.

"Wait a minute," Tanner said and ran his finger over the mirror. This time, it stayed dark. He let out a frustrated grunt and turned to me. "You know that place?"

"Sure, it's everywhere out here." I let go of Tanner's hand and blew out the candles.

"That's what I thought." He cleaned up his equipment, his movements angry and fast. "We'll just have to figure out something else."

I started toward the house. "My witch pack is upstairs. I'm not leaving it."

"I'll come with you." The truck's door shut behind me, and Tanner jogged to my side.

"No. She tried to run me out the window." I pointed to the window I'd almost fallen from.

Tanner faced me and leaned so close I could smell the orange breath mints he liked eating. He gripped both shoulders and gave them a gentle squeeze.

"I'm in this because I care about you. Don't shit on it." He kissed the tip of my nose, grabbed my hand, and pulled me into the house.

I followed, bewildered that he'd risk himself over a girlfriend he hadn't even had six months. His loyalty made my heart ache. I didn't deserve it. I knew that much. But I couldn't quite let him go to keep him safe.

We took careful steps across the porch. The front door was not only closed but stuck. No open invitation this time. Tanner struggled with it, lifting the door until the cords in his neck stood out. Either this was Loretta Nell's way of keeping us out, or she was off somewhere licking her wounds from the blast I gave her. Finally Tanner's efforts paid off. The door swung open, hinges groaning an off-key baritone.

Tanner shone his flashlight up the staircase and turned to me. "You climbed this?"

"It didn't look that bad in daylight." I gave him a weak shrug and started up the stairs. Tanner kept a firm grip on my arm as though it would keep me from falling through dry-rotted wood.

Then we were back in the room where Loretta Nell first attacked me. My witch pack and summoning supplies were right where I'd left them. I began gathering them as Tanner walked around the room.

"This shit's creepy. It's like whoever was here just left." He shined the flashlight on a picture hanging on the wall.

"The guy at the motel, Dwight, said a group of killer hippies lived out here in the early nineteen-seventies. The cops figured out what they were up to, came out here to arrest them, and ended up having to kill them." I zipped up my witch pack and slung it onto my shoulder, ready to go.

"That may be true, but this stuff here is not from the seventies." Tanner shined his flashlight on the nightstand where an electronic telephone base sat. "That's for a landline phone, but cordless phones like that weren't sold until way later. I'd say this floral wallpaper is from the nineteen-nineties. Somebody lived here after the killer hippies were killed."

I grunted. "We're probably about to find out more than we ever wanted to know about this place and what happened out here."

Tanner turned to me and shined the flashlight in my direction. "Why's that?"

"Summoning Loretta Nell to find the book didn't work.

Scrying for the book didn't work." I hurried for the rickety stairs.

"Wait up," Tanner called. "You'll end up tripping in the dark and falling." He caught up and slung his arm around me.

I wanted to lay my head on his shoulder and cry about the day. I didn't dare. Crying wouldn't help. I'd save the crying until I knew I'd found the book and was rid of Mohawk for good.

When we were back at our trucks, I said, "I have a room at the motel about ten miles back... Wait a minute. How did you find me?"

"I looked up Devil's Rest online. Got directions out here. Went to the little guest houses. Nearly got into a fight with some skinny asshole there. Then I went to the Devil's Slumber Inn where you rented a room." He shrugged and grinned.

Affable Tanner. Nicer than I deserved Tanner. I swallowed hard. No crying. Not now. Maybe not ever again if I didn't find the stupid book.

"Follow me back there. We'll unload and do some research." I opened the door to my truck and tossed in my witch pack.

"Now that I found you, I ought to go back there and beat up that little jerk behind the desk." Tanner let out a chuckle.

"What'd Dwight do to you?" I turned back to Tanner, smiling in spite of the dire situation I'd gotten myself into.

"Charged me fifty dollars to tell me where you were

and another ten to sell me a map to get out here." Tanner's husky voice dropped to an angry growl.

I started laughing, unable to help myself. Dwight had himself a regular little cottage industry going. I had to admire his entrepreneurship. Tanner got into his truck and slammed the door on my giggles.

———

BEFORE I HOOKED up with Tanner, I just thought I drove fast. Tanner drove like a man running from Hell. He beat me back to the Devil's Slumber Inn by enough minutes to have started an argument with Dwight.

"I'm not paying you another nickel, you little pissant. Not after what you charged me this afternoon to tell me where my girlfriend was." Tanner leaned into Dwight's face and jabbed the younger man's collarbone with one forefinger.

Dwight still wore the same smartass grin he'd had on when I met him. "The rules are the rules, mister. If you're staying with Miss..."

He gestured at me, eyebrows raised as though asking me my name. And I remembered something odd. Dwight hadn't asked me to sign a guest register or fill out a guest card. The asshat probably didn't report cash sales to the government.

I approached the two and crossed my arms over my chest. "I'm out of cash, Dwight. And it sounds like my honey is too. How much extra are you hitting me up for?"

"Twenty extra a night." Dwight took in my dirt-smeared arms and disheveled clothes but didn't seem surprised.

A little warning bell dinged in the back of my mind, but I ignored it. Tanner had his brows pulled down and his fists clenched. He'd hit Dwight if it came down to it.

Tanner crowded closer to Dwight, his eyes slitted and glittering. "Maybe you can apply the money you already charged me to what you *think* we owe."

Dwight stood a little taller and glared back. Tanner, a decade older and thirty pounds of muscle heavier, barely reacted. He'd beat Dwight until the younger man begged for mercy.

Dwight, seeming to sense this, slumped. "I guess."

"You guess," Tanner echoed.

I pulled my key out of my pocket and went to unlock my motel room.

"Wait a second," Dwight called after me.

I turned on the sidewalk but didn't walk back to him.

"I...uh...gave you the wrong room. Number five's already rented for the night." He reached into his pocket and pulled out a key.

Tanner snatched it. "Which room?"

"T-t-ten." Dwight pointed across the L-shaped row of rooms. "All the way at the end."

Tanner stomped to my truck and began unloading my things. He brushed past Dwight, knocking into him hard enough to make the younger man stagger, on his way to room ten.

Dwight squirmed. "He's really pissed, huh?"

I'd seen Tanner's face as he got my bags. Amused

rather than pissed. He'd beat Dwight at his own game and would crow about it all night. I gave Dwight a non-committal shrug. We watched Tanner continue the process of unloading the vehicles. Dwight's voice, when it came, startled me.

"I'm guessing you had no luck finding Loretta Nell's book?" He slipped his hands into his pockets.

"Nope. Not a bit." I thought about the way Loretta Nell's ghost had tricked me, about the blood on the ground outside the house. "How would I find out more about Loretta Nell and what happened to the Messengers?"

"I'll be glad to help. For a price." The smirk reappeared on Dwight's face.

Tanner came back and stood close to me. He lowered his head and stared at Dwight. The younger man tried to ignore the stare but began to twitch as though he had a fire ant crawling on his purple-headed warrior.

"There's a website called The Message," Dwight said in a sigh. "It was around way before the Crime Channel did a segment on the Messengers. Matter of fact, they cribbed most of their info from it." Dwight put his hands in his pockets and rocked back and forth on his feet, glancing at Tanner every few seconds.

I took out my phone and opened the notes function. "Is the website just the message dot com?"

Dwight nodded, overly helpful now. "I'll give you one more Devil's Rest tip. This one's free. Get on the ball if you want something more to eat other than convenience store food. They roll up the sidewalks by nine o'clock."

"You recommend anywhere, Dwight?" Tanner poured menace into his voice. He was playing this scene to the hilt.

Dwight squirmed again. "Seeing as you've been kicked out of Phil's, try Roderick's Bar-Be-Cue. Old Rod hates the Get Out of My Town Brigade. He'll serve you a good meal." He gave us directions, and we got into Tanner's truck and left.

Tanner and I drove back to town and found Roderick's with no problem. They were closing, but a white-haired guy with a red, porous drinker's nose—probably Roderick himself—offered to fix us two sandwiches to go. We thanked him and sat down to wait.

I took out my phone, saw Roderick's offered free Wi-Fi, and navigated to the message dot com. A cheesy, dark gray background with graphics made to look like bullet holes that dripped animated blood came up on my screen. Psychedelic rock from the sixties began to play.

Roderick came from behind the counter holding a large, brown paper sack. "Threw in some potato salad and a couple of pieces of our signature pecan pie. On the house."

He held the sack out to me and told Tanner how much our supper would be. Women's lib, and women paying for meals, had obviously not hit Devil's Rest. Tanner hauled out his wallet and gave Roderick some money. I watched the exchange wordlessly.

Roderick shoved Tanner's money in his pocket and said, "Heard the music playing on your phone. Y'all wouldn't happen to be visiting Devil's Rest because of Loretta Nell Grimes or the Messengers, would you?"

"Might be," I said.

"I ain't like some of the people in this town who'll put a boot up your ass just for coming here, but I'll caution you to be careful. They call this town Devil's Rest, and that's an apt name." He stared hard at Tanner, as though it was his responsibility to keep me out of danger.

"Thanks for the warning." Tanner walked to the door and held it open for me.

Tanner rarely held open doors. His California upbringing had taught him a different kind of manners. He was just as polite as any guy I'd been with, more in many ways, but I still teased him about his lack of old-fashioned chivalry. Now I winked as I walked past. He smirked at me and followed me into the parking lot.

As soon as the door closed behind us, a deadbolt clicked home. The parking lot lights turned off a few seconds later. Roderick really had been ready to close shop for the day. Tanner dug in his pocket for the keys to his truck. I walked along, swinging the bag against my legs.

"I wonder how many people Loretta Nell's ghost has killed out there at that farmhouse," I mused aloud.

"No telling." Tanner unlocked his door, and I went to my side of the truck.

I was going to tell Tanner that I wasn't sure I could beat Loretta Nell. But then I saw what was waiting for me on my side of the truck. I sucked in a surprised breath. Two of the three jerks I'd confronted when I took the wrong turn at Stephens Ranch crouched low, waiting for us to come back out.

"Hi, bitch. This is for Austin." Chubby rose and drew

his hand out of his pocket. It swung through the air and clobbered me on the side of the head before I had time to react.

The fist caught the upper part of my ear. It began to ring immediately. Chubby must've had something in his hand because the blow hurt way worse than a hit from a fist. Fiery pain spread. The punch itself jolted my brain hard enough to knock me off balance. I clutched one hand to my hurting head and staggered toward the beat-up sedan parked next to us. The sedan and I connected, and I sprawled backward to sit hard on the parking lot.

Pig-Face closed in. "You put Austin in the hospital. He's in a comber. Might not live."

He means a coma, I thought stupidly and wondered if Austin and Floppy Hair were one and the same. Considering his absence, I guessed they probably were.

Pig-Face reared back one of his roach stompers to give me a kick. Something hit him from behind. Pig-Face clapped both hands to his butt and sort of howled through his big-nostrilled nose.

Chubby hurried to his injured friend and grabbed Tanner around the waist. Tanner shook him off and gave Pig-Face another kick, this one in the knee. Pig-Face howled for real that time. Chubby froze, eyes wide. Pig-Face gripped his knee, tears streaming from his bug eyes, and went down for the count. Tanner kicked him again, this time in the face, spun around, and punched Chubby in the nose. The man bent over holding his face.

Tanner leaned over me. "You all right?"

I didn't know right then. The blow to my head still had me dazed.

Chubby recovered and rushed at Tanner, all flailing fists. Tanner hit him again in the nose. Chubby lurched backward, but Pig-Face picked that moment to jump on Tanner's back.

No, no, no. This couldn't be happening. I tried to get to my feet, but my injured head swam. I staggered back against the beat-up sedan.

I shook my head, trying to clear it. There was something special I could do. What was it? The black opal pulsed on my chest, and a raven cawed in the distance. Orev. Night was Orev's sleeping time, but he sometimes came to my aid. The black opal pulsed again.

My head cleared a little, and I remembered. I was a witch. And a damn good one, thanks to Mysti Whitebyrd.

I pulled on the mantle, felt the power gathering. But the day had whipped my ass. The energy building was nowhere near as strong as usual.

Pig-Face had one arm hooked around Tanner's neck. Tanner pulled on the arm with both hands, his face straining with the effort. Chubby, blood streaming from his nose, delivered a punch to Tanner's midsection. Tanner, his boxing training kicking in, tightened his torso, but his face still contorted from the punch.

I only had power enough to hurt Chubby or Pig-Face, but not both. I picked Pig-Face and imagined fire ants covering his body, stinging and biting and stinging again. Pig-Face, who'd had his eyes squeezed shut with the effort of choking Tanner to death, came to life.

He let go and fell to the ground, slapping at his burning skin. I focused the pain between his legs. He grabbed himself and let out a high, keening squeal. He rolled to his feet, ran across the parking lot, and disappeared into the darkness, still yelling.

A figure came from around the side of the building carrying something long and curved on the end. I doubled up both fists, magic spent, and prepared my body to take a beating. The figure ignored me, stepped up behind Chubby, and swung the object like a teacher swinging a paddle. I got a flash of white hair in the ambient light. Roderick.

Chubby quit pummeling Tanner, stiffened, and arched his back. Roderick reared back his weapon and swung again, hitting the same spot. The weapon made a meaty thud. Chubby yelped. Roderick swung his weapon back again, but Chubby put up one hand.

"No more, Mister Rod." His voice trembled.

"Then you best go home, Jayden." Roderick held the weapon, which I now could see was a crowbar, in position to strike again.

"These folks was trespassing out at the old Stephens Ranch," Chubby whined.

"That ain't none of your business. Just because you trespass out there all the time don't make that property your'n." Roderick swung his arm back, ready to let the crowbar fly again. "Now get on out of here."

Chubby climbed into the sedan I'd been leaning against and started it. Tanner dragged me off the hood and got me away from the car. Chubby gunned the car. It shot backward and almost hit the restaurant's dumpster. He slammed on the brakes, slid to a stop, and sped out of the parking lot.

"Food's ruined." Roderick stood over the bag. Someone had stepped on it and mashed the contents.

Tanner steadied me against his truck. I stood holding my head while he picked up the bag of ruined food, took it to the dumpster, and tossed it inside. He came back and held out one hand to Roderick.

"Thanks for helping us. I think they were about to whip our asses." Tanner put a little Texas swing on the last three words. He'd been working at imitating the way I said it for a while now. He was close, but I hoped he never really got there. I liked Tanner the way he was. I caught Roderick watching me watch Tanner.

"Two of you didn't do too bad for one man and a woman against those two thugs. Those boys are mean." Roderick's teeth flashed blue in the moonlight. "How about y'all come in for a real barbecue supper?" He gestured at his darkened business.

6

———————

RODERICK SEATED Tanner and me at a booth made of rough cut wood and varnished so slick our butts slid on the seats. "What I got's ribs. There's beans, potato salad, and coleslaw to go with that. That all sound good?"

"Nom nom nom." Tanner had developed a love for barbecue that went beyond my tolerance of the stuff. I kept expecting my body odor to start smelling like smoked meat.

Roderick hurried off to get the food. Tanner and I spent the minutes he was gone examining our injuries. Both Tanner and I tended to get into fights, so this wasn't a new practice.

A knot had risen on the side of my head. It was tender when Tanner probed it, but his fingers came away free of blood. Tanner had a few scrapes on his knuckles and a bruise forming on his neck.

Roderick set two plates of food in front of us and went back into the kitchen. He came back with three longneck beers, which he distributed. I didn't drink, not even beer, but I figured I'd keep my mouth shut and be a good guest. Besides, a few sips of beer might ease my aching head.

"Two of you act like you get into scrapes on occasion." Roderick took a pull on his beer. His lips popped as he pulled it away.

"She's got a bad temper," Tanner said in a hushed voice and jerked a thumb at me.

"He just likes to fight." I bit a hunk off one of the ribs. Tender, juicy, with just enough smoke for taste but not so much it made me feel like a fire-breathing dragon.

"How'd those fellas get it in for you?" Roderick drank out of his beer again, glancing between Tanner and me.

I wiped my mouth and hoped I didn't have bits of food stuck in my teeth. "Aw, I got in a scrape with them when I went out to the Stephens Ranch earlier today. Might've hit Pig-Face with my vehicle and made Austin wreck his four-wheel motorcycle."

Roderick chuckled. "That explains it. I'd advise against you going back out to the Stephens Ranch. It's a good place to stay away from."

"That so?" Tanner barely glanced up from his barbecue.

Roderick nodded. "It's dangerous out there. Not too long ago, a teenage girl fell outta the second story window. Died right there on the ground in front of the house."

The icy feel of Loretta's hands on me as she tried to wrestle me out the window came back. Chill bumps rashed over my arms, and I shivered.

Roderick gave me a shrewd nod. "Boy with her swore

something with glowing eyes pushed his girl out that window. 'Course the po-lice charged him for doing that very thing, and he got the death penalty. Convicted by a jury of his peers, right here in Devil's Rest, Texas."

"What do you think happened?" I ate more barbecue, even though Roderick's story had stolen my appetite. For one thing, not eating would insult him. For another, my magical abilities worked better when I had a full stomach and a good night's rest.

Roderick's wrinkled face creased in thought. His words came slowly, as though he had to weigh each one before he said it. "I think that place is like a disease, taints everybody who lives there. Maybe that boy did push his girlfriend outta that window. Or maybe a ghost did it." He snorted into his beer and took another long pull. "Maybe the devil himself did it."

The devil himself. The words sparked a memory. I scraped my mind for it and finally found it in my memory of the farmhouse. Over the flaking paint of one wall had been painted the words "Josie is the devil." I told Roderick what I'd seen. He nodded, finished his beer, and stood.

"Yep. That's another story," he said. "Lemme get another cold one, and I'll tell it to you. Y'all want one?"

Tanner nodded his head and finished the last of his beer. I shook my head and waved my hand over my beer, of which I'd had maybe five sips. It tasted worse than it smelled.

Roderick came back a few minutes later with three bottles. Inwardly, I cringed but made myself smile. Roderick winked and set a bottle of water in front of me.

I took a long sip and sighed. Much better than the beer. "Thank you."

"Next time, tell me you don't want beer." He shook his finger as he said the words and sat back down with a heavy sigh. "All right. You was talking about that 'Josie is the devil' business. I'm going to assume you have a vague idea about what happened to the Messengers."

I licked barbecue sauce off my fingers before I spoke. "They were murderers who the police killed."

Roderick nodded. "Good enough. The deputy who got the credit for figuring out those hippies was murderers was a feller named Freddy Stephens. Freddy ended up buying the farmhouse and all the land that came with it. No doubt he got the deal of a lifetime."

"And that's where the name Stephens Ranch comes from?" Regretfully, I took the last bite of barbecue rib.

"Yep. That little dirt road became Stephens Ranch Road. Now that you've got all the background, here's the story." Roderick paused for a sip of beer. "Freddy Stephens and his wife raised their only child out on that ranch, a little boy they adopted and named Freddy Junior. Freddy Junior grew up, got married, had two kids of his own. Freddy Senior and his wife got old, and she died. Freddy Senior started having a hard time taking care of himself. Freddy Junior lived over in Austin and decided to put his daddy in a retirement community close by so he could keep an eye on him. You follow me so far?"

Tanner and I both nodded. He curled his barbecue-stained fingers over mine.

Roderick watched, eyes squinting into a smile. "So the

whole family piles on down to the ranch to have one last good old family weekend before they moved Freddy Senior to the retirement community." Roderick drank again. "Things did not work out according to plan. Something happened that ended with every single Stephens dead except the granddaughter, Josie Stephens. Little college-aged thing. Cute as a button."

"Did Josie kill them?" I took out my cigarettes and showed them to Roderick.

He waved a hand. "Go on and smoke. Those no smoking laws are stupid anyway. Just ash on your paper plate there, and we'll throw it all away when we're done." Roderick took out a green and white pack of cigarettes and lit up. "To answer your question, there ain't nobody really knows if Josie killed those folks or not. Sheriff's deputy found her wandering the road, covered in blood, and about to die of heatstroke. Traumatized. When the po-lice went out there to the farm and found the carnage, suspicion started up about her doing the killings."

The vision I'd seen back at the Stephens Ranch let me know that Loretta Nell could have incited Josie into a killing rage. But I also knew that Loretta Nell was a powerful ghost, capable of murdering a living person. The murderer could have been either Josie or Loretta Nell.

Tanner's rough purr broke into my thoughts, nearly made me jump out of my seat. "What did the cops decide about Josie's involvement?"

"An aunt on Josie's mother's side of the family showed up with a lawyer, and they ended up dropping all charges. But Josie wasn't right no more." Roderick touched his temple to show us exactly what part of Josie had broken. "She's over at the state mental hospital. Probably be there for the rest of her life."

Pity for Josie and her ruined life hardened my stomach, making it feel overfull.

"I've answered your questions." Roderick tapped the table to draw me out of my reverie. "Now you answer one for me."

I nodded.

"What did you come out here looking for? Excuse me for saying, but you two're a good bit older than our usual visitors." He snorted, but the smile didn't reach his eyes.

Tanner and I exchanged a glance. He nodded. I gave a slight shake of my head.

He rolled his eyes. "If it hadn't been for Roderick here, we'd have been beaten to death in the parking lot."

I flushed, dug the picture out of my bag, and pushed it across the table to Roderick. "Looking for this book."

I'd expected Roderick to show surprise at the picture the way Dwight had, but he began nodding right away.

"I thought this was the Christian Bible first time I seen it." He took a long sip of beer. "When the Messengers first come to town, they came in here. Loretta Nell was carrying this book under her arm."

Roderick smoked and thought for a while. Finally he nodded to himself and began speaking again. "Loretta Nell...well, you see this picture. I was a young man back then, and young men think there might be a chance with every pretty woman they see. So I knew where the Messengers was staying. Hell, everybody in town did. Back then, it was the old Pilz Ranch."

Roderick stopped talking and shook himself. When he continued, his voice had lowered as though he was afraid of someone hearing. "I went out there. Looking to get in Loretta Nell's pants more than anything. They welcomed me like long-lost family. Including Loretta Nell. *Especially* Loretta Nell. We smoked a little of their wacky-tabacky, and Loretta Nell got out that book and started reading out of it."

I drew in a deep breath, and my stomach began to churn. From Loretta Nell's vision, I knew firsthand what the contents of Mohawk's book did to people. But I'd been able to leave the vision. Roderick had looked into the abyss and had to live with the aftermath.

Roderick took a trembling breath. "I've never felt that way, before or since."

I gulped, remembering the purity of the rage I'd felt in that vision, the way I'd wanted to hurt that boy Kevin. I'd wanted to see his brains splattered everywhere.

Roderick rubbed his hands over his face, shaking his head. "I decided the fella next to me was competing with me for Loretta Nell. I attacked him, and we fought. It was like something else, something mighty mean, just took me over." Roderick's eyes had gone glassy as he told his story. "I got that fella down and beat his head into the floor over and over again, hollering, 'In his name.'"

Tanner listened in stunned silence, eyes taking up most of his face.

"Did you kill him?" In the vision, I'd have killed Kevin if he hadn't killed me.

Roderick nodded, his faded eyes fixed on some distant hell.

It occurred to me that we were all alone with this man. He could pull a butcher knife out of his shirt and stab us to death right here. Maybe that's what he was building up to.

Roderick took a hard pull on his cigarette and crushed it out on my plate. "After that feller was dead, the room smelling of shit and blood, Loretta Nell came over, rubbing herself on me like a cat, all boneless." Roderick turned his gaze on me. His eyes, rheumy with age, blazed with fear of that long ago time.

"What happened to the body?" Tanner sat tensed as though ready to fight again.

"Those crazy motherfuckers dragged it out to the barn, strung it up, and started writing on the walls in that poor boy's blood," Roderick said to the table. "They tore him apart eventually. Ate pieces of him like animals. That was when I left. Ran home like the devil was after me."

"How'd you get away with it?" I wasn't sure why I cared. Roderick didn't deserve my judgment, and whatever he'd done forty-plus years ago didn't matter today.

"The guy wasn't from town, so nobody here missed him. During the day, I could pretend it never happened." Roderick wiped the sheen of sweat off his face with one trembling hand. "But nighttime was a different story. Loretta Nell would come to my window and tap on it. Then she'd motion me to come outside. I knew if I ever did, I'd be lost forever. So I pretended not to see her."

Now is when he'll attack us. I tensed my body.

Roderick's voice continued, softer than ever. "Month later, I joined the Navy. During Basic, I got a letter from Daddy saying what had happened to the Messengers. He asked if I'd seen anything funny out there. I never answered."

"But you never did anything else like that?" Tanner watched me out of the corner of his eye, no doubt remembering what I'd seen in the vision back at the barn.

"They was a war going on, boy. Don't you know what that's like? You kill people when you're at war." Roderick's eyes were like two deep pits, hundreds of years old and sad about it all.

Neither Tanner nor I answered. We hadn't been to the kind of war Roderick had. We couldn't possibly understand.

"I'd go into a red rage and then come to myself like I'd been asleep, always saying, 'In his name.' Loretta Nell would come to me in dreams, like she'd been that day at the farmhouse, all boneless and full of promises." He lit another cigarette.

"How'd you make her go away?" I'd worked with spirits long enough to know they didn't just take pity on their victims and leave them alone.

"The last time it happened, I swore never again. Went to bed that night. Sure enough, Loretta Nell came. I turned the rage on her, beat her and beat her. Killed her in my mind. Every time she tried to come back, I fought her. When that rage came, I fought it. After a while, she quit coming. Or maybe I quit seeing her." Roderick shook himself and made a rough sound in his throat. His eyes cleared.

He reached across the table and put one sun-spotted hand over my arm. "Reason I spoke of things I ain't never told another soul is that you don't want to find that book, young lady. I see Loretta Nell all over you, sense her. Don't let her come in. Get out of this town and never look back."

Oh, how I wished we could do that. Between the vision I had in the barn and Roderick's story, I knew we were dealing with something more powerful and mean than I knew how to beat. Worse, the book of the Serpent God would release mayhem into the world, make sane people do things they wouldn't normally do. But what was my other option? I wouldn't become Mohawk's slave. That left death. I thought about Hannah's gun. Maybe I should just kill myself. Tanner slid his arm over my shoulder and gave me a squeeze.

"We can't quite walk away," he said in his concise California non-accent. "We're under some pressure, outside pressure, to find that book."

Roderick watched us from behind a haze of smoke. "Never heard of life working another way."

I lit my own cigarette. "You ever hear any more about the book, what became of it?" I knew it was a long shot. Roderick wasn't even in town when the Messengers met their end.

He shook his head. "Might've gone into evidence. But don't go down to the sheriff's office asking a bunch of questions. When the Crime Channel came to town last year, Sheriff Hale threw one of them in jail for what she called loitering." He chuckled. "There's two kindsa folks in Devil's Rest. One group would just as soon lynch anybody who comes to town asking about the Messengers. The other group, which includes me, is willing to put up with them to keep their dying businesses afloat. If I were you two, I'd go to the library."

"The one downtown?" I remembered passing it right before I discovered Phil's, Home of the World Famous Monkey Burger.

"Same one." Roderick nodded. "Now if you go in there and old lemon lips Burris is behind the counter, ask if Mandy Drake is working. She's the one who'll help you." He smiled and winked. "Mandy's my niece. She loves the notoriety the Messengers give this town. Might be why I ain't so hard on those who come looking for the truth, whatever that is." Roderick checked the worn watch he wore on his wrist and raised his eyebrows.

Tanner immediately slid out of the booth and began gathering the plates. "Just tell us where to throw this away, and we'll get out of your hair."

We spent a few minutes helping Roderick clean up after our mess. His parting words as he held open the door for us to pass through were, "If you won't leave town, at least promise me you'll take care of each other. Seeing the two of you together reminded me of the good times with my wife, all six months of 'em."

We left laughing, and Roderick left the lights on until we got into Tanner's truck and started the engine.

———

WE STOPPED by the library on the way back to the motel. It was long closed, as expected. The sign gave the time it opened the next morning.

"I don't know what we'll do if tomorrow is Mandy's day off," I said to Tanner back in the truck.

Tanner, the voice of reason, said, "If Mandy's not working, we'll see if Roderick will tell us where she lives." He drove us back to the motel.

I checked the clock on my phone, its dull glow lighting the cab of Tanner's beat-up pickup truck. Closing in on twenty-four hours since Mohawk's visit. One-third of my time gone, and I was no closer to finding the book than when I'd started. I checked the time again.

Tanner took his eyes off the road. "Expecting a call?"

I tossed the phone on the dashboard. "I'm running out of time."

The words threatened to choke me. The idea of becoming Mohawk's prisoner hurt more than the idea of death. I glanced over at Tanner. He made the idea of death hurt pretty bad.

I wanted us to go see the Festival of Lights in Natchitoches this Christmas. And I wanted a future with him that stretched into the great beyond. Admitting that, even in the privacy of my mind, scared me. Getting attached to Tanner couldn't possibly have a good outcome.

The lights of Devil's Rest faded behind us. Soon nothing lit our way but the huge moon hanging in the sky and the headlights of the truck. As we neared the motel, the lights on the retro sign's arrow flashed in the darkness, pointing at Devil's Slumber Inn. The lights started at the top and cascaded all the way to the bottom. Then the entire arrow and sign would stay lit up for several seconds, flash off, and start again.

Tanner backed into a parking space facing the sign. We sat in the dark, listening to the truck's cooling tick and watching the arrow. He took one hand off the wheel and curled his fingers over mine.

Words I wanted to say to him but couldn't flashed through my mind. He'd sucked up his pride and come to help me. Even knowing the risk it involved.

If things went wrong, his life would be in just as grave a danger as mine. But I understood now that he wouldn't go. Asking would only insult him.

I tilted my head to watch the lights of the sign flash over Tanner's face. The dim glow cast pools of shadow over his face, rendering it unreadable. He'd acted as though we hadn't fought before I left. As though he hadn't threatened to end things because of my asshole behavior.

Though we'd gotten to know each other well, our relationship was still new. I didn't know everything there was to know about this man. The chemistry between us blew my mind. But I liked Tanner's personality almost as much as I liked looking at him.

Kind to a fault, fierce when the situation called for it, loyal even when it threatened his own safety. He was the other half of me. But I shied away from even vague plans for a future together. I wasn't convinced that was possible.

Tanner had a complicated history. The death of his wife and children had scarred him, maybe beyond repair. He'd made progress. Their deaths were no longer killing him with guilt. But he still mourned them and always would.

I knew all too well that Tanner might get up one morning and tell me it was time for him to hit the road. Fear of him breaking my heart kept me quiet. If I said the things I felt and then he left, I'd have to live the rest of my life knowing I wasn't enough.

Tanner, perhaps feeling the weight of my gaze, turned to me. He wasn't movie star handsome, but he had his own magnetism. An intensity burning behind his green eyes, a way of carrying himself that reminded me of a powerful animal stalking its prey. The heat I'd felt since the first second we met built between us.

Tanner took his hand from mine and caressed my cheek. In a soft voice, he said, "We can't do any more tonight."

I nodded and swallowed the flood of worries I wanted to spout just to get them out of me.

"Whatever happens, I'm going to be here." He scooted closer. The smell of barbecue and the heat of his skin enveloped me. He nuzzled the side of my face, his whiskers rasping against my neck. His whisper heated my skin. "Put your arms around me."

I did and rested my cheek against one shoulder. More words pressed at my lips, asking to get out into the world. *I should tell him he's the most important person in my life.* But I kept quiet and put one hand behind his neck, tangling it in his long hair, and kissed him. The salt of his sweat burned my tongue. I tried to memorize the way it felt, just in case.

Tanner had been in the motel room, but I hadn't. The

sign on the office door claiming the Devil's Slumber Inn had clean rooms was optimistic at best and a bald-faced lie at worst.

As I had suspected, the room made me wish I traveled with a clean bedspread and linens. A dark stain crept down one wall painted the color of cheap wine, and a spiderweb hung in the corner. A fuzz of white dust covered the dials on a TV at least my age.

Tanner had set my hatbox on a dusty dark wood veneer table. I opened it and dug for my flip-flops. I didn't want the carpet touching my feet. Tanner came up behind me and put his hands on my shoulders. I leaned into him but said, "Let me shower. I stink."

"I want to help you," he murmured.

Tanner pushed me to sit on the edge of the bed. He knelt in front of me and pulled off each boot, intense eyes fixed on me. He pulled me to my feet, dragged my stale shirt over my head, and unhooked my bra. The click of the clasp seemed loud in the quiet room. I pushed the flimsy garment off.

Tanner's eyes heated. His tongue teased the corner of his mouth for a second, leaving a patch of wetness. The smell of him filled my senses, chased away the awful day to the point where it was just Tanner and me. I reached for my jeans.

Tanner brushed my hands away, undid the button, and dragged them down my legs. I rested my hands on his back, sharing his feverish heat. The fabric rubbed harsh on my suddenly oversensitive skin. I gasped.

Tanner raised and held out one hand to me. "Let's get you in the shower. It'll make you feel better."

Naked and dreamlike, I shoved my feet into the flip-flops and let him lead me into the bathroom. He turned on the water, fiddled with it until it ran hot enough to steam.

"Take off your shoes." He held my hand to balance me while I did it and guided me into the shower. I did a slow turn and stood with my face turned up to the hot spray, staring at the ring of rust around the shower pipe and the permanent rust stain bleeding down from it.

The shower curtain billowed, sending a draft of cold air through the shower. Tanner's feet slapped down behind me. So this was how it was going to be. Not in the nasty bed but in the nasty shower. His fingers trailed down my side, through the water sluicing over my skin. I braced for him to push my legs apart.

But he reached round me, grabbed the paper wrapped bar of soap, and opened it. The soap slicked over my wet back. He rubbed it in slow circles, massaging the taut muscles between my shoulders. He worked his way down both arms and around to my chest. He brushed the tip of one nipple. My body tightened, and I gave a little squeak. He ignored both responses and moved on to my legs, strong fingers running over sore calves and thighs.

I moaned and put both hands on the stained tile to keep my balance. Eyes half closed, I waited for him to get down to business. I knew he wanted to. His arousal had brushed me several times. But instead he turned off the water and pulled the shower curtain back. The metal hooks rattled against the bar. He grabbed a towel and began to rub me dry with the rough fabric. I grabbed the second towel and tried to dry him.

"No. This is for you." He soaked all the water off me and then held my arm while I stepped over the tub. "Go wait for me in the bed."

Even drunk on desire, I still didn't want my feet touching the floor. I slid into my flip-flops and went into the other room where I pulled the bedspread off the bed and dumped it in the closet. The cool sheets rustled as I lay down on them. A few seconds later, Tanner came into the room, dots of water still shining on his body.

"Lay on your stomach," he said, his voice thick.

I did as he said. The hair on his legs tickled against mine as he knelt over me. Again I waited to feel him inside me. His hands ran over my shoulders, fingers digging in to find the knots of tension. I moaned into the pillow. Tanner's fingers found every sore stress point on my back and rubbed it into jelly.

Body relaxing, I let go of my worries and drifted, eyes nearly closed. I didn't even notice when he stopped. I only became aware of his breath tickling my ear, the heat of his chest against my back, and the thud of his heart. The smell of the cheap motel soap and Tanner's own hot, musky smell filled my senses. His lips brushed my cheek. I shivered.

Now. Admit you need him. Admit you were wrong about him coming here. Stubbornness lodged the words in my throat. If I said them, I left myself open to hurt.

But hadn't Tanner risked everything to come here? He'd saved my life and then rubbed me down like a high-end masseuse. He'd taken a beating for me and worshipped me like a goddess. Tomorrow he would try to help me save my own skin, all the while asking nothing in return.

"Let me turn over," I whispered against his lips. I needed to see his face.

Tanner raised enough for me to do what I wanted, the wet ends of his hair trailing my face. I rested my arms, now heavy and relaxed, over his shoulders. I practiced the words. None of them sounded right.

"You're the only person in the world I'd trust with my life," I finally said.

Tanner's only answer was to quirk one side of his lips. He raised himself to his knees and ran his fingers down my body, trailing fire. In a quick motion, he wrapped my legs around his hips. Bracing one hand on either side of my head, he said, "I'd do anything for you. You're my world."

We both gasped. The noise of our lovemaking filled the room, growing in intensity until it reached a white-hot crescendo where everything grayed out for a second.

Later, I lay smoking. Tanner took my cigarette and dragged on it. I touched my fingertips to his cheek and drank in those gorgeous eyes.

He pulled my fingers away from his face and kissed them. "Things are going to be okay."

"Because we're together." It might be the last couple of days I got to be with Tanner, so I cuddled against him and didn't know anything else until the morning sunlight streaked across my face.

7

———

"Sorry. But I come bearing gifts." Tanner stood in the motel room's doorway holding two cups of coffee and a paper sack. He came inside and deposited the items on the dusty little table. "Coffee pot didn't work. Dwight was nice enough to let us have these two cups for free. He sent you a pig in a blanket. Wanted to charge me for mine."

Laughing, I swung my legs out of the bed and groped for my flip-flops. At the table, I tried to give the pig in a blanket to Tanner, but he insisted on halving it.

"We've got a half hour before the library opens." He popped the last bite in his mouth and gestured at my untouched half of the pastry. "Eat it, or else."

Still not caffeinated enough to flirt with him, I forced down the food, drained my coffee, and got out my laptop. "I never did get to finish looking at the website about the Messengers last night. Might help us ask Mandy Drake better questions when we get to the library."

Tanner scooted his rickety chair next to mine as the

118

gray background and the bullet holes loaded. Again the psychedelic rock blasted out of the speaker. I had time to recognize it as The 13th Floor Elevators before Tanner reached over and muted it.

"Your Grateful Dead albums are bad enough." He gave me a smartass grin. I pretended to stick my finger in his ear.

I navigated to The Message's menu. The gothic red lettering had the blood animation where they seemed to ooze red stuff. I clicked red text that read, "The Day the Messengers Died." The page began loading.

Tanner had positioned himself at my shoulder leaning into me. He still smelled of motel soap from the night before. Remembering what had passed between us, I pushed his hair out of his face. I needed to tell him he mattered, that *this* mattered, just in case. My heart picked up speed. He turned to me. I ran one thumb over the shallow crow's feet at the corner of one eye. He waited, expression curious and open. Maybe even a little hopeful. Here it was. The right moment. I screwed up my courage. Just at that second, his gaze slid off mine. His mouth dropped open.

"What the holy hell? Who puts that up where anybody can see it?" Lips turned down in disgust, he pointed at the laptop's screen.

Shocked by his outburst, I turned my attention to the computer. It took every ounce of my self-control to keep from shoving the machine away.

Black and white photographs littered the screen. Every one of them showed dead people. Mousing over the pictures gave visitors a chance to click for more information. Just to get off the page of horrific images, I clicked on a picture of a row of dead bodies that looked to be full of bullet holes.

A new screen popped up. The title read "About The Messengers." A group photo was centered underneath the title. I clicked to enlarge it and stared into a dozen smiling young faces. Loretta Nell Grimes crouched on one end, grinning ear to ear.

All the people in the picture had long, straight, stringy hair. A few women wore floppy-brimmed hats. The men had bushy, unkempt beards. The women's clothes looked like something Mysti Whitebyrd would wear, only dirty.

The thing that struck me? Other than needing a good scrubbing, these people looked normal, like a college class on an outing. I took a closer look. A shiver ripped through my body.

"Holy shit," Tanner muttered.

Every one of the Messengers held a sharp weapon in his or her hand. Some of them, including Loretta Nell's, were stained with something dark.

I clicked out of full screen so I wouldn't have to look at those weird smiling faces another second. The webpage had a centered block of text underneath the picture naming each of the people and giving their age. Loretta Nell had only been twenty-six.

Underneath that, the words "The Rise and Fall of the Messengers" were centered on the page.

When the topic of killer cults comes up, names like the Manson Family and Superior Universal Alignment are usually bandied about. Most people have never even heard of the Messengers, yet they have a higher body count than both the Manson Family and Superior Universal Alignment put together.

The Messengers operated in the far southwestern corner of the Texas Hill Country but are believed to have gotten their start on the campus of the University of Texas at Austin in 1969 and 1970.

Their inarguable leader, Loretta Nell Grimes, is said to have approached students asking if they'd like to join a prayer circle. Most who joined dropped out of school and life and ended up dead on the grounds of the Pilz Ranch about ten miles outside Devil's Rest, Texas.

Not much is known about what the Messengers did on that ranch. The only well-documented piece of the Messengers' short history is of the day in 1973 when police raided the ranch. That day, armed members of the Messengers met police and opened fire. Police returned fire. The shooting continued until the entire group lay dead.

Once they could safely enter the ranch, police found a house of horrors full of altars that seemed to be dedicated to the worship of snakes. Inside the ranch's barn, corpses had been hung to dry. Pieces of meat had been stripped from the corpses, which began rumors the group had been cannibals.

Roderick's story filled my mind. Right after he killed for the first time, Loretta Nell had invited him out to the barn to become a member of the Messengers. Had eating human flesh been the initiation? If police found pieces of meat stripped from the corpses, maybe it had. An image of Loretta Nell with red-stained teeth flashed behind my eyes. I put one hand to my mouth.

Tanner raised one eyebrow. "You okay?"

I told him what I had on my mind. His face and lips paled. The half pastry I'd eaten swam on my stomach. I forced myself to keep reading.

Most of the Messengers' bodies remained unclaimed by embarrassed family members and received a pauper's burial in the Devil's Rest Cemetery. The biggest mystery of the Messengers' massacre remains what happened to Loretta Nell's body. There is no report of her remains being entered into evidence by the coroner or prepared for burial by the Devil's Rest Funeral Home.

The four sheriff's deputies who busted the Messengers testified to seeing Loretta Nell's lifeless remains and speculated that someone had stolen the corpse as a macabre souvenir of the day.

Whether or not they were telling the truth will likely never be known because every one of the four, including Freddy Stephens who led the raid, died on the very property where they shot the Messengers dead.

The final sentence contained a link, so I clicked it. It navigated to a new page with pictures of the four lawmen who'd stopped the Messengers' murder spree.

One group picture showed the four men standing over a pile of dead Messengers, their arms around each other, smiles on their faces. They reminded me of hunters standing over their kills.

Another black and white picture showed one of the deputies, a round-faced man with black hair. He had his arm around a plain-faced woman with frizzy brown hair. The man wore a broad smile. The woman looked like she wasn't sure what had hit her.

After the massacre, Freddy Stephens and his wife purchased the Messengers' old stomping grounds as a place to raise their young family.

Below was a picture of each of the other deputies involved in taking down the Messengers with a short blurb of how he'd died.

1985 — Dennis Muldoon drowned in a swimming accident in a lake on the Stephens Ranch property.

1999 — Ronald Jessup died in a hunting accident on Stephens Ranch. His gun exploded in his face.

2004 — Harris Coates died at Stephens Ranch when the all-terrain-vehicle he was riding rolled over on him, breaking his neck.

The final picture showed Freddy Stephens. He'd lost

most of his hair, and sunspots covered his red face. He wore his uniform and looked to be at a party of some sort.

2006 — Freddy Stephens, after retiring from the Devil's Rest Sheriff's Department, was stabbed to death on his property, along with his son, his daughter-in-law, and his grandson. The only survivor of that night was Josie Stephens, Freddy's granddaughter. Many believed she committed the murders, but she was never charged. Josie claimed Loretta Nell, thirty-three years dead at the time, did the killing that night.

Below that was a picture of the Stephens Ranch as I had seen it. The deserted farmhouse with graffiti on the walls. The deteriorating barn with its faded red paint and sliding door opening onto a black maw. In the center of the darkness stood a shadowy figure.

I held the screen close to my face and thought I saw a flash of Loretta Nell's blond hair. The text read:

If there is life after death, could a group like the Messengers, one who died a hard (albeit deserved) death, exact revenge on those who killed them?

This website has discussed only the deaths of the deputies who enacted the raid on the Messengers' lair. Not discussed are the fates that befell their wives and children.

By the time of the Stephens Family Massacre, there were no survivors.

Against my desires, I went back to The Message website's home page.

"What are you doing?" Tanner practically yelled, one hand gripping my shoulder like a kid he might want to yank away from something they shouldn't be seeing.

"I've looked at all this awful crap and still haven't found any mention of Loretta Nell's book. I need to make sure." I proceeded to click on every awful picture to see where the links took me.

The pictures of the remains found in the barn led to pages talking about the victims. Each victim had his or her own profile marked by that person's picture. The smiling people in those photos never imagined they'd get mixed up with the Messengers and die for it.

Another page featured an interview with one of the coroners who cleaned up after the Messengers. He claimed there were at least forty unique unidentified remains of victims found on the ranch. Authorities were unable to match them to known missing persons.

"The early seventies were really just a hangover of the sixties, and you had a lot of people just drifting," said the coroner. "We will probably never know who all those poor people were."

Another page featured graphic pictures of the Stephens Family Massacre.

"There's nothing else of use." I closed out the page in disgust.

"Okay. Any other ideas?" Tanner went to the sink to brush his teeth.

"If Mandy at the library doesn't know anything about the book, and I'm guessing she won't, we're going to see Josie in the mental hospital." I began dragging on clean clothes, still wishing for more coffee.

Tanner turned to me, toothbrush in his mouth, and said something. After a second, I interpreted his words as "How come?"

"The timeline doesn't make sense to me." I went to the sink and stood next to Tanner trying to do something with my hair.

He spat out his toothpaste. "Why doesn't the timeline make sense?"

"The Messengers were killed in the early seventies. Then Freddy Stephens buys the property and raises his family there without incident. Nothing happens in the house until the whole family was butchered—what— thirty-plus years later?" I put on eyeliner and deodorant, the only two required components of my daily routine.

Tanner watched me. "No incidents only counts if you ignore the three lawmen who lost their lives out there."

I grunted and finished drawing the thick black line before I answered. "But that's nothing like the Stephens Family Massacre. That shit was brutal. You saw those pictures."

Tanner put water on his fingers and used it to smooth down his long, straight hair. "So what are you saying?"

"Let's say Loretta Nell, or maybe the collective vengeful spirit of the Messengers, did kill the Stephens Family, just like Josie said. How did that family live in the house all those years safely? And what changed the night they were murdered?" I stared at Tanner in the mirror. "There's a piece of the story missing."

We packed our things and loaded them into my truck. I didn't trust Dwight not to go through them while we were gone. Then we left for the library.

———

WE PARKED RIGHT in front of the library. On the sidewalk, a mid-twenties woman struggled with a folding sign advertising the annual book sale, all funds to be used for the library renovation. She shared Roderick's hawkish nose and bore such a strong resemblance to him, she had to be Mandy Drake. We got out of the truck and approached her.

I asked anyway. "Ms. Drake?"

She turned to see who'd said her name, and the sign toppled over.

"Shit," she hissed under her breath.

Tanner hurried to help her get the sign upright. It didn't want to open. One of the hinges was stiff and needed a squirt of some kind of lubricant. Tanner forced it with the palm of one hand. Mandy breathed a sigh of relief.

"Mrs. Burris usually helps me set this out, but she had a

doctor's appointment this morning." She waved her hands at the sign, as though dismissing it, turned to me, and held out one hand. "To answer your question, yes. I'm Mandy Drake. You must be the young couple Uncle Roddy told me to expect."

Uncle Roddy? Tanner and I exchanged an amused glance. We shared a fourteen-year-old boy's sense of humor. This would be good for miles of giggles. Mandy's lips quirked as though she knew the joke well and had anticipated it.

"Let's get off the street. Someone might hear and get offended." She held open the library's door and motioned us inside.

Though the library's exterior was a downtown storefront, the inside resembled every other library I'd been inside. A circulation desk took up a large amount of space near the entrance. Beyond that stretched out shelf after shelf jammed with books. A staircase along one wall bore a sign telling visitors the genealogy center was upstairs with the non-fiction books.

Mandy led the way to the circulation desk, opened the little swinging door to let us come behind it, and then unlocked a door marked employees only. "I've got a few early morning regulars who come in to read the newspaper and gossip. They'll likely know who you are and be upset you're here. If they report me to Mrs. Burris..." She shrugged. "There's not many jobs in Devil's Rest."

Tanner and I nodded our understanding and went inside the tiny office. Mandy motioned to two chairs in front of a cluttered desk. We sat, and she went behind the desk. The name plate in front of the desk claimed it as Mrs. Burris's desk. Mandy caught me reading the sign.

"I'm just assistant librarian. I do have my papers—my degree, I mean—but Mrs. Burris has been the head librarian here since dinosaurs roamed the earth. I'm really just a glorified flunky, and my paycheck shows it." She tittered a little, but her eyes didn't smile.

"It's not my business, but why not go to one of the cities and get a job? Surely they'd pay more." Tanner asked in his perfect California-speak.

I didn't need to ask this question. I already had an idea of the answer.

"I'm hooked on the history of the Messengers. Mom grew up here and used to tell it to scare the wits out of me. When I got old enough, I started coming here and researching. The first attempts were kid stuff." She gave us an embarrassed smile. This one touched her eyes, crinkling them at the corners. It gave her generally unattractive features a little boost. "But I've gotten better over the years. There's a local group of us who are pretty into it. We meet once a month to exchange information. You're staying out at Devil's Slumber, right?"

I nodded.

"Dwight Carr's in our group." She laughed, a true laugh, throaty and full of life at whatever she saw on my face. "Yeah. He's an odd one, and he'll cheat you if he can. Try to get into your pants too." Her cheeks colored, and I guessed she'd fallen victim to Dwight's unique charm. "But Dwight's a good researcher. He tracked down Loretta Nell

Grimes's backstory. Where she grew up, went to school, that sort of thing."

"Did anything he found indicate what got her interested in..." I shook my head and shrugged at the end of the sentence, not sure how to say it without being crass.

Mandy finished the sentence for me. "In murdering people for Jesus?"

"Did Loretta Nell and the Messengers really commit murder for Jesus?" Tanner had been glancing around the office as though looking for something in particular. Now he turned his attention on Mandy.

Mandy's gaze flicked over Tanner. She caught me watching and her cheeks reddened. She cleared her throat and made a point to speak to me instead of Tanner.

"You've seen the website, right? The Message? Dwight loves it. He's always directing people to it. I find it a little tasteless, but..." She bared her teeth in an embarrassed smile.

I nodded. "We read through the whole thing before we came here."

"You found the eyewitness reports of Loretta Nell proselytizing on the campus of UT?" She asked.

Both Tanner and I nodded.

"That's what I mean by killing people for Jesus. We know nothing beyond that." Cheeks still pink, she stared at the desk several seconds, eyes moving. "I hope I haven't offended you."

"Not at all." Another connection clicked into place, this one inspired by the vision I'd had in the barn at Stephens Ranch. Loretta Nell had used Mohawk's book to get that church youth group, or whatever they'd been, to murder each other. She'd been practicing a religion, all right. Just not the Christian one.

A bell dinged in the library. Mandy excused herself, greeted someone from the door, and came back to sit down. "You're welcome to ask Dwight about his research into Loretta Nell's history, but he'll want to charge you for it. He wouldn't even allow the rest of the group to copy what he'd found."

"Is it worth paying for?" Tanner had assumed his usual thinking position, elbows on his knees, gorgeous biceps bunched, fists clasped under his chin.

"I don't think so." The door dinged again. Mandy greeted another patron. When she came back to the desk, she was antsy, probably ready for us to go. "Uncle Roddy said the two of you were looking for a book."

"Your uncle told us you'd know if it had been taken into evidence," I said.

She shook her head. "I looked at my list this morning after Uncle Roddy called, and there's no record of it."

Ugh. Another waste of precious time. My shoulders rounded.

Mandy spoke quickly as though she knew I'd probably get up and leave soon. "Uncle Roddy said you had a picture. May I see it?"

I dug it out.

Her eyes lit with interest. "May I get a copy of this?"

I nodded and watched as she snapped a few photos with her phone. When she finished, she pushed it back to me.

"Dwight's history of Loretta Nell Grimes doesn't include anything about that book. All our group has about it is Uncle Roddy's story, which he said he told you."

I wondered just how much of the story Uncle Roddy had told his niece. I bet not all of it.

Mandy stared at her phone and used her fingers to enlarge the picture she'd taken. "Well, look at that," she whispered.

"What?" I half stood, trying to see what she saw.

"Wait a minute." She tapped her phone a few times, and her laptop dinged. "I sent it to my laptop. Come here and look."

Tanner and I got up and crowded around her. She enlarged the picture until it was fuzzy and pointed with the tip of a pencil at a metal clasp holding the cover shut. A blurry key stuck out of it.

She tittered. "Just a book nerd thing."

I glanced at Tanner. He shrugged and tipped his head at the door. I gave a slight nod. Mandy was still engrossed in the picture.

I gathered my bag. Then I thought of something to ask Mandy. "Do you know much about the massacre of the Stephens family? I saw the graffiti on the house."

"Oh, you want to know about Josie. Now that's an odd story." She licked her lips and leaned forward.

My stomach twisted in disgust at her relish. That massacre had been a tragedy. Innocent lives lost. I worked to keep the revulsion off my face. Mandy began her story.

"Josie was found on the road right outside Stephens Ranch. If you've been out there, you know the ranch is a couple of miles off the road. She was barefoot and leaving blood tracks with every step. And—get this—her face was covered with gore. Like she'd taken a bite out of someone." Mandy's eyes widened, and her nostrils flared.

My stomach rolled.

"Had she?" Tanner's olive skin had turned a sick shade of green.

Mandy shook her head so hard her earrings clacked together. "Not that the cops could find. Wait a minute, I take that back." Her lips stretched into a greedy smile. "The victims had been...chewed on. But the gore on Josie's face didn't belong to any of her family members. Josie always said Loretta Nell was there with her. Seems there *was* someone else there." Mandy's eyes glowed with pleasure.

I wanted to get away from Mandy as soon as possible. Her delight in all this horrible, hurtful stuff sickened me.

"But that's not the kicker." Her smile widened, showing even more teeth. "When they found Josie, she kept screaming, 'Take me back. I need the book.'" Mandy held up her phone and showed us the picture she'd taken. "We knew from Uncle Roddy's story that there'd been a book. We've spent hours discussing what it was. This has to be it."

The bell outside dinged again. Mandy pushed back from her desk, a sure sign she needed us to beat it.

"Is there anything else I can help y'all with?" Her eyes darted to the door.

"Roderick mentioned Josie's in a mental hospital..." I began.

"Josie's at the state mental hospital in Austin." She walked to the door, peeked out, and held it open. I started to step out, but she blocked my way. "Wait a second. Mind if I ask why you're looking for the book?"

"A collector engaged us to find it." I knew that wouldn't do it. Mandy was too curious to leave it there. But I wasn't a good enough liar to think of something completely off-putting on the spot.

Sure enough, she clicked the door closed and whispered, "Who? And what do they want with it?"

Tanner saved me having to answer. "I've been in this business since I started working for my father back in California when I was fourteen. You learn not to ask."

Tanner cracked a crooked, charming smile for Mandy. I could practically see her heart fluttering. Wanting to leave before she thought of more questions, I squeezed around her.

"Wait." She led me around a corner and pointed at an exit hidden at the back of the room. "Sorry. The fewer patrons who see you, the better."

I nodded my understanding and hurried to the door, Tanner close behind me.

We managed to get out of the library without telling her anything more. Later, when it was much too late, I wished I had warned her.

8

———

BACK OUT ON THE SIDEWALK, Tanner took my hand and caressed it with one rough thumb. I gave him an impulsive kiss on the cheek. He hugged me. I hugged back, drinking in the comfort he offered.

Tanner was the best part of my life. And we'd just stumbled across each other. The twist of fate both fascinated and humbled me. Life wasn't all bad.

An elderly man wearing black horn-rimmed glasses stopped to stare at us. "You the one who caused the ruckus at Phil's Monkey Burger?"

Sweat tingled on my scalp. The smell of the cheap motel soap reached my nostrils as my body heated.

The man came a little closer. Tanner stiffened, shoulders expanding, arms lifting away from his body in silent threat. He'd hit if it came down to it.

The man stopped a couple of feet away. "Two 'a you need to get outta town. We don't take kindly to strangers coming in here snooping around."

"Understood." Tanner's deep voice didn't sound like he understood. It sounded like he was about one word from kicking this oldster's ass all the way to the city limits sign. The man must've heard it too. He made a wide loop around Tanner and me and went into the library.

This town gave me the creeps. Too many shades of Gaslight City. I couldn't wait to get out. Tanner gave me a gentle tap on the arm.

I spun around to face him and nearly yelled, "What?"

He put up both hands and took a step back. "I just asked if you still want to go to the mental hospital."

Wishing we could go back to holding hands and flirting, I tried to smile. "I guess. Unless you have a better idea?"

"Hate to admit it, but I don't. We don't have any other stones to turn over here in town." He slipped an arm over my shoulder and led me to the truck.

"You're right." I stared into the brightening sun, calculating how high it was in the sky, thinking about how much time had passed since Mohawk woke me up and told me I had seventy-two hours. I handed Tanner the keys and crawled into the passenger side.

Tanner climbed behind the wheel and began fiddling with his phone. "Damn. No signal."

"We'll have to wait until we get out of this devil's triangle to get directions." My mind tallied up the extra time lost and told me I needed to worry some more.

Tanner carefully followed the speed limit through Devil's Rest. Neither of us had voiced it, but this would be a bad place to have a run-in with law enforcement. Traveling with Cecil and Sanctuary had helped me develop a sense of such things. Tanner, who'd spent his entire adult life searching for magical items, had developed it for his own reasons, which I suspected were not always one hundred percent legal.

Once we passed the Devil's Rest city limits sign, Tanner sped through the parched landscape, at times going ninety miles per hour. He took chances I wouldn't have, passing when he wasn't supposed to and swerving onto the shoulder to get around slower moving vehicles. It scared me, but I wanted him to hurry. This trip to see Josie might be another piss in the wind. Then where would we be?

Tanner, as he did when he knew I was upset, babbled. "That Mandy chick was a new kind of weird."

I shrugged. "Look at Devil's Rest. Probably the only social life she has is dredging up that horror and going over every detail. The way she talked to us is probably the way she talks to the other members of that group."

Tanner nodded, gaze fixed on the road. He never dismissed an idea just because he didn't have it first. He'd mull over what I said and tell me days later he agreed or didn't.

"About that group." Tanner turned to me. "If you want the information Dwight has on Loretta Nell Grimes, tell me. I'll twist it out of him."

I nodded. Tanner was probably still mad about the way Dwight had gouged him for information on my whereabouts and directions to the Stephens Ranch. I hated to let Tanner strong-arm information out of Dwight. We were already leaving a way bigger footprint in Devil's Rest than felt safe. I began chewing on the fleshy part of my index finger, not hard, just enough to offset the pain of my tense muscles.

Periodically, I checked my phone. Finally it had a smidgen of service. I got directions to the mental hospital. We drove straight there. I gasped when it came into sight.

"Holy shit," I muttered.

"No shit." Tanner pulled into a parking place and leaned forward so he could see the whole thing.

The building was huge. Four stories and maybe an attic level. The building's front had snowy white Georgian columns across the front. To each side of the columns, a long wing jutted out. Despite the new paint and clean grounds, the place gave me the creeps.

I took out a cigarette with shaking hands and tried to light it, but my lighter hand trembled so hard I couldn't hit the tip.

Tanner reached over and steadied my hand. "This the same place you got sent as a kid?"

I dragged deep and shook my head. "Place I got sent was newer. And closer to where we lived in East Texas."

Tanner shook his head. "I'll never get used to all the distance in this state. East, West, South, North. Each part is considered a different place. I can't keep them straight."

I nodded, too wired up to formulate an answer. *It isn't like they're going to try to commit me. I can go in there, just like everybody else. It's a public place.* I drew hard on the cigarette, crushed it out in an ashtray full of butts, and turned to Tanner. "I gotta go in now."

He unbuckled his seatbelt.

I put my hand on his arm. "You don't have to come. Josie might talk more if it's to another woman."

But the truth was, I wanted that California cool Tanner could put on like a pair of shades.

Tanner ignored me, got out of the truck, and came around the side of the truck to open my door. "Let's do this."

I just sat there staring at the huge mental hospital, remembering my time in such an establishment. He gently pulled me out of the truck.

"I didn't know it would bother me this much." I tried to laugh.

"Most traumatic experience of your childhood? Please. I'm surprised you're walking." He took my arm and led me across the parking lot.

The building seemed bigger each step we took. As we neared it, fear slipped so deeply into my mind that I couldn't even read the signs telling visitors where to go. Tanner put one arm around my shoulders and led me through a double set of French doors in which the panes were so old the glass had dips and imperfections. Like the Georgian columns, the doors were whitewashed a blinding white. He walked me to a window with a sign that read "Visitors Check In Here."

I expected to see a nurse wearing a crisp white uniform, her hair done in a severe, old-fashioned bun. It would have completed the spooky vibe of the place. Had that person been waiting to check us in, I might have run screaming. As luck would have it, the lady behind the window had long, curly ginger hair and wore a set of brown scrubs with delicate yellow flowers.

"Help you guys?" She picked up a clipboard with a pen attached.

"We'd like to see Josie Stephens, please." Tanner put on his most polite smile, but his bar brawl nose and piercing eyes made the grin look more like a hungry tiger's than a friendly dog's.

The smile slid off her face. "I'll need to see some ID, please."

Tanner and I exchanged a quick glance. I nodded, and we both pulled out our driver's licenses and handed them over. The nurse, if that's what she was, read them carefully. She handed the IDs back and took a step away from the glass.

"Josie Stephens has a visitors list. We are ordered to follow that list to the letter. Anybody who's not on it can't get in." She gave us a flat-eyed stare.

I couldn't move. All this way, and I wouldn't even get to see Josie.

"Can't you just ask her if she'd be willing to see us?" Tanner's voice was still calm, but I heard the edge in it.

One look at the nurse gave me her answer. Sure enough she opened her tight lips and said, "No, sir. Ms. Stephens is not an attraction. She had an extremely traumatic experience, and she deserves to be left in peace."

Another nurse, this one wearing hot pink scrubs, came inside. She waved at the nurse behind the glass, walked across the room, and went up a staircase I hadn't noticed before. If only I could pass myself off as a nurse. A flash of inspiration hit me. I *could* do that exact thing.

"But this is important, ma'am, a matter of life and death." Tanner's voice rose just a little.

"It's okay, baby." I tugged at his arm. "This nice lady's right. Josie Stephens doesn't deserve to have a couple jerks like us piling in on her."

The nurse behind the glass smiled a little and nodded.

"But..." Tanner turned to me frowning, took one look at my face, and said, "Oh." He turned back to the woman behind the glass. "Thanks for your time, ma'am. We're sorry to have bothered you."

"No problem." The lady sat back down and started typing. She must've decided we weren't going to attack.

I took Tanner's hand and tugged him from the building. Once we were back out in the boiling sunlight, I said, "I'm going to do a spell to make myself look like a nurse. Get in that way."

———

BACK AT MY TRUCK, I dragged my witch pack out of the backseat, unzipped it, and dug around until I found the waterproof envelope where I kept Priscilla Herrera's grimoire. I pulled the envelope out of the pack and removed the spell book.

Soon as I touched the book, my ancestor's strong, determined energy flowed through my fingers and woke up the black opal. Somewhere behind me, a raven cawed.

The mantle opened up inside me, blossoming like an exotic flower and spreading its perfume through me.

Chilly wind came from nowhere, whipping both mine and Tanner's hair. I focused on the spell I wanted, the one commonly called a glamour spell, and opened the book. As usual, the book went right to the spell I wanted. A puff of age and old paper tickled my nostrils. The writing in the book looked more like symbols than anything in the English language at first glance, but as I stared, the words wiggled around like snakes and took a form I could understand.

I glanced over the instructions, noting they were different from the other time I'd used this type of spell. At the bottom of the page, words formed. "Don't forget the cost of this magic."

I nodded. The last time I'd done this spell, I'd gotten what I wanted, but I'd also enabled a murderer to take a life. The life taken was mostly unknown to me. But I'd had only the murderer's word that the person he killed was evil. Maybe I shouldn't do this.

Orev cawed behind me, resolute. He thought I should go for it. Priscilla Herrera's energy thrummed through me, ordering me to do it, even if it was just to hone my skills.

Tanner glanced over my shoulder at the spell book and rubbed his eyes hard. "Gives me a headache."

The whole thing gave me a headache too. According to the instructions, I'd have to find someone to impersonate. Not really wanting to try the lady we'd already spoken to, I stared out into the parking lot.

Several vehicles arrived at the same time. Hospital

employees wearing scrubs of all shades exited their vehicles and herded themselves into a building. It was either a shift change or the end of a meal break. I'd need to make up my mind quickly. The shift change, or whatever it was, would end soon. Coming into the hospital at an odd time would raise further suspicion.

Mind as made up as it was going to get, I began to walk toward a woman of my general height and age who also had a mane of long, dark hair. She'd separated from the crowd to gather it into a ponytail. I glanced back at Tanner and said, "Come on. Think of a question to ask this woman while you're walking."

We cut across the parking lot toward her, walking fast but not running. When we got close, I nodded to Tanner and mouthed, "Go."

"Excuse me, ma'am?" Tanner tried to do a Texas accent. He sounded about as authentic as Spanish rice made with ketchup.

The woman glanced up at him and made a face, almost rolling her eyes. Dislike came off her in waves. *Oh, no. We must've picked the bitch of the bunch.* But then she glimpsed me standing behind Tanner. The irritation fell of her face.

She smiled, brushed around Tanner, and spoke to me. "Y'all need some help?"

Struck dumb, I stared. I had no idea what Tanner had planned to ask her. *Think fast. Wing it.* "I noticed the historical marker outside the building and was wondering if there's tours."

As I spoke, I focused on her face, memorizing it as best as I could. The spell book had suggested a likeness. I didn't have one of those. But I knew from experience an item belonging to the person also worked for this spell.

The nurse, whose name tag said D. Homer, pulled her lips into a pout. "No. They ought to. The facility dates back to the eighteen-forties. But we still house and treat patients on site. It's probably a privacy concern."

That was it. There was nothing else for this woman and me to say to each other, and I still needed either a picture or a personal item.

D. Homer checked her watch and said, "I'm sorry not to be more help. Hyde Park's right over there. Lots of cool eating places, and it has a lot of history."

No idea what else to do, I smiled and nodded. "Thanks for the tip."

D. Homer walked away from us and toward the building.

I skulked back to my truck and glanced at the spell book, reading the directions one last time. Maybe I could make myself look like D. Homer just from memory. I closed my eyes and tried to call up her face.

"Need this?" Tanner held up his phone. On its screen was a picture of D. Homer, smiling as she spoke with me. "I'll let you use it. For a price."

I slitted my eyes at him and held out my hand. "If I told you to drop your pants right here, you'd do it. No deal."

Tanner blustered with mock outrage. "That's wrong. I'd at least make you take me behind some bushes."

I took the phone and set it down next to the spell book. One more read through, and I was ready. Oddly, there was no question in my mind that I could do it. The unknown ramifications concerned me more. I held out my hand to Tanner. "Let's share power. Might make it last longer."

Wordlessly, he put his hand in mine and closed his eyes. I closed mine and found the mantle nestled deep inside me, underneath its shroud of scar tissue. I pulled gently on the energy, teasing it out. It flowed through my body, blunted but still powerful enough to make me see the world that lay underneath ours.

A greenish haze of pollution overlaid the sky. But underneath, I saw the element of air. It rippled against the sky, rolling and somersaulting, pushing the wind. The earth, long covered by pavement, hummed beneath my feet. It could be hidden, but progress couldn't kill it. I drew both sources of power into me, letting them fuel the mantle.

Next to me, Tanner's body stiffened. His hand tightened on mine, and he took a deep breath and moaned as the power hit him.

Water flowed beneath the earth, endlessly recharging and renewing. I called for its cleansing magic and let it move through me and into Tanner.

The fire came last because it was inside me. It burned through my veins and called power from Tanner. The burn grew hotter, so hot that sweat popped out all over my body. It was time.

I let my eyes slide open and called up the digital picture of the nurse. I stared into her face, eyes roving over every feature, every sharp edge.

"Power of elements, I call on thee
Make it where they see her and not me."

I repeated the simple chant three times and then threw the power of the mantle into it, concentrating with all my might, on moving the energy that would make me look like the nurse.

My face began to tickle, then itch. The itch grew until it stung like ants on my face. I jerked my hand away from Tanner's and brought it up to touch my skin. My nose was wrong. Sharper and longer. I faced Tanner, but he still had his eyes closed.

"Tanner?" I shook his arm.

He opened his eyes. His mouth dropped open, and he backpedaled away from me. He stared hard at me and then came closer. He ran his fingers over my cheeks, frowning. He slid a hand down my body. "It is you. At first, I wasn't sure. But the body's yours."

I used the camera on my phone to look at myself. A gasp escaped my lips, and I nearly dropped my phone. It had worked. I was D. Homer. At least for a few minutes.

I stared at the hospital with dread. The last time I'd been in a place like this, they'd wanted to lock me away. Irrational fear bolted through me, trampling down all the confidence I'd built since that day when I was eight years old.

Tanner pulled me close. "You sure about this? There's got to be another way."

There probably were other ways, but I didn't have time to figure them out. Josie knew some stuff about Loretta Nell. According to Mandy Drake, Josie had at least known about Mohawk's book. She'd demanded to be taken back to Stephens Ranch to get it. Maybe she knew where I could find it.

Tanner waited for my answer. Even if he knew going in that hospital and scaring the shit out of myself was the best bet, he was too nice a guy to kick my ass all the way in there.

I gave him a squeeze and stepped away. It felt like taking the training wheels off a bike. "I have to do this. This spell won't last long, so I need to hurry." I marched across the parking lot and into the front door.

"Deena?" The nurse who'd told me I couldn't see Josie frowned. "Didn't you just come through?"

"I forgot something." The sound of my voice mixed with a little of Deena's made me stiffen. The spell had been so simple and low energy that it hadn't even disguised my voice. *This isn't going to work. They'll put you in a padded room and keep you forever.* My knees went watery at the thought, but I forced myself to keep walking.

"Guess I missed you going out," the nurse said to my back, but she didn't sound too sure.

I hurried up the same stairs I'd seen the other nurse use and acted like I knew where I was going. Soon, I knew I'd overplayed my hand. The hospital was huge, and I had no idea how to find Josie. Asking another nurse would blow my cover.

I wandered the halls, drawing curious glances from Deena Homer's co-workers, but nobody called me out for not being wherever Deena was supposed to be. A TV blared nearby, and I peeked into a room full of chairs and realized, as I glanced over the patients' faces, that I didn't even know what Josie looked like.

My spirits sank. In my hurry to get this done, I had made every possible mistake. I had no idea what Josie looked like, didn't know where to find her.

"Deena?" The voice came from right behind me.

My stomach jumped. Sweat popped out all over my body. If this person wanted to converse, it could go so very, very badly. I slowly turned to face whoever'd caught me.

A middle-aged woman wearing a starched white nurse's uniform glared at me. Her name tag read Fitch, which I first mistook for Bitch. "Why are you in the women's wing, Deena? I thought we talked about this."

"Uhhh...I forgot something in my car." The sound of my own voice jolted me. The glamour was already wearing off. Fear spread through my body. It would make the spell wear off even faster, but I didn't have the self-control to stop it.

Fitch frowned. "You don't have to come through the women's wing to get to the children's wing." She pulled a spiral bound notepad from her pocket. "I'm going to make a note of seeing you up here. Two more times, and I'll make a formal complaint. I'm tired of you young nurses playing more than you work."

Shit. I'd gotten Deena, who seemed perfectly nice, into trouble. Another glamour spell, another batch of trouble. At least nobody was dead yet.

Fitch stopped writing in her notepad. "Come on. I'll walk you out." She did just that, leaving me outside a locked door.

"Fuck," I muttered and stomped off, no clue where I was going. If Josie was anywhere, she was behind that door with Fitch the Bitch and now off limits to me. I passed a row of windows looking out on a courtyard. My reflection showed regular old Peri Jean Mace starting back at me with scared eyes.

Perfect. Footsteps approached. I turned down a hallway, ducked behind an open door, and watched through the crack between the doorjamb and the door. Fitch the Bitch passed by, craning her neck, probably trying to catch the errant Deena Homer doing shit she wasn't supposed to be doing. The only bright side was that I now looked like me. Deena Homer wouldn't get into further trouble for my shenanigans.

Fitch approached. I stood as still as I could. She went into one of the patient rooms and came out, leaving the door open. She stared right at the door I was hiding behind. I held my breath, heart thudding so loud in my ears it was hard to believe Fitch couldn't hear it. But she didn't seem to. She passed by, rubbing at chill bumps that had risen on her sun-spotted arms.

I came out from behind the door and crept in the direction I'd seen Fitch come from. This wing was being renovated. Scaffolds lined the walls. An unopened box of tile sat next to a neatly folded drop cloth. This would be the perfect place to hide out while I figured out what to do next. I ducked into an empty patient room and took out my phone, ready to hit the web for all my research needs. My phone's blank screen stared at me. I let out a disgusted grunt.

Since getting one of the fancy full-featured smart-phones, I had trained myself to think the phone held all the answers just because I could access the internet. But there wouldn't be a recent picture of Josie online. Nor would her room number here at the hospital be posted. I rolled my eyes.

Behind me, a small voice said, "You looking for me?"

My whole body jerked, and I nearly dropped my phone on the hard tile, which surely would have busted it into a million useless pieces. I juggled the glass and plastic albatross before finally getting control of it and tucking it into my pocket. Heart hammering, I turned to see who'd spoken.

———

THE GIRL SAT lotus position in the corner of the empty room, a hand of solitaire laid spread at her knees. At first, I thought Loretta Nell's ghost had somehow found me here at the asylum. But a closer look revealed fuller lips, a broader nose, and darker blond hair.

"Josie Stephens?" I stared at the slight woman with thin red scars all over her face, her hair long and unkempt but clean.

She nodded. "Are you the lady who came earlier wanting to see me? The one Ilsa wouldn't let come up?"

I gaped at her. "How'd you know? And what are you doing in here?"

Josie smiled, showing small, neat teeth. "Ten years in a

place like this, and you learn the ropes. As for your second question, waiting on you."

Cold fingers walked up my back. "Why?"

"Loretta Nell said you'd be coming." She swept the cards into a pile and began shuffling them.

The chill spread to the rest of my body. Soon I'd be shaking. *Stay calm. Pretend it's all cool.* "You've been in contact with Loretta Nell?"

"We talk every day." She giggled at whatever she saw on my face, putting a hand criss-crossed with thin, red scars over her mouth. Her stormy blue eyes gleamed with something that made my skin crawl. Then it was gone. "Go on and ask."

"What do you think I'm here to ask you?" I felt sorry for this woman who'd had her life cut off the day she got thrown into this place. Had it not been for Memaw, the same thing could have happened to me.

"All kinds of people come to see me. They all ask the same questions. They want to know about the night my family died, and they want to know why I said Loretta Nell Grimes did it. Why would you be any different?" She slapped some cards down on the floor.

I crouched on the floor so Josie and I could see eye to eye. Standing over someone indicated a dominant position, and I wanted her to trust me enough to talk.

"I'm different because I know Loretta Nell murdered your family."

She lowered her chin. Her chest rose and fell with her breaths. "So what do you want to know?"

I nodded. "Did you ever see Loretta Nell before the night she killed your family?"

Josie bared her teeth in another smile. It somehow reminded me of an animal waiting for a chance to bite. "Oh, I get it. You're one of those."

A warning bell went off in my head. I let it ring. It was too late to do anything but play this out. "One of what?"

She continued playing her new game of solitaire. "Ghost hunters. Paranormal investigators. You've been out to Poppy's house. Maybe heard footsteps. Or didn't you say you'd met Loretta Nell?"

I didn't want to give Josie any more information about myself. This whole setup felt wrong. More than ever, I wanted to get away from Josie, go back to Tanner.

"If you've met her, she's going to kill you." Josie turned over a card. "See, I didn't know to leave her alone."

"You brought her ghost back, didn't you, Josie?" I whispered.

She ducked her head but nodded. "It started six months before the night she killed my whole family. We'd gone to visit Poppy. Nana had just died, and Poppy said I ought to go into the attic and see if I wanted some of Nana's stuff from when she was young. There was nothing I really wanted, so I started poking around."

I said nothing. Josie spoke mostly to her cards, laying them down, picking them up. She wasn't really playing solitaire. She was just moving the cards around. She seemed to have forgotten she was talking to a real person.

"I saw the door behind a wardrobe. One of those tall ones so big a person could stand in it. Took me an hour to get enough stuff out of the wardrobe so I could move it, but I did." She stopped playing with her cards and stared through me. "I wish I had just left it alone. But I didn't. I opened the door and found that room, that awful little room. There were pictures cut out of magazines and posters on the walls. It wasn't too much different than my dorm room at college. And I could feel her in there, maybe listening to records or reading." She raised her head, and we stared at each other. She whispered, "I'd heard about Loretta Nell and the Messengers all my life. But for the first time, I got curious about who she was. Biggest mistake of my life."

"What did you do?" My voice shook. I didn't want to hear this story. Normal people, the ones who didn't have to live with freaky talent like mine, never knew when to leave well enough alone. The unlucky ones ended up where Josie Stephens now sat.

"I bought an Ouija board," she told me, wide-eyed.

I held in my groan. It just got worse and worse. An Ouija board gave a powerful ghost like Loretta Nell an engraved invitation to wreak havoc. No wonder things ended the way they did.

"She visited the first time we used it..." She paused, and I thought I'd have to prod her to continue, but then she started talking. "That was when cameras in cellphones were pretty new. My roommate and I took a lot of pictures. When we looked at them, they all had *her* in them. If the picture was of my roommate, Loretta Nell would be next to her. Just standing there. No expression on her face." Josie lowered her chin and set her eyes on me again. "Like this."

A shudder ripped through me. When Josie did that, it heightened the slight resemblance between her and Loretta Nell.

She blew out a breath. "Then Alex—that was my roommate—died."

I drew in a whoop of air. This wasn't what I'd expected. "How?"

"Single car accident. They couldn't figure out what happened." Josie stared at the window behind me so intently I turned to make sure Loretta Nell wasn't there. When I turned back to Josie, she was smiling again.

"After Alex died, I got obsessed with what happened to the Messengers. I spent a lot of time in the library, reading news articles, poking around on the internet." She licked her lips. "Then I started using the Ouija board to talk to Loretta Nell by myself."

I wanted to tell her to stop, to beg her not to say another word. Or to just get up and leave. But I hadn't even asked her about the book, and it seemed Josie had been in fairly direct contact with Loretta Nell for quite some time before she ended up here.

My voice came out cracked and trembling. "What did Loretta Nell tell you?"

Josie shrugged. "It was just letters that didn't make words. Then it just became places."

"Places?" Cold sweat rolled down my body as Josie talked. The stuff matched other stories I knew about spirits gaining control of people. Was I sitting unprotected in a room with a mass murderer, even one who got duped into what she did? I inched away from Josie, hoping she wouldn't notice.

Josie nodded. "The library. The theater building. A few days afterward, things would happened to people there. They died." She started humming, eyes on her cards.

"What about your family? Did Loretta Nell warn you in advance what was going to happen to them?" I tried not to hear the humming or to acknowledge that the song was a gospel standard called "Power in the Blood."

She raised her eyes to mine. The smile came back. "No. By that time, I was having blackouts. All I remember is Loretta Nell coming out of the walls of Poppy's house to take her revenge."

I stiffened. The words didn't bug me so much. The smile did. Knowing and feral, it made my knees wobble. It was time to go, past time. But I still had questions.

"That night, the night your family died, did you see a book? Or did Loretta Nell read to you from a book?" I watched Josie for a reaction.

Josie shuffled the cards again, gaze fixed on the floor. "Book?"

That didn't make sense. Mandy had said Josie begged the deputy to go back to the house for the book.

I took the picture from my bag and held it where Josie could see it. She put down the cards and leaned forward, tilting her head to one side. Magic flashed through my black opal right about the time I noticed Josie had tilted her head too far for it to be comfortable.

I tried to scoot away from her, but the linoleum was slick and new, and I lost my balance. Josie snatched the picture away from me and crumpled it to a ball in one hand. Her lips stretched into an ugly snarl, and she changed positions to crouch on her knees. Her face contorted, and she looked more like Loretta Nell than ever.

"You'll never have the Serpent God," she growled. "You're unworthy. You don't even love him."

The black opal pinged uselessly on my chest, its warning too late to do me any real good. I cowered away, trying to remember how much space was between me and the door. But I'd been too focused on my stupid phone and then Josie to notice such a small detail. I inched backward.

Josie crawled forward, eyes shining with cunning. She leapt and pinned me to the floor, stronger than I ever could have imagined. Eyes wild and shining, she leaned over me. Something tugged at my brain. It tapped around the edges, trying to get in.

Panic shocked me into action. I grabbed at her arms. She whipped them out of my grasp and snapped at my hand. I doubled up a fist and swung at her, but I was on my back, at the wrong angle to really hurt her. She slapped my ineffective punch away and settled her mad eyes on mine.

The tugging came again. I gathered my energy and pushed against it. Josie's head snapped back. She shook herself and locked eyes with me. Sour terror filled my mouth. I had to bite my lip to keep from screaming. Josie wasn't holding me down anymore. Josie had not physically changed, but Loretta Nell stared out from behind Josie's eyes.

The room flashes twice and is gone. I'm back in the barn at the Stephens Ranch.

Dim light filters into the barn from a floodlight outside. The empty room I saw before is now filled with all manner of junk. The bloodstains on the walls are not as shining and fresh as when I saw them. My mind latches onto that, but before I can figure out why that's odd, I hear the girl whimpering.

A much younger and less weathered Josie crouches against a dark-colored farm truck, her teeth chattering. Sweat plasters her long hair to her face. In one hand, Josie girl holds a sickle. Something moves in my peripheral vision. Josie and I both gasp.

Loretta Nell flits around the room, manifesting then disappearing again. She darts in to tap Josie's shoulder. The poor girl screams, body jittering from fright.

"You can't have me, you crazy bitch." Josie's voice is guttural with pure animal fear.

"You've been mine since the day you were born, just like all the other children of those bastards who killed me." Loretta Nell manifests in Josie's face.

Josie screams again but gets control of herself and crawls to her feet.

"No. I'm not yours." She hefts the sickle and takes on a warrior's stance, sides heaving with exhausted breaths.

Loretta Nell's spirit manifests, solid as a real person, and races toward Josie. The girl's eyes widen. She rears back one arm and swings at Loretta Nell.

The sickle sinks deep. Loretta Nell clutches at her chest. Phantom blood seeps from the wound. Loretta Nell staggers backward and sits down hard.

Josie advances on Loretta Nell, eyes gleaming with mad fury.

"You killed my family. Whether you're a ghost or not, I'm going to kill you," she grates in Loretta Nell's face.

Loretta Nell, at first glance, seems afraid. Her eyes are wide and shining. Her mouth is open in a little o. But I can see things Josie, the panicked teenager, cannot. The hand Loretta Nell is holding to her chest is not cradling a wound, it's holding the sickle in place. And behind her wide eyes is something close to fear but not the real deal. Behind Loretta Nell's wide eyes is greed. She needs this little scene to play out and is terrified it won't.

Josie grabs a hanging pulley attached to the ceiling and drags it to Loretta Nell. She ties the rope around Loretta Nell's torso and hoists her body into the air. Loretta Nell hangs still, throwing in a reasonably convincing twitch every few seconds, hand still holding the sickle to her chest.

I want to scream at Josie to stop, that it's a trick. But this is a vision. I'm seeing the past, and I can't change what's already happened.

Josie digs the sickle deeper into Loretta Nell's chest and pulls it all the way down to her pubic bone. A half-transparent flow of glistening guts and blood spill from the body. Loretta Nell's head flops to one side as though she's dead, but her eyes stay bright and aware.

Josie showers in the blood and entrails, rubbing them on her face, eyes shining with madness. She raises her hands to her face and licks the palms.

Josie leaves Loretta Nell hanging, goes over to the work table, and comes back with a long knife, the kind used to skin animals. She peels off a piece of Loretta Nell's flesh and lifts it to her mouth.

I can't keep quiet. "No, Josie, no. It's what she wants you to do."

Not hearing me, Josie eats the piece of flesh. Loretta Nell's still eyes come to life as she watches her victim feed on her. Josie's face ripples, becoming Loretta Nell's for one second.

She lets out a wild roar and sticks her head into Loretta Nell's open chest, burrowing. Loretta Nell's body moves lifelessly underneath the wild attack. But her eyes. Her eyes are bright with glee.

The vision fades, and I'm back in the mental hospital with Josie leaning close enough to kiss me.

"That book is not for you. It's not for the last survivor. It's for Loretta Nell and the Messengers." Josie delivered her words in a high, sweet lilting country accent.

But they were all dead, rotting in their graves for the last forty-plus years. I dared not say that. Josie had the upper hand. She might eat me the way she had eaten Loretta Nell in my vision.

Caw caw caw. Orev's presence came into my mind. A tapping sound came from the window. Orev must've landed there and was hitting it with his beak. I didn't dare take my gaze off Josie. She inched closer, saliva dripping from her mouth to plop onto my face and slide down my cheek.

"J-J-Josie, if you tell me where the book is, I can get you free of Loretta Nell." My voice trembled so hard I barely recognized it. "Maybe even get you out of here."

Josie smiled, blue eyes cold as rain in January, now all Loretta Nell. "I will rise again. And I will kill both the last survivor and you for trying to take what's mine. And then I will cleanse the earth of the undeserving."

She fitted one hand over my throat and began to press down, her face straining with the effort. I coughed against the sudden loss of oxygen and punched at Josie. She didn't move.

"But first the last survivor." She breathed a cloud of foul breath into my face. "The last survivor is key."

Even with my consciousness fading, I knew this was important. I tried to ask what she meant by key. A weak croak escaped my lips.

Fitch the Bitch slammed into the room, walkie-talkie gripped in one hand.

She yelled into it. "I found Stephens. We need Winston in the unfinished wing right now."

Fitch grabbed Josie under the arms and tried to pull her off me. Josie twisted in her grasp, arms and legs flailing.

"She's just like the last survivor," Josie screamed.

Fitch's eyes widened. The nurse's body jerked as though she'd been goosed. It was enough for Josie to twist and sink her teeth into the nurse's arm. Fitch yelled and let go of the wild thing. Josie got to her feet and ran out of the room, bare feet slapping the linoleum.

Fitch pointed one finger at me. "Stay right there. You and me need to talk." Then she ran out of the room, yelling into her walkie-talkie again.

I wasn't staying anywhere and waiting for Fitch to tell me off. I grabbed the wadded-up picture off the floor and hightailed it out of the room.

9

I RACED DOWN THE HALLWAY, shoes squeaking on the shiny, new linoleum. The hallway ended at a T, and I went left, toward the parking lot and Tanner. My smoke-singed lungs screamed for oxygen, but I pushed on, picturing Tanner and the warmth of his arms. I called up the soft purr of his voice, the music of his laugh, his strong thighs, the taste of sweat on the back of his neck.

Tanner had come to equal safety and stability. *When did that happen?* Maybe the long nights we'd laid together in the darkness, fingers laced together, talking.

I ran past the row of windows, my reflection transparent. Queenie had been right. I was a ghost in my own life. I needed to put my whole self into my relationship with Tanner and quit holding back because I didn't want my heart broken again. I needed to quit being afraid of what I was, of my power. The fear might help me avoid hurt and scary things, but it would always hold me prisoner. Just like if I had spent all my growing up years in a place like this one.

Footsteps pounded behind me, coming nearer each second. My pace slowed as my smoke-damaged lungs failed to provide the oxygen I needed to keep running full blast. My pursuers were barely a turn behind me.

I came to a door marked "Exit" and slammed through it. A huge man stood on the other side. The contrast of his dark skin against his white uniform almost burned my eyes. His name tag said K. Winslow.

"There you are." K. Winslow reached for me with a hand roughly the size of my head.

I tried to duck around him, but he caught my arm and yanked me off balance. I let out a shrill yell. K. Winslow gave me a hard shake.

With his other hand, he pulled out a walkie-talkie and said, "Nurse Fitch? Winslow here. I got the intruder."

Fitch's voice came back. "Good job, Kevin. Bring her to my office."

I doubled up a fist and swung it into Kevin Winslow's stomach, using my whole body the way Tanner recommended. The impact rang up my arm as though I'd hit an iron wall. Winslow tightened his grip, pulled me off the floor, and dangled me in front of his face.

"Hit me again, and I'm gonna beat the white off 'a you. Got it?" His voice, low and menacing, echoed in the stairwell.

Fear flooded my bloodstream, pushing my heart so hard and fast my skin tingled.

Winslow gave me a teeth-rattling shake. "Hear me, girl?"

I nodded.

He let go of me. I fell hard on concrete floor, most of my weight landing on one knee. Pain shot through my body. I howled. Tears spurted from my eyes, and I rolled over onto one side clutching my injury. By tonight, the knee would probably be twice its normal size and the color of an eggplant. My tormenter clicked his tongue.

"Aw, hell. I didn't mean to do that." He grabbed me by the same arm, which had begun to throb from how hard he'd gripped it, and hauled me to my feet. He leaned into my face. His breath smelled like corn chips and salsa. "You gotta mind me, or I'm gonna hurt you. Understand?"

I nodded again, crying from the pain in my knee.

He put an almost gentle hand on my shoulder. "You know my name. What's yours?"

"Peri Jean Mace." My voice trembled.

"You done got yourself in deep shit, Peri Jean Mace. Josie Stephens is Nurse Fitch's pet project. Or peeve. Hope you have a damn good reason you broke in here to see her." Kevin Winslow hauled me up the steps and stopped in front of a door like the one I'd slammed through an eternity ago. He held it open and pointed toward a closed door a few feet away with a sign that read Suzanne Fitch. I stumbled toward it. Winslow took one arm to hold me upright.

"Peri Jean, I want you to understand something." He continued talking as he tugged me along, never looking at my face. "Suzanne Fitch is my boss, and this is a good paying job for a guy like me. You're gonna tell her what she wants to know whether you like it or not."

I nodded, gasping from the pain in my knee. What kind of damage had Kevin Winslow done to me? I wanted Tanner. Just the thought of him took away some of the darkness and gave me a little comfort. Kevin doubled up one roast-sized fist and knocked softly on Nurse Fitch's office door.

"Bring her in, Kevin," Nurse Fitch sang.

Kevin opened the door and pushed me inside. Nurse Fitch set her pen aside. "Seat her in front of the desk, please."

Kevin used both hands to fold me into the chair. Nurse Fitch watched the same way she might have watched someone pat a hamburger patty before throwing it on the grill.

"How'd you get in here?" she asked.

I shook my head and shrugged.

Nurse Fitch glanced at Kevin and gave a slight nod. Something slammed into the back of my head hard enough to knock me forward. My forehead smacked the edge of her desk. I slid to the floor, banging my already throbbing knee on the floor. I yelped like a kicked dog.

Kevin grabbed me under the arms and pulled me back into the chair. I couldn't sit up straight.

"I've told you not to hit them so hard," Fitch hissed at Kevin.

"Didn't seem hard to me." I heard the shrug in his voice.

"He's a big dude," I slurred, thinking about Wade Hill. "They don't know how hard they're hitting."

"Uh-huh. She's right," Kevin said from behind me, where he might have been getting ready to clobber me again.

Fitch watched me from across the desk, gaze still clinical and cold. "Tell me how you got in here." Her eyes flicked to Kevin Winslow standing behind me.

I couldn't take another hit. But if I told Fitch how I got in, she might lock me up for being crazy. The scared eight-year-old who'd been sent to a mental hospital began to scream. Hysteria buzzed around my thoughts, a swarm of bloodsucking mosquitos, ready to help me do something crazy.

Then I remembered who I was. Peri Jean Mace. Great-great-great granddaughter of Priscilla Herrera, a witch of considerable power. Peri Jean Mace. Raised by Leticia Gregson Mace, a fierce little woman who could have backed down the devil himself. Peri Jean Mace. A badass witch who had more power than these two clowns could imagine.

"I'll give you one more chance, Miss..." Fitch said in a bored voice.

"It's Peri Jean Mace," Kevin Winslow supplied.

"Miss Mace then. Tell me how you got in here, or Kevin will convince you to talk." She settled her gaze on mine, probably thinking it was intimidating. For the record, it was.

But I didn't do humility too well.

"I'm a witch." I watched her face go slack with shock then hard with angry disbelief. "I used a glamour spell to fool your gatekeeper downstairs." I waited for her to call me a liar. Maybe she'd even go for the gold and call me a crazy liar.

Suzanne Fitch didn't do either. She picked up a framed picture off her desk and stared at it with her lips pressed together.

This was it. My opening. I drew on all the bad energy the hospital had and concentrated on the glass of that picture. A satisfying clink came from Fitch's desk.

She flicked her gaze to me. "Am I supposed to believe you caused that?"

I pulled myself up and sat in my chair again. My knee screamed in protest, but I pretended not to feel it.

"You don't have to. I'm not finished." I called on the element of air and got a funky, electricity charged wind blowing in the office. The mantle glowed and strained behind the scar tissue spell. It called to me, asking to be let out. I pulled at it.

Suzanne Fitch's office took on a hazy glow. Ghosts marched through, wearing clothes of their era, trailing cold air with their passage. All the hurt and fear people had felt in this place hung overhead like storm clouds.

I breathed in, gathering my focus, and called down a bolt of lightning. It hit a stack of papers at the corner of her desk. Both Fitch and Winslow let out screams. A wisp of smoke trailed from the papers. Intent on me, Fitch didn't notice. The papers began to belch smoke. A flame licked around them.

Winslow shot forward, his huge feet pounding the floor. He grabbed a file and slapped at the papers. Suzanne Fitch recovered faster than most would have. She grabbed her own file. She and Kevin beat out the fire before it got big enough to set off the smoke alarm.

"Kevin, please open the door to let the smoke out." Her voice came out a little breathless, but her face stayed calm and in charge. Kevin did as she asked and stood in the doorway as though daring anybody to ask what was going on.

Suzanne Fitch moved her jaw as though chewing on her words. "Fine. You've some sort of psychokenesis. Why did you use it to get in here to see Josie Stephens?"

I'd hidden what I was all my life because I feared ending back up in a place like this. Coming clean with someone in charge of keeping mentally ill people under lock and key scared me. But I had a few questions of my own to ask Suzanne Fitch, and she was, by God, going to answer.

I took a deep breath. "Josie Stephens might have knowledge of a book I need to find. And when I say need, I am talking life and death."

Suzanne stared across the desk at me but didn't call me a liar.

Planning how I could make Suzanne Fitch stroke out if things went sour, I took out the now battered picture of Loretta Nell Grimes holding the book and set it on Fitch's desk. She picked it up and studied it, mouth thinning into a hard straight line. She slid the picture back across the desk and leaned back in her chair, making it groan. Before she could speak, the walkie-talkie on her desk came to life.

"Nurse Fitch?" A new voice twanged over the speaker. "Sam Adamick here. Got the other 'un."

My heart stuttered as icy fear coated it. They had Tanner. He wouldn't be riding to my rescue. Worse, they might hurt him. Anger melted my fear in a quick flash.

Fitch keyed the walkie and spoke. "Bring him up."

"Nurse Fitch?" I sat very still, anger pumping hard now, and waited for her to acknowledge me. She did with a flick of her eyes. I spoke slowly, my East Texas brogue worse than usual. "If you hurt my man, I'll kill you, Winslow, and this Adamick. But you'll be first. I'll make your eyeballs pop right outta your head."

She flinched and paled. Winslow moved out of the doorway. A massive guy dragged Tanner into Fitch's office. Tanner took one look at me, eyes widening, and spun to face the guy I assumed was Sam Adamick.

"You said if I came with you, she wouldn't be harmed." Tanner hands hung by his sides, not fisted yet, but I knew the tone of voice. He wasn't far from violence.

Adamick shrugged. Tanner doubled up one fist and let it go, his whole body twisting with its delivery. His feet came off the ground when the punch hit. Adamick, who might have been fit twenty-five years and a hundred pounds ago, staggered backward, holding his jaw.

Tanner jerked away from Adamick, grabbed my arm, and yanked me out of the chair. Kevin launched himself at Tanner.

"Stop it, all of you," I yelled. The energy building in me swirled another harsh wind into the room. Another bolt of lightning cracked onto Suzanne Fitch's desk. She screamed.

Winslow and Adamick froze. Tanner edged me closer

to the door. I pressed myself hard against his side. He gripped me with one arm, protecting, but also drawing strength. We needed each other.

Stop being scared to love him. The voice didn't even sound like mine. It sounded suspiciously like Priscilla Herrera.

Winslow stepped in our way. "Nope. You ain't going nowhere."

I turned back to Fitch. "What do you want from us?"

"You're trespassing on state property. I'm supposed to involve police." She leaned away from the smoking papers on her desk.

"But you're not going to." Otherwise the police would have been waiting for me in Fitch's office.

Fitch shook her head. "Josie Stephens is a problem patient. Weird things happen around her. She gets out of locked rooms, out of restraints. She hurts staff members."

I shrugged. Nurse Fitch probably wouldn't believe how Josie was doing it if I told her.

"I don't care how she's doing it." Fitch seemed to read my mind. "I care about running a safe hospital."

"We're not killing Josie for you." Tanner spoke up from beside me.

I glanced at Fitch, expecting to see horror but only saw irritation.

"Neither of you look very upstanding. If I call the authorities into this, what other kind of trouble will you be in?" She leveled her gaze on me like someone used to getting her way.

If I had been a drinker, this would have been where I said, "Hold my beer."

Instead, I drew on the mantle in silent concentration, pulling it to the point of painfulness, and aimed it at Suzanne Fitch. I imagine fire ants and red wasps crawling over her body and stinging. All at once.

She let out a shrill cry. "Winslow! Adamick!"

I turned my attention to the two big men. Winslow took one look at my face and took off running. Must not have been that great of a job after all. Adamick reached for me. Tanner slammed a fist into his flabby midsection, but I concentrated on his eyes. I imagined them burning. Adamick clapped his hands over his face and staggered out of the doorway.

I turned back to Fitch's desk. Her eyes widened, the fear bright behind them, but she kept her face placid. I admired that.

"Now that we're alone, you're going to tell me why you looked like somebody rubbed sandpaper over your asshole when Josie started talking about the last survivor." Far as I could tell, this last survivor was the only clue I'd be getting from this whole shit show.

Fitch took a shaking breath, licking her lips at the same time. "Please. Both of you, sit."

Tanner and I glanced at each other, each silently asking the other what to do. I sat first. He followed.

I found my voice. "Tell me about the last survivor, or I'm going to fuck this place up so bad that you'll never be able to explain it away."

Beside me, Tanner chuckled.

Fitch closed her eyes and let out a sigh. When she opened them again, they held a sad resignation.

"A very dear friend of mine was Josie's therapist." Fitch turned around the picture whose glass I'd broken.

In it, a younger and more carefree Suzanne Fitch embraced an attractive woman. The two laughed at the camera, hanging on to each other the way Tanner and I did. Fitch pressed her lips together, eyes sad.

"Josie talked to Colleen at length about the book and the last survivor." Fitch continued staring at the picture.

"Bring her in. Let us speak to her." Excitement built in my chest. This could really go somewhere.

"Colleen no longer works for the hospital, or anywhere. She was traumatized by her experience with Josie. She sees very few people." Fitch said no more, but her fierce expression said it all. She'd protect this woman with everything she had.

I admired Suzanne Fitch. We had a lot of the same traits. For that reason, I hated myself for what I needed to do.

"Ms. Fitch, if you don't put me in touch with Colleen, I'm going to report you to whatever board governs this hospital. Your poor security allowed me to get in, and then you allowed your flunkies to assault my boyfriend and me." I swallowed hard, cringing inside. I sounded imperious—and like a pussy—even to my own ears. "You will lose this job faster than a cat whips a dog's ass."

For the first time, Fitch didn't have a response at the ready. She searched my face, probably looking for a crack of weakness she could wedge her way into and talk me out of my threats. I stared steadily back.

Her face hardened. "Get out while I make a phone call."

I stood. "Fuck with me, and I'll make you wish your daddy liked condoms. Hear me?"

She flinched at my vulgarity but gave me a slight nod. Tanner and I stepped outside the room.

"That was mean," he whispered.

My face heated. It wasn't just mean. It was ruthless, just like Priscilla Herrera. I rubbed at my stomach. My ancestor still scared me silly. But the more things I survived, the more I understood her.

We all made wrong turns. Sometimes it just couldn't be helped. Getting turned around and headed back in the right direction took whatever it took. The world Priscilla and I lived in was dog eat dog. A woman either had to show her inner steel to the world or be buried beneath it.

Minutes crept past. I expected to hear police sirens any second. But the door finally opened, and Fitch came out holding a slip of paper.

"She's expecting you." She held the paper just out of my reach. "Now you listen to me. If you traumatize my loved one further, all the magic in the world won't save you."

"Understood." I snatched it out of her hand.

Tanner and I walked out of the hospital and into the blistering sun. It took my breath away and burned my skin. Heat baked through the soles of my boots to warm my feet uncomfortably. It fit the shame I felt for the way I'd treated

Fitch, even though being the bigger bully had been the only way.

I could only hope Colleen was worth the effort. If she wasn't, I didn't know where I'd turn next.

————

THE SHORT WALK to the truck made my knee throb. By the time we reached it, I gripped my thigh and practically hopped.

Tanner had to lift me into the truck. "You need to see a doctor."

I shook my head. Mohawk's clock never stopped ticking. A hospital emergency room or doctor's office would cost me too many hours.

"We can find a drugstore on the way to see Colleen Pellingham." I tapped the address into my phone's map to get directions. A robotic voice began telling Tanner how to get back to the main road.

He sat fingering the steering wheel and doing nothing to start the truck.

"Why aren't we moving?" I gave him a pat on the arm.

"I keep wondering who this last survivor could be. The website said every one of those cops and their families were dead. Josie is the only surviving descendant of any of those cops." He put one hand over his mouth and ran it over his stubble beard.

"Only one way to find out." I buckled my seatbelt to let Tanner know I was ready to go.

Tanner stuck the keys in the ignition and started the

truck. He reached over and put one hand on my leg. "You know I'll drive you across hell if you need me to. And I'll take you to see this Colleen Pellingham. But what if it's a trap?"

I put my hand over his. "I have to try. Not finding Mohawk's book is the end for me anyway."

Tanner's head rocked back as though I'd slapped him. He pulled his hand away and began driving. My phone's navigational system sent us through unfamiliar streets. Tanner stopped at a drugstore and bought me a bottle of over-the-counter pain pills and some analgesic cream. I swallowed a handful of pills and pulled my pants down to rub the cream on my knee while he drove.

When our electronic navigator told us to make a right and the destination would be on the left, Tanner pulled to the curb, shut off the engine, and tucked a lock of hair behind his ear. He unbuckled his seatbelt and twisted to face me.

"We need to talk. You're talking like you die if you don't find the book. What am I missing?" His eyes, always intense, carried a hurt deeper than I'd seen in a long time.

"I'm not going with him." I pulled out my cigarettes, lit one, and offered the pack to Tanner.

He lit his with shaking hands. "What does that mean?"

I let out a breath it felt like I'd been holding since I left Sanctuary. "Hannah loaned me a pistol. It won't kill Mohawk, but it will kill me."

Tanner's whole body jerked. He dropped his cigarette in his lap. I snatched it and brushed off his jeans. His mouth worked, but nothing came out. He shook his head repeatedly. I crushed the cigarette in the ashtray.

"You've got to understand...I can't. I can't go with him. I can't let him do what he wants to do to me." The idea of being forced to have a child sired by Mohawk made me want to barf in my mouth, so I pushed it away.

"But even if you have to let him take you, there's still a chance you can get away." He grabbed my hand and held it tight. "If you're dead...there'll never be anything else." He let go of me and twisted away, rubbing at his eyes with the back of his hand.

"I can't live like that." I reached to touch his back, but he flinched away from me.

Then he turned around and glared at me through wet eyes. "But if you're alive, there's always a chance. Don't I mean enough for you to be willing to try?"

He did. But what kind of life would I have if Mohawk took me as a slave? Made me birth a monstrosity made of both of us? Before I could formulate an answer, Tanner grabbed me and pulled me to him.

"I can't do it again," he whispered over and over.

It didn't take telepathy to know he was talking about losing his family—a wife and two daughters—in one ugly swoop. But I couldn't make promises, not on such an unsteady future.

I held him tight, aching with guilt over making him feel this way, and stroked his hair. "Let's just take it a little at a time, see how things go."

These weren't new words. I said them to Tanner every time he talked about what we'd be doing over Christmas, where we'd be next spring. I said the words, smiled at him, and hoped for the best. I didn't know what else to do.

Stop living like a ghost in your own life. I jerked to attention. Where had that come from?

Tanner drew in a deep shuddering breath and raised his shirt to wipe his eyes. I stared at the scars on his chest, injuries he'd gotten in the wreck that killed his wife and two daughters.

Almost to himself, he said, "It's gonna be okay."

He started the truck again and drove to Colleen Pellingham's house, hunched over the wheel as though he was driving me to my death right then. I loved this man, hated that I was making him hurt, but didn't know how to change it.

Colleen lived on a pristine white concrete street of identical row houses made of light-colored brick. They all had brown shutters and brown garage doors. Colleen's unit was discernible only by the number next to the fancy porch light.

Tanner pulled to the curb and cut the engine but made no move to get out. I unbuckled my seatbelt.

"Wait," he said, gaze still focused on the street.

I did as he asked.

Tanner turned to me. His eyes had dried as we drove, but the red rings around them attested to his emotional state. "I'll meet you all the way. Whatever happens, I'll be right there. That's my promise."

My heart froze, then pounded hard. I gulped back a rush of stupid words. Anything I said would cheapen

Tanner's selfless pronouncement. I'd had to kiss a lot of toads to find him, but he was worth the wait.

Finally, I thought of something to say. "And I'll defend you to my dying breath."

"Let's hope you don't have to." He held his fist out, and we bumped.

Tanner deserved so much better than me. He got out of the truck and waited on the sidewalk. I joined him and took his hand. We marched to the front door. It opened a crack as we approached, and a wide dark eye peered out.

"Peri Jean Mace?" The voice quavered. Fitch had indicated Josie hurt Colleen Pellingham so badly that she no longer practiced as a therapist anywhere. Colleen had seemed so vivacious in the picture Fitch showed us. I dreaded seeing what Josie had done to that laughing, happy woman.

"I'm Peri Jean." I stepped around Tanner so Colleen could see a fellow woman.

"Your ID, please?" Colleen held one thin, trembling hand through the crack in the door.

I dug it out and handed it to her. A second later, the door opened. I saw Colleen's entire face for the first time and had to hold in my gasp of shock.

A livid red scar bisected her face. The jagged split had gone over one of her eyes, and I was willing to bet the eye in the socket was a prosthetic. Colleen stared at Tanner, taking in his scuffed work boots and his faded blue jeans.

"This is Tanner Letts. He's my...boyfriend." I took his hand again. It felt funny calling a nearly forty-year-old man a boyfriend. But lover sounded worse.

Tanner's lips quirked in a smile, and he gave my hand a little squeeze.

Colleen motioned us into a dim living room. The mini blinds were closed, and heavy dark drapes covered them. The only light came from a lamp sitting on a sofa table. On the table was a picture of Colleen and Suzanne Fitch locked in an embrace in front of a Christmas tree. I recognized this room in the background.

Colleen motioned us to sit on a burgundy love seat. She sat in a matching recliner and reached down beside it. A weapon. This woman was probably as scared of us as we were her.

"Suzy said you'd had a run-in with Josie Stephens." She swallowed hard.

Hearing the formidable Nurse Fitch being called a curlicue name like Suzy almost made me smile. But I held it back. I let go of Tanner's hand and leaned forward, making contact with Colleen's one functional eye. "Josie attacked me. Held me down on the floor. If Nurse Fitch hadn't found us when she did, I'm not sure what would have happened."

Colleen took a trembling breath and nodded. "Suzy called again after you left her office. She said you had a picture of Josie's book."

I took it out and passed it to Colleen. She positioned the lamp to shine on it and stared hard at it, face going pale. Her breathing quickened. "Suzy and I both thought maybe the book was part of Josie's psychosis."

"It's real, and I need to find it." I held out my hand for the picture, and Colleen passed it back. "Nurse Fitch also said you were aware of a last survivor. Josie carried on about this last survivor when she attacked me. She said the last survivor was key. I'm looking for any information you have about either."

Colleen's breathing quickened, and she began to twist the fabric of her slacks between her fingers. "You understand that Josie thinks she's Loretta Nell sometimes?"

I nodded. No need to tell Colleen that Josie and Loretta Nell were psychically merged. She might think I was off my rocker and clam up.

"Josie reminded me of my younger sister. She pulled me in so deep. It all happened before I knew what was going on." She lifted a shaking hand to wipe at the damaged side of her face.

"She fooled me too, and I thought I was ready for her." I caught Colleen's gaze and gave her what I hoped was a nod of solidarity. Colleen's condition wasn't something I'd avoided out of smarts or toughness. I'd simply been lucky.

Colleen crossed her right leg over her left and then hooked that ankle around the left leg. Something a child would do. It had the effect of making her seem smaller. When Colleen spoke again, her voice came out in a soft squeak.

"I thought it would be therapeutic to let Josie work through her delusions about Loretta Nell Grimes. Josie told me all about Loretta Nell and her nasty book. Names, dates, information she should have never known. Told me where to find things, who to ask." Colleen stopped speaking and swallowed. "She was obsessed with what became of the lawmen who'd helped dispatch the Messengers."

Tanner smiled a little at her play on words. I didn't think it was funny.

"According to the website, all the deputies there that day and their descendants are dead. Except for Josie." This was what Tanner and I had discussed coming over, and I wanted to see if Colleen agreed.

"That horrific website." A little smile played on her lips. "It's wrong. Josie somehow knew there was one last survivor."

Neither Tanner nor I spoke.

Colleen seemed to take our silence as some kind of judgment. "You don't understand what she was like, the things she'd say. It was like I'd fallen under a spell."

In as sympathetic a voice as I could manage, I asked, "Did Josie ever explain her obsession?"

"Not really. She just said the book was useless as long as the last survivor lived." Colleen sat back in her chair, pressing herself hard against its plush back.

Tanner and I exchanged a glance. He looked as confused as I felt. I'd seen Loretta Nell using that book. It didn't matter if this last survivor, whoever he was, lived or not. I could understand Loretta Nell wanting the lawmen who stopped her tirade of terror dead. But saying they rendered the book useless? That didn't make sense.

I turned back to Colleen. "Josie convinced you to find out who he was, didn't she?"

Colleen reddened, and her good eye lowered. "He's the son of Harris Coates. On record, Coates was childless and unmarried. But he had an illegitimate son. The mother left town before the baby was born and raised him on her own. They were long gone by the day of the massacre."

"Any idea where he lives?" Tanner threw me a quick, nervous glance.

"How do I know the two of you aren't somehow caught up in Josie's thrall? I lost an eye over this man. How do I know you aren't just going to kill him?" Colleen's voice raised a little.

"You don't," I said. "But I'm going to die day after tomorrow if I don't find that book."

Colleen's skin turned ashen. "How do I know you're telling the truth?"

I sat back, already ashamed of what I was about to do. "You don't. But you do know I'll get *Suzy* fired from her job if you don't pony up whatever information you've got."

Colleen's eyes narrowed. "You're not going to do that. It almost made you sick just to tell me that."

Annoyance flashed behind my eyes, kindling another headache. "All right. How about this? If I can track down this book, I'm also going to banish Loretta Nell Grimes's ghost from this plane. She'll leave Josie alone and make Suzy's job easier."

Colleen unwound her legs and clasped her hands on top of them. She sat that way for so long, I considered prodding her with magic. Without warning, she took a sheet of paper off the table next to her chair and held it out. Tanner stood and retrieved it. He handed it to me and sat back down. Harris Coates's son was named Aaron Todd. He lived in Devil's Rest.

"How'd he end up there?" I shook the paper at Colleen. It contradicted the story she told us about the expectant mother leaving Devil's Rest to raise a child on her own.

"I don't know. But I can't believe he doesn't know who he is." Colleen sat still except for her chest rising and falling.

I stood. "Thank you for speaking with us."

Colleen stood. "What are you going to do?"

I shook my head. "Go see Aaron Todd. He might be the answer I'm looking for."

Colleen didn't look too convinced. I didn't mind. I wasn't either.

10

———

THE JOURNEY from Colleen's front door couldn't have been more than twenty yards, but it felt like a million miles. The dark townhouse where Colleen spent her days and nights felt like a prison.

Tanner walked with his head down, hair swinging in his face, but it didn't hide his downturned mouth. Needing a little ray of light in my life, I hurried to his side and took his hand. He pecked my cheek.

"I felt sorry for her," he almost whispered.

"Me too. It's like she stopped living the day Josie hurt her." Another thought crowded into my mind before I even stopped speaking. At our cores, were Colleen and I so different?

Tanner and I climbed into the truck in silence. I searched Aaron Todd's address. He'd been there all along, right in Devil's Rest, just blocks from Phil's Monkey Burger. I started navigation.

Tanner listened to the directions with a blank look on

his face. He'd stuck the keys in the ignition but hadn't started the truck.

"It's a trick, isn't it? You'll run around in circles until you run out of time, and that'll be that for both of us." His words came faster and faster at the end.

Dread settled at the pit of my stomach like a lead cannonball. So far, I had successfully avoided this train of thought. There was no point in it. It wasn't like there was some chthonic being quality control line I could call and complain about Mohawk being unfair. Either I'd manage to outplay him, or I wouldn't.

"I suspect you're right, but I will absolutely not lose by default." I stared at Tanner's profile.

He sat with his fists clenched. He'd have fought Mohawk right then—and died—if he could have.

"There is a way to work this out. It'll likely involve cheating Mohawk, but I don't have a clear enough picture to know what to do. So let's go see Aaron Todd." I lit a cigarette and leaned my head back.

Tanner drove too fast all the way back to Devil's Rest. We found Aaron Todd's tidy, slate-colored, mid-century bungalow with no problem. On the front porch, the smell of fresh paint mingled with the freshly turned soil in the flowerbeds. I knocked and got no answer other than the endless, patient bark of a dog several houses away.

"Aaron ain't here." The voice came from the other side of the porch.

I had to back several steps away from the door to see a man staring through the stark white porch railing at me. His white hair puffed over the top rail like a bunny's butt, and the way he had his hands wrapped around the rails reminded me of someone in jail.

I checked my watch. Mid-afternoon. Tick-tock. Tick-tock. "Where can I find Mr. Todd?"

The old man huffed. "What're you selling, lady?"

I got a glimpse of myself in the door's glass top half. Tight jeans, boots, tight-sleeveless T-shirt. Tattoos on my arms. Hair a wild, dark mess trailing down past my shoulders. A bruise forming on my forehead. I sauntered toward the guy. "What's it look like I'm selling, mister?"

Tanner came up the walk, head lowered, staring at the guy from under his brows, a snarl set on his fine lips. He had one fist doubled up.

The oldster took another look at me, his mouth hanging open. "A-a-aron's got a honky-tonk out past the Devil's Slumber Inn."

A frustrated scream built in my throat. I knew the exact place, having passed it on my way to and from the Stephens Ranch. "The Devil's Dance?"

Never in my life had I wanted to roll my eyes worse. I'd wasted hours tussling with Josie, Suzanne Fitch, and Colleen Pellingham. And for what? So I could come back to Devil's Rest and go to a place I'd noticed within my first few hours of being in town.

The old guy, focused on Tanner, who'd advanced to the point they were standing chest to chest, could only nod.

Tanner, radiating danger, leaned into his face. "We can find Aaron Todd at the Devil's Dance honky-tonk?"

"Y-y-yep." The guy turned away from Tanner and hurried in the other direction. The sound of the dog barking got louder for a second, only to be cut off by a slamming door and the man's scolding voice.

"Let's go." Tanner started walking back to the truck.

I followed, feet sinking into the lush, green lawn. Aaron Todd's neat house and his manicured lawn were not what I expected from the bastard son of a deputy who'd had a ghost's target on his back. What would Aaron Todd be like?

I climbed into the truck next to Tanner. He sped out of town and down the road to the honky-tonk. When we passed the Devil's Slumber Inn, Dwight stood in the parking lot talking to two girls who looked just about old enough to get themselves in hot water and too young and stupid to get themselves out. They both held Dwight's homemade maps.

The sight made something wiggle at the back of my mind, some connection. But then we passed the motel, and it slipped way. A few minutes later, the sign for the Devil's Dance Roadhouse came into view. It was roadhouse. Not honky-tonk. Stupid old man.

The sign featured the requisite red devil, pointing a finger at a dog dick red building. Underneath the devil, another sign read "Bikers Welcome." Figured. It was just the sort of place a bunch of road hogs would love.

A surge of missing Wade rose up and evened out before I had time to really think about it. He wouldn't have been any more help than Tanner, and he might have been more trouble. I glanced over at Tanner, only to find him watching me, that same sad expression on his face.

"Come on." I tried to make my voice brisk. "We find that

book, maybe we can get a motel room in San Antonio. Take a few days before we rejoin Sanctuary."

Tanner tried to smile, disbelief dulling his normally brilliant eyes. "I'd go for that."

In the roadhouse parking lot, Tanner grabbed my hand and wound his fingers through mine, and we crossed the gravel without talking. A spring screeched as I pushed open the door, and the smell of stale beer and staler air conditioning rolled out. Reminded again of Wade, I took the first step inside the darkness. A darkened glass window with a slot to pass money and probably IDs sat to our right. Next to it was a sign that read "Cover charge $10 when a band's playing." Our feet whispered on the concrete as we passed by the window, down the dark hallway, and into a large open area.

The sound of a shotgun being pumped echoed through the room. "You found me."

Tanner stopped and put his hands up. I snorted and walked toward Aaron, daring him to shoot me. Tanner grabbed at me, but I danced out of his grasp.

I sat down at the bar. "That old bastard tell you I was coming?"

Aaron didn't answer. Thin lips pressed in a line, he leveled the gun at my face, nostrils flaring with each breath.

"Put it down and let's talk." I tried to pretend my heart wasn't trying to chisel its way out of my chest. In the mirror, Tanner still stood, hands raised and eyes wide with almost comical horror. I twisted around so I could speak to him. "Aaron ain't going to shoot us. Come on."

Tanner hesitated, chest rising and falling fast. He lowered his arms.

Aaron dropped the gun's barrel. "She's right. Shooting her would put me in a tub of hot shit." He shoved the gun out of sight, took a ring of keys out of his pocket, and began flipping them on his hand.

I laughed, dizzy with relief. This whole ordeal was making me crazy. Aaron laughed with me, and something in it caught my attention. Aaron and I took each other in.

The rough, weathered skin around Aaron's mouth twitched but never turned into an actual teeth-baring smile. His faded blue eyes twinkled. I didn't necessarily go for men nearly old enough to be my daddy, but Aaron had a weird kind of charm. The done it all, seen it all kind. He probably had to beat women off with a stick.

Aaron winked. I pretended not to see. Tanner slid onto the barstool next to me. I clasped hands with him and kissed his cheek. Aaron, eyes still locked on mine, gave me a sage nod.

"So what do you want with me? And what do you want to drink? You need to drink if you're going to sit in here." Aaron set cardboard coasters emblazoned with red devils in front of us.

"Iced tea and lemonade?" I shrugged. Tanner pointed at a bottle advertising a locally made beer. Aaron busied himself getting our drinks. I spoke to his lean back. "What I came here for is going to sound crazy."

Aaron set my iced tea and lemonade in front of me, raised his eyebrows, and gave me that almost smile again.

"Do you know how many times women have said that to me?"

My mouth started to curve. I bit my lip and glanced at Tanner. He sat very still, gaze fixed on Aaron like a dog guarding a favorite toy. *Come any closer, buddy, and I'll snap.*

Aaron saw the look and shook his head. He might think Tanner a wimp because he had been afraid of the gun. He'd regret his mistake if he disrespected Tanner.

"I know your father was Harris Coates." I blurted the words out to slap some of the cockiness out of Aaron. Sure enough, the I'm-so-sexy smirk dropped off his face.

"And?" He got the keychain back out and swung it around his index finger. Once. Twice. He flipped the keyring into his hand and curved his fingers around it.

"I'm looking for a book that belonged to Loretta Nell Grimes and the Messengers. You know anything about it?"

Aaron swung the keys around his finger again. "Just that if you're in a jam over it, you're a dead woman." He tipped his chin at Tanner. "You too."

Tanner blew out a snort that reminded me of a bull getting ready to charge. And he might have been. He spoke to me. "Let's go. He doesn't know anything."

"That'll be ten for the beverages." Aaron didn't sound like he was fooling around either.

I did roll my eyes then. "Stop the shit. Both of you."

But Tanner stomped through the bar and slammed outside.

With Tanner gone, Aaron smirked again and leaned on the bar and stared into my eyes. "I'll tell you anything you want to know, you drink a shot of tequila with me."

I shook my head. "Talk to me anyway."

The door screeched, and Tanner came back in. He slammed a crumpled ten dollar bill on the bar, sat down on the barstool next to me, and took a long pull on his beer. He clunked it back down on the bar and glared at Aaron, mouth set in a snarl. Aaron laughed.

I took the crumpled picture of Loretta Nell holding the book out of my pocket and laid it on the bar. "I'm looking for this book."

Aaron picked up the picture and frowned at it. "Loretta Nell Grimes. She sure was a looker. What makes you think I'd know about this book?"

"Because Loretta Nell says you're the key. She wants you dead." I knew the words would get a reaction out of Aaron.

His ruddy skin turned pasty, and he pushed the picture back at me. "Bullshit."

"Nope. It's true. I'm a spirit medium. I've been in contact with Loretta Nell Grimes, and she says you're the key. What does that mean?" I leaned on my elbows and watched Aaron Todd the same way I'd watch a snake.

"What do you want the book for?" Aaron brought the shotgun up to sit on the counter between us. Next to me, Tanner went still, his grip tightening on his overpriced craft beer. I put one hand on his back and looked at Aaron like he was almost as scary as a roll of toilet paper.

"I'm working for a collector who wants the book." The clock ticked endlessly in my head, and I begged the universe for this not to be another runaround.

Aaron Todd shook his head, and I knew I was sunk. "I don't know nothing about any book."

I tipped my head back and put my hands over my face.

Aaron put one cold, rough hand on my arm. "Now I didn't say I ain't got some ideas for you, honey."

"She ain't your honey," Tanner growled.

Aaron Todd laughed. "Every woman's my honey, mister."

Tanner shot out of his seat.

"Will the two of you just can it?" I nudged Tanner. "I'm not interested in him." I pointed at Aaron Todd to make clear who I meant. "But I do want to hear what he has to say."

Aaron's smirk almost broadened into a smile.

I stared into his faded eyes. "And you. Stop fucking with my man, or I'll kick your nuts up so high they'll look like a chin implant." The smirk fell off Aaron's face. I gathered the power of the mantle. "Tell me what you know. Now." The lights behind the bar flickered, and thunder boomed in the small room. A hot wind picked up and fluttered Aaron's carefully shabby hip clothes.

Aaron's eyes darted around the room. "What is that? What are you doing?"

"What I do." I made lightning pop behind the bar. "Tell me what you know, or I'll do more."

Aaron grabbed on to the old wood and squeezed his eyes shut. "Fine. I didn't grow up with my father. Met him during the last couple of years of his life. Daddy always said he was marked for what happened that day."

I shook my head. "But the Messengers were bad people. And Loretta Nell was worse."

"The shoot-out wasn't all that happened. It was what happened after that." Aaron took a shot glass from beneath the bar and poured a shot of amber colored liquid into it. He took the liquid in one gulp and shuddered. "Loretta Nell snuck away during the shoot-out. They found her in the barn. She had the book with her." Aaron poured himself another shot. "She started reading out of it, and my daddy said he snapped. Like a crazy rage. He said him and those other men did things to her, made her die screaming." Aaron stopped speaking and shivered all over. "When she was dead, they knew they could never let anybody see the body. Freddy Stephens suggested they hide Loretta Nell's remains. He promised to come back later and bury her."

Aaron quit talking and poured himself a third shot of the strong stuff. He offered the bottle to me, but I shook my head.

I didn't need liquor. The confession had fuzzed up my brain, made it thick and slow. But I knew one thing for sure. If Freddy Stephens had disposed of Loretta's body, he'd likely disposed of the book too. I'd have to contact his spirit. If it went as swimmingly as contacting Loretta Nell's spirit had, Mohawk might not have to come after me. I might already be dead.

Back to us, Aaron stared at himself in the mirror behind the bar. He spoke to our reflections. "My daddy never trusted Freddy Stephens after that day. He did everything he could to stay away from Stephens Ranch. But the last time I talked to him, he said he was going to have to go out there and see Freddy. He never came back."

"Why'd you come here, to this awful little town?" I swallowed against the bitterness Aaron's story had made me taste.

"Inheritance." Aaron's shoulders slumped.

The conversation was over. Aaron Todd was another waste of time. I got off the barstool. Tanner did the same. I turned back to Aaron, maybe to thank him, maybe to tell him to go to hell, but he was still staring at himself in the mirror. Tanner and I left.

———

TANNER DROVE us out of the Devil's Dance Roadhouse parking lot without asking me where I wanted to go next. I asked no questions. Contacting Freddy Stephens's spirit had me worried.

Aaron had said his father never trusted Freddy Stephens after the day he and the other sheriffs killed Loretta Nell. I didn't blame him. Freddy seemed to have spent the rest of his life carrying out Loretta Nell's revenge. Until the night Josie brought Loretta Nell home.

Thoughts of Freddy slipped from my mind, and I focused again on Josie and her survival. She *and* Aaron Todd were the last survivors. But Josie had spoken as though it was only Aaron Todd. Why would she exclude herself? It didn't make sense.

There was something I wasn't catching on to, and damned if I could figure out what it was. My scrambled brain repeated one option: contact Freddy Stephens's spirit. Ask him about the book. After everything I'd seen, I hated to take the risk. But what else could I do?

Tanner pulled into the motel parking lot. I turned to tell him my plans. Before I could get any words out, he put one hand behind my neck and pressed his lips to mine, his passion fierce enough to hurt.

"I want you. Now." His breath burned hot against my lips. To punctuate his sentence, he gave my lip a light nibble. I gasped and dug my fingers into his arms. He drew back, eyes burning hot. I drank it in, running one thumb over the stubble on his cheeks. He kissed me again. "Say you want me."

I breathed in his musky scent and said his words back to him. "I want you. Now."

He dragged me across the truck, out the door, and into the trashy little motel room. Door barely closed between us and the rest of the world, he kissed me harder than before, arms wrapped so tight around me I could barely breathe. He let go and tugged my flimsy tank top out of my jeans. I raised my arms and let him pull it over my head.

Tanner needed this right now. Facing losing me, maybe his own death, and dealing with an asshole like Aaron Todd had washed every bit of cool Zen king off him. He needed me to belong to just him right then. And I needed to be wanted that way.

He tangled one hand in my hair, pulled my head back, and kissed my throat openmouthed, his teeth grazing the tender skin. We moaned together.

He shifted his grip, lifted me, and tossed me onto the

bed. I moved to undress, but he brushed my hands away and yanked off my clothes. By the time I lay naked on the thin sheets, my breath came in ragged gasps. Tanner stood over me, still fully dressed.

I stared into his eyes, finding all the things I loved about him. The warmth. The kindness. And the passion. I held open my arms to him. "Come here."

Smiling, he crawled onto the bed, his clothes rasping against my bare skin. I twined my arms around his neck. His lips tasted like cigarette smoke and hops from the beer. He worked his way down my body, sucking and nibbling.

I propped my head on the pillow and watched him, mesmerized at the contrast of his tawny skin against my deep olive, at the way his tongue left wet trails on my belly. And how my body felt hot enough to melt. His mouth found my hipbone. I jerked and cried out. Raising his eyes to mine, he gripped one ankle in each hand and planted them on his shoulders.

Body quivering with anticipation, I opened myself to him. We watched each other while his tongue teased, and my breaths sharpened. I reached for his hand. He took it off my ankle and twined his fingers through mine. Body stiffening, I screamed loud enough I'm sure Dwight heard me in his office.

The sound of Tanner's zipper going down broke the rhythm of my gasps. I raised myself on my elbows and murmured, "Just pull down your pants."

He did what I said and climbed between my legs, pulling them around his waist.

"Squeeze me," he whispered.

The whole world narrowed down to our breath mingling, our eyes locked. With maddening slowness, his lips brushing mine, he slid into me. I dug my fingers into his shoulders and screamed again.

Bodies sliding together, we made promises neither of us could keep. The ticking clock ceased to matter. All that mattered was spending time with the man I loved.

Afterward, we lay naked on the rumpled mess we'd made of the sheets, sweat drying on our bodies. Tanner ran one finger through the beads of moisture.

"This is us together," he whispered.

I nodded. The feeling of us together was so big right then it ached. It wasn't just the lovemaking, though that helped. It was the rightness between us all the other times. I wanted to tell him I loved him, even if it ended ten minutes from now. I wanted him to know how much this time with him had meant.

Tanner cut off any words I might have said. "Was I too forceful? Tell me if I was."

I shook my head.

He blew out a breath. "I don't get jealous, but the way Aaron looked at you, like it was a done deal." He frowned. "And the way you looked at him."

With one hand, I caressed his cheek. "You matter more than he ever could. Guys like Aaron Todd are a waste of time. Aaron only cares about Aaron. Women want him because they think they can be The One who'll make him change. But he never will." I continued caressing Tanner's hot, damp skin. "You, on the other hand, are worth every second I spend with you. I wish it could be like this all the time, every day." I slid one hand down his ribs.

He closed his eyes, but then opened them right away. "Yeah?"

I nodded. "More than you know." A little of the worry lifted. I'd been wrong for wanting to take care of this book business all by myself. Tanner not only helped, he might end up saving my life. Or at least my sanity. He deserved better than me.

Tanner sat up. "I want a shower. Come with me?"

I deadpanned at him, "If we're going to find this book, we're going to have to get to work. Go. And hurry."

Tanner padded into the bathroom. I waited until the shower turned on to text Hannah. "Tanner gets my RV and my truck. And half my money. Give the other half to Finn and Dillon."

Her message came back a few seconds later. "Going that well?"

"Even better." I sent a sad face.

Her message consisted of two words. "Love you."

Mine was one. "Same."

The shower cut off, and I took my turn, rushing. I tried putting makeup over the bruise forming on my forehead from Winslow's roughing me up at the mental hospital. My efforts only made it look worse. Finally, I wiped off the concealer and slapped on my usual heavy eye makeup, which Hannah called tramp tracks.

I found Tanner sitting on the bed, smoking and using my laptop. He glanced at me. "What's the plan?"

"All I know to do is contact Freddy Stephens's spirit.

And I don't want to." I sat down next to Tanner and rubbed at my tightening shoulders until he took up the cause.

"Then don't. Let's try to approach it from another direction." Tanner's hands kneaded the muscles.

I moaned as he hit a particularly tender spot. "The only other direction we have is Aaron Todd. Why does the last survivor need to be dead? Why is he key? I don't understand how Aaron Todd is holding anything or anybody back."

"That story Aaron told about what those sheriffs did to Loretta Nell? I mean, I can see why her spirit wants revenge." Tanner rubbed harder.

I hung my head, moved with the rhythm of Tanner's massaging, and thought about what he'd said. "Then maybe it's not about him holding her back but a meaningful sacrifice." That still didn't sound right.

"Or maybe he knew more about the whereabouts of the book than he said." Tanner stopped rubbing and gave me a light pat. "So what are we doing next?"

"We can go beat more information out of Aaron Todd or find where Freddy's buried and make contact." I still didn't feel too confident about contacting Freddy's spirit.

Tanner moved away from me and picked up the laptop. "While you showered, I researched Freddy Stephens." He moved the laptop so I could see the screen. "I think Freddy was using the book somehow." He tapped a few buttons, and a news article came up. The title was "Devil's Rest Jail the Deadliest in Texas?"

The article, written for a college newspaper, chronicled a series of odd deaths starting in 1975.

"Not too long after the Messengers met their grisly end," I said in a dramatic TV-announcer voice.

The article went into a great deal of detail about jail cell suicides, usually of transients, of which there seemed to be many. It made sense.

A town like Devil's Rest would attract its share of seekers. The town's name alone was bait. The Messengers just made it worse. I thought about the way I'd been treated at Phil's, Home of the World Famous Monkey Burger. Had those people been carrying out a celebrated Devil's Rest tradition above and beyond anything to do with the Messengers? I shivered.

"You cold?" Tanner rubbed his hands over my arms.

"Mmm." I read a little further. Freddy Stephens had been the arresting officer for all but a few of the dead people. Aaron's father had arrested those.

"Those were sacrifices," I muttered. "Freddy and that other guy, Aaron's father, made them under the influence of the book."

"Maybe." Tanner got off the bed to put on his boots. "Or maybe killing Loretta Nell and the other Messengers just taught them they liked taking human lives." He held out my cowboy boots. "What do you want to do?"

"I don't want to contact Freddy Stephens's spirit." I slid the boots onto my feet. "After what happened with Loretta Nell, and what you've found out here, I'm afraid of what will happen." My face heated at my cowardice.

"I wouldn't do it either." Tanner pulled himself onto the dresser. It gave a loud pop under his weight. His eyes widened, and we both laughed.

"I've got four options." I began ticking them off on my fingers. "I can contact Freddy's spirit. I can contact Aaron's father's spirit. We can go whip Aaron Todd's ass and see if he'll tell us more. Or we can use non-magical methods to figure out what happened to the stuff in Freddy's house." I was leaning toward the last one. "Freddy probably wasn't expecting to die that night. He didn't have time to hide the book. So whatever happened to the rest of the stuff in the house probably happened to the book."

Tanner lowered his head in thought. "Could be hidden somewhere in the house. Or some scavengers could have picked it up. If it's the latter, we'll never find it."

"I say no to scavengers. Mohawk would be satisfied if someone else had found the book. All he wants is for his creation to be causing mayhem and murder." I got off the bed and picked up my keys from the table. "Mandy Drake is going to help us again."

"She's scary. Pass." Despite his objection, Tanner followed me out of the room and got into the truck next to me.

I was halfway back to downtown Devil's Rest before I spoke again. "Mandy's not half as scary as me."

"I'll second that," Tanner muttered behind one hand. I poked his ribs where it tickled. He squirmed away from me.

The library, with only ten more minutes to be open, had no patrons. Mandy sat at the circulation desk, her attention focused on her computer screen. She didn't move when the entry chime dinged. Tanner and I stood at the circulation desk.

"Hi Mandy," I said to get her attention.

She jumped and peeked around her screen. "Oh, hi. How's the search for your book going?"

"I haven't given up yet. You got a minute for another question?"

She shrugged.

"After Freddy and family were dead and Josie was in custody, what happened to the stuff in the house?" I tried to keep any urgency off my face. Tanner's feelings about Mandy resonated big time. No matter how nice she acted, I didn't trust her.

"The contents of the house were auctioned off. Josie was the last Stephens, so the property legally went to her. But she'd been declared mentally incapacitated, so an aunt on her mother's side of the family arranged the sale of the property and contents. I think they used it for her legal defense." Mandy smiled, but it wasn't the greedy, salacious smile that had scared Tanner and me when we first met her. This one was normal. I relaxed a little.

"Does a record exist of the items auctioned off?" I leaned on the counter.

Mandy frowned and held up one finger. "I can't believe I never thought of looking that up. That would be an awesome topic for our discussion group." She began clicking on the keyboard. Her shoulders sagged after a few seconds. "No. It was a private auction. Would you like the name of the auctioneer? He's local."

"Yes. Thank you." I grabbed a flyer for a library book sale and flipped it over to write on the back.

Mandy gave me an odd look, like she might want to

scold me for wasting a flyer, but then just read off the address.

A few minutes later, Tanner and I were back in the truck. The auctioneer, a Jeb Pugh, lived only a mile from the library.

"Running around in circles," Tanner muttered as he drove.

"I'm gonna figure out how to turn it around. I promise." I concentrated on my promise as though that made it more likely to come true.

11

———

DARKNESS HAD FALLEN by the time we got to Jeb Pugh's house. Though Pugh lived only a few blocks from Aaron Todd's spiffy bungalow, his house was the polar opposite of Aaron's.

To start with, Jeb Pugh's vintage house was a late nineteen-seventies ranch house. Nothing cute about that. To make matters worse, Jeb had let his house go. Dirt dulled the red bricks. Black mildew streaked the sidewalk leading to the front door.

Tanner and I both had to leave the sidewalk to edge around a knockout rose bush so neglected it had only a few leaves. The concrete floor of the postage stamp-sized porch was so black with mildew it could have been paint. I rang the doorbell and was rewarded with the sound of shoes slapping on a hard floor. The door opened, and bright light beamed out on the gloomy entryway.

A man wearing square wire-framed bifocals gave us a trusting smile. "Help you young folks?"

I stared in shock. I had expected someone unkempt, with dirty clothes and maybe body odor. This guy, with his carefully trimmed white hair, and his tucked-in checkered shirt didn't fit the house. "Yes, sir. I'm Peri Jean Mace, and this is my boyfriend, Tanner Letts. We need to ask you about an auction you performed some time back."

Pugh's smile dimmed but stayed in place. I took that as a hopeful sign. Sure enough, he stepped back and held the door open. "Why don't you come inside? Mosquitos'll set up a dictatorship if I stand here with the door open much longer."

Tanner and I followed Jeb Pugh down an entry hall with outdated linoleum. It opened into a combination living room and dining room with a too-big table. In the living room part, a woman with a fluff of short, cottony hair sat in a recliner with her feet up. She worked the lever to put down the footrest.

"Oh, company. You should have warned me, Jebediah." She stood and used both hands to smooth down her light blue slacks.

I glanced at the clock on my phone and winced. These folks were probably just about to go to bed. "We're sorry to have disturbed you so late, ma'am. We've got a few questions for Mr. Pugh, and he invited us inside."

Jeb Pugh motioned at the heavy dining table. "I'm Jeb. Not Mr. Pugh. Y'all have a seat."

The lady joined us and held out one arthritis-swelled hand to me. "I'm Cheryl Pugh."

I shook her hand. "Peri Jean Mace and Tanner Letts."

Cheryl Pugh practically pushed me into a chair. She sat

down at the far end of the table. "Jeb, you're not going to get them something to drink?"

"Now Cheryl, I ain't had the chance to see what they want." Jeb's voice raised, but the smile never left his face. "Coke? Milk and cookies? That is what I'm going to have."

"Milk and cookies," Tanner agreed before I could speak. I glanced at him and realized I'd forgotten to eat again. Poor man was probably starving.

Pugh went into the kitchen, rattled around a bit, and came out holding a tray with four tall glasses of milk and a box of store-bought iced oatmeal cookies. He set out the refreshments and took a seat at the head of the table. Tanner immediately grabbed a handful of cookies, pulled his milk to him and went to work. Both Pughs watched with amusement.

"I'm guessing you folks want to ask about the Stephens auction." The good humor left Jeb's eyes with the words, but he didn't seem angry as many of the town folks did when the topic of Devil's Rest's true crime history came up.

I nodded that we had.

"What do you need from me?" Jeb watched me steadily.

As soon as I'd seen Jeb Pugh, I'd known candor would be the best approach. I took out the bedraggled picture of Loretta Nell Grimes holding the book and slid it across the table. I waited until Jeb Pugh picked up the picture to speak.

"I need to find that book. I've gotten in trouble with... someone bad. Both Tanner and I are in danger." I threw a glance at Tanner, silently asking what he thought of me just laying it all out.

He was so busy with his cookies, he barely shrugged.

Jeb stared at the picture some more. "Where'd you get this?"

"The man who wants me to find the book gave it to me, and he's not the kind of man you question." I wished fervently for a cigarette but saw no ashtrays in the Pugh house.

Cheryl Pugh held out one hand to her husband. He hesitated but passed her the picture. Her face stilled at what she saw, and she whispered, "That's her. That's Loretta Nell. She could look so normal." She handed the picture back to me.

"Did you auction off this book?" I asked Jeb.

He shook his head. "I seen that book only once in my life, and that was the day I took my teenage self out to the ranch to see what all the fuss was about." He glanced at his wife, flushed, and looked down at the shiny surface of the table.

Cheryl Pugh didn't seem all that shocked. "Oh, Jeb, who cares? I barely knew you then." She turned to me. "Loretta Nell Grimes flashed herself around town, invited young men out to the ranch. They came back bragging about orgies. Later they complained about catching the clap."

Tanner snorted. I shook my head at him and caught Cheryl smiling at us.

"You want to know what made my skin crawl?" She didn't wait for an answer. "The way Freddy Stephens bought that death trap and dragged his wife and that inno-cent little baby they'd adopted out there. Then they all died—the whole family. Except that Josie, and she probably killed them."

The room went quiet except for Tanner crunching on those stupid cookies. The air conditioner kicked on. It seemed to spur Cheryl into talking again.

"I helped Jeb put on that auction, and I can assure you that book was not one of the items we auctioned off. Most of it was the kind of stuff you'd see at a moving sale." She finished her milk and set the glass aside.

Jeb snapped his fingers at his wife. "But remember that young man who kept bidding on stuff?"

"Oh yes. He acted like everything there was a collector's item." Cheryl spoke to me. "Tell you who it was. Guy who owns the Devil's Slumber Inn. I know you've got to be staying there."

Dwight. The king of the moneymaking scam. That nasty little troll. He probably sold the stuff to people who couldn't get enough of the macabre.

"I see you know who we mean." Jeb laughed. "He didn't get anything of value. I expect any souvenirs worth having got removed by that lawyer."

I cocked my head but didn't ask the obvious question.

Cheryl spoke in answer. "The house was sealed after the murders. But once they decided not to charge Josie, everything went to her. The aunt who'd taken up custodial care of the girl opted to sell it all and put the money in a trust for Josie. That's when we got called in."

"I know just what you're about to say. Hush up. I want to tell it." Jeb shook one crooked finger at his wife. "The day we showed up for the house to be unsealed so we could prepare for the auction, a lawyer met us there. He said he came to retrieve some property that went to another party named in Freddy Stephens's will."

Cheryl took up the story. "That lawyer had a locksmith with him and everything. They went upstairs and opened Freddy's safe and got some stuff out. I asked him who'd been named in the will, and he wouldn't tell."

"He didn't know who he was dealing with." Jeb smiled at his wife.

Cheryl patted at the table, smiling. "I knew his secretary. Our daughters were best friends in high school. All I had to do was take her to coffee and ask. She swore me to secrecy, because her boss would know where the leak came from if it got out, but she told."

I smiled. Nosy little ladies in small towns always had an in. "Who was it?"

"Aaron Todd. He owns that bar out past..." Cheryl trailed off at the look on my face. "What is it, hon?"

I turned to Tanner. "I'm going to beat his fucking ass."

Cheryl's mouth fell open at the force of my anger. I tried to cover it, but the real me was out of the bag and into the world.

"He lied to us," I growled at Tanner.

Tanner stood. "Mr. and Mrs. Pugh, thanks for the midnight snack. It really hit the spot."

The Pughs, unable to cover their shock at my change in personality, showed us to the door.

I stopped and spoke to Cheryl. "What did Aaron Todd get from Freddy Stephens's estate?"

Cheryl recovered from her shock at my outburst

enough to say, "She claimed her boss wouldn't tell. One of the stipulations of the will."

I sighed. "Thanks."

Tanner and I turned to go.

"Good luck," Jeb Pugh called to our backs as Tanner and I hurried back down the walk.

———

WE DROVE out to the Devil's Dance only to find the parking lot empty and the bar dark. A piece of white paper had been taped to the door. I got out of the truck to read it.

The page, which had been typed on a computer and printed out, read "Went on an errand. Will reopen at eight p.m."

I didn't have to check my phone to know Aaron Todd was running a couple of hours late.

"He may have left town," Tanner said from behind me.

"Why?" I didn't give him a chance to answer. "Let's check his house."

We got back in the truck and drove to Aaron's neat bungalow. Lights blazed through the gaps in the curtains. Tanner parked at the curb, and we hurried to the front door. I doubled up one fist and gave the glass storm door several raps.

"Open up, Aaron. We need to talk." I listened for movement inside the house and heard none. The sound of a door slamming came from nearby.

"He's going out the back door." Tanner took off running toward the back of the house, me on his heels. A chain link fence bordered Aaron Todd's backyard. Tanner hit the gate running, barely pausing to undo the latch. He left it hanging open.

We raced into the backyard to find the back door gaping wide, dim light streaming from it. My eyes adjusted to the gloom. A bullet-shaped barbecue pit and a couple of trash cans lurked near the door. Otherwise the yard appeared empty.

"He must've jumped the fence and went into the woods." I wasn't enthusiastic to explore the greenbelt behind the house.

Tanner ignored me and took graceful, silent steps toward the back door. He took the last step running and kicked one of the trash cans. Someone grunted. A man-sized shape rose from behind the trash can, shoved Tanner out of his way, and launched himself across the tiny yard.

Tanner recovered and raced after him. The man vaulted the fence within a few seconds and disappeared into the greenbelt behind the house. Tanner and I hit the fence and climbed over.

We plowed into the thick growth, trees tearing at our bare arms. The sound of someone crashing through the greenbelt seemed to come from everywhere. Then it stopped. The only sound I heard was my pounding heart and Tanner's heavy breathing.

I dug in my pockets and got out the tiny flashlight I used to unlock doors at night. It was such a rinky-dink thing it didn't even have an on-off switch. A button had to be held down for the light to come on. I pressed it and saw the blood on Tanner's face.

"You're hurt." I leaned in, looking for the wound.

"Huh?" Tanner touched his face and held out his bloody fingers. He felt around some more. "This isn't my blood. It was on him."

I wasn't so sure and tried to look closer, but he shook me off and took several steps deeper into the woods. He cupped his hands over his mouth and yelled, "Aaron Todd, we just want to talk."

A branch popped nearby. A rock whistled into the clearing and smacked Tanner in the chest. He grunted and put his hand to the spot where it had hit.

I ran in the direction the rock had come from. "That's it, Aaron. I'm gonna rip your dick off and make you eat it with soy sauce."

I didn't even see the rock coming. It clipped me in the chin and knocked me off balance. I staggered and grabbed on to a tree. A branch snapped, and another rock hit my thigh. Hard enough to elicit a yelp.

That pissed me off. I ran in the direction the rock must have come from. Gnarled tree limbs tangled in my hair. Cursing my decision to grow it long, I stopped to pull them out.

Tanner appeared next to me and gently untangled the limbs. "Let's get out of these woods."

I twisted to face him. "No. He threw rocks at us. Fuck Aaron Todd."

Tanner leaned so close our cheeks brushed. "I don't think it's Aaron."

"Huh?" I tried to pull away from Tanner, but he wouldn't let me go.

"I think Aaron's dead." His hot breath whispered against my ear. He lowered his whisper to almost nothing. "And whoever's out here with us killed him." He gave me another tug. "Come on. He knows these woods, and we don't. He might be five feet away from us right now."

I swallowed hard and looked around. Darkness obscured any hint of another person nearby. Tanner gave me a light tug, and we crept back through the little copse of trees. I spent the short walk looking over my shoulder. We climbed back over the fence a lot more slowly than before and trudged to the back door. Tanner pulled me to a stop.

"Don't go in. If I'm right, Aaron's body's in there." He took out his phone. "We need to call the cops."

Despite the situation, I smiled. "If Cecil heard you say that, he might revoke your membership in Sanctuary."

Tanner held his phone in one hand, fingers poised to dial. "We need to let them know we had nothing to do with this. That older couple, the Pughs, knew you were pissed when we left their house."

He had a good point, but I still wasn't ready to give up precious hours to a police investigation. Especially not a murder investigation. It could keep me from finding the book. Not that I was close. Best I could tell, I wasn't even in the same country.

Josie's face appeared behind my eyes. The last survivor had to die. She'd said he was key. Her use of the word kept coming back to bother me. Something was off about it, but I couldn't figure out what. One thing was for sure. Aaron was likely now dead. If I could figure out why it had been so important for him to die, I might still be able to find the book in time.

"Come on," I begged Tanner. "If I call the cops, I'm not going to find the book." I peeked inside the open door. Blood spread in a widening pool on the light-colored tile.

He shoved the phone back in his pocket but didn't follow. "We're going to leave traces of ourselves everywhere."

I nodded my understanding, climbed the steps, and stepped inside, careful to avoid stepping in the blood.

The kitchen had been remodeled to look old, with mid-century style tile countertops and white cabinets. It was a nice room, if you ignored the smell of raw sewage and the dead body sprawled on the floor like a broken doll.

Aaron Todd had died on his side, eyes open and one hand reaching toward something visible only to him in his last moments. The killer had etched the word "PIG" on Aaron's forehead.

Whoever had thrown rocks at Tanner and me in the woods had cut open Aaron's stomach and left his guts in a greasy pile in front of him. That explained the smell. Aaron had been de-gutted, same as the bodies nailed to the wall of the Stephens barn in my vision. The killer, who'd been as alive as Tanner or me, had acted in Loretta Nell's stead. Cold spread through my body.

Loretta Nell had done a good job of erasing every link to the men who killed her. She only had one heir left to go —Josie. What did Loretta Nell have in store for her? That still bothered me. I shook it off and pulled myself into the moment.

Tanner stepped into the kitchen, got one look at Aaron, and clapped his hand to his mouth. He gagged. I rushed to him and dragged him in front of the sink, careful to keep him out of the blood.

"If you need to puke, do it here. Neatly." I stood with Tanner at the sink, hand on his shoulder as though he needed my help, but I really didn't want to look at Aaron Todd.

Tanner stood in front of the sink, breathing hard, swallowing every few breaths. "We were in the woods with whoever did that."

He gagged again. This time he lost his milk and cookies. I got a few steps away from him, wondering why I didn't care enough to vomit. Had I already seen too much? Done too much?

I forced myself to walk back over to Aaron Todd. This time I searched for the presence of a spirit. My black opal sent a light shock into my chest. I stared into Aaron's glazed eyes. Ghostly translucent eyelids blinked over his open eyes. I startled.

Embarrassed heat rushed to my cheeks. What kind of psychic medium witch was I? Not a very tough one for sure. A shadow fell over my face. I glanced up to see Priscilla Herrera watching the scene. She gestured at Aaron.

She didn't have to speak. I knew her well enough to understand the message. Don't be intimidated. Make him talk to you. And she was right.

I knelt next to Aaron and searched for the power that made me different from most people. The scar tissue covering my power had been worn so thin it now leaked in a half dozen places. I directed the mantle through it, which ached like a wound being stretched open, and let its electric charge flow through me. It opened my second sight. A spot in the middle of my forehead burned as my third eye opened.

I turned it on Aaron and saw the flirt I'd talked to a few hours earlier. We'd talk now, really talk. I had too much power pushing at his spirit for him to try to fuck around with me.

"I'm dead." Ghost lips moved over Aaron's still, dead ones. He tried to smile.

"You're dead," I agreed. "You should've given me the book."

He wrinkled his nose. "I never had the book."

What? I had thought for sure he'd lied to us about having the book. What else could the lawyer Cheryl Pugh mentioned have given him? Before I could insist he tell me, Aaron's ghost looked down at his mutilated body.

His see-through features contorted in horror. His spirit form flashed once, then twice. Too many brushes with the truth, and he'd beg to move onto the next plane. I had to get what I could out of him before he did that.

"If you didn't have the book, where is it?" I reached out to the spirit with my magic, hoping to hold it just a little longer.

"The only time I've ever seen it is in that picture you showed me," he said, still focused on his corpse.

"Then what did the murderer want?" I gave a little more forceful pull on the spirit.

Aaron's hand reached for his pocket, probably looking for those stupid keys he'd kept playing with in his bar. "Is this all there is? I don't want to spend eternity like this."

I slumped. He'd processed his death and was ready to move on. I'd help, of course. Dealing with spirits was my talent. But couldn't Aaron give me a little more information?

"I'll help you cross over," I soothed. "But first, tell me who killed you and why."

"I don't know who it was." Aaron rose from his body and stood looking around the room. He pointed in the corner. "Is that real?"

I stared in the direction of his finger, opening myself fully to the spirit world. A blinding light grew in the corner, getting ready to receive Aaron.

"Don't go over there yet," I said. "Tell me who killed you and why."

"It was a man, but he had on some stupid mask. It doesn't matter now." Aaron wandered toward the light.

It did too matter, damn it. I got to my feet and chased after him.

"Hey, wait. Why did this guy kill you?" At least I could get one good answer out of him.

Aaron turned back to me. The ghost's eyes had already darkened with death. He didn't speak but pointed at his corpse's head. *PIG.*

"Loretta Nell?" Even as I said her name, I knew I was wrong. Loretta Nell was dead. Unless she had control of someone. That wasn't right either. The only person I knew her to have control of was Josie Stephens, and Josie lived in a mental hospital. The person Tanner and I had chased was twice Josie's size.

Aaron's ghost flickered again. The light in the corner brightened. He reached one translucent hand into his pocket but came up empty.

"You want your keys?" If it made the ghost stay a little longer, I could dig in a corpse's pockets.

Aaron's ghost nodded.

I went back to the corpse and tried the pocket he wasn't lying on. A condom. A wadded receipt. No keys. Cringing with revulsion, I rolled the corpse. The blood-soaked shirt made a sticky sucking sound as it separated from the floor. The corpse flopped onto its back. I gagged but forced myself to reach into the other jeans pocket. Another condom. Aaron had believed in being prepared. I dug around some more. Empty.

I turned to find Aaron standing right in front of the light. He was ready. If I held him too much longer, the opportunity would pass and I'd have to tap serious magic to get him across the veil.

I went to stand next to him. "Your killer took the keys, didn't he?"

The ghost turned to me and said something, but no sound came out. His ability to speak was leaving along with the magical spark of life all of us held for one brilliant season.

"Just nod if I'm right." I let my magic pull on Aaron's spirit again. He nodded. I had a million more questions for Aaron, but there was no point asking them. He was ready to go, and it was time. I broke the magical connection between us and said, "I don't think it hurts. You just start walking, and it takes you."

The ghost turned back to me. His eyes were completely gone, replaced by black holes. His ruddy skin had turned the color of oatmeal. He raised one arm and pointed at the wall next to me. His lips moved again. I shook my head.

"It's fine, Aaron. Thanks for your help." I motioned at the white light. "Go on."

Aaron's ghost took an uncertain step into the glow, and it flowed over him. He took another step and turned back to me.

"Go on. It's fine," I told him.

He did as I said, and the glow took him over, erased what he'd been, and winked out. I stared at the empty spot. Would the light come for me after I'd breathed my last? Or would it be the darkness? I might have a chance to find out sooner rather than later.

12

TANNER JOINED me to stare at the wall. "That womanizing prick tell you anything worth knowing?"

I bit back a laugh and faced him. Tanner had splashed water over his face. Beads stood out on his dark skin, still an ashy gray, and dampened his hair. The light would surely come for my sweetie. Even speaking ill of the dead, he was too nice for anything else.

"Aaron never had the book, but the murderer took his keys." I wanted to scream in frustration.

"Why the keys? Think he had something back at the bar?" Tanner stared longingly at the door, likely itching to get out of the murder house.

"I don't know. Right before he left, he pointed at this wall." I showed Tanner how Aaron had pointed.

Tanner walked to the wall, knocked, and took pictures down to see if there was a safe behind them. He stilled and shook his head. "The garage. It's right out there." He pointed at the wall.

We hurried outside to the small structure next to the house. Sure enough, the door light spilled from the open door. I ran inside, ignoring Tanner's order for me to wait.

The garage had been too small to park a modern car inside, and Aaron had used it as a storage room. Someone, probably Aaron's killer, had tossed the room. Papers and files lay everywhere. A gray file cabinet had a foot-sized dent in it.

A presence rolled over me, pinging my black opal. Aaron. Because we'd shared such an intimate moment so recently, I recognized him right away. My vision flickered, and the spot between my eyes burned. He wanted to show me something. I let the vision take me.

A man wearing a pink pig mask rages around the tiny room. Aaron watches, eyes full of terror. He tries to sidle to the door. The masked man stops searching and points a pistol at him. Aaron freezes. The masked man marches toward Aaron and puts the barrel of the pistol to his forehead.

"Freddy Stephens gave you something other than those keys. I know he did." The masked man's voice seems vaguely familiar, but I can't place it. "He left directions to the place where he buried Loretta Nell."

Confusion clouds my understanding of what's going on. Who cares where Loretta Nell is buried? Nothing matters but the book. Another realization slams into me. Aaron's killer, likely with Loretta Nell's help, is trying to beat me to Mohawk's book. The implications flood my mind, but I don't have time to contemplate them because Aaron picks that moment to speak.

Aaron shakes his head, lips trembling. "Freddy Stephens left me nothing but the keys."

The masked man jabs the pistol's barrel harder into Aaron's forehead. "Then give me the keys."

Anger at the masked man thuds in my temples. I hate people like this. Want to hit them and hit them.

Aaron closes his eyes and lets out a shuddering sigh. He seems to know it's the end of the line for him.

"They're back by the front door, right where I dropped them when you shoved me into the house." Aaron's voice shakes, but he still manages to sound sarcastic and bored. I admire him for it.

The masked man steers Aaron out of the garage. As he does, Aaron throws a glance at the file cabinets, relief evident on his face. The vision fades.

I came back to myself with Tanner gripping both arms, face less than an inch from mine, and breathing his barf breath on me.

"You're going to have to brush your teeth, sweetie," I mumbled.

Tanner flushed. He let go so quickly I nearly fell down onto the concrete floor. I caught myself just in time to keep from bashing my head on the dented file cabinet. I spread my hands on the cool metal and leaned against it. Aaron had used my own power to show me what he wanted me to see. The sound of casters rolling across concrete came from behind me.

Tanner took my arm. "I got you a chair even though you made fun of my breath. Sit down." He helped me into the chair and came around in front of me, staring into my eyes. "You're getting too tired."

"It doesn't matter. We're not just racing against

Mohawk anymore." I struggled against the waves of fatigue threatening to put me down for the night.

Tanner pressed his lips together, brow wrinkling, and began to shake his head.

"Whoever killed Aaron wants to beat us to that book." My skin burned with the fever of worry.

Tanner took a step backward. He rubbed his forehead with one shaking hand.

"No," he breathed.

I gave him a few seconds to accept the truth before speaking.

"Aaron's murderer thought Freddy had given Aaron the location of Loretta Nell's grave. Turns out, all Freddy left Aaron was a key." Talking made my head swim. I put my elbows on my knees and tried to get control of myself.

"A key to what?" Tanner glanced around the mess.

"I don't know, but I think there's something important in here. As the killer took Aaron out of the room, he glanced back and looked relieved." The dizziness came and went in waves. Nausea came on the tail of them. When was the last time I'd eaten an actual meal? Roderick's. Had a good night's sleep? Before I met Tanner.

Tanner watched me, frowning. "So?"

"Aaron did everything he could to get his killer out of this room. He was hiding something." Ignoring the most current flood of nausea, I stood. "And we're going to find it."

Tanner nodded. "Okay. What are we looking for?"

"What the key goes to? I'm not sure, but something's bothering me. Aaron's killer wanted to know where

Loretta Nell was buried. Not the location of the book." I took out my cigarettes, but another wave of nausea hit me. I put them away.

"I don't get it." Tanner's eyes narrowed, their green growing more intense as he thought. "Is her corpse needed for some ritual with the book, to make it work?"

I shook my head. "I don't know. But here's what I do know: Aaron wasn't surprised when the killer asked where Loretta Nell is buried. That makes me think the answer to all our questions is somewhere in here."

Sifting through Aaron's storage room went slowly. He hadn't had much of a filing system. Business receipts and profit and loss sheets mixed with personal bank statements and receipts from the renovation Aaron had done on his bungalow. From the amount of money he'd spent on the latter, he'd apparently planned to stay. That set up another layer of the mystery. Why would Aaron stay?

The deeper I dug, the clearer a picture of Aaron emerged. He'd lived in a cycle of boom or bust. The Devil's Dance was one of many businesses he'd owned. Aaron had filed bankruptcy, been sued for nonpayment of debts, and owed some woman exorbitant alimony payments. But none of it answered the looming questions about Loretta Nell's burial site or what Aaron's key opened. I tossed the files onto the floor where they scattered, spreading into a big mess.

Tanner wandered over, probably to offer comfort, but bent to pick up something off the floor. He held up the large brown envelope. "What's this?"

"It's got a lawyer's name on it. Aaron was constantly in legal trouble..." I let a tired shrug finish the thought.

"The return address is in Devil's Rest. It could be the lawyer Mrs. Pugh mentioned." Tanner pulled a sheaf of papers from the brown envelope and read off the top page. "Says here Frederick Richard Stephens had left Aaron Wayne Todd an antique skeleton key, a sealed letter, and a manila file with 'Shawn Grimes' written on the tab."

I leapt to my feet and crowded in, trying to see what else he had. He tried to turn his back. I tickled him. We wrestled, giggling. For those seconds, we weren't sitting in the same property with a murder victim. Mohawk was a campfire story designed to scare stupid teenagers. Then I snatched the papers and skimmed over them.

I found a cheap white envelope so thin the blue security backing showed through. It had Aaron's name scrawled on it in looping old folks' script. "This must be the sealed letter. I don't see the file. And I guess we both know what happened to the key."

Tanner grabbed the envelope. "Aaron said his father didn't trust Freddy. Why would Freddy leave him this stuff?"

"One way to find out," I said.

Tanner withdrew a sheet of paper covered with a blue ink scrawl and began to read. I came close and read along with him.

Aaron,

You told me at your father's funeral that you blamed me for his death. You were right about everything. I'm a weak, selfish man. You were right to call me a murdering son of a bitch.

Right now, I need you to put aside your feelings for me and pay very careful attention.

Once I am dead, you and this key I'm giving you are the only things keeping Loretta Nell from doing what she promised that awful day in 1973.

Harris said you knew what we did to Loretta Nell, so I won't waste time rehashing it. But I will tell you the last thing she said, just to make sure you know.

Loretta Nell turned around to us, all bloody and torn up and said, "I will rise again. When I do, the Messengers and I will do to Devil's Rest what should have been done in the first place."

Well, I buried that book with Loretta Nell. But I kept the key in hopes that anybody who found her wouldn't be able to get it open.

Tanner stopped reading.

I shivered hard, scrubbing at my arms. Tanner and I exchanged a glance.

He said, "That's why the killer wants to know where Loretta Nell is buried—the book is with her."

"And now he has the key to get the book open." I took up the reading.

Now we need to talk about Shawn Grimes, the son of Loretta Nell Grimes. Yes. Even trash like Loretta Nell has kids.

After the shooting stopped, after we'd killed Loretta Nell, I found the boy hid up in the attic. Had a picture of his momma holding that book clutched in his hands, shaking all over. That kid knew his momma was dead.

He said to me, "You're gonna pay for what you did to my momma. She's gonna get you. And I'm gonna help her."

That kid's words chilled me to the bone, but I tried to play it off. Told him he was young, didn't know what he was talking about. If he was wise, he'd do everything he could not to be like Loretta Nell.

This kid curled his lip, eyes blazing like somebody who's killed all his life—maybe he had—and said, "The Serpent God will guide my path."

I grabbed up that kid and stowed him in the back of a squad car until children's services could come collect him. I never saw him again. But I've always felt him out there waiting for the right time.

I stopped reading to give my heart a chance to quit pounding.

Tanner's wide eyes suggested the story had made him feel the same as it had me—witnessing evil. I started reading again.

I've kept track of Shawn Grimes over the years. The file included will have his current address at the time of my death.

Aaron, I know your daddy left you that rattle trap house of his. I need you to set yourself up in Devil's Rest and keep a watch on things. You might think you want to blow me off, but if they ever decide to take their revenge, they'll come for you too.

At the bottom of this letter is a number. It goes to a bank account that I've put money in over the years. Nobody knows about this money but you and me. The name on the account is someone who doesn't even exist anymore. One of those damn Messengers. Use it to start yourself a business. And don't fuck around. Keep it solvent.

This key opens the gate to hell. Guard it with your life. Stay off the Stephens Ranch. That's where all the deaths have occurred so far. I hope that if you stay off the ranch, Loretta Nell won't be able to get to you. If Shawn Grimes, or any of his like, ever comes sniffing around, you kill him.

Best Wishes,

Freddy Stephens

Tanner and I sat in stunned silence for several minutes after we finished reading Freddy Stephens's version of a last will and testament.

Tanner spoke first. "Do you think Aaron's killer is Shawn Grimes?"

"I don't know." Icy bands of fear wrapped around my heart. They squeezed and choked. My mind cut off in self-defense, allowing me to watch the drama raging around me from far away.

"I don't understand why this is happening. Loretta Nell's been killing people out at that ranch since 1973." Tanner's voice rose with each word as though volume would make all our problems go away.

"Those killings are small compared to what the book is capable of causing. Mohawk wants to see huge, crazy violence. A massacre." I turned to him, movements slow and forced, still distant from it all.

"But why now?" he demanded.

"Time and season. Mohawk has me in his sights. It's a perfect opportunity for them to make a comeback." I stifled an almost hysterical giggle.

Tanner's small, intense eyes narrowed, glittering. "That's not going to happen. I will not let it happen."

I continued without acknowledging his fury. That distant place my mind had gone was nice and cool. "But there's more. Events are, for some reason, favorable for Loretta Nell's revenge plan to take place."

"Then what do we do now?" Tanner set the letter aside and stared at the floor.

"Shawn Grimes is our only lead. We do whatever it takes to find him and hope like hell he leads us to the book." The cool distance was fading. My reality break was over. Time to get back to work.

———

TANNER and I went through the package Aaron had received from the law firm. No matter how many times we looked, the Shawn Grimes file was not part of it.

"That file is somewhere in this room." I surveyed the mess of spilled papers and overturned boxes of junk.

"Unless the killer came back in here after Aaron was dead and found it." Tanner's gaze met mine. "Do you think the guy in the woods was Shawn Grimes?"

His words seeped into me, cold as ice. That we'd been

playing rock toss with Aaron's killer back in the woods was nothing new. But knowing it had probably been Shawn Grimes somehow made it worse. Especially after reading what that kid had said to Freddy Stephens. We had to find him and end him. That would put a cramp in Loretta Nell's plans.

"How are we ever going to find anything in this mess?" The words came out of me in a strangled whisper.

Tanner shrugged and sat down on top of the file cabinet. The cheap, thin metal crimped under his weight.

I raised my eyebrows at him. "First the dresser back at the motel and now this. It's all that barbecue you eat."

He wadded up a paper and tossed it at me. The tension broke a little. I handed him a pile of papers to search through. He fumbled them and let them slide out of his hands. They cascaded to the floor in a fanned out mess.

Annoyance flashed, but I took a deep breath. Tanner hadn't meant to do that, no matter how damn dumb it was. I knelt to pick up the papers. Tanner slid off the file cabinet to help. We went through the papers as we picked them up.

"There's nothing here." Tanner went through the last pages.

"But there's something sticking out from behind the file cabinet." I pointed at the discolored edge of something that looked like paper.

Tanner and I moved the file cabinet. Behind it was taped a dirty white mailer. The summer hadn't been kind to the tape on top, and it had begun to let loose, making the corner visible. I ripped the mailer off the file cabinet and pawed it open. Inside was a file labeled "Shawn Grimes."

I gave Tanner a hard hug and drew back to stare into his eyes. That had been the first thing that attracted me. Those clear green eyes.

He laughed and ducked away from me. "Don't get too excited. It might not even help."

"You kidding? Aaron Todd went to some trouble to hide this. It's hard for me to believe there isn't something useful in here..." I trailed off. Tanner and I stood staring into each other's eyes. The connection between us loomed bigger than life again, aching in my chest.

Tanner took the file and opened it. On top of the thin sheaf of papers sat a picture of Shawn Grimes as a kid. He held the picture of Loretta Nell that Mohawk had given me clutched to his chest.

"Looks like Loretta Nell, doesn't he?" Tanner squinted at the picture. He noticed resemblances between parents and kids more readily than I did.

I looked for Loretta Nell in the kid and found her in the spray of freckles across Shawn's nose and cheeks. His eyes, though dark instead of Loretta Nell's blue, blazed with a fury I knew well from my few encounters with Loretta Nell's ghost. Oddly, Josie's ferocity came to mind.

I picked up the picture of Shawn and read the back: "Shawn Grimes, age six. Taken the day he was made a ward of the state."

I cringed. In other words, this poor kid had just watched his mother die and the world he knew crumble, only to be kidnapped by a bunch of well-meaning strangers who snapped a picture of him like an animal in a zoo as he sat in their offices.

The reports stacked underneath the picture said about what I'd figured they would. Nobody wanted to adopt Shawn. His age and what he'd seen in his short life marked him as undesirable. He bounced from group home to foster home and spent some time in juvenile detention facilities.

The progressive decline of Shawn's existence and the waste of his potential depressed me. If I hadn't had Memaw to love and raise me, I might have ended up much the same.

Wait a minute. I couldn't let this poor man's disadvantaged childhood distract me. My life hung in the balance.

I flipped through the rest of the pages and saw nothing of use. Shawn's changes of address stopped around the time Freddy Stephens died. I glanced at Tanner and shook my head. "Another waste of time."

Tanner, the soul of patience, flipped to the last page in the file again. I'd mistaken it for yet another memo from one overworked state employee to another about Shawn's inability to quit doing bad things. Instead, it was a letter addressed to Freddy Stephens from a Linus Bramwell, Author.

"Read this part." Tanner tapped the middle paragraph.

In my efforts to write an accurate account of the Messengers, I tracked down Shawn Grimes, the son of

Loretta Nell Grimes. He told me quite a wild story about that day.

You've never done many interviews about your involvement in putting an end to the Messengers reign of terror. I'd love the opportunity to get your take on what happened.

The letter was dated two years before Freddy Stephens was murdered, which made it a good twelve years old. It was still worth seeing if Linus Bramwell, Author, was alive. I dragged out my phone and typed his name into the browser.

Tanner, who'd already started a search, held his phone up to my face. "Says here he lives in Austin now."

"Smartass," I muttered at Tanner.

He smiled and stood up a little straighter. "You know it makes you hot."

I squinted at the address. It had shown up because it was part of an announcement of a writers group meeting three months earlier. The internet was a great way to stay connected, but it was also a scary motherfucker for people who might not want to be found.

"Think we should barge in on this guy tonight?" I glanced at the time on my phone and saw it was headed toward midnight. One more full day, and then I faced Mohawk. I wasn't going to find the book in time.

"I'd say we need to think about what we hope to get from Linus Bramwell before we waste precious time on him." Tanner put his hands on my cheeks and caressed my face with his thumbs as though we weren't standing a few yards away from a dead body and a world of trouble if the cops barged in. Much as I hated to admit it, he had a good point.

"Aside from maybe seeing a recent picture of Shawn Grimes so we'd know who to watch out for..." I trailed off, mind working. "We're going to have to get that key from him. Mohawk won't give us a pass on it."

Tanner nodded. "Bramwell might also be able to offer insight into Shawn Grimes. Sometimes knowing about someone helps you anticipate what they'll do next."

"Let's go see Bramwell," I said with fake enthusiasm and pumped my fist for emphasis.

Instead of answering, Tanner pulled me to him. "Stop worrying. We are going to make it," he whispered.

I hugged him hard, not because I believed him, but because I needed the comfort right then.

"I've got an idea," I said without letting go. "Let's get out of town before they find Aaron's body. We'll find some-where to sleep on the way."

"That's a bad idea." Tanner followed me back into the house and watched me wipe the doorknobs with the hem of my shirt. "The Pughs know you were headed over here. That neighbor, Mr. Nosyheimer, got a great look at you this morning and knew you were asking about Aaron Todd. Cops are going to be looking for you."

I stopped in front of Tanner and put my hands on his shoulders. "Baby, don't you think Sanctuary can disappear like they never existed?"

"But..." Tanner shook his head and said no more. He

followed my pass through the house, face stiff with disapproval.

We drove back to the motel. Some kids were having a party and had their door open, blasting music for the entire motel to enjoy. Tanner and I exchanged an eye roll, and things were okay between us again. He'd been involved in the paranormal all his life. Surely he'd walked away from sticky situations from time to time.

Fifteen minutes later, we'd loaded our vehicles. I dropped the keys to our room into Dwight's overnight slot. However things turned out, we wouldn't be needing them anymore.

"Leaving like thieves in the night?" said a voice behind me.

I jumped and spun around, expecting to see a cop with his gun in one hand and handcuffs in the other. When I saw it was Dwight, I laughed to cover my fright.

"Yeah. The book's a loss." No way I'd tell him we might be back. If we did come back, I wanted to sneak in and out of town as quietly as I could. "I'm paid up, right?"

"Sure. Y'all didn't buy any porn, and you didn't use the phone. We're square." He laughed.

Tanner stood a short distance away. "You ready?"

I walked away from Dwight and patted Tanner on the chest on my way past. He stared at Dwight a few more seconds, got into his truck, and followed me out of the parking lot. I turned on my truck's radio and listened to the voices fading in and out of the static most of the way to Austin. My truck was new enough to have satellite radio, but I liked the static and the way music and voices came and went. It reminded me of life.

I chased Tanner's taillights back to the outskirts of Austin. We stopped at a huge truck stop and parked far away from the building.

Without a word, we crawled into the back of my truck, curled together, and slept with the windows down. The sound of tapping on metal invaded my dreams a few hours later. I jerked awake to see a golden strip of dawn on the horizon.

A cop stared into the window, shining his flashlight on us. "Sir? Ma'am? This is private property, and the manager would like you to hit the road."

Tanner and I dragged ourselves to a sitting position. Heart hammering, doing everything I could to look normal, I gave the cop a nod.

The Devil's Rest police might have already found Aaron Todd's body. They might be looking for us right now. Sleeping in this parking lot had drawn attention and had been foolish. Cecil would have bawled me out for it.

"Sorry about that." I prayed my voice sounded normal.

"Y'all get going, okay?" The cop clicked off his light and walked away.

"Think it's too early to visit Linus Bramwell?" I waggled my eyebrows at Tanner.

He giggled. "Yeah, but it won't be if we go get breakfast." He made no move to get out of the truck.

"What is it?" I was already lighting a cigarette and wishing for coffee.

"What do we do if Linus Bramwell's no help?" Tanner swallowed hard.

"I don't know," I said honestly. "We might be out of plays."

Tanner got out his phone and found us a place to eat breakfast. We ate our greasy meal talking about everything but what would happen if we couldn't find Shawn Grimes.

13

FORTY-FIVE MINUTES LATER, Tanner and I sat in the parking lot of a shopping center one mile from Linus Bramwell's house. We'd parked Tanner's truck and driven past Linus's subdivision.

A guard shack sat at the entrance. I didn't need to go talk to them to know they wouldn't let us in without Linus's okay. I watched the clock on my phone roll over to seven o'clock.

"It's early, but we can't wait any longer." I glanced at Tanner, looking for approval, but caught him staring at me with the saddest expression on his face. I took his hand and kissed it. Then I dialed the number Linus Bramwell had allowed to be listed online.

It rang once, twice, three times. A man who sounded ten times more chipper than I felt answered. "Yes?"

"Linus Bramwell? The one who was writing a book on the Messengers?" Now that I had the guy on the phone, I felt more unsure than ever. There was no way the guy would agree to see us.

"Who exactly are you, and where did you get my name?" He no longer sounded chipper. He sounded suspicious and a little afraid.

I gathered my nerve and started talking too fast. "My name is Peri Jean Mace. Mr. Bramwell, I've been researching Freddy Stephens's involvement in what happened with the Messengers, and your name came up. I was wondering..."

"I've never heard of you." He sounded annoyed, and people who felt that way usually hung up.

I kicked myself into high gear. "I know you suspected Freddy Stephens of some wrongdoing in relation to the Messengers, and I've got a file on Shawn Grimes in my hand right now. Freddy Stephens had it prepared."

Silence met my words.

I decided to go for broke. "I'm at the shopping center a mile from your house. Call down to the guard shack. Tell them to let me in."

A silly nursery rhyme played in my head. *Little pig, little pig, let me in.* I had to stifle hysterical laughter. This earned a raised eyebrow from Tanner. He took my hand again. I drew on his support the same way I'd draw on my magic.

"Come on, Mr. Bramwell. You know you're curious. Let's talk." I spoke with more confidence than I felt.

He sighed. "What did you say your name was?"

I repeated it, even spelling it for him.

"Go to the guard shack, and they'll be expecting you." He cleared his throat. "But Ms. Mace?"

"Yes?"

"I'm armed. Any bullshit, and I'll kill you." He hung up.

Tanner and I drove through the subdivision. The robotic voice from my phone giving directions was the only one doing any talking. We found Linus Bramwell's house and stared in silence. The newly risen sun made the Austin stone, Spanish-style structure glow like all the gold in El Dorado. Tanner pulled into the circular drive and stopped at the front door.

He tucked a lock of hair behind one ear and tried to smile at me. "House like this would cost several million back in California. What do you think it costs here?"

I shrugged. Real estate had never been on my radar. Until the last year or so, I couldn't have afforded even a plywood shack.

Tanner ignored my lack of a reaction. "Bet it's worth at least half a million. Maybe a million."

I understood his point. "Bramwell may have never written the book about the Messengers, but he must've written something that did mighty well."

"You ready?" He offered me his hand.

We got out of the truck and walked to the front door. I held the Shawn Grimes file in my free hand and slapped my leg with it. Tanner knocked on the door.

Little pig, little pig, let me in. I stifled the same crazy giggle from earlier. Facing my own death, I was losing it.

The door swung open. A white-haired man, face the color of chalk, stepped into the space. He held a handgun pointed right at Tanner and me.

I stiffened at the sight of the gun, and Tanner's hand jerked in mine. I squeezed tighter. He squeezed back.

"Mr. Bramwell, I'm Peri Jean Mace. This is my boyfriend, Tanner Letts." Sweat formed between my hand and Tanner's. Was this how it ended? Shot to death in some bland Austin subdivision?

Bramwell glanced at the file in my hand. "What's in there?"

I took out Shawn Grimes's picture and showed it to him. He nodded and tipped his chin at the file again. I showed Bramwell his letter to Freddy Stephens. He looked like he might throw up.

"Where'd you get this?" His voice trembled.

"Freddy Stephens left this to a man named Aaron Todd. He was..."

"Harris Coates's bastard son. He dead now too?"

I jerked in surprise and guilt.

Bramwell clapped one hand over his mouth and coughed. Between gasps, he said, "Look, I've changed my mind about this..."

Tanner and I exchanged a glance. Another mistake. More time wasted. I turned to go, pulling Tanner with me.

"Wait," Bramwell called. "Come in. Damn writer's curiosity. Gonna be the death of me yet."

Tanner and I stepped inside and followed Bramwell through the house. I gaped at the exposed beams, stone walls, and stone floors. Though the odor of brand new still hung in the house, it had been made to resemble some rich person's idea of a Spanish mission.

We came into a kitchen that could have housed a family of five. Bramwell opened one of the rustic wood cabinets and took out a coffee cup. He turned to speak to me.

"Can you wait to kill me until I've had some coffee?" Without waiting for our answer, he stepped in front of a fancy coffeemaker and filled his cup.

Tanner prowled into the breakfast nook, put his hand on the rustic wood table, and stared out the wall of windows at Bramwell's pool and hot tub. I tried to read Tanner's posture but couldn't pick up much more than sadness. Had he lived in a place like this with his wife, the beautiful Bea, and his beloved daughters?

He never went into much detail about his life before he met me. I knew he'd made good money selling arcane items and antiques to rich California people, and he'd lost it all after his wife and daughters died in a car wreck. He caught me watching him and winked. I walked to him and let him fold his arms around me.

Linus Bramwell spoke from the coffeemaker. "If the two of you hadn't been holding hands, so obviously in love, I wouldn't have let you in."

Cheeks heating, I turned my attention to him but didn't answer. What do you say to something like that?

"Do either of you want coffee?" Bramwell gestured at the machine.

"If you're going to kill us, I might take a cup before you do it." I was paraphrasing Bramwell's earlier quip, hoping to break the ice.

Bramwell didn't laugh, but he poured me a cup of coffee and brought it and his cup to the table. He spoke to Tanner. "Mr. Letts?"

Tanner glanced quickly at the gun, still sitting on the counter next to the coffeemaker, and shook his head. Bramwell nodded and sat down at the table, motioning me to do the same. We both took sips of our coffee. It was so good I closed my eyes to savor it.

Bramwell took another sip before he spoke. "I'm not going to kill either of you."

"I knew that when you opened the door." I leaned toward him and lowered my voice. "You ain't got that killer vibe."

Bramwell blanched and threw a look over his shoulder at the gun he'd left behind. "Before we go any further, I'd like to know what you want out of this conversation."

I considered giving him a hard time but was too tired and scared. I took the picture of Loretta Nell Grimes holding her book of horrors out of my back pocket and handed it to him.

"I've been tasked with finding this book. It's a matter of life and death for me." The entire story hovered on my lips, right along with the terrible need to cry, but I pushed it down.

Bramwell nodded and slid the picture back to me. "What makes you think I'd know where to find it?"

"I don't. But I hope you know where to find Shawn Grimes." Just the mention of Shawn's name brought back the image of Aaron Todd's gutted corpse. The coffee soured on my stomach. If Shawn did that to Aaron, he was a dangerous man, likely a psychopath. And here I was looking for him.

"What do you want with Shawn?" Linus's eyes had gone flat with some emotion I couldn't quite identify.

"I think he killed Aaron Todd over the book." I watched Linus carefully. He could be helping Shawn Grimes, even hiding him. If that was the case, we were going to have to fight for our lives in a few seconds.

"You saying Aaron Todd had the book?" Linus still had that flat look in his eyes, but now something lively danced behind it. Writer's curiosity?

"No. Look at this picture." I took the picture back out and tapped the book. "Freddy Stephens left Aaron a key to open the book. Aaron was killed last night and the key taken."

Linus picked up the picture and squinted at it. "What makes you think Shawn had anything to do with Aaron's death?"

I drew out the letter Freddy Stephens had left for Aaron Todd and passed it to Linus. His eyes, now shining and dancing, moved fast as he read. He raised his head. "Wow. Shawn told me about this—this prophecy. Now it's coming to pass."

"Prophecy?" Tanner finally turned away from the pool. "I thought it was just revenge."

Bramwell made a face. "Can't prophecy and revenge go together?"

Tanner and I both shrugged. I didn't care. I just wanted the craziness to end.

Linus glanced between us, deflating a little. "The two of you really are in danger, aren't you?"

Tears welled in my eyes. I cursed my own weakness and swiped at them.

Linus nodded. "No more games. I'm going to tell you everything I know about this Shawn Grimes business. I'm not sure it's going to help you the way you think, but maybe something..."

I searched for guile and saw nothing but a man who'd gone from curious to deeply sympathetic in a few seconds. I nodded. "I'd appreciate that."

"Before we start, answer a question for me. Do you know what I write? Either of you?" Bramwell glanced between Tanner and me.

Tanner nodded. "I looked you up. You write books about the occult. Fiction and non-fiction."

Tanner's words surprised me. I turned to stare at him. He hadn't said a word.

Linus smiled and nodded. "In the early 2000s, I was researching cult activity in prisons. A young man, who turned out to be Shawn Grimes, approached me. He told me about the book, about his mother's murder. It was from him I first heard of the Serpent God." Bramwell's eyes had quit twinkling. Fear now darkened them. He got up to get more coffee and could barely hold his cup steady enough to pour. He spoke with his back to us.

"Shawn's story didn't fit into my current project, and I blew him off. But meeting him haunted me. I looked up the story of the Messengers and became interested in writing a book about occult murderers. I tried to see Shawn in prison but learned he'd been released. I tracked him to a shack, literally a shack, in Austin where he was living with a woman and her child." Bramwell returned to the table. "Shawn and I became friends. Well, friends as much as anybody can be friends with a human being like him.

"Now we're back to prophecies," Linus said. "Would you like to hear the one Shawn told me?"

I didn't want to hear, but I nodded anyway.

"According to Shawn, the day lawmen came to raid the Messengers' compound, Loretta Nell knew they were coming. She conjured up this half man, half snake." Linus shivered. "This *thing* promised Loretta Nell that she'd rise again to continue their work. It promised her that she and Shawn would host a festival of blood and suffering. After that, they would live like gods." Linus raised one trembling hand to his mouth. "It would be many years before this came to pass. Loretta Nell would know it was time because a woman who was also a raven would come."

My breath caught in my throat. Waves of dizziness filled my head.

Linus pointed at the raven tattoo on my arm. "That's you, isn't it?"

Nausea climbing up the back of my throat, I managed to nod.

"When the woman with the raven came, it would be time for the sacrifice of the last survivor—Aaron Todd—and then the book could be used again." Linus, unable to contain his excitement despite any sympathy he felt for me, leaned forward, a smile hovering on his lips. "Now I see that the last survivor held the key to the book, and it was useless without the key."

"Let's back up," I said. "I don't understand this thing about Aaron being the last survivor. What about Josie?" I had finally tired of slapping the loose end away.

Bramwell raised his eyes to mine. The crow's feet at their corners narrowed, and his blue eyes twinkled. He was loving every second of this. "Josie is not who you think she is. You've been to see her, haven't you?"

I nodded.

"I'd be surprised if you hadn't. Those stories about her screaming to be allowed back on the ranch to find the book are pretty compelling." Pushing back his chair, Linus said, "Let me show you something."

He got up, went into a room off the kitchen, and came back carrying his own file. He took out a picture of a dark-haired man with intense eyes sitting at a metal table with a beer resting between his muscled arms, staring right through the camera at me. The dead-eyed man in the picture could be nobody but Shawn Grimes all grown up.

"Does he look familiar?" Linus did smile now, likely enjoying the mystery.

"He does, but I just can't place him." Shawn Grimes as an adult reminded me of someone else, all right, someone I didn't know well. It was in the brows and the lips. The identity of this other person hovered at the edge of my consciousness but I couldn't quite lure it out.

"Like I said in my letter to Freddy Stephens, Shawn told me a really wild story about what happened that day. Would you like to hear it?" Bramwell settled back in his chair, still watching me.

Chest tight, I nodded. This whole thing had my head spinning.

"Shawn said the deputies just showed up and started shooting people. There was no attempt at arrest. Loretta Nell hid Shawn in the attic, told him to stay there until the real cops came." Bramwell snorted at that. "Shawn said the shooting stopped, and the men went into the barn. He heard his mother screaming." Bramwell's throat clicked as he swallowed. "Freddy Stephens carried Loretta Nell's body out of the barn and off into the woods."

The woods. I tried to remember the layout of the ranch. In what direction had the woods been? Linus's soft, cultured voice cut into my thoughts.

"When Freddy came back from the woods, he went into the house and looked until he found the baby." Linus raised his eyebrows. This was the punchline.

I snapped off the thoughts about the woods. "Baby?"

"According to Shawn, Loretta Nell had given birth very recently." Bramwell gave me a minute for it to sink in.

"Freddy's child," I muttered. Just saying the words made another piece click into place. "Freddy and his wife adopted the baby. He grew up to be Josie's father."

Linus pointed one finger at me like a gun to let me know I had the right answer.

This was why Josie wasn't dead. Though she might

have shared DNA with the lawman who'd killed Loretta Nell, she also carried Loretta Nell's genes. When Josie ate whatever facsimile of flesh Loretta Nell could manifest as a ghost, that bound them even further. Now Loretta Nell intended for Josie, her granddaughter, to carry out her revenge plan. I thought about Josie wandering the halls of the mental hospital. *After a decade in this place, I've learned the ropes.*

The feeling of being a puppet having my strings pulled came back. Mohawk had lured me out here to carry out plans he'd made decades ago. He'd pitted me against people who knew their mission and couldn't wait to carry it out. Mohawk had put me at a disadvantage from the very beginning. Well, he was going to get a Peri Jean Mace surprise right up his ass. I wouldn't just give up and let him win. I began to assess where I stood.

Shawn Grimes had the key to the book, probably the book as well by now. He'd pick up his last remaining family, and he and Josie would go on a murder spree fueled by that book. Mohawk planned not only to feast on the destruction but on my misery after he took me as a slave. I'd played the fool, and now I'd probably never set things right. But I'd eat catshit and onions before I quit.

"Mr. Bramwell, I appreciate all you've helped me understand, but I need to find Shawn. Now. He's about to..." I tried to call up words but saw only blood and dead bodies in my mind's eye.

"You see, that's why I'm so disturbed about what you're telling me. Shawn Grimes is dead, has been for a good five years." Bramwell raked his fingers through his thick, white hair, blinking rapidly.

Shock spread in my chest to tingle against my nerve endings. I shook my head, denying Bramwell's statement.

"It's true," Bramwell said. "Shawn Grimes was murdered. It was a sad situation. He'd been straight for a while, but one morning he went out to start his car. Someone walked up to it and shot him to death."

I wanted to scream denials, but I saw the truth on his face. Here I was, my freedom in its last hours, and I was just as lost as I'd been from the beginning.

"May I see that picture again?" Bramwell held out his hand.

I gave it to him, put my hand in Tanner's, and stared out at the fancy pool and hot tub. It was a nice fantasy. Escape here.

Bramwell held up one finger and hurried out of the room. This time he came back holding an old photo album. "You need to understand something about my relationship with Freddy Stephens. About two weeks after I sent the letter asking for an interview, my ranch in Dripping Springs burned to the ground." Bramwell's face turned the color of paste. "Killed my wife, my horses, even my dog. I had a speaking engagement in San Antonio that night. Wasn't even home."

"Freddy Stephens did it?" Fury burned hot just underneath my skin. I was glad Freddy Stephens and I hadn't met. I hated people like him.

Bramwell did a thing where he wiggled his shoulders and almost nodded.

"I'll never really know. Not long afterward, I got a message in my voicemail. This rough voice said, 'Back the fuck off or you're next.' Shawn Grimes swore the voice on the message was Stephens." Bramwell did the odd motion that wasn't quite a shrug or a nod again. "But I told you that so maybe you can better understand what I'm going to tell you next."

"Mr. Bramwell, you don't have to explain yourself to me. I'd have hunted Freddy Stephens down like a rabid dog." The hot anger under my skin would have carried me beyond fear.

"I believe you." Linus almost smiled. "Well, here's my story. When I heard what happened to Freddy Stephens, I went to the auction of his house."

He paused as though Tanner or I would act shocked. I couldn't believe he'd done so little.

Bramwell continued. "There was a guy at the auction buying stuff left and right, and he ran up the bids on everything. But I managed to get this one thing."

He flopped the photo album down on the table and flipped through it. The album showed a bunch of pictures from people wearing plaid pants and flare collars. The women wore bell-bottoms and had beehives. I recognized a picture of a much younger Freddy Stephens and another of a man who looked a lot like Aaron Todd.

Bramwell kept flipping pages. "At first I thought I'd paid too much for an album full of pictures of a guy who'd killed my wife and animals. But then I saw this." Bramwell held the album where I could see and picked at the edge. He pulled it back. "He'd hidden his secret pictures in here."

The pictures behind the cover showed a young Freddy Stephens and an alive Loretta Nell Grimes in a variety of poses. All the pictures had been taken in a spot that looked vaguely familiar. Some of them had Loretta Nell holding the book.

Bramwell held my picture of Loretta Nell up to the ones from his photo album. Both were taken in the same location. He flipped a few pages in the photo album and pointed to one of the whole family. It was the same spot. This time I recognized it. This was the spot where I'd first encountered the thugs who'd tried to beat Tanner and me to death in the parking lot of Roderick's barbecue joint.

"This is where he buried her," I muttered to nobody in particular. Then I turned to Tanner. "After everything we've been through, Loretta Nell—and the book—have been in one of the first places I visited after I came to Devil's Rest."

Anger was my default emotion, and I wanted to be furious about the way I'd been led around in circles. But I was too scared. Mohawk was winning. He was beating the shit out of Tanner and me.

"We need to get back to Devil's Rest and dig up the book before whoever murdered Aaron figures out where it is." Tanner pushed his chair back and stood. He held out one hand to Linus. "Sir, thank you for your hospitality and your help."

Linus shot out of his chair, his gaze focused on me. "If you're willing to come back and tell me your story..." Bramwell trailed off with a bow of his head.

"I'll think about it," I told him. In truth, I'd have to talk to Cecil, see if he had any thoughts. Sometimes my great-uncle saw trouble on the horizon better than I did.

Linus walked us out to the truck and shook both our hands again. He asked for my phone number, and I gave it to him, even though he had it on his caller ID.

Tanner and I left Linus Bramwell's fancy subdivision and drove back to the strip mall.

The acres of concrete had filled up with people going and doing. They sped through the parking lot, walked into stores as fast as they could, and generally had a pinched hurry-up air about them. Today, I was like them. I needed to hurry if I wanted a chance at survival.

"Let's take your truck back to Devil's Rest," I told Tanner. "Mine's the one more people have seen. If the cops are looking for me..." I shrugged.

Tanner and I spent too many minutes brainstorming a place to leave my truck, one where it wouldn't get towed or rouse suspicion. We decided on a parking garage a few miles away. Turned out, driving a few miles in Austin took almost an hour. But we emerged from the garage without my truck, holding a ticket to get it back.

We got into Tanner's old beater and rolled down the windows. The air conditioning only worked sometimes. I got the GPS working on my phone and began talking Tanner out of Austin.

———

ONCE THE PACKED-TOGETHER buildings of Austin ended, we

headed south for Devil's Rest. I watched the landscape speed past.

I understood what my great-uncle Cecil loved about this place. This open, empty land made up a hypnotic panorama. The lonesome, crooked highways screamed desolation. The blazing sweep of sky, the sun a merciless burning corona at its center, didn't forgive mistakes easily. The whole place felt like a secret.

My phone's ringing jolted me out of my daze. I answered, "Peri Jean Mace."

"Ms. Mace? This is Linus Bramwell." His voice broke up on the last few words.

"Yes, sir. We're getting out into the wilds, so the signal's not too good. What can I do for you?" I stared out the window at a bloated deer carcass on the roadside.

"I'll make this fast then. Since you left, I haven't quit thinking about who murdered Aaron Todd. With Shawn dead and Josie locked up, who else would care about all this stuff?" He said something else, but the signal scrambled it. I turned to Tanner. "Pull over before I lose him completely."

He did as I asked.

"Linus, I didn't catch that last part." I lit a cigarette and watched buzzards circling the dead deer. Pretty soon, they'd dig in. Bon appetit. *Ick.*

"I said that I had forgotten all about Shawn's son," Linus said.

I dropped my cigarette in my lap. Tanner slapped at it, but I snatched it up before he could ruin it.

"Shawn had a son?" Even as I asked the question, I

remembered Linus telling us about hunting Shawn down at a shack in Austin where he was living with a woman and a boy.

"I never really knew, to be honest. Shawn brought the boy to several of our meetings, and the boy seemed versed in the subject matter." Linus paused several seconds. "I took a picture of Shawn every time he came to talk, and I am positive I had one of Shawn and the boy. Maybe I don't. Getting old sucks. My advice is don't do it."

If I couldn't get the book, I wouldn't be getting old. Neither would Tanner.

"Aha," Linus shouted. "Here it is. I'm going to send it. Hold on." The sounds of Linus moving around came over the phone. "Okay. It's sent. I know you're headed to dig up that blasted book. If I think of anything else useful, I'll call."

We said our goodbyes and hung up. Tanner took off driving again. I held my phone in my lap, watching one bar of service fade in and out. At this rate, Linus's picture would never come through. The picture finally popped into existence, as though by magic. I opened it. At first, the preteen next to Shawn Grimes looked like every other gawky, dorky boy with his sweaty cap of hair and red, freckled cheeks. Then I saw the eyes, and bile rose up the back of my throat.

"It's Dwight Carr," my voice rasped out, barely a whisper.

Aaron Todd's killer, Loretta Nell Grimes's grandson, had rented me a motel room and flirted with me. If Linus had been right and Shawn Grimes had fed Dwight the story of Loretta Nell's demise and the prophecy for her resurrection, Dwight had probably known who I was the second he saw my tattoo. And I'd stupidly done everything right under his nose.

Now that I'd made the connection, Dwight's resemblance to Loretta Nell, his grandmother, made the hair on the back of my neck stand up. He looked like a male version of her with dark hair.

Tanner swerved over on the side of the road and grabbed my phone. "That little shit."

I put my cigarette to my lips with one shaking hand and dragged deeply. The burn of the smoke in my lungs pushed down my urge to scream and claw at my face.

"Dwight sends people out to that farmhouse for Loretta Nell to kill them." Tanner closed his eyes, fingers on the bridge of his nose.

"He killed Aaron." I rubbed at the headache forming in my neck. "He has the key to the book. He's probably already dug it up."

"I don't think so." Tanner set the phone aside and faced me. "Somehow Loretta Nell can't show him where she's buried. So he's waiting for us to lead him to the book the same way we led him to Aaron Todd and the key."

Tanner started the truck, got us back on the road, and sped toward Devil's Rest. The minutes dragged past, but my thoughts raced.

The truth of it all sunk in deep. Dwight had been keeping track of us the whole time I'd been in Devil's Rest. I'd been so wrapped up in my own drama, I hadn't even realized it. Stupid. He had done a better job of tricking me than Mohawk had. And he was winning.

The Serpent God's prophecy was coming true. Dwight had the key, thanks to me. Now all he needed was the book. Then he'd... The indescribable pictures of blood and gore floated behind my eyes again. I shuddered. No way I'd let that happen. I'd beat him in the end.

But something else nibbled at the edges of my thoughts. Some detail I'd forgotten. We passed a billboard showing a young woman leaning against a wall, her hair in her face. Josie. That was it. How did she play into Loretta Nell's plans?

Then I saw it. Josie had eaten part of Loretta Nell's spirit. Taken Loretta Nell into her as surely as Dwight had joined himself to Loretta Nell by being her grandson and sending her people to murder. The memory of Josie becoming Loretta Nell in those last moments I spent with her filled my head. I shuddered.

Loretta Nell would need Josie out of the mental hospital to finish the possession. Then whatever was left of Josie Stephens would be no more. She'd be all Loretta Nell Grimes, and she'd go on to help Dwight fulfill the Serpent God's prophecy.

I tried again to imagine what that would entail. That scene from my vision in the barn, where the kids in that church youth group tore each other apart, was the only information I had to go on. It was horrible enough.

Then I thought of something worse. What would Josie do to get out of the mental hospital to come help Dwight create carnage? I needed to warn Suzanne Fitch that Josie would try to break out soon. Maybe even tonight.

Disgust pumping through me with every beat of my heart, I took out my phone and called the mental hospital.

Barely listening to the automated menu, I pushed zero until I got a human voice and said, "Suzanne Fitch. This is an emergency."

One ring. Two rings.

"Suzanne Fitch. How may help you?" Suzy Fitch sounded frazzled.

"Josie's going to try to escape today or tomorrow," I said.

"Who is this?" Fitch's voice sharpened.

"Peri Jean Mace. I used magic to set some papers on fire in your office. Remember me?"

Fitch drew in a sharp breath, and her voice dropped to a near whisper. "How do you know?"

Too tired to explain, I said, "I just do. The guy who's going to break Josie out is named Dwight Carr. He's her cousin."

Fitch let out a sigh. "It's okay, Peri Jean. You don't have anything to worry about. Dwight Carr has been banned from visiting Josie for almost a year now. He was caught being inappropriate with her."

My stomach gave another disgusted lurch. "Keep an eye out for him anyway."

"Oh, we will. I'll tell Winslow and Adamick right now. Is that all?" Her voice had sharpened now that she had a plan.

"Yes," I said. Fitch hung up on me. I turned to Tanner. "Let's stop by the Devil's Slumber Inn. If Dwight's there, we'll make it where Fitch doesn't have to worry about him coming to get Josie."

Tanner drove like a speed demon all the way to Devil's Rest. We screeched into the parking lot of the motel, parked the truck lopsided, and ran to the office. The door was locked. Tanner and I got on either side of a concrete planter, lifted it, and swung it at the aluminum and glass door. The glass shattered inward in a crumpled sheet. Tanner unlocked the door, and we went inside.

I climbed behind the partition, hurried through the office, and slammed into Dwight's living quarters. The living room consisted of a gross couch with a cowboy roping cattle embroidered into the leather and wooden wagon wheels on each end.

A laptop sat open on the couch next to a stack of papers. I picked up the one on the top and recognized the ginormous list of email addresses I'd seen the day I checked into the Devil's Slumber Inn. The next page showed the same thing.

"What is it?" Tanner said from behind me.

I handed the paper to him and went to the little apartment's tiny bedroom. It reeked of sex and marijuana. The bed was unmade, stained sheets in full view. I checked the adjoining bathroom but found nothing more than another mess. I went back out into the living room to find Tanner studying the email addresses.

"Let's go," I told him. "Dwight's on the way to Austin already. Hopefully Adamick and Winslow can stop him from getting Josie out."

Tanner let the paper he was holding flutter to the floor. "Those two could stop an eighteen-wheeler."

We exchanged a smile. Though the timing was wrong, and we had miles to go on this journey, I went to Tanner and hugged him, just wanting to enjoy that split second of life with him. He laughed and hugged back.

"Let's do it," he said.

We got back into his truck and started the drive to Stephens Ranch.

14

TANNER'S and my good mood died as soon as we got to the top of the hill and saw Pig-Face and Chubby from Roderick's barbecue joint. They must have recovered from their beating enough to come back to their favorite hangout. Austin—aka Floppy Hair—must have still been languishing in his "comber."

Now that I knew Loretta Nell and her book were buried here, these men's aggression made more sense. Another clue I hadn't seen. I wasn't going to survive long if I didn't pay better attention.

Purple half-moons hung under Pig-Face's eyes, and he had a piece of tape over his broken nose. Chubby held his back where Roderick had whipped him with the crowbar. They carried weapons, Pig-Face a baseball bat and Chubby a hatchet. At least they didn't have guns.

Tanner shoved the gearshift into park and unbuckled his seatbelt. He leaned forward and pulled on the top of the bench seat. I leaned away so he could get behind it. He pulled out a tire iron and a length of chain. He offered me my pick. I took the chain. He opened his door.

I grabbed his forearm to stop him from climbing out. I needed to say something, to let him know how much he meant to me. Just in case. He turned back to me, face expectant.

My brilliant, romantic words were, "If this is the last five minutes of my life, there's nobody I'd rather be with."

He winked and nodded. "Same for me."

We climbed out of Tanner's worn-out truck together. Soon as my feet touched the ground, fury came out of nowhere and worked its way through me, its flames licking at my self-control. The black opal pinged. This savagery was stronger than anything I'd felt so far. Did the book know it was about to come into play?

I glanced at Tanner for reassurance but found his face twisted hatefully. My stomach did a cartwheel. Despite how often Tanner found fistfights, he rarely got angry. He'd told me he couldn't allow himself the luxury of anger. He knew he could really hurt someone.

Tanner smiled then, but it looked more like the way a dog shows its teeth before it bites. His small, intense eyes squinted as he focused on Chubby and Pig-Face.

"Hey, you dickless pieces of shit. Want another beating?" Tanner sing-songed the words, his voice raw with rancor.

Chubby hefted his hatchet. "We gonna do the beating, asshole."

Tanner adjusted his grip on the tire iron. The four of us walked toward each other, arms out from our bodies. My rage reached its boiling point and ran over, its venom flooding through me. My self-control snapped off with a click. I wanted to see these two petty assholes hurt.

I called to the mantle. It moved inside me like a coming storm. The magic pricked through my body. Energy from the earth came up through my legs. Bruise-colored clouds rushed over the burning sun. A streak of red lightning lit the sky.

Pig-Face's eyes followed it. I had expected fear, but third-degree hate blazed from his eyes. He didn't care.

That was okay. I'd make him care before this was over. I called down another bolt of lightning. It hit the ground between the thugs and us. The mantle swirled in my chest, expanding with each furious breath I took.

"Get in your truck and leave now." My voice boomed off the hills like a clap of thunder.

Pig-Face and Chubby jerked in surprise but didn't back down. Their eyes darkened with anger and pleasure at that anger. Good. I felt the same way.

I channeled the mantle into the chain. The metal grew hot as though I'd laid the thing in fire. The burn didn't matter right then. My anger was like a tidal wave rushing toward these assholes, and I was riding it like a surfer from hell. I took one step forward and swung the chain at Pig-Face.

He raised one hand and caught it. The heat seeped into his skin. His eyes widened, and he let out a pure, high, satisfying scream and dropped the baseball bat he'd held.

Dark joy pounded along with my anger. I bared my

teeth in semblance of a smile. "Damn, that was a good scream. Think you can do it that way again?"

The fire of wrath blazing, I jerked the chain and swung it again. It hit his midsection, which included one bare arm. Smoke rose from his arm. He screamed harder.

I glanced down at my hand. Smoke rose from it. The chain was burning me too. But I wanted to hear Pig-Face scream again, wanted to relish the shine of fear in his eyes until I beat them out of his head. This bloodthirstiness felt good. Too good. No wonder so many people did mean things.

I reared the chain back for another blow. Pig-Face saw it coming and pealed out a scream. It sounded like the best opera I'd ever heard. The chain hit his neck with a dull *thwack*. I pulled it away and delivered another blow. Pig-Face blocked with his arm. When I pulled the chain away, a stripe of skin came with it. I knew what it meant to feel like a goddess.

Chubby rushed Tanner with a wild scream, raising his hatchet as he came.

Face set in fierce lines, Tanner swung the tire iron fast. It hit Chubby across the lower half of his face. Blood foamed from his mouth. The hatchet thumped on the dirt. Chubby dropped to his knees bawling, hands cupping his jaw, blood hanging in a slobbery line stretching toward the ground.

I stopped beating Pig-Face, who'd quit letting out those high girly screams anyway and watched. Bloodlust stormed inside me.

Tanner approached Chubby, smiling that awful toothy

smile, and swung the tire iron in an upward arc right over the guy's family jewels. The hit made a soft thump. Chubby collapsed howling, face turning the color of beets. He clutched at himself.

My rage spiraled high. I ran at Chubby, dizzying inferno of hate clouding my thoughts, and kicked him in the nuts as hard as I could. The bones of his hands felt like brittle sticks. I kicked again.

"You cheated. You cheated." Chubby broke off his words to let loose a howl that would have been the envy of any self-respecting coyote.

Tanner leaned down, vein thumping in his neck, and growled, "We don't care."

He swung the tire iron again and hit Chubby in the arm. The bone made the same sound as a wet branch snapping in two. Chubby's face knotted into a scream, his whole body shaking, tears streaming from his eyes. Tanner smiled at me, and I smiled back, feeling more love for him than I'd ever felt for anybody, even Wade.

Wait a minute. That's wrong. This isn't us. The words, barely more than a whisper, came from deep inside, almost too far away for me to hear. The red delirium faded just enough for me to realize that voice knew its stuff.

Something was bad wrong with both Tanner and me. We got into fights with other people. Lots of them. But neither of us was cruel by nature. We didn't enjoy hurting people.

I spent a lot of time mad at the world, and I had killed people. But never just for pissing me off. They had to really, really do something awful. Hurt someone I loved. Prove themselves a permanent threat.

Kill them, another voice whispered. *Kill them both. Eat their hearts.*

Saliva shot into my mouth, and my stomach rumbled. Every thought turned red and hot. The desire to spill blood heated me, not unlike sexual desire.

Pig-Face got to his feet again, eyes burning with stupid hate. He picked up the baseball bat off the ground, using one hand to wrap the injured fingers of his other hand around the shaft. Chubby, broken arm hanging, somehow got to his feet. He picked up his hatchet with the arm that wasn't broken. There wasn't a shred of humanity on either man's face. They wanted to kill us too.

Tanner walked toward the two men, steps light and graceful, smile splitting his face. "Come on," he rumbled. "Let me kill you."

Before I could stop myself, I called the mantle into the chain again. My hand ached as the metal burned the skin. The pain didn't matter. I walked toward the fight, hand tight around the too hot chain. The need for violence boiled away all coherent thought.

Sacrifice them to me. I'll let you keep your freedom. The voice came again, sly and prodding. The haze of fury dimmed just a little. That voice belonged to Mohawk.

I snapped back to reality, really saw what I was participating in. Cold revulsion splashed over the hateful fury. My stomach tightened into a cold ball. I let the chain fall to the ground.

Tanner and Pig-Face marched toward each other like

soldiers of the scrap yard, their makeshift weapons raised. Chubby stumbled along behind Pig-Face.

No. Tanner had to stop before he killed Chubby and Pig-Face. Killing them was exactly what Mohawk wanted. The deaths would bind Tanner and me to Mohawk. We'd become his new killers. I knew this the same way I sometimes knew a magical spell would work.

The realization drove away a little more of the madness. My hand began to throb where I'd burned it with my own magic. I turned my hand over to see the shape of the chain branded onto my palm. My shoulder ached from swinging the chain with all my force.

The horror of what I'd done sank in. Bile stung my throat. Tanner, Pig-Face, Chubby circled each other, taking swings and dodging with inhuman speed. *Stop them.*

I ran for the truck. My smoke-singed lungs ached within a couple of steps. I hit the truck hard, clambered in, and gave the key a vicious twist. The truck's old engine blasted to life. I jerked it into gear and jammed my foot down on the accelerator. The truck leapt forward, hitting a pothole and jouncing my hands off the steering wheel. I grabbed it again, fighting for control, and steered toward Tanner, Pig-Face, and Chubby.

Tanner swung the tire iron at Chubby's one good arm, knocking the hatchet from his hand. My sweet, decent boyfriend smiled, murder in his eyes, and scooped up the hatchet. Pig-Face tried to rush him with the baseball bat. Tanner chopped at the arm holding the baseball bat. The bat fell to the ground with a thump.

The sight tickled at the ball of fury I'd tucked away.

That anger wanted to come out for another round. I forced myself to look carefully at Pig-Face and Chubby. These were human beings, not so different from me, give or take a hundred IQ points. The poor men's sides heaved. They were beat. Tanner was about to kill them just to be doing it. Then he'd belong to Mohawk.

The idea of Mohawk taking away the man I loved, shitting up my life after all, brought the rage roaring back. Only this time it was directed at doing good instead of evil.

I laid on the horn to get Tanner's attention. His head jerked in my direction, eyes dead with anger. I blasted the horn again and sped toward him. Tanner's mouth dropped open, and he leapt out of the way. Chubby and Pig-Face finally saw the truck.

They ran from it, but in the wrong direction. I wanted them to go toward the road leading away from the hilltop. If they stayed here, we'd kill them. I had control of the rage but didn't think I could hold it. I chased Chubby and Pig-Face around the clearing, having to go extra slow not to hit Chubby. He ran with one arm flopping and the other hand holding his ruined nuts.

Finally we made the entire circle of the hilltop clearing. A few more steps, and we'd be back at the road leading down the hill.

Tanner waited at the intersection to the road, holding the tire iron in one hand and the hatchet in the other. As the men ran and limped toward him, he raised both. The men bellowed battle calls and rushed Tanner. He swung the hatchet and chopped Pig-Face in one leg, laying it open. Somehow, Pig-Face kept his feet. It had to be the rage pushing him along. Otherwise both of these losers should be lying in the fetal position while they waited for an ambulance.

I drove the truck closer to Pig-Face and Chubby, blaring the horn to let them know I could run over them. The two men stumbled down the road leading away from the hilltop, barely able to stay on their feet. I used the truck to herd them down the road.

Their truck appeared in my rearview mirror, head-lights flashing, horn honking. I saw Tanner at the wheel. My stomach squeezed into a cold, nauseated ball. I didn't want to watch my sweet boyfriend murder these two.

We came to a wide spot, and the truck flew around me. Tanner skidded to a stop next to Pig-Face and Chubby. Tanner bailed out of the truck, holding the hatchet aloft. But Pig-Face and Chubby must have finally come to their senses. They both put their hands up. This seemed to calm Tanner. He motioned at the truck. They climbed in and sped off, tires kicking up a fan of dust.

Before I knew what I was doing, my foot slammed down on Tanner's truck's accelerator. It jumped a few feet. *What the dunderfuck am I doing?* Mohawk's laughter rang in my head. Using the same focus I used to call my magic, I pinpointed the lunacy and shoved it aside.

I pressed my foot on the brake and watched them go. Tanner turned to face the truck, sides heaving. We stared at each other through the glass. He stomped toward the truck, eyes still slitted like a gunslinger's.

I tensed. Having just seen what he was capable of, the beast that lurked within, there was no question whether he could kill me. He threw the weapons into the back of the truck. They clanged on the metal, and I jumped.

Tanner stepped away from the truck, some of the tension gone from his shoulders. He mouthed, "You okay?"

He'd seen the beast within me too and had every right to be scared. I rolled down the window, mind flashing with images of him reaching into the truck and putting those strong hands around my neck.

But trust was a two-way street. He was willing to trust me again. If I couldn't afford him the same respect, I didn't have any business telling myself I loved him. Calling as much courage as I could, I reached through the open window, extending one hand to Tanner.

"I'm fine. Are you okay?" My voice sounded more normal than I would have imagined.

Tanner took my hand and nodded. He tried to smile. A rush of love, one stronger than the rage, filled me. It chased away the last of the black-tinged red fury. I let it go with relief.

"They might come back any time," I said. "Let's dig up Loretta Nell and get the book as fast as we can."

Tanner hurried around to the other side of the truck and got in. We joined hands, and I backed up the hill, marveling at how my love for Tanner had shifted the tide of emotion.

———

I BACKED into the clearing where Freddy Stephens and

Loretta Nell Grimes had once taken pictures, the place where Freddy had picnicked with his family.

Had Freddy fed on this place the way those thugs had? Maybe he'd come up here and soaked it in, let it convince him to kill people he arrested and to bring his friends to the ranch to get killed.

I parked the truck in nearly the same spot Tanner had when we'd first arrived and got out. Tanner came around to my side of the truck, head hung.

"I can't believe I did that. Sometimes I get into fights, sure, but never..." He shook his head.

"I think I'd have killed them had I not heard Mohawk's voice." My skin tightened at the memory. "He told me to sacrifice them to him. He told me he'd let me keep my freedom."

Tanner nodded. "I heard him too. That's why, when you were chasing those men with the truck, I waited at the mouth of the road back down the hill. I figured either I'd make those guys leave or kill them. Didn't matter which."

The feeling of having my strings pulled came back. I thought I finally understood. "The way this hit us when we came up here together was different than what I felt when I came alone. Then I was just scared."

"The two of us together made it stronger." Tanner shoved his knotted fists in the pockets of his jeans, face flaming.

"I think if we had sacrificed those assholes to Mohawk, we'd have become the new owners of the book." A shiver worked its way up my back.

How close had I been? If I was honest with myself, very

close. I hung my head and took deep breaths. Even now, I still felt it. Anger nibbling at my brain, irritating, trying to get me to react.

How had I been so stupid? A being like Mohawk had plans within plans, manipulations beyond what I could imagine. The anger got bigger. My skin flushed. If I let myself, it would rage into a tower of hate nothing would douse until I hurt someone. Maybe myself.

Ignore it. Priscilla Herrera's voice came from inside my head. *Let it go. Think of the things you love. Nice things. Think of your young man.* Her voice lowered at that last sentence, full of insinuation.

Normally, I'd have bristled at the implication. In order to pass on the family magic, I needed to have a child. Tanner was perfect. Decent, proven fertility, and with his own magical talent. But then we'd be tied together. What if we decided we never wanted to see each other again?

Negative thoughts and fears crowded in. I shut them down and took a deep breath. The side trip into the land of failed romance had done its trick. The anger burned low, manageable. I raised my head to find Tanner watching me.

"We're about to come into direct contact with this book," he said. "Do you think we can keep it from controlling us?" He turned away to stare at the dimming daylight, showing he didn't expect an answer. I moved to stand next to him.

The hills stretched into the distance, softly rounded tops blending together. White mist veiled the farthest ones. The darkening sky shone a soft pink over them. Now I understood why Tanner stared out. The beauty of it tamped down the bloodlust we both had brewing inside us. We stood side to side, shoulders brushing.

"What should we do to keep the book from controlling us?" I worked to keep my voice calm, taking deep slow breathes.

"I've got something in the truck. Not sure how much it'll help." He snorted. It was almost a giggle.

I chanced looking at him. A smile stretched across his face.

"Remember when I went with Gus and Cliff to play cards?" He still wouldn't look at me.

I nodded. Gus and Cliff were the only same-sex couple in Sanctuary. They liked to gamble and occasionally invited Tanner or me to join them at card games. I always refused because I sucked at cards and didn't want to ruin the evening. Tanner sometimes accepted because, as a dealer of arcane items, he might come across something valuable.

"I won a jeweled scarab beetle. Folklore says they protect against evil. It's not very magical, but we can try it." He started toward the truck.

"While you get it, I'll start looking for Loretta Nell's remains." I had to hurry. The sun now hung over the hills, blazing a deep cheese color. I sought the mantle and found it weak and tired.

I called to Orev anyway. He swooped out of one of the squat trees and landed on a boulder, head cocked, black eyes fixed on mine.

Too tired to use our telepathic connection, I spoke aloud. "There's a body buried up here. Can you find it?"

The black opal pinged at his presence but went still. The bird flew around the small clearing a few times and perched on a rock at the far edge. I walked to him, black opal heating with every step.

I stood next to the rock where Orev had perched and gasped. The ground dropped off here, providing a stunning view of the hills and the sunset. The black opal sent a shock of magic into my skin.

This was the prettiest spot on the overlook, yet we'd steered clear of it. We must have sensed the evil on the lizard level of our brains. I opened myself to Loretta Nell's spirit in hopes she'd lead me to her grave. Nothing.

It didn't surprise me. She seemed most active near the house and barn where she'd met her end. She might not have even realized where Freddy buried her. Some spirits became disassociated with their human shells almost immediately following death.

Footsteps crunched in the dry grass behind me, signaling Tanner's approach. He held out one closed hand. I cupped my palm underneath. He dropped the beetle into it.

The thing wasn't even an inch long. Made of some metal, perhaps brass, it was crafted down to the finest details. I'd have been willing to believe it was an actual beetle dipped in brass. It gave off age and experience, but was without real magic as Tanner had said.

I carefully slipped it into my pocket. "Orev says she's buried somewhere over here. I can't get a sense of her spirit."

Tanner snorted, eyes dull with scorn. "Of course not. Nothing's ever easy."

We walked, searching for a sunken spot or an area where it seemed the rocks had been removed to dig for a grave. Nothing.

Caw. Caw. Caw.

I glanced at Orev, still perched on the rock. He'd want to find somewhere to roost soon. Was he rushing me?

Caw. Caw. The bird tilted his head one way, then the other. The gist of his thoughts came. *Look at me.*

I walked toward him. He looked the same as usual. Deep black feathers, so black they seemed to absorb light. He hopped around on the rock.

What did he mean? I came closer and took my first close look at the rock. It was a big one with a long flat base and a peak where Orev had perched. I touched the rock. The black opal gave me a sharp enough shock to knock me back. My hand fell away. As it did, my fingers ran over something uneven. I leaned close. There, almost faded by wind and rain, was the shape of a crude flower.

"Tanner?" I called. "She's under this rock. Help me move it."

Tanner hurried over. We stood side to side, put our hands on the rock, and pushed, both of us grunting with effort. The thing didn't budge. Tanner walked back to his truck and came back swinging a pry bar.

"Doubt this'll work." He shoved the flat part of the bar under the rock. I put my hands next to his, and we tried to dislodge the rock. The rock moved, but not enough.

I let go of the metal and walked a few feet away, panting. "I wonder if just knowing the location'll be good enough for Mohawk?"

Tanner put his hands on his hips and shrugged. He wouldn't outright tell me no. He was too nice for that. Besides, I knew the answer.

Mohawk wanted me for breeding purposes. He'd twist things any way he could to get his way. It was up to me to outsmart him.

"Let's try again." I walked back to the rock. Tanner joined me, but with significantly less enthusiasm than the first time. We pulled and grunted. The rock lifted a little but nothing like we needed for it to get out of our way.

Priscilla Herrera appeared on the other side of the rock, smiling. "It won't be so bad when he takes you. You'll grow used to the situation quickly. Your cowardice will come in handy."

"Cowardice?" I quit pulling and rose to my feet. "How could you call me a coward?"

"You're too afraid of your natural gifts to use them to move this rock." She did something awful then. She put her hands on her hips, arched her back, and laughed at the sky. It went on and on. Finally she straightened up and settled her dark gaze on me again. "At least you'll have an heir to pass the mantle to. This one will have more ability than any of us. Of course, it'll probably also turn into a snake and crawl on its belly from time to time."

"Why are you so damn hateful?" I clenched my fists. "Can't you just tell me what to do instead of being an asshole?"

She smiled. My bravado dropped, and cold fingers

crawled up my back. Priscilla Herrera, my third-great-grandmother, rushed at me and slammed into me. The ghost knocked me onto my back. The first blow slammed into my chest and knocked my breath out of me.

"Wake up." Her scream came from inside my head and all around me. "Each step you take, each decision you make, is you creating your own destiny." She hit me in the chest again, even harder. "Stop walking as a ghost. Live in your life."

As suddenly as the attack began, it ended. Priscilla was gone. I lay staring up the sky, noting it had turned the color of blueberries cooked into pie filling.

Tanner dropped to his knees beside me, eyes big, spitting out questions faster than I could process them. "What happened? Was that Loretta Nell? Are you okay?"

"I'm okay," I managed between gasps. "That was just a visit from Priscilla Herrera."

Tanner, who knew about Priscilla, glanced around, as though she might come do something nasty to him.

I gripped one of his wrists, closing my fingers over the strong tendons, to get his attention. "I'll have to use magic to make the rock move. Orev's going to help me."

Caw. Caw. Caw. The bird put his whole body into each cry. I'd finally hit on the right answer.

Tanner pulled me to my feet. "Okay. What do I do?"

What could he do? The answer came without much effort. *Share magic with me.*

Tanner and I were connected. Our souls and our magic had touched. Whether he stayed with me forever or left sometime, the bond was here right now. Not enjoying and living in it was the stupidest, most cowardly thing I could do.

Priscilla was right. She wasn't nice, but she always had good advice. My fear of Tanner eventually hurting me had convinced me not to enjoy him as much as I could, to put up a wall so he wouldn't hurt me. The wall would eventually destroy anything we might have.

"Why do I keep doing this?" I muttered.

"Doing what?" Tanner stood a distance away watching me carefully, as though I might sprout horns.

"Shutting out people, shutting out my magic, shutting out anything that scares me. It's counterproductive." I tried to laugh. It didn't work.

Tanner took a tentative step toward me. "When the most important people in your life shit on you, you end up not trusting yourself."

I flinched at the nakedness of his assessment. He knew me. That in itself scared me. *Stop it, Peri Jean.* I shook off the weird, vulnerable feeling and held out my hand to Tanner. "Do you trust me?"

He closed the distance between us, took my hand, and nodded. "Even though you're scary."

"Okay then. We need to combine our power to make that boulder move." I glanced at the horizon. The sun had turned the color of blood. I gave Tanner's hand a squeeze. "It's going to hurt. We'll feel terrible afterward, probably have to eat and sleep to get better."

Tanner nodded. His breathing deepened. He was already putting himself into the trance state he'd need to access his magic. No questions asked. No fear. He was just going forward.

An aching, bittersweet emotion I couldn't quite describe welled in my chest. It hurt and felt good at the same time. It left me wanting, hoping I'd feel it again. This was the man and the ease I'd stumbled around looking for all this time. I kissed his cheek to thank him, even though he'd never understand quite what I felt.

I lowered my head and closed my eyes, pulling my conscious down deep inside. Sweat popped out over my body with the effort.

The mantle shone behind the thin layer of the scar tissue spell, blinding brightness escaping through cracks and holes. The spell was damaged, dying, but it still held back the majority of my power. I coaxed the mantle out through the cracks of the scar tissue. The pain receptors inside the scar tissue screamed as they stretched. I stiffened against the ache but let it come.

Wind picked up, drying the sweat on my face. The earth vibrated power beneath my feet. The magic began to work its way up my legs. Tanner's hand tightened over mine.

"It's going to be okay," I murmured, hoping I wasn't lying.

I called water, and a light mist came from the sky. Fire came by itself, from within me. It crackled though my veins and hit Tanner hard enough to make him cry out.

"The book," I said. "Call to it. Make it push the rock away."

"I can't." Tanner tried to pull away, but I tightened my grip.

"I'm going to do it too." Without warning him, I latched onto his power. Unlike my power, which glowed a blinding white, Tanner's was jewel green like his eyes. It danced like smoke, graceful and dangerous.

I pushed it out to find the spark of magic Mohawk had instilled in the book. He'd bitten me once with his snake fangs, and I knew his magic when I brushed against it. Dark purple, the magic of the book held no light whatsoever.

I let Tanner's and my power brush against the magic of the book. I teased, coaxed, and promised. The book's magic leapt after me. It would capture me, use me, the most powerful acolyte it had had in centuries. Shaking with effort, I jerked Tanner's and my magics away before that dark force latched on and claimed us. We escaped with it breathing down the backs of our necks. It grabbed for us one last time.

I raised my head, hoping the book's greed had moved the rock to get at Tanner and me. The rock raised a little. The book's darkness seeped out of the crack, searching for what I'd promised. The rock dropped back into place. A howl of rage answered the dull thump of the rock settling back into place.

Wisps of dark smoke worked their way from under the rock and crept along the ground, searching for us. Wind scattered the smoke.

The rock vibrated, and a ripping sound issued from beneath it. Tanner's hand closed around my upper arm, and he yanked me backward. The rock tipped over the same way Tanner and I had nearly given ourselves hernias trying to make it do. It rolled down the hill, picking up momentum as it went. After several dozen yards, it blended with the gray twilight.

15

———

N OT QUITE KNOWING what to expect, Tanner and I approached Loretta Nell's final resting place. I turned on my little pocket flashlight, which was almost the same as nothing, and shone it into the dark patch of earth. Pity filled me.

Loretta Nell's corpse reminded me of a small animal killed on the road and run over so many times it was flat and unrecognizable.

I tried to swallow my emotions. "Asshole Freddy didn't even bury her. He just set that rock over her."

Tanner hunched his shoulders. "But she was a pretty horrible person."

She had been, but who deserved this? I got the beetle out of my pocket and cupped it in my palm. The book lay on Loretta Nell's chest, a little dirty but perfectly recognizable by the lacy silver corner caps winking in the dying light.

I took a step forward, but hesitated, my cowardice

getting the better of me. What was going to happen when I touched this thing?

Nothing, not if you don't let it. Priscilla's voice echoed in my head. *It plays on weakness. You may be a coward, but you aren't weak.*

I steeled myself and reached for the book. The skeleton twitched. I jumped and yelped. The skull, which had a fist-sized hole in it, twisted to face me. The air cooled. Loretta Nell was here.

Hand quivering, I reached into the grave and pulled the book away from the skeleton. It made a sticky, ripping sound. My fingertips numbed with the evil it held. A clump of dirt fell from it and thumped to the ground.

Whispers, louder than any ghost I'd ever encountered, hissed in my head, their words chilling and clear as a January night. *Nobody can understand you like the god of the serpent can. He wants you to have power, love, and bounty. A sacrifice. Just one. The god of the serpent does the rest.*

The book, oversized and thick, was cumbersome. But I didn't dare put my other hand on it. If it had this much power with me holding a protective amulet, I hated to think what it would do to the unprotected hand.

The book's metal corners cut into the skin of my straining fingers. I adjusted my one-handed grip and regretted it immediately. The leather cover was pliable and warm, like living skin. I didn't want to know what kind of skin it had been made of. Didn't even want to think about it. But I did. Sweat rolled down my back and arms.

The sun winked out at the edge of the horizon, deepening the night. Coyotes howled nearby. Their crazy laughter raised the hair on the back of my neck. I turned to Tanner to tell him it was time to go, but another voice interrupted me.

"Turn around real slow, Peri Jean. Both you and your man." Dwight's voice came from behind us.

Still struggling with the book, I turned around. Dwight Carr stood in the last dregs of ambient light pointing a semi-automatic pistol at us. Josie Stephens stood next to him. She held the sickle. They both wore the same smiles the Messengers had in that creepy picture online.

Winslow and Adamick had failed to stop them after all.

I threw my head back and let out a frustrated yell. "You have to be kidding me."

Dwight would make me give them the book. Of course he would. He had Loretta Nell's revenge to carry out, and I had just filled in the last puzzle piece for him. Mohawk would be here in mere hours. And I'd be dead or a concubine because of these two stinky, greasy little turds.

Josie smiled and shrugged. "Nope. No kidding."

"Bring the book here." Dwight sharpened his voice to sound like a TV bad guy. He failed miserably. He sounded like a constipated elk.

I made my decision. I'd die here, save myself the humiliation and misery of being taken slave by Mohawk. I hardened my voice, did my best to embody King Tolliver, and said, "Come and take it."

Tanner swiveled his head to stare at me. "No! Not yet. There's still hope."

"No, there's not," I argued, glaring at Dwight. "I'm not letting go of the book. Kill me and take it."

I took a few steps toward him so he'd get a good shot. "Do it. And let Tanner go."

Tanner gaped at me several more seconds. Then his eyes narrowed, and he turned to Dwight. "Kill her, and I'm beating both of you to death."

Dwight turned the pistol on Tanner, not sure which of us to shoot.

"Just let it go," I told Tanner. "We had a good run. But you don't need to die over it. You've got a great life ahead of you. I-I—" I turned my face to him and gave into the weakness I'd been trying to stave off for at least a month now. "I love you. These weeks with you have been the best of my life. I'm sorry this is how it ends."

"It doesn't end this way," Tanner shouted.

Dwight shot in the air. "I'm killing you both. Give me the book."

"Fuck you." I stuck out my chin, pretending my heart wasn't hammering in my chest.

Tanner lunged at me, hit me hard enough to knock me to the ground. The air left my lungs in a combination *whoosh* and cry of pain. He wrestled the book away from me and slung it away from Dwight. Josie ran for it.

"Why did you do that?" I tried to say. No sound came out of me other than a pained wheeze.

Tanner grabbed me around the waist, threw me over his shoulder, and took off running. He ran like people in the movies, zigzagging back and forth. Dwight took two shots at us. Both came close enough that I felt the air move. Maybe Tanner didn't have too bad an idea with the running back and forth.

Tanner ran past Loretta Nell's grave and down the hill. He raced along as though he wasn't carrying a hundred pounds of me slung over his shoulder.

Dwight shot two more times. This time, the bullets didn't come close enough for me to feel them.

"Come on, Dwight." Josie's shout floated through the quiet night. "Forget them."

A vehicle started somewhere nearby, revved, and sped away.

Tanner kept moving until he had us behind some trees. He dumped me on the ground.

"You're heavier than you look. It's all the fried food y'all eat down here." He flopped down beside me and gasped for air, holding his side.

"Then quit saying y'all and trying to talk like us if you don't like it here," I mumbled.

Tanner chuckled and finished catching his breath. He turned to me. "Did you mean what you said up there?"

I frowned and shook my head at him. "Heat of the moment."

"Liar." He tried to lace his fingers between mine, but I jerked away.

"Why didn't you let me die up there?" I hissed at Tanner. "Mohawk's going to come in a few hours. If I don't have that book, he's going to take me into custody. Do you know what he's going to do to me?"

He let his head fall back and stared up at the starry night. "You're always putting the cart before the horse. And everything's so full of doom and gloom. How do you know we can't get the book back between now and then?"

I rose to my knees. "Once the power of that book gets in Dwight and Josie, how easy do you think it's going to be to best them?"

Tanner held both hands up. "We'll figure something out."

I ignored him and crawled to my feet. My ribs hurt where Tanner had hurled me to the ground, and I still smelled him on me. Made me want to kick him. My phone buzzed with a text message.

It would probably be Hannah or Finn and Dillon saying they were coming to the rescue. Then I'd have to worry about everybody I knew dying in a misguided attempt to help me. I dragged the phone out of my pocket.

The message was from an unknown number. "Linus Bramwell here. Please call."

My phone had one bar of service showing. It flickered off and changed to no service. I let out a disgusted snort and started walking.

Tanner leapt to his feet. "Where're you going?"

"To get the book back." I stomped back up the hill, madder than I'd been in a long while.

Tanner ran past me and stopped at the top of the hill with a sad moan. I hurried to his side. We gaped at his old truck together. It sat on four flat tires. The hood was open, pieces of the engine strewn on the ground.

"You should've let him shoot me," I muttered.

"Oh, come on. You can't be blaming me for this," Tanner shouted.

I didn't, not really. But the frustration of this whole fiasco had come home to roost. I wanted to have a meltdown, fall on my knees, and scream. Tanner was an easy scapegoat.

I finally shook my head at him. "We'll have to walk back to town. And once we get there, I don't know what we're going to drive. My truck's in a parking garage in Austin."

Tanner put his hands on his hips and leaned his head back. His angry posture. A rush of love for this man hit me hard.

I rubbed one hand over his flat stomach. "It's gonna be okay, sugar." I said the words saccharine sweet with just the right little twist of smartass.

Tanner dropped his arm and stared at me, eyes narrowed. One corner of his mouth twitched. I knew what was coming and tried to run, but I had smoked for fifteen solid years. I didn't get far.

He grabbed me around the waist and swung me, yelling, "What did you just say to me?"

I laughed and played along with him. It didn't hurt a thing to enjoy my last few hours on earth. We got everything that was valuable out of Tanner's truck and walked off the Stephens Ranch together. We found the road back to Devil's Rest and walked down its empty middle.

My phone buzzed again. I pulled my hand from Tanner's, checked it, and found not only three bars of service, but another message from Linus Bramwell.

"Dwight Carr is the son of Shawn Grimes, the grandson of Loretta Nell Grimes. He's broken Josie out of the mental hospital."

Linus didn't realize I'd recognized Dwight as soon as I

got the picture. I'd been too focused on stopping Dwight to call him back.

I thumb-typed a quick message. "They already found us and took the book."

Tanner and I started walking again. My phone rang. I answered on speakerphone. "Linus?"

His panicked voice crackled over the line. "Are you and your young man all right?"

"We're both fine," Tanner answered.

"You say those two crazies got the book from you?" Linus was practically shouting.

"Yep. We're walking back to Devil's Rest to try to stop them." Flashes of the vision where Loretta Nell made the church group turn on each other flashed. That's what Josie and Dwight would try to do. I had to stop them. Just the thought of the battle ahead made my bones ache.

"How did you know Dwight had broken Josie out of the mental hospital?" I asked.

Linus spoke so fast his words sounded like another language. "I've a contact at the mental hospital. An orderly named Winslow."

I closed my eyes. Of course. Winslow was an enterprising kind of guy. He'd make himself available to whoever had money.

"Winslow says that Josie and Dwight killed a man named Adamick and a nurse named Fitch. Dwight and Josie were screaming 'In his name' at the time of the murders."

All the spit in my mouth went dry.

Linus kept talking in my silence. "You know that I write

about the occult. This book you're trying to get your hands on operates on sacrifice. The more sacrifices, the stronger the bond between the person and the book. You've got to find a way to break that bond."

Headlights peeked over the horizon.

I spoke quickly, ready to end the call. "Linus, I'm going to do everything I can to stop them..."

"Just a minute," he cut in. "Breaking the bond will take...consuming the..."

The phone beeped as the call dropped. I stared at the screen. It read "Call failure."

I thought I had heard Linus say the word "consuming." Was I supposed to eat the book? If that's what it took, I'd do it. But it sure would be a hard meal to swallow.

The headlights were closer now, and the driver had slowed. I shoved the phone back into my pocket and turned to face the next few minutes of my life.

———

THE TRUCK'S headlights turned the world white. I threw up one hand to shield my eyes.

"Run," I yelled at Tanner. Before he could protest, I waved my arms over my head. Tanner glared at me for a second and then did the same. I wanted to kick him in the ass but was too tired.

The truck rolled to a stop. Roderick leaned across the seat and opened the door, activating the dome light.

Before he spoke, I had a second to feel relief. *Where did that come from?* The encounter a few months earlier with the hag that almost killed Hannah had left me not really caring if I lived or died. It had been liberating. I glanced at Tanner. He was the reason for my change of heart. I didn't know how to feel about that.

Roderick was talking, his voice high with panic. "Seen your truck drive through Devil's Rest. Then you never came back. Thought you two were dead or hurt." He took a good look at us and made a face. "You are hurt. What happened?"

I saw no reason to lie. "Dwight Carr came for the book. Tried to kill us. Maimed Tanner's truck." The rest was too complicated to explain.

Roderick nodded slowly. "Well, let's go get that book. He don't have no more right to it than you."

I wasn't so sure about that, but we needed a ride. Tanner and I barely got the truck's door closed before Roderick took off, burning rubber. Tanner and I had been walking almost forty-five minutes. Not five minutes later, the Devil's Slumber Inn sign flashed in the darkness. A crookedly parked car sat in front of the motel office. Maybe we'd caught Dwight after all.

"Stop off here." I tapped Roderick's arm.

He gave me an odd look but did as I said.

We crept through the broken door and into the office. The sign outside lit the room in flashes. Unless Dwight and Josie were hiding underneath the counter, we were alone. We hurried down the narrow hallway to Dwight's little apartment.

The only light in the room came from the screensaver on his laptop. I tapped a few keys to wake it up. A spreadsheet appeared on the screen. Those email addresses again. I didn't get it. Roderick came to stand behind me, watching me scroll through the addresses.

"There's my email right there." He pointed.

I scrolled some more, amazed at the number. There had to be at least a thousand addresses here.

"I think this is everybody in town, or damn near." Roderick's hand hovered over the keyboard. "You mind?"

I passed the laptop to him. "Be my guest."

He scrolled for several long seconds. When he spoke, anger laced his words. "So that's what he was up to. Damn it, Mandy."

"Pardon?" Tanner stood a safe distance from Roderick, body tensed as though he was waiting for anything.

"See, Mandy's real taken in by Dwight Carr. Does all kinds of things for him she shouldn't. This is one of those things." Roderick's nostrils flared.

I'd play, even though I didn't really want to know at this point. "Like what?"

"The Devil's Rest Library is run by the City of Devil's Rest. So Mandy used her access to their computer system to get every single email address they had." Roderick glared at the laptop as though he'd like to throw it.

Tanner made a face. "Why emails?"

Roderick shook his head as he delivered his rant. "Dwight said he wanted to send out a mass mailing about being nicer to people coming to town curious about the Messengers."

Dwight's plan fell into place. I moved toward the laptop. "Excuse me." I practically pushed Roderick out of my way. He went willingly enough. I minimized the spreadsheet program. Open on the screen was a service for mass emails. There'd only been one email sent.

I got so lightheaded I had to sit down on Dwight's couch. The squeak seemed loud.

"What is it?" Roderick leaned over my shoulder.

I opened the email Dwight had sent to everybody in Devil's Rest. The email contained no text, only five pictures of pages from an open book. I couldn't see the gross leather cover or the silver corner caps, but I didn't need to. The images couldn't have come from anywhere but Mohawk's book.

I didn't want to look at the pages, was afraid of what they'd awake in me, but I couldn't help myself. Each page had a few symbols on it. Nothing I knew the meaning of offhand. But these symbols tapped at my lizard brain, trying to coax my fury back to full flame.

My mind supplied ideas of the ways I could kill both Roderick and Tanner and use their blood to paint those symbols on the walls of this room. I hit the off button on the laptop and pushed it aside.

Roderick stood staring with glazed eyes. Faster than I'd have thought him capable of moving, he snatched a metal ruler off the desk and came at me with it.

"In his name," Roderick screamed.

I jumped up and shoved the rolling chair into Roderick. It didn't faze him. Tanner hit him from behind, knocking him to the floor. The expression on Roderick's face never changed from dazed madness. I stomped on the hand holding the metal ruler. Roderick didn't react.

"Do it again," Tanner yelled.

I didn't want to hurt Roderick. He'd been nice to us, and I liked him. But I did as Tanner said, bringing the hard sole of my cowboy boot down on the back of Roderick's hand. I felt and heard the bone snap.

Roderick let out an agonized scream. Bile shot up the back of my throat, followed closely by sour, hateful guilt. Roderick stopped screaming and began to flail, trying to escape Tanner's grip. Tanner grunted with the effort of keep Roderick in check.

I left them and ran around the room, looking for a way to restrain Roderick. But few people have handcuffs or lengths of rope lying around. I found a supply closet and ran back to Tanner.

"Let's get him in that closet over there." Without waiting for his answer, I began to tug on Roderick. He snapped at my hand, the click of his teeth somehow more horrifying than his attempt to kill me with the metal ruler.

Tanner helped me haul Roderick to his feet. He kicked and jerked in our grips. I lost my patience and slapped him across the face.

"Snap out of it. Let it go, or it'll kill you," I yelled.

Roderick's eyes lost some of their maniacal shine. He struggled again, and I slapped him again.

"Stop it." I spoke the same way I sometimes spoke to members of Sanctuary. "Stop it, or we're going to lock you in that closet. It's over. Let it go."

Roderick relaxed in our grip, but neither of us released him. The older man stood panting, his shoulders slumped.

"It'll all right. I'm done." His voice didn't sound like a

madman's, but I'd been fooled too many times in the last few days to trust anybody. I kept my grip on Roderick's arm. He said, "You can let go. I won't attack you again. I'm so sorry I did that." The remorse in his voice convinced me. I let go.

"If Dwight sent those images to everybody in town..." I didn't want to think about what it meant, not after what we'd just been through with Roderick.

Roderick cradled his broken hand. "Mandy. She checks her email twenty-four hours a day. I've got to go see if I can help her."

"And we have to get that book from Dwight." Tanner checked the time on his phone. "And you've only got a few hours before Mohawk comes for you."

Roderick glanced between us. "What are you two really up to?"

I shook my head at him. "You don't want to know. Give us a ride to town?"

To my surprise, Roderick agreed. We stowed the valuables we'd taken from Tanner's ruined truck in Dwight's apartment. We'd either be alive to come back for them or not. Roderick drove us the last few miles to Devil's Rest.

On the outskirts of town, we passed the first row of burning houses. One of them had someone hanging from a cross out front. My stomach sank. We were too late to help anybody.

16

FLAMES BELCHED from the windows of houses. Doors hung open. A small, still form lay on one of the lawns, fine blond hair blowing in the night breeze. One of her little shoes had fallen off a few feet from her.

Cars sat with open hoods, flat tires, and broken windows. Flames licked at a few. Human forms sat slumped over in more than one.

Roderick passed it all, face grim and still.

Something didn't add up. This kind of carnage had taken time to get rolling. Some of the cars had finished burning and sat smoking. How had Roderick bypassed getting caught up in it? I put my hand on Tanner's leg to signal him. He slipped his arm over my shoulders. Otherwise, I kept as still as I could.

"This wasn't going on when you left town?" I asked Roderick.

He stared at the road ahead, seeming not to see the ruined town. We had reached the edge of the downtown area. He spoke without looking at us. "Dwight said if I brought you two back, he'd give me Mandy and let us leave town."

The passenger side door clunked open. Tanner jumped out of the truck and dragged me with him. We hit the ground hard. Pain flashed in my elbow as it connected with the pavement, the hard packed surface shearing off a layer of flesh. Tanner dragged me to my feet.

"Hey!" Roderick slammed on the brakes. He clambered out of the truck and barreled around it.

Tanner and I ran, hands clasped. We cut between two buildings. Roderick's footsteps pounded behind us for a couple hundred yards. Then he yelped in surprise. The sound of a body hitting the ground came out of the darkness. Roderick began to scream in earnest.

"No, no, no." His words struck pity in my heart. He'd not been a bad man. Just one who loved his family enough to do whatever it took to save them. I understood that. Roderick's screams cut off abruptly.

Tanner and I ran until we found ourselves in the parking lot of a dentist's office. I put my hands on my knees and tried to catch my breath.

"I'm gonna quit smoking," I gasped.

"No, you're not." Tanner stood next to me, panting but not as hard as me.

Little by little, the stitch in my side eased. I stood up straight. Something rattled nearby. I jerked to attention and tried to place the noise. It sounded like a raccoon raiding a trash can. But I couldn't dismiss it. Not tonight. I stared into the darkness, willing my eyes to adjust.

They soon did. A shadow stood next to the dentist's office, swinging one arm. The arm passed the trash can, and it rattled. My eyes adjusted a little more. The whites of the person's eyes shone in the darkness. Their lips split in a smile, and their white teeth glowed in the dark.

"Let's go." I started backing up.

The person standing in the darkness let out a wild scream and raced at us, knife held aloft in the arm they'd been swinging against the trash can. I didn't have time to move. Tanner took one step toward the knife-wielding maniac. His fist moved so fast I couldn't see what he did.

The woman sprawled forward, taking big steps, trying to regain her balance. She stepped in a pothole and went down. She somehow landed on the knife, stabbing herself in the chest, right underneath the ribcage. I expected screams. They didn't come.

The woman reached across her chest and pulled on the knife. It came out with a sucking sound. She slowly got to her feet and came toward us, holding the knife out again. Tanner and I both backed away, too stunned to run.

The woman shambled toward us, each step less graceful than the last. Her bladder let go. Urine slashed the pavement. She dropped to her knees, eyes still wide and wild, and tossed the knife at us.

"In his name." With those guttural words came a line of slobber and blood. She shuddered and fell forward.

I backed away from the dead lady, not wanting to meet her ghost. Tanner stood rooted to the spot. I went back and took his hand.

"We gotta go." I gave him a light tug.

Tanner turned to me, mouth open. Nobody had to tell me the scene had been too much for him. "She was probably a nice person."

"I know." I gave him another tug.

He pressed his lips together. Tanner knew how to whip the ass of a person, but he also hurt deep for them. Usually it touched me. Tonight it scared me because any hesitation could get us killed.

The sound of a vehicle approaching came from the darkness. That snapped Tanner out of his gloom. We hurried to hide in the pocket of shadow on the porch in front of the dentist's office.

A convertible rolled into sight. Two young men sat in the front seat, and two young women sat with their feet on the backseats and their behinds on the trunk of the car. They saw the dead woman and rolled to a stop. The boy in the passenger seat pulled out a pistol and fired several rounds into her dead body, then a couple more at the dark sky. They drove away howling like coyotes.

The hair stood up on the back of my neck. Tanner shivered next to me. In the distance, a voice came over a loudspeaker. Though I couldn't understand the words, the speaker's cadence reminded me of the fiery sermons Memaw had dragged me to when I was a kid. And I knew the voice.

"Dwight." I started walking toward the sound. Tanner walked behind me, saying nothing. I stuck my hand in my pocket to make sure the snub-nosed pistol Hannah had loaned me was still there. It might not work on Mohawk, but it would damn sure work on Dwight and Josie. If I could hit them.

Tanner jogged a few steps and fell in beside me. I let go of some of the gloom to smile at him. Horror raged around us, but we still had a smile for each other. I was glad I'd picked this man. And that he'd returned my feelings.

If I died, I'd lose something I really liked: Tanner. Tonight would have been easier if we'd never met. I shook off the thought. We had met. We'd met, fallen in love, and now I was angry that I might not get to see how things played out.

Then there was my family and Sanctuary. Sure I had a lot of duty there, but I'd chosen it. If I died, I'd miss so many things.

The truth was out. I didn't want to die tonight. And I wouldn't let Mohawk take me. I'd have to do whatever it took to get out of here alive and with my freedom. All this time I'd looked for the book, I'd thought I was doing everything I could. But I wasn't. I needed to live out loud.

I hadn't used every bit of my power to battle Loretta Nell's ghost. She'd caught me by surprise the first time. But I should have been ready for her when we'd encountered each other in the mental hospital. She was just a nasty old ghost, not even a true chthonic being like Mohawk.

And Dwight. I should have fried his brain back at the Stephens Ranch, no matter how tired I was. He was a worthless person. Whatever he'd done to turn the citizens of Devil's Rest into lunatics proved that.

Tanner and I reached downtown. Neither of us could

speak for several seconds. The sight in front of us was just too much.

Not ten feet from me, a woman beat a man with a golf club. His head had a dent in it, and blood was spreading in a pool around his body. But she kept right on swinging, hollering, "In his name, rise."

Rise. That was different. The rest had just been saying "In his name." Where had the "rise" come from?

On the street, one of the boys from the car who'd passed by the dentist's office chased one of the girls. He was laughing. She wasn't.

Tanner yelled, "Hey!"

I elbowed him as hard as I could. He took it with a pained *umph.*

"Don't get their attention," I said in a low voice. "Let's find Dwight, get the book, and stop them then."

That satisfied Tanner enough to get him moving. We walked in the direction of Dwight's preaching. The highs and lows were really no different than what I'd heard in the churches of my youth. But his words were.

"You feel the Serpent God's spirit. Let it take you. Let it use you," Dwight's magnified voice boomed. "Look upon the man next to you. Has he sinned against you? Then you deserve to avenge it."

Dwight said a string of words in another language, his voice guttural. The spark of rage from back at the Stephens Ranch woke up and burned bright. Mohawk's voice whispered in the back of my mind. I pushed it away.

All around us, the citizens of Devil's Rest did the opposite. They tore the flesh of their neighbors and family, broke the bones of people they'd known all their lives. They did it yelling, "Rise," calling the Serpent God to power in Devil's Rest. Their eyes shone with animal insanity.

Tanner and I moved underneath the awning of the buildings, our steps as swift and silent as we could make them. Dwight's voice got louder and louder until my eardrums rattled. We found him standing in the bed of a truck behind a wooden podium. The book was open in front of him, a portable PA system piled around his feet. Josie Stephens sat on the cab of the truck, swinging her legs in time with Dwight's shouts.

He yelled into a microphone, "The Serpent God rewards those who sacrifice to him. Those who survive this night will live like royalty. The Serpent God will bless us and keep us. So sacrifice, sacrifice for him."

Bloodcurdling screams rose over Dwight's commands. I stepped into a doorway and pulled Tanner with me.

"What is it?" His breath tickled on my face.

"I need to see what I'm up against." The heat coming off Tanner's body turned me on, despite the awful scene in front of us. I wanted to spend the night in his arms, not dead. That meant giving it all I had, not living like a ghost in my own life.

I settled my gaze on Dwight and opened my second sight. Loretta Nell moved just underneath his skin. I focused on Josie and saw the same thing. Loretta Nell's ghost was in two places at once. How could that be? It didn't matter. All that mattered was getting the book away from those two freaks, killing them if that's what it took.

Evil emanated from the book like an egg salad fart. But I felt more than just evil baking off the leather cover and pages. Power surrounded the book and its current owners. Loretta Nell's body had protected the book all these years. She'd formed a relationship with the power in it. Now that power belonged to her ghost.

"Spill blood," Loretta Nell screamed in Dwight's voice. "Spill blood in his name, and he will rise in this town."

A chorus of screams started up and quickly cut off. The hair on the back of my neck bristled. I had to put a stop to this.

I called to the mantle. Orev's caws came from nearby. He'd probably perched on top of a building. His presence met mine. Though ready to help, he was almost as scared as I was.

The wind on the street picked up, spraying grains of sand on all the revelers and murderers. Now or never. I stepped out from the doorway and walked toward Dwight, gathering power as I went.

Tanner walked with me, one hand in his pocket. I understood now I couldn't keep him away no matter how hard I tried. He had a right to choose his fate as much as I did. The two of us marched into the middle of the street in lockstep.

The city fountain stopped flowing as I passed. The water boiled and steamed. Earth magic came up through the concrete. My steps rang as loud as a giant's might have.

Dwight stopped talking and smiled. Loretta Nell's spirit flashed over his face.

"Hi, Dwight." I spoke as though we were at a church

service. Calm and sweet. Just one member of the flock greeting the other.

"Peri Jean. I see Roderick failed at his task." His lips pulled down in a mock scowl.

"So what? You killed Mandy anyway," I sneered. Thunder rumbled in the distance, as though agreeing with my accusation.

Dwight's smile broadened. He bent at the knees, grabbed something out of the bed of the truck, and held up Mandy's severed head. She'd died screaming. He lobbed the head at me. Josie shrieked with laughter and clapped her dainty hands.

Tanner let out a repulsed yell, but I focused on not letting the head hit me. Human heads were heavy. It would hurt. The head slapped on the pavement and rolled underneath an abandoned car.

I stepped back in front of the podium. "Give me the book, Dwight." I held out one hand.

He made a pouty face and shook his head. Josie gave me double fuck-you fingers behind him. I wanted to send it back but figured I could be adult about this.

"Loretta Nell's making you feel all pumped up like you're getting revenge for her. But this isn't some movie. The cops are eventually going to show, and you're going to die." I held out my hand for the book again.

Dwight gave me the finger and went back to preaching, Loretta Nell roiling behind his face.

Fine. We'd do this the hard way. I drew on the waiting power I'd built up, pulling magic from everything around me, including Tanner. The power built until my eyesight changed into what I called LSD-vision. Everything came to life.

I called fire. It flamed bright inside me, powered by all the other elements. I aimed it at Dwight and let it fly. The young man jittered as though he'd picked up an electrical wire, his arms flung out from his sides. I kept pushing power, expecting his eyeballs to burst or his skin to melt. Instead, Dwight began to laugh. Loretta Nell's mad howl mixed in with his laughter.

I quit pushing my power at Dwight. It wasn't hurting him. It was only tiring me out. But why?

My only guess was that Loretta Nell's power and the book's power outranked me. Fine, then. What now? My body still trembled from the wasted effort. One more good blast, and I was done. I'd better make it worth it.

Dwight picked up the book off the podium, walked to the edge of the truck bed, and knelt down. He crooked one finger for me to come closer. I did but stayed out of reach, hand on Hannah's gun.

Dwight fixed knowing eyes on me and spoke in a low voice. "The Serpent God wants me to deliver a message to you. You ready?"

Sweat broke out on my forehead.

"The Serpent God says there's no way for you to win this and that he'll be along to collect you directly." Dwight rose and walked back to the podium.

How I wanted to bite him and claw out his eyes. But jumping him wouldn't get me anywhere. Right then, Dwight, Josie, and Loretta Nell created a triumvirate of evil I couldn't whip.

My fingers caressed the pistol. The idea of whipping it out and pulling the trigger flashed in my mind over and over. Two things kept me from it. One, I was no longer sure the pistol would kill Dwight or Josie. Not after my magic failed to do the job. Two, I still had to face Mohawk.

My magic still seemed the best solution. But I needed to quit farting around and bring out the serious firepower. My problem? I had no idea what to do with it. One glance around me indicated I was going to have to figure it out. And fast.

———

I STOOD on the street like a moron while Dwight went back to convincing the townspeople of Devil's Rest to do horrible things to each other. He ignored me as though I was no more important than a fly. In his current state, I suppose I carried about the same threat.

Suddenly I understood what Linus Bramwell had meant about breaking the bond between the book and its users. It would level the playing field.

I leaned to speak in Tanner's ear. "I've got to banish Loretta Nell."

As though he'd heard me, Dwight stopped speaking and glared down at me. "Leave now, Peri Jean. You're under the protection of the god of the serpent. But Tanner there?" His smile chilled me. "At my word, these people will fall on him like a pack of wild dogs." Loretta Nell's voice blended with Dwight's, gave it a demonic burbling effect.

The corpses littering the sidewalks and the streets

came into focus, their glazed eyes seeming to stare right at me. Dwight wasn't lying. The same folks who killed them would tear Tanner to bits in a matter of seconds. All my bravery dropped to my feet where it puddled and cooled.

A cold hand pressed against my back. Priscilla Herrera's voice whispered in my head. *Ignore your fear. Think of all you win if you fight.*

Tanner faced Dwight with his fists clenched, not willing to back down even with the threat of Dwight siccing the crazies of Devil's Rest on him. He was here for me, willing to face this horror right alongside me.

Someone that brave deserved bravery in return. I pulled myself together.

There had to be a way to catch Dwight off guard. I grabbed Tanner's hand and started to back away. He resisted, but I caught his eye and shook my head. We walked away. Once we passed Dwight, I called on the mantle and on Orev. He'd have to help me pull Loretta Nell out of Dwight, Josie, and the book.

I'd already called the elements. They were ready to help me. I used my physical connection to Tanner to pull on his magic, letting its warm energy seep through me. Still walking away from Dwight, I took a deep breath and spoke a banishing incantation I'd created on the spot.

I said in a low voice,

"Loretta Nell Grimes,

from the living plane I banish thee,

Loretta Nell Grimes,

With the power of North, West, South, and East

I banish thee,

Loretta Nell Grimes,
With the power of above and the power below
You must go."

Behind me, Dwight stopped his chanting to kill, kill, kill and said, "Peri Jean Mace, are we not finished playing yet?"

I turned around. Dwight leapt onto the truck's cab, climbed over it, walked down the hood, and hopped to the pavement in front of me. Josie came right behind him. Both stalked toward me.

Were they really going to make it this easy? The closer they got, the more power I could direct at them. I called to Orev.

The bird swooped down from whatever rooftop he'd been perched on and landed on Dwight's head, digging in his claws. Dwight screamed and danced, grabbing for the bird's legs. Orev's wings flapped. I sent my magic out to the bird, and we connected.

Through the bird's primitive mind, I saw Loretta Nell's spirit within Dwight. I grabbed onto her and pulled as hard as I could.

Loretta Nell dug in deep, summoning the power of the book she'd managed to absorb. Dwight threw his head back and screamed, the whites of his eyes blooming red as the blood vessels inside exploded.

I sunk my claws, Orev's claws, deeper into Loretta Nell and kept pulling. My body began to shake with the effort. I ignored the pain and kept on without care for what it did to Dwight's body or mind. I just pulled with all I had.

A burst of Tanner's power warmed me, replenishing

me. I gave one last hard yank. Loretta Nell came out of the top of Dwight's head, exploding it as neatly as a shotgun blast. Dwight's body slumped and thumped to the pavement. The smell of fresh sewage hit me.

Intent on survival, Loretta Nell wiggled away from me and snapped her full presence into Josie. The girl-woman jolted, body stiffening as though caught in the throes of an explosive orgasm. She shook from head to toe as the spirit absorbed.

I hurried toward her, Orev cawing right behind me. Josie recovered and raced for the truck, slipping in the gore from Dwight's exploded head. I stayed right on her heels and caught her as she tried to vault onto the truck's hood. She flipped over and clawed at me, snarling like an animal.

She dug her fingers into my neck. "Now it's time for you to die. Your only true purpose was to find the book. I'm the Serpent God's favorite daughter." She spoke through bared teeth, flecks of spittle flying into my face.

I reared back and hit her in the mouth. Blood spurted onto her teeth.

On the other side of the truck, the screams ceased. In their place rose a chant. "Holy, holy, holy."

"Holy fuck is more like it," Tanner muttered.

Josie-Loretta Nell let go of me and hurried to see what had changed her acolytes' focus so quickly. She scrambled back onto the truck to see over their heads. I followed and immediately wished I had stayed ignorant.

The biggest, whitest snake I'd ever seen slithered down the middle of the street. Easily the length of a car and the girth of a tree, the snake's belly made a rasping sound on the pavement. People knelt on either side of the street and salaamed it. Tongue flicking, woody brown eyes fixed on me, the snake came right for us. As Dwight had promised, the Serpent God was coming for me.

Fear crowded out all rational thought and ate the little bit of courage I possessed with relish. The primitive part of my brain blared one message, *run, run, run.*

But it wouldn't do me any good to run. Not now. Mohawk was right here, more powerful than I'd ever be. He'd catch me with no effort at all.

The snake morphed into the shape of a human man as it came. Mohawk ran the last few steps to the bed of the truck where Dwight had been preaching.

"I ssssee you killed one of my disciples." He showed me his snake fangs.

Josie-Loretta Nell grabbed the book and held it against her chest, eyes glittering, lips stretched into a crazy grin.

Shaking head to toe, I pointed at the book. "Here's your book. I retrieved it for you."

Mohawk laughed so hard the punk chains on his leather jacket clinked. "Yes, you did what I wanted. You found the book. You did this." He swept his arms wide. "But you don't possess the book. I ordered you to possess the book. Loretta Nell Grimes, through the body of Josie Stephens, still possesses the book. Your freedom is forfeit."

Tanner and I huddled together. I don't know which of us shook harder. Dizziness filled my head, cool and light. Black dots danced in my vision.

"No," I managed to whisper. "I got the book. I dug it up. I found it. That's what you said."

Mohawk glided closer. "When I gave you this task, I knew you would fail. Loretta Nell's spirit and the book's power are fused together. You cannot possess the book. Therefore, I'll possess you."

The pieces clicked together, each one making me a little sicker. Mohawk had had a plan from the first second he gave me seventy-two hours to go on this wild goose chase.

Dwight and Josie were primed and ready to use the book to drive the town of Devil's Rest right into apocalypse. Aaron Todd had the key to open the book. All I had to do was locate Loretta Nell's body and get the book out of the ground. And I had done it.

I slipped my hand into my pocket and pulled out the little pistol Hannah had loaned me. This was it. Faced with human slavery, I'd rather die.

Tanner put his arm around me. His body trembled against mine. I let him see the pistol. He nodded. We'd die together. I put the gun to my temple and placed my finger through the trigger guard.

"Oh for Pete's sake." Mohawk flicked his fingers. The gun pulled out of my grip and flew toward him. "You can't think it would be that easy. Do you?" He flashed his snake fangs again.

Josie-Loretta Nell pealed a victory whoop, followed by a volley of mad cackles.

Through the fear, a little embarrassment sparked. Actually, I had thought it would be that easy. Fury chased the sharp shot of embarrassment. This sucked. Mohawk had tricked me, made me complicit in the deaths of

Aaron Todd and a bunch of other innocent people. How dare he?

The answer came right away. He didn't dare. He just did. He had the power to take, and so he did. Josie's hoarse laughter cut off like a switch flipped.

"You should've just let her kill herself, your majesty. You don't need her to sire your offspring. I am your favorite daughter." Josie threw back her shoulders and arched her back. The posturing would have been funny had Loretta Nell's face not been rippling right beneath the surface of Josie's, driving her laughter and foolish actions.

Mohawk's eyes grew wide. Energy crackled around him. "Things will go the way I say they will and no other way. If you want to continue as the high priestess of my message, you will obey me without question."

Mohawk's voice boomed off the buildings and echoed in the black pit of this night. Every voice stilled at its command, even Josie-Loretta Nell. Bottom lip juiced out in a pout, she nodded.

Mohawk smiled, showing his snake fangs, and crooned, "That's my favorite daughter. Such a good girl."

Josie-Loretta Nell threw me a smirk of triumph.

I wanted to kill her. Everybody won tonight, except me. It sucked, and it made me furious, but I had to face the truth. I had lost.

The human mind is a torture device unlike any other. Mine went to work, making a chronicle of how things would go.

Mohawk wanted to sire a halfling with me. In my current state, I couldn't conceive. After my miscarriage, I hadn't gone to the doctor and had developed an infection. It had rendered me infertile.

Mohawk would have me supernaturally healed. Then he'd do things to me. Horrible things that would chip away at my sanity. In the end, I'd probably be a giggling mess just like Josie-Loretta Nell.

I wanted to put my hands over my face and scream. Everything I'd endured, everything I'd learned. All of it was rendered worthless tonight.

Tanner squeezed my hand and whispered, "It's going to be okay. No matter what, it's going to be okay."

I squeezed back but spoke to Mohawk. "Let Tanner go. Let him walk out of here."

Mohawk threw his head back and laughed. He turned his back to me and spoke to the people kneeling behind him. "Fetch some nails and wood to make a cross. Large nails."

The rumble of a few hundred bodies going into motion, all eager to please the Serpent God, killed the quiet.

"I can't let Tanner go," Mohawk said. "For one thing, he knows too much about all this. For another, we'll need a sacrifice to allow Loretta Nell to become Josie."

"You can't," I breathed.

"Oh, I ca-an," Mohawk sang. "I'm boss motherfucker right here and now. I'll do whatever works."

He was right. Nobody could stop him. I turned to Tanner. "Run!"

He shook his head. "I was dead from the time I lost my

wife and daughters until I met you. You saved me. I won't leave you to face this alone."

I opened my mouth to scream at him, to call him names, to hurt him so he'd leave. But Mohawk motioned at Tanner, and three burly members of his fellowship surrounded us.

Tanner stood his ground until one got close. He snapped two fast punches into the guy's nose. The crunch of it breaking set the other two into motion. One of the other guys, who probably outweighed Tanner by a hundred pounds, jumped onto his back.

"Fucker," I screamed, pounding at his ribs.

My punches had no effect on the big man, so I bit his arm. The final guy clubbed me in the back. The force of the blow knocked me on the ground. I fell on my injured knee. Pain shot through my entire body, a bolt of lightning shearing away rational thought. I lay there panting, able to do nothing more than watch. One of the men kicked Tanner's legs out from under him. Tanner fell to the ground with a pained grunt.

We stared at each other, beaten, both of us facing the end of the road. A tear spilled out of one eye and rolled down my cheek.

"I love you," I mouthed at Tanner.

He pressed his lips together, eyes shining as tears filled them. He nodded as one tracked down his face.

"How sweet," Mohawk crooned.

"Shut up, you stinky old pussy fart," I shouted, acting a lot braver than I felt.

They dragged Tanner away. I scrabbled after them,

determined to fight some more. Mohawk appeared in my face, more snake than human.

"Stop it, or I'll have them pull him limb from limb right now." He backed me onto the bed of the truck and made me sit on its edge, not far from Josie-Loretta Nell. He climbed on the truck's bed to face his favorite daughter. With one long-fingered hand, he caressed the girl's face. She smiled up at him. He kissed her mouth. "Only a little longer, my beauty. You'll be restored to your former glory."

I winced at the idea of Loretta Nell back in any kind of power. She'd been crazy in life, even crazier in death.

"I know what you're thinking." Mohawk tapped his temple. "Loretta Nell's too insane. Things'll just blow up for her again. But she learned from the first time, didn't you, pet?"

Josie-Loretta Nell nodded. Mohawk kissed her cheek. His snake tongue flicked against her skin.

I turned away, stomach tossing. To hell with them. They were all crazy. I needed to focus on a way to get Tanner out of this. One of us needed to survive this night.

Something moved next to Josie-Loretta Nell. My father's ghost came into view. I startled. I'd seen very little of him since the night he'd helped me defeat the Coach-man. Daddy put one finger to his lips.

Shhhhh. His soft whisper filled my head. *You don't have much time, baby, and neither do I, so listen close. You have power over the spirits. Use that to turn the monster's power against him.*

A commotion rose. Some of Mohawk's new followers had raided the hardware store and stolen cross ties and a nail gun. Now they nailed the thick beams to a wood base and began constructing a cross on which to crucify Tanner.

My sweetie's eyes had grown big. He'd die a horrible death tonight if I didn't do something to stop it. I glanced back at my daddy, looking for clarification of what he'd told me to do.

He was fading but gave me a smile before he winked out of existence. I didn't know what Daddy had meant about using Mohawk's power against him, but I had my own idea.

If I pulled Loretta Nell out of Josie and broke her connection to the book, nobody would own it. Then I could possess it, and Mohawk would have to admit I'd won. I began to make plans.

17

———

THE CONSTRUCTION of the crucifix halted when two of the carpenters got into an argument. One of them shot the other in the eye with the nail gun, which resulted in another crazy trying to get the nail gun away from the first one.

Mohawk stood over them, a beatific smile on his face, paying no attention at all to me.

This was my chance. I opened my second sight and studied Josie. Loretta Nell's ghost wore her like a living garment. But her hold was tenuous. She couldn't quit glancing at me, hating me for being something she wasn't. I could do this.

Orev let out an encouraging caw from nearby. He knew what I had planned and would help in any way he could.

I went deep into myself where all the magic hid, dropped all clutter from my mind, and concentrated on my lungs inflating and deflating. Then I focused on my third eye. It opened and streamed bright light on Josie. It

316

showed me exactly where Josie ended and Loretta Nell began. Even better, it showed me the crackle of jealousy over Mohawk's desire for me that weakened her hold on Josie. My black opal heated, and the smell of my own burning flesh reached my nostrils.

"Loretta Nell." I spoke in a low voice, hoping not to distract Mohawk from his orgy of carnage.

She half turned and bared Josie's small teeth in a sneer.

"How does it feel for every important man in your life to betray you?" I plowed on, not giving her a chance to answer. "I mean, we're not just talking about Freddy Stephens. The Serpent God, the being you gave up your life to follow, picked another woman over you. How do you pick up your dignity after that?"

A low growl came from her, increasing in volume by the second. The hair on the back of my neck bristled, one animal ready to fight another, but I ignored it and used my third eye to watch Loretta Nell's connection to Josie. The second it was at its weakest, I fashioned my hand into a claw, drawing on Orev's power as a guider of souls, and reached into Josie.

Loretta Nell let out a furious howl. She frantically tried to regain her hold on Josie, but it was too late. I grabbed on to her and pulled, the same way I had with Dwight. She had a lot of power because of the book, but I dug in, determined to be brave.

Loretta Nell whipped around like a snake, writhing to throw me off. I held on for all I was worth and began to drag her out of Josie. She quit trying to resist and mounted her own attack.

She dug psychic claws into my hand and used them to rip and tear me open. Power leaked out of me in a ghostly wisp, and my spiritual core ached with the damage. Loretta Nell used her hold to pull me deeper into Josie, effectively trapping me.

Josie snapped into motion. She pulled a shining silver knife out of a hidden pocket and swiped at my arm with it, laying open the flesh. I yowled and tried to pull away, but Loretta Nell had me in her grip. Josie slashed with the knife again. I grabbed at her wrist with my free hand. Our flesh smacked together. Sweat slicked both Josie's wrist and my hand, and I almost lost my grip on her. But I dug in my fingernails. Josie's teeth gritted in pain. She kept straining to bring the knife down on me.

"Stop it." Mohawk rushed over and pulled us apart. He took a deep breath, nostrils flaring. He frowned at me. "What do you think you're doing?"

Down on the street, another fight broke out near the crucifix. The nail gun *whoosh*-hissed as it shot a nail. Someone screamed.

I glanced away from Mohawk's angry face. Tanner had gotten the nail gun away from his executioners and held it on them. Every time one of them came forward, Tanner shot him with a nail. Head shots. A fan of bodies had begun collecting at his feet.

Mohawk spun away from us. I had only seconds to do whatever I was going to do.

Daddy said I needed to use Mohawk's power against him. The power of the book belonged to Mohawk. Loretta Nell harnessed that power right now. Maybe Daddy had meant for me to steal the book's power from Loretta Nell and use it against Mohawk.

I had to try. Centering my power again, I grabbed for Loretta Nell's spirit. She pushed me away easily. Powered by madness, Mohawk's book, and Josie, she far outranked me. My body and spirit shook with exhausted trembles. My muscles ached like I'd been hauling roofing bundles all day. I grabbed again, and Loretta Nell wiggled right out of my grasp.

I used the last of my power to lunge one final time. Loretta Nell ran but wasn't fast enough. I got a tenuous hold on her. This time was going to have to count for everything. Loretta Nell struggled against me. My psychic muscles ached. I began to lose my grip.

Priscilla Herrera's voice filled my head. *Eat Loretta Nell. Consume her. Absorb her power.*

Linus Bramwell's words echoed in my head. *You must consume...*

Their meaning became clear. Revulsion swept over me. Even as a spirit, Loretta Nell oozed evil and magic. She stank of it like a hundred-year case of body odor. I didn't want her inside me.

Priscilla read my thoughts. *Do it or become the Serpent God's bride. You choose.*

Put in those terms, the choice was pretty easy. The spirit thrashed against my hold. I dug deeper, grinding my teeth with the effort.

The mantle moved inside me, eager and more interested than I'd ever seen. It turned over and over until it beamed out of the cracks in the scar tissue spell. It worked its way up my throat and forced my mouth open. It reached out in a shining arc and dove into Josie. It hooked into Loretta Nell's spirit and took up the tug of war.

"Stop that right now." Mohawk's shout rumbled through my whole body. "I'll kill you."

I ignored him. He wasn't going to kill me, no matter what I did. Then he'd never sire a halfling with me.

He changed tactics. "I'll hunt down every Gregg and kill them. I'll make you watch while I kill Tanner."

I had a feeling he'd do those things anyway. Mohawk quit yelling threats and pulled at me. He beat at my back with his fists. He bit me. But he was too late. The mantle sank sharp teeth into Loretta Nell's spirit and took the first bite.

Her scream ripped through my head. The force of it nearly scrambled my brain. My whole body filled with the roar and shook with the force of it. Evil squirted into my mouth. It tasted sour and had an after bite like old coffee. But some deeper part of me relished this taste, considered it the taste of victory.

Eat, Priscilla ordered.

I gave the mantle teeth, and it took bite after bite of Loretta Nell. She wailed like a dying animal for what felt like an eternity and had to be at least a full minute. My magical core filled with her essence and darkened to an amber color with the taint of her evil.

I burped. Hot bile raced up the back of my throat. I clapped my hand over my mouth to hold it in. I wouldn't let her go that easily.

Loretta Nell's life flashed through my mind. She'd

killed and killed and killed. Hated everything and everybody. Disgusting images of her taking lives and using people flashed behind my eyes. My knees buckled, and I dropped to the bed of the truck, landing in something wet and warm.

Before I could analyze what I was kneeling in, my chest twinged. I put my hand over the sore spot.

Spirits don't have a heartbeat, but they have a rhythm all the same. Loretta Nell's energy pulsed inside me. Each pulse came slower. She was dying for the second time in her conscious existence. Her being shook and writhed in agony.

The pain, rather than physical, was emotional. Loretta Nell didn't want to die. She wanted to go on and on, spreading all the evil and misery she could. Wild, blood-soaked images flashed in my mind, trying to make their place, battering at my sanity.

I pushed back at the horror that had been Loretta Nell Grimes. The mantle came to help. It forced her will into a flat, calm line. Loretta Nell screamed like a dying panther. Her energy pulsed slower and slower, until she just stopped.

Loretta Nell was dead. What's more, she had died inside me. Horror spiked in my brain. The idea of joining with Loretta Nell had almost as much appeal as eating a dog. It was wrong, went against my nature. Would what remained of Loretta Nell eat away at what was good about me?

A cold, calculating part of me woke up. It tamped down the horror and analyzed Loretta Nell's remains. The power she'd gained from her use of Mohawk's book pulsed an ugly, stained amber. But it was all mine now to control and use as I saw fit.

I delved into this new aspect of my magic. The contents of the book and the ways to use it now belonged to me. The desire to use it burned deeper than any other urge I'd ever experienced.

My father's voice rose from the shouts and calls for blood. *Control it. Control yourself. There's more of you than her.*

He was right. He had to be. I knelt there, warm wetness seeping through my jeans, and took deep breaths until I controlled the urge to rip and tear and make things bleed. Little by little, my head cleared. I opened my eyes and took stock of how badly I was hurt.

The place where Josie had cut my arm oozed a steady stream of blood. It would need to be closed. My hands, where I'd pretended to have Orev's claws, were covered with ugly shallow scratches. Nothing huge or life-threatening.

The warm wetness continued to dampen my jeans. I glanced down and nearly screamed. I was kneeling in bloody clumps of dark tissue. I felt my chest and head, studied my hands and arms again, taking extra care to look at the knife wound. My injuries weren't that bad.

Then something moved in my peripheral vision, and I saw what was left of Josie. I screamed until I ran out of air.

Josie Stephens reminded me of a sock turned inside out. She was nothing but gore and blood. Chunks of bone lay scattered about. The metallic smell covered me, invaded my nose, took up every part of my mind.

The part of me that was now Loretta Nell Grimes screamed in grief for her dead granddaughter and grandson. It filled me, hurting, burning, overflowing. I opened my mouth with the idea of screaming again, but a cold hand clapped over it.

Priscilla's voice came. *Do not scream again. Get up and show them all who you are.*

I put my hands in the cooling blood, stomach heaving, and pushed myself to a standing position. Wiping my hands on my jeans, I walked to Dwight's podium. The book sat on it, unbloodied, unharmed. Last I'd seen it, Josie had it. Had it brought itself here?

Soft whispers brushed against my mind. The book could do anything. Convince anybody of anything I wanted. All I had to do was pick it up, use the key, and open it.

The key? Last I knew, Dwight had that. My pocket grew hot. I reached in and found the skeleton key there waiting. It had found me, same as the black opal found me if I took it off for too long.

The book's familiar whispers started back up. Perverse. Evil. Wrong.

I stood behind the podium and stared out at the Devil's Rest crazies, who'd killed each other this night in honor of the Serpent God. Mohawk. I looked around for the son of a bitch. We needed to have words.

Instead of finding Mohawk, I found Tanner. He'd set

the cross made for his execution on fire and was using the burning wood to stave off the crazies surrounding him.

Something fifty times more intense than anything I'd ever felt for Wade, Dean, Chase, or any other man chased away the evil thoughts. It warmed me, made me smile. I walked to the edge of the truck bed.

"All of you, step away from Tanner Letts right now." I jerked at the sound of my own voice. It didn't sound like me. It was deep, commanding, sure of itself. More me than I had ever been.

The crazies responded to it, though. They scattered and ran to stand on the side of the street, all watching me with fearful eyes.

"Come on." I motioned to Tanner.

He stared at my face for several long seconds. "Is it still you?"

That was a good question. Was it? I searched inside and found all the old insecurities, all my memories, all my worries. They lay in a pile on one side of my consciousness. On the other side was the shining sheet of the mantle, trapped behind the scar tissue, which was more tattered and ragged now than ever. A few threads of dark amber cut through it, all that was left of Loretta Nell Grimes.

"It's me, Tanner. Come up here. Stand with me." I held out my hand to him.

He paused. "Is that your blood?"

I dropped my hand, confused. Why did he care? I'd vanquished our enemies. Then I got it. He thought I was an animated corpse. "It's not mine. It belonged to Josie Stephens."

Josie who was now dead because of me. The regret of her loss hit me again, but this time it wasn't just some residual emotion of Loretta Nell's. This one was all me and strong enough to feel true grief for a person who tried to kill me. That reminded me I was human and could overcome this and anything else. We all carried a seed of evil. But our universal connection allowed us to think before we acted, to help instead of hurt.

Tanner walked to the bed of the truck. I held out one hand. He took it and leapt onto the truck with me. I wanted to hug him but hated to smear blood on him. I settled for squeezing his arm and kissing his cheek. It left a smudge.

Footsteps rang on the pavement. I saw nobody at first. Then the movement of the snake caught my eye. This one was black with a poisonous viper's head. It continued wriggling toward us, growing until it took on Mohawk's human form. He stopped a few feet from me and bowed.

"The Gregorius Witch has finally emerged in your pitiful shell." He showed me his snake fangs. I was too tired to feel repulsed or scared.

"Yes." I meant to call him Mohawk, but another name came out. His real name, one some ancient part of me knew.

Mohawk's crazies rumbled with a moan of religious ecstasy.

Mohawk glanced around at them, smiling. "You see the power you could have?" He walked toward me. "It's all right there in that book. Everything you need to do. You'd be a goddess on earth."

"Admit I've fulfilled our bargain. Release me." That commanding voice came out of me again. It shook inside me.

Tanner glanced at me with his eyebrows raised, his intense gaze unsure for once.

"Ahh, Gregorius Witch. I cannot release you." Mohawk, or whatever his real name was, had taken on a more formal speech pattern. He had adopted something almost like an accent, but its rhythm was unfamiliar.

My daddy's words came back to me. *Use his power on him.* How could I do that? I checked the mantle and found it fully charged. It had enjoyed Loretta Nell's spirit in a way that scared me. *Use his power on him.* I drew on what was left of Loretta Nell, easily finding the magic of the book, and let it flow through me. I raised my head to stare at Mohawk.

"I command you to concede I have fulfilled our arrangement." My voice shook the ground.

Mohawk laughed. "I cannot. The book was once Loretta Nell's to control. Now it is yours. You must either make use of it or give it to someone who will." He cocked his head at me. "This is what I told you from the beginning, if you'll remember."

But he'd lied about so many things. How was I supposed to predict which ones were true or not true?

He came closer. "Would you like me to advise you on finding a successor?"

"Are you going to try to cheat me?" My hand darted out

for Tanner's, but I pulled it back. I had to do this myself. I was the Gregorius Witch, whatever that meant.

He shook his head and held out one long, skinny hand. "If you wish to be free of me, Gregorius Witch, let me help you."

I tried to climb off the truck. My abused muscles let out a scream. Tanner put his hands under my armpits and lowered me. Mohawk reached for me. I recoiled but then reconsidered. I had control of this situation now. I put my hand in Mohawk's, the hair on the back of my neck standing up like a dog's hackles, and let him lower me to the ground.

———

TANNER SLID off the truck and pulled me away from Mohawk.

"Tell us how to get rid of the book." I spoke in the same commanding tone but heard the thunder fading from my voice.

Mohawk sniffed the air and made a face. "The two of you smell terrible. I can't deal with you like this."

He motioned to a man made unrecognizable by the blood covering him head to toe. The guy came without hesitation.

Mohawk spoke to him in a dismissive tone. "Find them clean clothes and a place to wash themselves. Get me someone who can cook and open the diner. We're all hungry."

The man stared at Mohawk, swaying back and forth, eyes glazed.

"Now, now, now," Mohawk screamed.

The bloody man jumped into action, grunting and gibbering at other gore-streaked people. I tried to understand the words they said to each other and couldn't. They'd regressed to language not quite human.

A woman missing one eye stumbled over to us. She grunted something and motioned us to follow.

Tanner and I exchanged a glance. We clasped hands and followed.

The woman led us up some stairs at the back of one of the buildings and showed us an apartment. A framed picture on the wall showed the same woman, perfectly normal and smiling with her arm around a cute guy wearing a baseball cap. One night, and all that was over for her. She led us through the apartment and pointed out a bathroom with a shower stall. Grunting and gibbering to herself, she left.

I turned to Tanner, wanting to put my arms around him and rest my face on his chest but stopped as I remembered the way he'd feared me back at Dwight's makeshift podium.

"You scared of me now?" My voice had lost all semblance of command. Now I was just a squeaky little woman, afraid of the future, afraid of having her heart broken.

Tanner closed the space between us and put his hands on my waist. "You know you've got the right woman when you're a little scared of her."

He pulled me to him and brushed his lips against mine. I kissed him back because I wasn't sure who I was right then and needed everything to feel normal. We got in the shower together.

Our touches, tentative at first, asked the big question: Are we still okay? But as our breaths sharpened and our pulses sped up, the need to make sure we were both still alive blotted out any other concerns.

When we got out of the shower, two sets of folded clothes lay on the floor outside the bathroom. On top of mine lay an unopened box of wound-closing bandages. I found some rubbing alcohol in the bathroom, and Tanner dressed my wound.

"I dislike the idea of giving that book to someone who'll use it," I said as Tanner used the strips to pull the wound together.

"The conundrum of adulthood." Concentrating on his task, Tanner's voice was little more than a husky whisper.

"Huh?" I tried not to wince as Tanner slapped a larger bandage over the strips holding the knife wound closed. Tanner sat back to look at me.

"Life is rarely pure black or pure white. The choices we make day to day are mostly gray. We allow some bad stuff to exist in exchange for what we deem most important." He took my hand, his meaning clear.

"Is this living out loud?" I tried on the words for size. They might have been a little big, but I could get comfortable in them. I'd chosen Tanner and me over martyring myself to stop an evil that could never be stopped.

Tanner kissed my hand. "We did the best we could."

I leaned in and brushed a kiss over his lips. "And we're leaving together."

"That's what's important." He kissed me, really kissed me, and I let the argument be over for right then.

An hour later, we sat in Phil's, Home of the World Famous Monkey Burger. The maddening smell of frying bacon came from somewhere in the back. Tanner and I held hands on top of the table. Mohawk sat across from us sipping coffee as though he wasn't a monster who had caused a massacre and killed a few hundred innocent people.

He watched me over the top of his mug and set it down on the table with a clunk. "You don't look like the Gregorius Witch any more. You look like a scared little girl again."

I glanced at the book, which sat at the far end of the table on top of a plain black tote bag, the key attached to the one of the lacy silver corner caps with a bit of yellow string. It radiated wrongness. Chill bumps marched over my skin.

I pointed at it. "How do I get rid of that? Do I have to banish Loretta Nell?"

"There is no banishing. She's part of you now." Mohawk held up his coffee cup.

Phil approached. He had a broken nose. Several missing patches of his hair revealed a bloody scalp. Three of his fingers were gone. Teeth marks covered his hands. He filled Mohawk's coffee cups, eyes rolling, gibbering madness.

Mohawk motioned him away and spoke to me. "I should charge you for the information."

"Suck it. You got exactly what you wanted out of this whole fiasco." I sipped at my coffee, which was actually quite good, considering the circumstances.

"I want a halfling with you." Mohawk sat back to allow the woman who'd let Tanner and me use her apartment deliver our plates.

We all got the same breakfast. Three slices of bacon, three sunny side up eggs, two pieces of toast. Tanner stared at his. Mohawk and I dug in, glaring at each other.

"Not happening. Ain't paying you either, not if I have to find someone else to bestow that walking nightmare on." I jabbed a piece of toast dripping egg yolk at the book.

Mohawk's features flattened, his face widening. He let me see fang.

"And don't even show me your snake face. Right, baby?" I elbowed Tanner.

He jumped but pulled himself together. "Absolutely. We've had enough. You said you had some ideas. Let's hear them."

I gave him an approving smile. He took the first bite of bacon.

Mohawk rolled his eyes. "Love is overrated. You know that, right?" He leaned forward. "Six million dollars for the halfling. I'll get you a condo on the beach. Or the mountains. In your name. We'll never have to talk again."

"Tell me how to get rid of the book." I ate a piece of bacon like I had this conversation every day.

Mohawk sat back, lips set in a pout. He stuck his fork

under his eggs and slung some at me. It landed on my clean shirt. I narrowed my eyes at him and tossed the remainder of my coffee in his face.

"Tell me how to get rid of the book." I leaned over the table and growled.

Mohawk dug several napkins from the metal dispenser on the table. "I should kill you for that." He mopped off his face and tossed the soggy napkins onto the table.

Glaring at him, I dipped a napkin in my ice water and dabbed the egg off my shirt. I tossed the dirty napkin on his and sat back in my seat.

Mohawk let out a hissy giggle. It quickly deepened into full-chested guffaws. He reached inside his leather jacket and took out a tattered slip of paper. It fluttered to the table. "These are just suggestions."

I opened the paper and found three names and addresses, all nearby. "Who are these people?"

"Who cares?" Mohawk ate his eggs and stared at the wall over my shoulder. "They'll do whatever they're going to do, and the next person will get the book."

I tossed the paper back on the table. "No deal."

Mohawk rolled his eyes. "Hanson Shadix is a seventeen-year-old boy who likes setting fires and killing animals. He's ripe to do more and will make a great disciple." He stopped speaking, dipped his toast in the portion of eggs he hadn't thrown at me, bit it off, and chewed. "Hanson will be good for a school shooting or maybe a mass poisoning."

"He's a kid. He needs help, not encouragement." I pushed my plate away, wishing I hadn't eaten as much as I had. The greasy food tossed in my suddenly tender stomach.

Mohawk shrugged. "William T. Buckmeyer has a ranch near the Mexican border. So far, he's kidnapped one hitchhiker and plucked out her eyes for being a prostitute. He's looking for one to stone to death. He'll be a great serial killer."

The idea of someone, probably a woman, being stoned to death made the food I'd eaten grow heavy. I took out my antacids and crunched one between my teeth.

Mohawk watched, smiling. "Danna Donahue is a schoolteacher. Very popular with her coworkers, the parents, and even her students. There's darkness in her she doesn't even know about yet. She might have a cruel social experiment in her." Mohawk wiped his last square of toast over his plate and popped it in his mouth. He chewed with his mouth open.

Sitting there in the soft morning sunlight, with his punk hairdo and punk clothes, he looked like a kid who'd spent all night partying. Not an ancient creature who got off on directing murder and mayhem. Then I noticed the pattern of snakeskin right under his human skin.

No, not human and not a kid. Make your decision carefully, Priscilla Herrera's voice whispered in my ear.

I didn't want to give any of these three people the book. The first two might already be evil, but helping them become more evil went against my nature. The idea of hurting that last lady made me hurt. Left alone, she might never hurt a fly.

"That's wrong," Mohawk said. "She's got it in her. The book doesn't work unless the evil's already there."

"That's horseshit." Tanner balled up his napkin and tossed it onto the table. "That book made us almost kill those dumbasses."

Mohawk grinned, showing off flat short teeth. "Look deep inside yourself, Tanner Jackson Letts. There's evil. Most of you never do anything about it. That's why I've handpicked these three. They'll be the easiest to turn."

I shook my head. "I can't hurt anybody like this."

"Then you become my slave." Mohawk shrugged. It was win-win to him.

Tanner spoke to me as though we were alone. "Years ago, I heard about an artifact auction here in Texas. Supposedly someplace in San Antonio."

"The book will still find the right person." Mohawk used his napkin to scrub the grease off his mouth. "Don't you want to know whose life you influenced?"

I didn't know what to do. Back at that apartment, with Tanner dressing my wounds, it had all seemed so simple. Choose myself. Choose Tanner. Live out loud. But with it right here in my face, I saw people and hurt. Any exchange of the book would cause misery beyond what I wanted on my karma score sheet.

Tanner spoke into my ear. "If you do the auction, the book will be chosen. Anybody who chooses that thing..."

"They're still going to do bad stuff with it." I lowered my voice. "Hurt people."

Tanner nodded. He'd lost his first family because of another driver's carelessness. He knew all about how people can hurt each other, even when they don't mean to.

"If you sacrifice yourself to this thing—because that is what you'll be doing—is the book going to be taken out of play?" Tanner didn't wait for me to answer. He turned to stare at Mohawk.

The monster wearing the young punk's skin lowered his chin and looked up at us. A smile grew on his face, and his eyes changed from human to snake eyes. He laughed. It was answer enough.

As usual, Tanner was right. I could give myself to Mohawk, and he'd give the book to someone, or I could put the book back into play myself and stay free.

Tanner leaned close. "Live out loud. Survive."

I hated spreading evil. Sure I did bad things, made bad decisions. We all did. But the deliberate spread of mayhem? I couldn't get comfortable in it.

Tanner put his arm around me. "I'm with you. Whatever you do, I'm with you."

I twisted to face him. "Can you find out how to get the book in the auction?"

It was like buying meat in a grocery store. Some animal had suffered greatly so that the clean, cellophane-wrapped package could be there for me to buy. But I hadn't had to see the animal's suffering.

Was it the more honorable choice? No. Tanner had called it the adult conundrum. There was no honorable choice. There was choosing myself and living out loud or dying in every way but the one that would free me. I chose the auction because, for the first time in a long time, I wanted my life, especially the part of it that entwined with the man beside me.

Tanner motioned for me to let him out of the booth, dragging out the fancy phone I paid for him to have. He walked a few booths away and sat down.

Mohawk smiled at me. "Young love."

"Eat dog turds, snake man," I snarled at him. "What happens to this town? The people in it?"

"I'll clean it up." Mohawk made a sweeping gesture at the plate glass window. "Other than you having ingested Loretta Nell, it'll be like the last three days never happened. Tanner's truck is beyond repair. I'll have it destroyed so it's never traced back to him. I got you something to drive out of here. Look for a convertible in front of the dentist's office a few streets over. " He rose in his seat and leaned toward me. "Drop the scared little girl act. Let me see the Gregorius Witch again."

I recoiled from him, not sure what he wanted. But when he said that name, something flared inside me. It felt a lot like the satisfaction of eating Loretta Nell Grimes's spirit. The thing inside me grew bigger. The lights in the diner flickered, and a little breeze moved the wadded napkins on the table.

Mohawk leaned forward, nostrils flaring. "Leave with me."

I raised my middle finger. The lights flickered again and buzzed.

Mohawk laughed. "You're a fool not to marry your fortune to mine."

I turned away from him.

Tanner rejoined us, much happier than the situation warranted. He almost glowed. He'd enjoyed stepping back into his old life for a few moments. What did that mean? I shook off the thought. *Save it for another day.* Tanner put his arm around me and kissed my cheek.

He whispered in my ear, "Everything's going to be all right." He drew back, mischief sparking in his eyes.

I jabbed him in the ribs. We wrestled, both of us laughing, and I let the stress of the moment slip away.

A bell dinged. I turned away from Tanner to find the seat across from us empty. The slip of paper with the names was gone.

Mohawk walked across the parking lot, staring out at the demolished cars and the smoking buildings. He waved both arms and shouted a word in another language.

It was as though a light switch flipped. Gunfire popped in the distance. A woman screamed, loud and long. A truckload of people holding garden implements careened around the corner. They slowed in front of Mohawk but then burned rubber trying to get away from him.

18

———————

TANNER and I walked to the dentist's office still holding hands. The woman who'd tried to kill us the night before, but ended up killing herself, still lay in the parking lot like someone's forgotten trash. Nearby sat the convertible we'd seen the night before when it had been full of kids driving around looking for trouble. The keys swung from the ignition.

"I don't know how I'm going to pull my camper," Tanner said as he slid behind the wheel.

"Let's figure it out far away from here." I buckled my seatbelt, got out my phone, and typed in the address Tanner'd gotten for the auction. The auction was in China Grove, Texas, a small town right outside San Antonio.

Tanner cranked the engine and got on the road. The last of the hellish summer heat hung in the wind combing through our hair. But like everything else in my life, it hung on the cusp of change. The brilliant blue sky had already shed its white haze of summer humidity. It spread

338

clear and cloudless over us. The gorgeous day ate at our gloom and eventually swallowed it whole.

We talked and laughed like a couple going to a picnic. The car's radio played all happy songs. We sang the words, even though neither of us could really sing. But the passing miles gave my worries time to sneak back in. I stared out at the passing landscape more and sang less. Finally I turned down the radio and spoke aloud what bothered me about all this.

"Don't you think it's a little coincidental that they're having an auction when we need it?" It might not bother Tanner, but I wanted warning if this was going to turn into some kind of brawl.

Tanner stared at the highway stretching out in front of us and licked his lips. "This auction isn't..." He stopped speaking and seemed to rethink. "This auction is run by a guy like Mohawk. It goes on all the time. Dave, my friend, said to go to this address and give them the password."

"What's the password?" My head swam with the new knowledge.

Two years ago, I'd had no idea anything more other-worldly than me being a medium and a few people being telepaths existed. Now I learned about something new every time I turned around. My world had broadened along with my own growing gifts. In times like this one, I felt like a lost child in a big forest full of predators, endlessly seeking a place to hide. The problem? There was nowhere to hide.

Tanner, with no idea of my inner vertigo, smiled and said, "The password is Santa Claus."

We both laughed, and it swept away a little of my tension. I turned up the radio, found a station playing redneck rock and roll, and sat watching the miles pass. The DJ broke in after a stretch of songs by the Allman Brothers and said he had breaking news. Something inside me twisted. I turned up the radio even more.

"From Devil's Rest, Texas. A convoy of tankers carrying fuel exploded sometime last night and burned down the majority of the town. At least two gas stations exploded after catching fire." The DJ, who'd been speaking excitedly, stopped and sighed. "So far, no survivors have been found. Authorities have closed off the area and declared it unsafe. If you have friends or family in Devil's Rest, authorities ask you to *not* go rushing out there..."

I spun the dial and turned off the radio. As promised, Mohawk had cleansed the town of Devil's Rest, hidden the horror that had happened there. Authorities and cleanup crews wouldn't find a single living soul. They'd be left to wonder exactly what had happened and to spend a bunch of money cleaning up the mess.

How many deaths had I made possible just by going to Devil's Rest? Too many. Jeb and Cheryl Pugh came to mind. So did Roderick and Mandy. Shame heated my skin and made my stomach feel full of poison. I took out my antacids and crunched one.

"Stop beating yourself up." Tanner put a hand on my thigh.

I didn't bother to answer, just sat with my head down. This was living out loud. This was choosing me. Many innocent people had paid the price for my selfishness.

Could I live with it? I'd have to. I wanted my life too bad to do otherwise.

China Grove turned out to be a lot less exotic than the name. The address for the auction had a gated entry. Tanner pulled up next to an intercom box and pressed the button.

A creaky expressionless voice came back almost immediately. "Password."

"Santa Claus." Though we'd laughed about it earlier, it was no longer funny at all. Nothing was.

The voice came back, still devoid of emotion. "Mr. Letts, please park to the right of the house. Someone will be out to see you and Ms. Mace inside. Please wait for your escort."

I froze. Whatever was on the other end of the intercom knew my name. I turned to ask Tanner if he'd told them, but his gray skin and tight lips gave me the answer.

The gates slowly swung open. Tanner drove us inside the property. The driveway wound through beautifully landscaped grounds and opened to a tennis court-sized parking lot. A huge manor loomed over it, so big it looked like it belonged in a movie about rich people in the English countryside.

I immediately understood why we'd been told to park in the lot to the right. The left side had nothing but paneled trucks. To the right sat rows of vehicles way fancier than Tanner's and my stolen ride. Tanner pulled into a parking space and cut the engine. A stiff-postured man wearing a dusty black suit rushed around the side of the house and hurried toward the convertible.

Tanner made no effort to get out. "Dave—my friend from California—said not to react, no matter what we see."

The man reached the car, and I had to hold back a gasp. His skin had a decidedly greenish cast, and a jagged scar ran across his throat. He bent to stare into Tanner's face.

"Your contribution to today's auction belongs to the Serpent God, yes?" His voice was the one we'd spoken to on the intercom.

I leaned forward to answer. The man's eyes found me, the whitish-gray corneas locking on my face. My skin prickled, and the words died in my throat. I gave a short nod and leaned back in my seat, heart pounding as though I'd narrowly missed some horrible fate.

"Where is the book, please? I must verify the authenticity."

Tanner, staring straight ahead, said, "It's in the trunk. The tote."

The man turned and walked to the back of the car. Tanner used a lever on the floor to open the trunk. The man rustled around. Then silence. Tanner and I exchanged a glance. Sweat stood out on his upper lip, and his chest rose and fell with quick breaths.

The man returned to the front of the car, the tote bag tucked under one arm. "Follow me inside. Mr. Silas is waiting."

Tanner got out, came around to my side of the car, and held open the door for me. He hadn't been raised to play doorman, so I could only assume he didn't want me far from him. I had no problem with that. I let him take my arm as I slid out of the car. We joined hands and followed the man to the house's front door. It swung open as we approached.

A woman wearing a short black and white maid's uniform stepped aside to let us enter. She had the same greenish skin and a faded, round scar at her temple. Her grayish-white eyes never settled on us. She stared at the sky behind us. We went inside, and the door closed behind us with a final sounding *clunk*.

Our feet rang on gleaming marble floors. A chandelier as big as my RV's kitchen twinkled from a cathedral ceiling. A tall, slim man stood from a maroon, satin-covered sofa with dark wood trim. His pencil-thin mustache and slicked back hair reminded me again of old movies where people lived in impossibly big houses.

"I'm Black Silas. Welcome to my home and to the auction." He held out a hand to me. "Peri Jean Gregg?"

He had the first two names right, but why Gregg instead of Mace? The freak outside had called me Mace. Something to puzzle over later. I took his hand and shook it, relieved the skin was pink and warm—hot, in fact—instead of the greenish cast of the two servants.

He smiled, revealing a row of straight white teeth. "Tanner Letts, correct?"

Tanner nodded and shook Mr. Silas's hand.

"I knew your grandfather, Jackson, quite well. Great man." Silas held Tanner's hand an extra second. "You returned to Texas after the accident that claimed your family?"

Fear pumped through my heart. Maybe Tanner's

friend, Dave, had told Black Silas our names, though that still didn't explain him calling me Gregg instead of Mace. But there was no reason for Silas to know about what happened to Tanner's wife and daughters.

"Yes, sir." Tanner's face had gone shiny with sweat.

Silas stepped between Tanner and me, pressing a hot hand to each of our backs, and pushed us toward a set of double doors across the room. "The auction is already in progress, of course. The Serpent God's book will be up after the current bid closes."

When we got within a few feet of the doors, they swung open, seemingly on their own. A blast of chilly air met us. Silas pressed us inside. I stared in awe.

This one room was at least as large as the house I'd shared with Memaw back in Gaslight City and filled with people. The auctions I'd been to were usually noisy. This one was stone quiet, except for the auctioneer's soft words.

The auctioneer, tall with a fringe of white hair around the lower half of his scalp, stood on a slightly raised stage centered at the far end of the room.

"Now taking bids on the knife used by the killer known as the Baytown John." He held up a dark-bladed fillet knife with a wooden handle. "For those who've never heard of him, Dennis Neil killed twenty prostitutes before he was caught. This is the knife he used to dissect them in his home. It was made by Dennis himself."

Rows and rows of chairs, not a one empty, stretched to the back of the room where Tanner, Black Silas, and I stood. Near the middle of the room, a hand holding a red marker raised.

Silas ushered us around the perimeter of the room. Some of the bidders turned to stare, but most were intent on the Baytown John's knife. A man about my age wearing all black and a grim expression on his face continued to hold up the marker.

The auctioneer nodded. "Bidder number seventy-five starts the bid at red, which is tier three. Any others?"

Silas parted a black curtain to the left of the stage and pointed to a short row of theater style seats. "You'll be able to watch from in here."

He gestured to the opening in the curtain. Though it had appeared opaque before we crossed through, it was sheer on this side. I had a perfect view of a sweating guy wearing an ill-fitting suit holding up a black marker on the front row.

"Bidder number thirty raises the bid to black, tier seven." The auctioneer's voice, perfectly audible behind the curtain, sounded just as calm as it had at the sight of the red marker.

Black Silas's eyes widened. He took out his phone, pressed a button, and spoke into it. "Bidder number thirty has live cargo?" His eyes grew as he heard the answer. He hung up, leaned forward, and spoke into my ear. His breath was ice cold. "You're free to leave once the book has been sold. Your payment..."

I shook my head. "Keep the money. Donate it. I don't care."

Black Silas moved away from me and stared at my face. He cocked his head. "Your wish is our command." He held out a black business card. "If you ever need my services again, contact me directly. No need for intermediaries for you, Miss Gregg."

I took the card, and Silas swept away. We watched the bid markers raise to yellow. The auctioneer pointed out that yellow was tier eight.

A couple who couldn't be far out of their teens won the knife. The girl, with mad eyes and who wore a short skirt with no underwear, jumped around and squealed. The other bidders watched with straight faces and little interest.

The auctioneer set the knife aside and picked up Mohawk's book. The key had been cut off the twine and stuck in the keyhole.

"This tome is one of three created by ancient worshipers of the Serpent God. This cult made sacrifices in exchange for favor from the god. The followers of the god of the serpent have risen and fallen several times over the history of civilization. This particular book was last owned by Loretta Nell Grimes of the Messengers." He held the book over his head, turning slightly left and right so everybody got a chance to see it.

A slight rumble went through the room.

The auctioneer set the book down on a tall table next to him. "The authenticity of the book is guaranteed by Black Silas himself. Shall we start the bidding?"

Mohawk's book garnered much more excitement than Baytown John's knife. Mouth dry, I watched as it received a total of thirteen bids. The final marker, a gold one, was held up by a silver-haired man wearing an expensive suit.

The auctioneer acknowledged the bid with a sober

nod. "Let the record note that bidder number six has bid gold, tier thirteen. Because bidder number six is the only person in this room who has gold tier standing, he has won the book."

Something in me, the little bit of Loretta Nell that remained undigested, spasmed at the loss of the book. I took that as my sign to get the hell out of this creepy place. I stood and held out my hand to Tanner. His hand, when it closed around mine, was slick with sweat. We walked the perimeter of the room, still attracting little notice, and left through the door we'd come in.

The huge entry hall was empty and silent. But the feeling of someone watching crawled up my back and gave me chill bumps. I quickened my pace. By the time Tanner and I reached the door outside, we were running.

We raced to the car, slammed open the doors, and clambered inside. Tanner gunned the engine and peeled out. He raced toward the gate. I twisted in the seat, watching behind us, as though we were being followed by a mob carrying pitchforks and torches. We both breathed a sigh of relief when the gates opened to let us out.

Tanner drove fast away from Black Silas's mansion, not speaking until he pulled into a convenience store. "To Austin to get your truck and get rid of this thing?"

"I hate driving this car even to Austin. Seems like we're just asking to get pulled over." I took out my cigarettes.

"The car's owners are dead. Nobody's looking for it yet." Tanner played with the keychain, metal cut in a feather shape and painted bright colors.

I tried to imagine the person who'd bought that

keychain, shying away from thoughts about how they'd likely died. Instead I focused on my boyfriend, thankful for surviving to have this moment with him.

"Let's do it." I made myself smile.

Tanner sped out of the parking lot and cut into traffic like a stunt car driver.

THE EIGHTY-MILE DRIVE between China Grove and Austin passed with me making phone calls.

I first talked to Cecil. He barely reacted to my story about what happened to the citizens of Devil's Rest and what I'd had to do to beat Loretta Nell.

"What did you do with the book?" he asked instead.

"Auctioned it at a place in China Grove," I said.

"You got into Black Silas's auction?" Cecil's voice rose with surprise.

"Tanner arranged it." As much as I hadn't wanted Tanner to join me on this trip, he'd saved my ass in more ways than one.

Cecil grunted at that. "Didn't I tell you he'd be a good addition to Sanctuary?"

Shelly, Cecil's wife, spoke up. "And a good match for you?"

I hated being on speakerphone, and Cecil loved using the feature. But I made sure to keep my voice polite. "You were both right." I glanced at Tanner. "About everything."

"Get him to take on the mark of the raven." Cecil lowered his voice. "Ask him to stay."

I wasn't ready for that yet. But I said, "I'll do it. Talk to you in a few days?"

We hung up, and I called Hannah. She answered right away. "Peri Jean? Is it really you?"

"Yep. The book's gone. My debt to Mohawk is paid." Just saying the words made relief flood through me again.

A male voice, one I thought belonged to Leon Blackfox, spoke in the background.

Hannah's voice trembled. "Leon and I heard the news about Devil's Rest and were sure you were gone."

"No, but I lost your gun." Truth was, I hadn't tried very hard to get it back. Things got too weird to worry about it.

"To hell with it. All that matters is you're alive." Her voice had that overly bright sound it used to get when she was with a man. It was one of the best sounds I'd heard in a long time.

As soon as I hung up from Hannah, my phone buzzed with a text message. "This is Queenie from Natchitoches. The Wanderer says congratulations. He'll be watching you."

At least one good thing had come of all the bad. I had a chance at meeting the person, or thing, that could help me shed the scar tissue spell once and for all. I thanked her and spent the rest of the drive watching white clouds pollute the perfect blue sky and thinking about what I'd done.

Tanner had been right about the adult conundrum. Good and evil danced cheek to cheek. They coupled in honky-tonk parking lots under the blink of neon signs. They broke up the next morning over their tequila hangovers. Then they got back together the next weekend. It wasn't pretty, but it was the way the real world worked.

The good guys—Tanner and me—had won this particular joust between good and evil. As much as we could anyway. That mattered more than some misguided self-immolation. There were times to fight for the underdog, the way I had for Hannah, which put me in Mohawk's crosshairs, but there came a time when every heroine had to fight for herself.

Victory came with sacrifices, heartbreaking ones. But sacrificing myself meant the good I added to the universe would be gone forever.

I, Peri Jean Mace, was worth saving. I was a loyal friend. A talented witch with untapped power that frightened even me. A fierce warrior.

Maybe a little evil had to be allowed in order for there to be good in the world. And maybe this was all some massive justification for being selfish, for choosing my own life and Tanner's. In which case, I would call the black mark on my conscience the cost of survival.

Then I need to make it count. No point in surviving if I couldn't let it go. Quit living like a ghost in my own life.

We found the parking garage and left the convertible a few blocks away with that metal feather keychain swinging from the ignition. Time to say goodbye to Devil's Rest and all that had occurred there. But, like Lott's wife in the Bible as she and her family fled Sodom and Gomorrah, I turned back for one final look.

The shiny paint threw my reflection back at me. A skinny woman with long black hair, holding on to the hand of a man with powerful shoulders. Tanner tugged my heartstrings in a million ways, for a million different reasons. After kissing a mountain's worth of frogs, I'd finally found the right man. I smiled.

Something moved behind us, coming so fast it was a blur. My heart jumped. I twisted to face the threat. The sidewalk was empty except for normal people rushing around, phones plastered to the sides of their faces. I turned back to the car.

The reflection in the paint, again, was different from what was really there. A dark, cloudy sky roiled in the reflection. Lighting zagged across the sky. A horde of shapes on horseback followed the lightning, a pack of dogs with fiery eyes running alongside them. They raced closer. One horseman pulled ahead. As he sped toward us, his face came into focus.

Oscar Rivera. The Coachman.

My nerves spasmed. Adrenaline flooded my bloodstream. I let out a yelp, jerked my hand out of Tanner's, and spun around. Again, the sidewalk was empty.

"What is it?" Tanner scanned the street, body tense and alert.

"I don't know." I opened my third eye and scanned for magic or supernatural baddies. But Tanner and I were truly alone on this random street. My heart slowed, as did my panicked breaths. It was okay. For now. Tanner put his hand on my hip.

"Do you see something?" Tanner, brow furrowed, stared into my eyes, searching for what was wrong.

"We're okay for now. Maybe a little supernatural indigestion?" I forced a smile and let him take my hand again.

I followed Tanner into the parking garage, silent, my thoughts churning and bubbling. Oscar presented a true threat. A narcissist at best, and a psychopath at worst, he would go to any lengths to achieve his goal.

He *would* be back. There was no doubt about that. It might not be today. Maybe not tomorrow. But sometime. If only I understood Oscar's endgame. Maybe then I could anticipate his next move. Fight him better.

But you don't. And you can't. All you have is now. The thought pushed its way to the surface of my mind like an angry sign-carrier at a protest. It was right.

All I had was that moment with Tanner. I wanted to enjoy our relationship. Living in fear of the next week, the next month, even the next year was a waste of what we could have.

We reached my truck and unlocked it.

Tanner turned to me. "Back to Sanctuary?"

I thought about what I was going to say next. Tanner and me being together within Sanctuary was one thing. And so was him traveling with me to take care of business. What I was about to suggest went beyond that. It was living out loud.

"Why don't we take a few days off in Austin? No work. No drama. Just us?" The words felt dry as dust on my tongue. It wasn't that I was afraid of refusal. It was that I was afraid of elevating Tanner's status in my life.

Tanner thought it over, frowning at the dirty cement wall of the parking garage. "I'd like that. A lot."

"And after we do that, why don't you sell your camper and move in with me?" I held my breath, waiting for Tanner's reaction.

All of a sudden, the huge parking garage, so empty my voice echoed off the concrete walls, seemed too close of quarters. The knife wound on my arm picked that moment to start aching. My nerves ground like concrete on tender skin.

Other than my asshole first husband, I'd never lived with a man as a romantic partner. Wade, who'd come the closest, had just been a roommate. But this needed to happen between Tanner and me. I needed him. Fighting evil didn't matter as much without him by my side.

After what seemed like an eternity, during which I'd had time to imagine every awful outcome of my suggestion, Tanner picked up my hand and kissed the back of it.

"After Bea and the kids...I didn't think I was going to feel like this again." The skin around his eyes crinkled, and his eyes sparkled with mischief. "I'm glad I decided to give you a chance."

"*You* gave *me* a chance? Puleeze." I rolled my eyes. But then I dropped the act. I didn't want Tanner feeling like moving in with me was his only choice. If he didn't want to, it was better he didn't. I squeezed his hand.

"You can say no to moving in with me. We can replace the truck you lost in Devil's Rest, no problem." I gave what I hoped was a brave smile.

Tanner shook his head. "Nah. I want to live with you."

He pulled me to him. We kissed hard to seal the deal.

In Tanner's arms, Oscar and his stupid endgame seemed less dire. Maybe something I could handle when it came.

Wrong turns and the bad places they led to were part of the war of life. Just the way things went. But war could kill the spirit long before the body stopped living. The man in my arms reminded me that I wasn't dead yet, that I had a reason to find the way home.

Keep reading for a sample of the final
Peri Jean Mace Ghost Thriller.

LAST EXIT EXCERPT

I struggled to get the "Closed" sign open. It popped out of my hand and clattered to fall on my feet. Damn Cecil and these cheap-assed open/closed signs. I had warned him. Told him you get what you pay for. He'd gone behind my back and bought them anyway.

Calm down. Cecil and the signs weren't the whole problem. They weren't even that big of a deal in the grand scheme of things. The tension aching between my shoulder blades came from another source. I cut off the train of thought. *Not now.* I'd have to live through the dreaded event soon enough.

I focused on the night sky. A cloud cover rendered it starless and murky. It had been one of those blustery, windy days, a storm grumbling on the horizon. If the weather forecast and my poor aching bones were right, this storm would usher in the first cool weather of autumn. We needed the break. That gorgeous Texas Hill Country sky blazed hot enough to melt glass by the end of summer.

But I wished the rain could wait until tomorrow, after Tanner and I finished our little errand. The flood of worries came again. I slammed the door shut on them. Best not to dwell on it. It wouldn't do any good. I picked up the sign to try again.

Wind whipped my hair into my face, delivered stinging lashes to my cheeks. I ignored it and put some muscle into my task. The wind strengthened. It caught the sign and slammed it closed on my thumb. I bit back an ugly word and let the sign fall to the dirt again.

Injured finger clutched to my chest, I glanced around to see who'd been watching. A few Summervale revelers glanced in my direction. None showed any interest.

They had other things on their minds. Though Samhain was still five days away, many wore costumes. Their excitement lent a mystical charge to the air. Everyone had a spring in their step, drawn by the moon and the shadows that lurked in the darkness.

A woman wearing a red leotard, tail sewn on the ass, came toward me. She'd attached manufactured goat horns to her head. She held the chubby hand of a toddler wearing a purple and gold satin costume and a pointed hat with bells on it.

I smiled at the kid. She—or he, the costume made it hard to tell for sure—gave me that wide-eyed stare kids give strangers. I nodded to the mother.

"Too cute." I pointed at the kid.

She giggled her thanks and kept walking, probably afraid I was going to try to pull her into my tent and take her money. If only. I stared the tent where Tanner ran his arcane items business. Usually I loved hanging out with my scorching hot boyfriend. But I had a bad feeling about what we had planned for tonight.

My worried thoughts swelled. They tapped at my defenses and begged to come out to play. I gave up and let them come.

Some friends of Tanner's from California were in Texas. Staying at a hotel in Austin, not too far away. Tanner and I would be going to visit them shortly.

But that wasn't what worried me. It was the way Tanner had acted about the whole thing. He had waited until this morning to tell me, almost as an aside, over breakfast. After everybody was at the table. So I couldn't ask many questions. Worse, his invite to tag along was half-hearted.

I could have just refused to go. But no woman can resist that sort of bait. We live on curiosity. And we have to know the whole story, even when it would be best if we didn't. I had a gut feeling this whole adventure would end badly. But there was nothing I could do other than play it out.

So I did the only thing I could. I snatched that el-cheapo sign off the ground and put my anxiety into it, forcing it open, even bending the frame a little. I attached it to the little pole that would keep it from blowing away.

A loud clap of thunder forced my attention off the blasted sign. I stared into the impenetrable night. Lightning flashed. Carnival goers shrieked and gasped. They scattered like a pack of buzzards surprised by a car.

From the newly emptied dirt throughway, familiar eyes

stared at me. Panic flashed brighter than the lightning. No. It couldn't be. I held my hands out in a warding off gesture.

"You're dead," I whimpered. Unable to stand it another second, I scooted back into my tent and closed the flap. Heart pounding and my mouth cotton dry, I went back over what I had seen.

Barbie. Standing there giving me that evil glare she reserved for when I'd committed a mortal sin. My mother had been a bitch, a thief, and a murderer. She had abused me and abandoned me as a child. Was she my personal boogeyman? Probably.

Thinking rational, logical thoughts calmed me enough to think. Barbie was dead. I had watched her die. If I had really seen her, she was a ghost. Which turned her into something I could control.

Not only was I a powerful spirit medium, I was a witch. And not just any witch. Mohawk—that sleaze bucket— had called me the Gregorius Witch. I didn't know quite what that meant, but the name gave me a tingle of power unlike anything I had ever experienced.

I, Peri Jean Mace, would go back outside my tent and banish Barbie. I would fling her into the deepest, darkest pit, and she would never find her way out. Then I'd go with Tanner to meet his friends. Get the mystery over with. I pushed my shoulders back and marched toward the tent flap. Just as I reached it, someone came inside.

I screamed and backpedaled. My feet tangled together, and I pitched to the ground. I landed with a grunt and raised my arms to protect my head. Now it would happen.

My mother's ghost would kick me, pound me with freezing fists.

"Are you okay, honey?" The voice didn't belong to Barbie. Relief flooded me.

I raised my head to see who my visitor was. Queenie, a witch from Natchitoches, Louisiana. Someone I trusted way more than my mother's ghost. I climbed to my feet, brushing off my pants and trying to retain my dignity. Impossible task. I'd just busted my ass in front of her.

So I sucked it up and forced a smile to my face. "Miz Queenie! What are you doing so far from Natchitoches?"

She gripped me in a hug and kissed both my cheeks. "All week long, I had a feeling I needed to come see you."

She let go of me and set her quilted bag on top of my séance table. From it she withdrew a smaller cloth pouch, which she laid on the table. She turned back to me, smiling, but it wasn't a comforting smile. Her faded eyes, darting around my tent, said she had serious business with me.

"Are you here about the Wanderer?" Nervous tendrils spread through my stomach. This was even worse than meeting Tanner's friends.

I didn't know who—or what—the Wanderer was. But Cecil and Queenie both seemed to think he could relieve me of the spell blocking me from the full power of Priscilla Herrera's mantle. No telling what kind of horror that experience had in store for me.

"I think it might be." Queenie smiled. From the cloth pouch, she pulled a deck of Tarot cards. "I'll pass on his message by reading your cards. Are you game?"

I glanced at my cell phone. Two minutes until it was time to meet Tanner. Any other time, I'd have messaged him and told him to go on without me. But I wanted to see firsthand what he didn't want me to see. On the other hand, whatever Queenie had for me could save my life. I shoved the phone back in my pocket.

"Of course I have time." I went to the séance table and sat down.

Queenie took the chair across from me. The two candles I kept on the table flamed to life. I jerked with surprise. Queenie, acting as though she hadn't seen, calmly shuffled the cards three times. She set them in front of me. "Cut them, please."

I did as she said, and she directed me to do it two more times. Queenie laid out a spread of three cards in front of me.

"You choose which one to turn over first."

I let my hand hover over each card. The one on the left made my eyeballs burn. I pointed at it, and Queenie turned it up.

The image of a burning tower, a man and woman falling to their deaths in a tossed ocean greeted me. I recoiled. My scant knowledge of Tarot included the meaning of The Tower. My skin tightened.

"Upheaval, clearing the way for something new." Queenie's voice raised the hair on the back of my neck. "Turn the next card."

Again, I passed my hand over the two remaining cards. The one on the right sent a charge of bright energy flowing through me. I pointed to it. Queenie gestured her permission for me to see what waited.

The image on the card turned my stomach. A man lay prostrate, ten swords sticking out of his back. I didn't know the meaning of this card offhand, but the image was clear enough. Bad shit coming down the sewer pipe.

Queenie stared at me across the table. Her lips trembled. She licked them and spoke. "Ten of Swords. Betrayal. Loss. Ending. Turn over the final card, please."

I did as she asked. After The Tower and the Ten of Swords, the sight of the skeletal horseman with his scythe didn't surprise me. Still, I jumped when Queenie spoke.

"The Death Card. You clear away what is old and used up so that something else can regrow in its place." She swept a hand over the three cards.

I did my best to stay calm, but worry fogged my brain. "What would you say the Wanderer's message is?"

The candle sputtered as though someone was blowing on it. Queenie watched as though it was talking to her. She gulped. Just as I suspected. Nothing good. She took a deep breath and began to speak.

"A storm is coming." Thunder clapped, as though to underscore her point. "You're going to lose things that are very important to you right now. If you survive, you will become someone new."

Upheavals, losses, death. There'd been so much over the past couple of years. I had lost almost everything there was to lose. Everything good anyway.

No, wait. Some good things had come after losing

things and people I had thought I would never get over losing. But the idea of more tragedy coming down the road, headed for me, terrified me. I didn't think I could withstand it. I wiped at my face, surprised to find sweat there.

Queenie reached across the table and squeezed my hand. "None of us relishes upheaval. But it is something each of us must endure. You must learn to believe that you will come out on the other side." She took her hand off me. "Now as for what it has to do with the Wanderer, he won't lend his help until you reach this point." She tapped the Death card.

Wordlessly, Queenie packed her tarot cards back into their pouch, which she dropped in her large, quilted bag. She stood from the table. She was done.

"I have a flight out of Austin to Mexico City late tonight. I winter in Mexico each year." She winked at me. "If I want a quick visit with Cecil and Shelley, I'll need to hustle."

She turned and hurried out of my tent. I clambered after her. But by the time I got outside, she was already gone.

I sent her a silent well wish. The early Samhain revelers jostled past me. They had forgotten the coming storm and were back to the business of having fun. Just the few minutes Queenie and I had been inside our tent had called forth even more in costume.

My phone vibrated in my pocket. I pulled it out. There was a text message from Tanner on the screen.

"I waited on you a few minutes, but you must've changed your mind. See you in a few hours."

No way. He wasn't getting off that easily. I ran through the crowd, determined to catch him before he left. Urgency drove my short legs through the pre-Samhain carnival goers, earning more than a little ire. I flashed them glares but didn't back up my silent threat. Right now, catching Tanner mattered more.

Just about the time my smoke-damaged lungs set up a true protest, I saw Tanner's broad, squared shoulders going through the carnival's exit.

I followed at a dead run, no idea that tonight was the last night I'd ever work for Summervale Carnival. Or that years would go by before I passed through its gates again.

Available now
Order Last Exit from your favorite bookseller.
ISBN: 978-1-947462-21-2

Visit Catie's website:
www.catierhodes.com

Find Catie on Facebook:
http://www.facebook.com/catierhodesauthor

Follow Catie on Book Bub.
https://www.bookbub.com/authors/catie-rhodes

Join Catie's email list:
http://smarturl.it/lrdenewsletter

ABOUT THE AUTHOR

Catie Rhodes writes southern-fried urban fantasy with a strong dose of horror and a side dish of humor.

She is the author of the Peri Jean Mace Ghost Thrillers. Her short stories have appeared in *Tales From The Mist, Let's Scare Cancer to Death, and Allegories of the Tarot.*

Catie was born and raised behind the pine curtain in East Texas. She comes from a family of world champion liars.

Their tall tales molded Catie into a purveyor of her own brand of lies and legends. One day, she found the courage to start writing down her stories. It changed her life forever.

Catie Rhodes lives steps from the Sam Houston National Forest with her long-suffering husband and her armpit terrorist of a little dog.

Find Catie online:
www.catierhodes.com

www.ingramcontent.com/pod-product-compliance
Lightning Source LLC
Chambersburg PA
CBHW070739190726
48292CB00002B/340